LET IT BE ME

"Marcus, this was the most wonderful night," Vera said breathily. "It was absolutely wonderful!"

Marcus looked down at her and smiled. He closed the front door and leaned back against it. "Did you have a good time? Were you surprised?" he asked in his deep, sexy voice.

She turned to Marcus with a huge smile on her face and assured him that she had indeed had a most delightful evening and she'd been completely surprised. Walking toward him, she counted off points on her fingers. "I looked fabulous, I had the best-looking man in the world as my escort, I had a wonderful meal, even though I didn't get to eat your dessert, and everybody in Atlanta saw my boobies," she added, giving the neckline of her dress a small hitch. "It was a swell night, Marcus."

By now she'd reached Marcus, who was still leaning lazily against the door. He suddenly stood up straight and, without another word, reached out and put both his great big hands around Vera's small waist. Pulling her into his hard, muscled chest, Marcus bent his head and kissed her. Vera was too shocked to resist and he pulled her even closer, until their bodies were like one.

Let It Be Me

MELANIE SCHUSTER

ARABESQUE

BET
BOOKS

BET Publications, LLC
http://www.bet.com
http://www.arabesquebooks.com

ARABESQUE BOOKS are published by

BET Publications, LLC
c/o BET BOOKS
One BET Plaza
1900 W Place NE
Washington, DC 20018-1211

All Kensington Titles, Imprints, and Distributed Lines are available at special quantity discounts for bulk purchases for sales promotions, premiums, fund-raising, and educational or institutional use. Special book excerpts or customized printings can also be created to fit specific needs. For details, write or phone the office of the Kensington special sales manager: Kensington Publishing Corp., 850 Third Avenue, New York, NY 10022, attn: Special Sales Department, Phone: 1-800-221-2647.

First Printing: March 2004
10 9 8 7 6 5 4 3 2 1

Printed in the United States of America

Dedicated to Debbie Renee Sims,
A true friend in every sense of the word
and the best proofreader in the world!
Thanks a million,
Debbie

ACKNOWLEDGMENTS

As always, there are so many people to thank for their continued support that I hardly know where to begin.

Thank you to everyone who had written to me to let me know how much they've enjoyed my work. Your support and kind comments mean the world to me.

A special thank-you to Leslie Cannon for her unstinting spiritual support and friendship.

Another thank-you to Sabrina Demps, for her friendship, her cheerful and enthusiastic FAMU info, and for the tickets! Go, Rattlers!

Thank you to my brother Dwight Woods for research help when I needed it, and also for my three beautiful nieces.

Thanks always to my mother for her continued support.

To Danny Watley, my sincerest thanks for continued friendship.

To Erica Taylor, see, I told you I wouldn't forget!

A very special thank-you to Chuck and Toni Waters for appearing in my book, and to their exceptional creator, Janice Sims, for her wonderful friendship.

And as always, to Jamil. There aren't enough words to thank you for always being there for me. Thank you for always making everything feel like a celebration. You are truly the best.

Chapter 1

The last of the vivid sunset vanished over suburban Atlanta, leaving the purpling dusk typical of early spring. The spectacular view from the top floor of The Deveraux Group took in miles of sparkling lights, a veritable vista of the prosperity of the new South, of which The Deveraux Group was an integral part. The company started by Clay Deveraux Sr. so many years ago had exceeded all expectations. From a motley collection of weekly newspapers and monthly magazines geared exclusively toward the African-American community, the company had grown into a media monolith under the canny leadership of the Deveraux brothers, Clayton Jr., the twins Malcolm and Martin, and the youngest brother, Marcus.

Now the corporation handled newspapers, magazines, cable television, films, music, and investments. Each brother headed up a division of the corporation with the help of other family members and highly skilled and trusted executives from outside the family. In what was viewed by industry insiders as a surprise move, Marcus Deveraux, the youngest of the brothers, had been named chief executive officer, in charge of the entire corporation. Nearing thirty years of age, Marcus was where he had wanted to be since he was a child. He'd always known that the leadership of the family business would be his; the fact that circumstances dictated it happen earlier rather than later was of no consequence. He was more than ready to take on the challenge and his decisive brand of management had seen even more growth in the eighteen months since he had assumed his new role. So why was he sitting alone in a darkening executive suite, lost in his own thoughts?

Leaning back in the oversized Moroccan leather desk chair, Marcus faced the breathtaking view from the floor-to-ceiling windows of his office and saw nothing. More and more, he was the last person to leave the building. His brothers had left hours before, each rushing home to his wife and children, something Marcus did not desire or envy. Marcus wasn't interested in marriage; he had too much fun dating.

Like his brothers, he towered over the six-foot mark, and he was handsome to the point of being beautiful, with his Creole coloring and thick, wavy black hair. Unlike his lean, muscular brothers, however, Marcus was built like a linebacker. He was broad-shouldered and heavily muscled and looked as if he could bench-press a pony. And he showed no signs of settling down like his brothers; he had his pick of charming and beautiful women not only in Atlanta, but practically everywhere he did business, and as The Deveraux Group was an international company, he traveled extensively.

His health was excellent, his family was thriving along with the business, he had achieved his major career goal at an age when most men were just figuring out what they wanted to do with their lives, and yet there was something missing. Too often he found himself brooding when he should have been reveling in all he'd achieved and all he was going to accomplish.

He took a deep breath and stretched to get rid of the malaise. He had a date in less than two hours, and here he was, moping around like an adolescent. Larissa Morgan wouldn't appreciate him in the mood he was in, and he couldn't blame her. She was vivacious, intelligent, and ambitious; in short, a great date. They had been seeing each other for a couple of months and he thoroughly enjoyed her company as well as her energetic lovemaking. Marcus stood up abruptly, stretched again, and ran his hand over his jawline. If he put some foot in it, he could make it home in time to shower, shave, and change into something casual for their date.

The thought of seeing Larissa cheered him up as always and he started singing as he left the office. He had almost reached his BMW in the parking structure when his omnipresent cell phone rang. After his usual brief greeting, Marcus froze.

"She *what?* Which hospital? I'll be there in fifteen minutes," he said tersely as he tossed his suit coat into the back of the car and started the engine.

Vera Clark Jackson winced, the pain of her injured ankle obvious. Taking a deep breath, she smiled. "Well, it was worth it. Ooh, what a rush! I highly recommend skydiving, guys, you should try it," she said gamely as she adjusted her position on the narrow and uncomfortable emergency room bed.

Her two companions, Aidan Sinclair and Paris Deveraux, looked at each other and made identical expressions of distaste before replying in perfect unison, "No, thank you." Aidan, always the most outspoken person in any room, got in the last word.

"I know what it feels like to trip over a giant rock, I don't need to strap a big ol' nylon bag on my back and fall ten thousand feet to end up in traction," he said sarcastically.

Vera made a face that was part pique and part pain.

"That's right, kick me while I'm down. You couldn't offer up a little sympathy, could you?"

Aidan laughed at her expression and shook his head. "Oh, no, Miss Girlfriend, that would be too much like right."

Paris was quietly minding her own business, too quietly, considering her usual outgoing personality. Just then, the curtains around her bed were pulled opened by a tall, very good looking orthopedic resident.

"Mrs. Jackson, I'm Dr. Bohannon and I . . . Oh, wow, Vera, is that you?" He stopped in the middle of his introduction when he recognized his patient.

"Oh, my goodness, Dante, is that *you?* I can't believe it! You really did go back to school, didn't you?" Vera's words were cut off as she and the doctor embraced tightly, which caused Aidan and Paris to look at each other with the raised eyebrows of the terminally nosy. Vera didn't sense anything amiss as she hastened to make introductions.

"Dante, this is Paris Deveraux. And this is Aidan Sinclair," she said. "Meet Dante Bohannon, who played football with John. He always said he was going back to school to become a doctor and look at him!" she said with admiration. The little silence that followed might have been awkward, as the man Vera referred to was her late husband, John "the Tank" Jackson, who'd been tragically killed in a plane crash over two years before. But Dr. Bohannon was so obviously glad to see Vera, and she him, that the moment passed quickly.

"So, Vera, how did this happen?" the doctor asked as he began examining her injury.

Vera winced, but managed to get out the story. "Well, it was a charity thing. You raise money by taking pledges from people who want to see you jump out of an airplane. Oh, I know it sounds reckless, but you get a week of classes before the jump. And there were some very sober citizens doing it, too: two bank presidents, a college dean, a couple of lawyers. Anyway, we were raising money for my favorite charity, Habitat for Humanity, ouch! Oh, no, I'm fine," she lied breathlessly when Dante stopped probing her ankle to look at her flushed face.

"Really, it just hurt a little bit," she said bravely.

Dante seemed to read her thoughts. "Vera, I know it must hurt like the devil, so I'm going to get you down to X ray as soon as possible. As soon as your films are back and we know exactly what we're dealing with, we'll get you more comfortable, okay?"

He smiled at Vera and shook his head in admiration. "You jumped out of an airplane to raise money for charity. That takes guts, girl."

Vera beamed back at him and said proudly that her landing was perfect. "But there was this big ol' boulder out in the field and some photographer yelled my name and I turned around and bam! Here I am," she sighed.

"Someone will take you to X ray in a few minutes. We'll have you out of here as soon as possible," Dante promised.

The handsome doctor had no sooner left than a loud voice outside the examination cubicle made them all jump. The three of them were all startled, but Paris was the only one who also tried to look innocent as the voice carried closer to Vera's chamber.

"Jackson. Vera Clark Jackson. Which room is she in?"

The sound of the deep, all-too-familiar voice made Vera groan and close her eyes, made Aidan turn even paler than usual, and caused Paris to start rummaging in her huge tote bag as though she hadn't heard a sound.

Vera opened one eye and looked directly at Paris. "Why did you have to call him? Isn't this bad enough without him getting into the act?"

Before Paris could formulate an answer, the curtains surrounding her bed were jerked open and Marcus Deveraux towered over them, looking like the very wrath of God. Without looking at Aidan and Paris, he ordered them to leave.

"You two, out. I want to talk to Evel Knievel alone," he said in a tone that left no room for compromise. It was rather unnecessary, though, as Aidan had already headed for the hall and Paris knew her cousin Marcus well enough to do exactly as he said. Paris scooted out into the corridor to join Aidan and opened her mouth to speak.

Aidan forestalled her by holding up a hand. "Uh-uh, talk to the left 'cause you ain't right! Why in the world did you call him? You knew he was going to go off as soon as he walked in the door! You're family, he can't fire you. I'm just a pathetic little art director and I'm totally expendable. What do you think he's going to do when he finds out that we knew about this escapade?"

When Aidan finally drew a breath, Paris smiled weakly. "Well, we're about to find out," she mumbled.

As Marcus pulled the curtain closed, Vera looked him over carefully. He was dressed expensively, as usual, in custom-tailored clothing, although his suit coat was missing. His wavy hair was slightly tousled due to his running an agitated hand through it on the way to the hospital. His thick black eyebrows were a straight line of anger, and his high cheekbones bore the faint reddish tint that meant he was truly furious. And as always, he looked like he needed a shave; no matter how often Marcus shaved, he had a faint shadow on his cheeks that most women found irresistible, especially when combined with his thick, glossy black moustache. Vera, however, wasn't admiring him; she was trying to see how mad he actually was.

"Vera, what in the world is wrong with you? What put it into your head to go jumping out of an airplane? An *airplane,* for God's sake. You could have been killed. You could have broken your neck, your back, you could have been killed, damn it!'"

"You already said that," Vera said helpfully.

Her calm little comment only served to fuel his fire. "Look, woman, don't start with me! You seem determined to maim yourself with these lunatic stunts. First it was race-car driving, then white-water rafting, and then rock climbing! Why don't you want to stay in one piece? Why can't you take up something like line dancing or tennis, something sane? What is this obsession you have with risking your life?" Marcus was pacing back and forth like a stalking panther as he delivered the angry words and his deep, mellow voice got louder with every word, something Vera pointed out to him.

"Marcus, can you talk a little louder? I'm sure they didn't hear you in Decatur," she said acerbically. "And can we have this discussion some other time? I'm a bit uncomfortable right now," she said through clenched teeth. The ankle was really beginning to throb.

"That's why we need to talk about this *now*," Marcus retorted. "This is the end result of your craziness. You're in pain? Good! Maybe it'll teach you not to be so careless. Maybe you'll learn something from this after all!"

He stared at her rumpled, helpless form and tried to forget the nasty rush of adrenaline that had come after hearing she was injured. Vera was more than an extremely valued employee; she was, outside of his brothers, his best friend. An extremely careless friend, he remembered, the anger returning. Then he looked at her again and he knew he couldn't stay mad. Despite her tousled hair and the crumpled hospital gown, she was gorgeous.

She had short black hair that was so well cut it looked chic even when mussed, thick, arching black brows over long-lashed brown eyes that were bright and sexy, even when filled with misery as they were now, baby-soft brown skin that currently bore a trace of ashy paleness, due no doubt to pain; everything about her was adorable, even in her current state.

Vera narrowed her eyes at Marcus. "Okay, that's about enough of that, mister. May I remind you that you are *not* my daddy? I have one father and he lives in Saginaw, Michigan. You may be my employer, but you are not the boss of me!" She crossed her arms across her full and tempting breasts, looking oddly like a defiant little girl. "What I do and when I do it is not your concern, Marcus Deveraux. And I'll have you know that I made an excellent landing after my jump! Tripping over the rock was a completely separate issue," she said indignantly.

Just then the orderly arrived to take Vera down to radiology to be X-rayed and his timing couldn't have been better. It was about to turn really ugly in the confining emergency room space; Marcus was getting angrier instead of calming down. The orderly detected nothing out of the ordinary and blithely suggested that Marcus might like to accompany his wife down to X ray.

Vera's eyes got huge and she was about to correct the young man when a look at Marcus's still angry face made her think better of it. "Yes, *dear,* would you like to come with me?" she said sweetly.

Marcus ground his teeth briefly and bared them in a feral smile. "Of course, *darling*, I'm not leaving your side until this ordeal is over," he said grimly.

Marcus allowed the orderly to assist Vera into a wheelchair and then followed them out into the corridor. Catching sight of Aidan and Paris sitting in the waiting area like two children about to be called up in front of the principal, he pointed a long index finger. "You two, don't even think about leaving here until we get back."

After watching the odd little procession head to the elevators, Aidan turned on Paris. "Have I thanked you yet for all the fun I'm having? Now tell me, what put the bright idea into your twisted mind to call Marcus Deveraux in the middle of all this? He's like the last person on earth who needed to be invited to this little party."

Paris took a deep breath before speaking. "Well, I just thought that he should know what was going on," she offered. "After all, he is her boss, and since she really doesn't have any family here, I thought someone from The Deveraux Group ought to be notified," she said primly. "I just called him, I didn't tell him to come over here or anything."

Aidan mumbled something impolite under his breath and lowered his head into his hands. Looking at Paris out of one eye, he added, "And why were you looking at that big ol' doctor man like he was a turkey sandwich?"

Paris looked at him with no remorse. "Because I'm hungry," she drawled, leaving no doubt that her hunger had nothing to do with food. "Oh, cheer up, Calamity Jane. We'll be out of here in a couple of hours and I'll get you a cosmopolitan and a boca burger," she promised.

Aidan sat up straight at that. "With cheese?"

"Enough to clog every artery in your body," she affirmed.

Dr. Bohannon brought the X rays to the emergency room and Vera brightened considerably upon seeing him, which didn't improve Marcus's already foul mood. Vera didn't sense anything amiss as she hastened to make introductions.

"Dante, this is Marcus Deveraux, my dear friend and my boss. And, Marcus, this is Dante Bohannon, who played for the Falcons with John. He always said he was going back to school to become a doctor and look at him!" she said with admiration.

Marcus managed a good imitation of a smile and shook the man's hand. After a few more minutes of idle chat, however, he was ready to get down to business.

"So, Doctor, how bad is her ankle?"

Dante explained that Vera had a severe bruise and sprain of the ankle, which would probably make her life uncomfortable for a few weeks. "We'll tape it up and give you some nice crutches to use while it's healing. Try to stay off it for the next few days, and keep it elevated."

Vera made a face at the mention of crutches. "Actually, I have a couple of sets at home. And a cane, too, so I don't think I need any more. Can I take Tylenol for the pain?"

Dante immediately wrote out a couple of prescriptions for her, adding that the one would help her through the first night and the other could be started the next day to reduce inflammation.

"Vera, I can't tell you how good it is to see you," he said warmly.

She flashed him a brilliant smile in return. "It's wonderful to see you too, Dante. Let's get together and have dinner. A good home-cooked one, I know how you residents eat," she added with a laugh.

They exchanged phone numbers and another hug while Marcus stood by looking none too thrilled with the reunion. After Dr. Bohannon left, Marcus turned to Vera with a scowl on his handsome face. " 'Will' and 'Grace' are out there in the waiting room. I'm going to send one down to the pharmacy to get these prescriptions filled, and the other one can help you get dressed. I'm going to get the car. And don't think we're through discussing your little adventure, because there is plenty left to say on the subject," he warned her.

Vera thought of several hot retorts but settled on "Yes, Daddy," which she mumbled under her breath. Luckily, Marcus didn't hear her as he was already on his way out of the door. In a little over an hour she was at home in her own bed with a minimum of drama. That didn't mean that the rest of the evening was without incident.

She and Marcus barely spoke on the ride home; he had to threaten to throw her over his shoulder so that she would consent to being carried up the stairs of the carriage house where she lived; her little dogs, Kika and Toby, barked furiously and ran around under everyone's feet; and Marcus coerced Paris into going home to get a change of clothing so she could spend the night with Vera. Finally everything was arranged to Marcus's liking and Vera was in the middle of her prized antique bed, wearing an oversized white T-shirt and pink cotton pajama pants patterned with little dancing cats. Her injured leg was propped up on two pillows and she was yawning widely, the result of the prescribed pain pills.

"You didn't have to bully poor Paris into staying here, you know. It's just a sprain," she added sleepily. "I hate sleeping on my back. And I hate sleeping in clothes," she complained, pulling at the neckline of the T-shirt.

"Oh, yeah? What do you usually sleep in?" Marcus asked, amused in spite of himself. She really did look like a little girl.

"My *skin*," Vera said grumpily as she tried to get comfortable in the alien position.

Marcus pretended to be shocked. "I can't believe it! You sleep in the raw?" he asked playfully.

"Booty-butt naked," she answered with a huge yawn.

Marcus looked down at her and was momentarily blindsided by a rush of warm feeling. She looked innocent and lovable, yet totally sexy, a heady combination. He sighed and shook his head, then turned to her dressing table where he inspected himself in the mirror.

"I figured out why you look so damned young, Vera. You give the rest of us all the gray hair, especially me.

Look at this new crop, all courtesy of you," he said as he ran his hands through his hair.

Vera laughed sleepily at his comment. Marcus did have a lot of prematurely gray hair, especially at the temples. And he had inherited the same blaze of white hair in the front that made his mother, Lillian Deveraux Williams, so distinctively elegant.

"Now you can't blame that on me. I have nothing to do with your genes," she said groggily.

"Yeah, but you're making it worse. You've got to stop doing these things, Vera. What would your father do if he knew you were jumping out of airplanes and carrying on?"

Vera's eyes had closed as she submitted to the powerful effect of the pills, but Marcus's last statement made her open them slightly.

"Oh, Daddy knew all about it," she said earnestly. "I wouldn't do something like that without telling him."

Marcus was stunned. "You told him you were going to commit this madness? I don't believe you! What did he say when you told him?"

Vera closed her eyes again and smiled. "He said . . . whatever you do, don't tell . . . Marcus. He'll . . . have a . . . fit," she murmured before drifting off to sleep.

Marcus stared down at Vera's sleeping form and clenched his hands at his sides. As though he had no will of his own, he leaned over and kissed her on the forehead. He was rewarded with a sweet smile and the sound of her voice murmuring his name. He backed out of the room and pulled out his cell phone as he did so.

"Larissa? Sorry this took so long, but I'm all done here. If you still feel like company . . . great. I'll be there in thirty minutes." He'd no sooner pressed the end button on the small phone than he realized that the only place he wanted to be that evening was the place he was leaving.

Chapter 2

Vera awoke slowly the next morning, tossing her head back and forth and murmuring, "No, no, no." She sat up abruptly and tried to get out of the bed, only to recall painfully the events of the day before. It felt as though this sprain would be around to remind her of her actions for some time. Issuing a sound of frustration, she lay back down, trying to rearrange her pillows as she did so. Even with the addition of a powerful painkiller, John Jackson still haunted her dreams. Vera blinked and hastily dashed away the hot tears of frustration that were sometimes a part of her awakenings. She would dream about her late husband and wake up in a state of anxiety. Seeing his former teammate, Dante, had probably triggered this one. What a place to run into him, the darned emergency room.

A particularly painful throb from her bound ankle actually cheered her up for her own private reasons. *One more down, only a couple to go,* she thought, and with difficulty pulled open the drawer of her nightstand. Taking out a folded piece of paper, she scanned the list in satisfaction. She could cross skydiving off the list, thanks to yesterday's exploit. The sheet was titled *Things to Do Before I Turn 40,* and she'd managed to achieve most of them in good time, since her fortieth birthday was coming in a couple of months. Some of the items involved benign things like traveling to places she'd always wanted to see, viewing selected art exhibits, achieving certain financial milestones, and other practical things. Some were purely for pleasure, like learning to tango and taking piano lessons. Others involved physical endurance like learning to rock-climb, to white-water raft, to skateboard, and to run a number of marathons.

Vera, like many other people, didn't want her milestone birthday of forty to pass without her having marked certain accomplishments. And if she were to be completely honest with herself, she'd have to admit that part of the motivation for the list was John; after he died she was trying to keep herself so busy she wouldn't have time to grieve. For some reason, it seemed critical that she test her courage, her ability to withstand pressure, which led to some of her more reckless stunts. No one knew about this list and Vera had every intention of keeping it that way. Some things were just too difficult to explain.

Vera stared at the paper in her hands without really seeing it. *John*. Big, handsome, funny, and strong. It was still hard to believe he was gone. The events surrounding his death in a plane crash were so surreal that it had taken almost two days before Vera could accept that he'd been killed in the mountains with the other occupants of the ill-fated plane. She closed her eyes briefly and said a quick prayer for the man she'd loved so deeply. John had been her college sweetheart and the biggest part of her life for the eighteen years they'd been together. They'd packed a lifetime of memories into those years, some wonderful, some terrible. Vera had managed, with great difficulty, to accept the changes his death brought about.

She knew she'd never again be able to be happy in the sprawling suburban house they'd lived in together, so she sold it and bought the much smaller carriage house in which she now lived. She threw herself into her work even more, segueing from *Image* magazine to the publication she'd conceived titled *Personal Space*. *Personal Space* was her baby, a magazine devoted to lifestyles and matters of the home. It had succeeded beyond anything her employers could have hoped for and had even evolved into a weekly television show. She could admit to being truly happy with a fulfilling career, a loving family, and exceptional friendships. So why did she feel adrift, like a boat that had lost its mooring?

Vera pushed the thoughts aside and dealt with more pressing matters, like the fact that she needed to go to the bathroom. With some difficulty she slid out of bed and hopped to the room by holding on to various pieces of furniture and doorknobs until she'd managed to arrive at her chosen destination. She decided to take a shower while she was in there. Kika and Toby seemed to still be asleep, improbable as that was, so this was the opportune time to get bathed and dressed before she had to figure out a way to get them walked. The pain in her ankle was terrible, although not so excruciating that she was going to stay in bed. Besides, she was hungry, her normal state every morning. Vera loved breakfast.

Unwrapping the ankle took a few minutes, but Vera would have no problems rewrapping it, as she was well practiced in the art after years of being married to a football player. She gamely got into the shower and took a hot, soapy one, although not as long as her usual marathon ablution. She then managed to pull on a pair of cotton knit workout pants and another oversized white T-shirt. Next, she tackled the stairs. After an attempt to walk down them normally, she handled the obstacle in typical Vera fashion—she slid down on her butt. It was a bumpy ride, but efficient.

"Ouch," she muttered as she landed. Grabbing the stair rail, Vera hoisted herself up and was preparing to hop into the kitchen when Paris entered the front door with Kika and Toby.

"Paris, bless your heart! Did you take these little monsters out? I told you being my assistant was going to have its moments, but I'll bet you never thought you'd be reduced to dog walker," she said ruefully as the dogs barked their joy at seeing their mistress.

"Okay, okay! I'm glad to see you, too!" Vera hopped into the living room and plopped on the chaise longue. She picked up the two little dogs, which did their best to cover her with kisses. "Were you good doggies for Paris? Did you have a good walk?" she inquired.

Paris laughed at that. "Oh, they were good doggies, all right! They barked at everything in sight, they threatened the mailman's life, and they tried to attack a few joggers, all of whom were *fine,* by the way. If they were bigger, they'd be dangerous," she said lightly.

Vera made a face at the small dogs. They were an adorable mix of miniature spitz and Pomeranian who didn't seem to know they were smaller than most people's feet. They thought they were big dogs, big fierce ones at that. "I don't know why they hate men so much," Vera commented. "The only male they can stand is Marcus and that's because he gave them to me. I think they think he's their daddy or something."

Upon hearing Marcus's name, Kika and Toby immediately took off in search of him.

"Good-bye, little pests," Vera said fondly, before turning to Paris. "Thanks for walking them. And thanks for spending the night even though it was totally unnecessary. This is not what being my assistant means," she assured the younger woman.

Vera had been an employee of The Deveraux Group for over twelve years. Starting as a feature editor at *Image* magazine, the high-fashion monthly, she had become the editor in chief of that publication, as well as developing a few others along the way up to and including *Personal*

Space. From feature editor to editor in chief and vice president in charge of publications at The Deveraux Group, Vera was often considered the most indispensable member of the executive team other than the talented and driven Deveraux brothers.

In order to keep her world running smoothly, Vera had two assistants, one editorial and one personal. Her personal assistant, Trina, was taking six months off after the birth of her first child, which left Vera in need of a replacement. Paris, a Deveraux cousin from Lafayette, Louisiana, was finishing her training program at The Deveraux Group after completing her MBA. She had interned at a number of publications and was willing to take on any assignment to further her knowledge of the company. From all appearances, it looked like her new slot as personal assistant to Vera would be her most interesting.

Glancing at Vera, she noted the time and suggested that breakfast was in order. "Would you like me to fix you something? An omelet or bacon and eggs or whatever you'd like," the younger woman offered.

Vera smiled gratefully. "Paris, thank you, but that's not necessary. I eat the same thing for breakfast almost every day, a bowl of Kashi with skim milk, a carton of fat-free yogurt, and some fruit. And usually a cup of green tea. It tastes like boiled grass, but it's full of antioxidants," she said with a grimace. "Supposed to be really good for you, I guess. I think I'll treat myself to coffee this morning, though. A great big cup," she said with satisfaction.

Paris made a face. "Umm-umm, I don't eat or drink anything that isn't delightful to the taste, which is why my rear end is the size that it is," she admitted. "And I never eat breakfast. I just can't gag it down," she said with a shudder.

Paris was a big, beautiful woman, tall and definitely plump. She had the look of a Deveraux, although the roundness of her face hid the sculptured cheekbones that were a family trait. In addition to a beautiful complexion, she had a wealth of hair, a thick cascading flow of wavy black silk, or it would have been if she hadn't confined it to a ponytail every single day. She looked at Vera with a combination of admiration and envy.

"I wish I was more disciplined about what I eat. Maybe I could get a figure like yours," she said frankly.

Vera had a beautiful body. Even as she neared her fortieth birthday, she was trim and toned, still resembling the cheerleader she'd been in high school and college. She was tall and lithe but stacked, with a small waist, full breasts, and curving hips that led down into legs that were firm and shapely. An admirer once remarked that Vera's body was so amazing she looked as if she were moving when she was standing still.

Vera barely acknowledged Paris's compliment, though. Rising with effort, she accepted the cane Paris offered her and headed to the kitchen to fix her cereal and coffee. "Honey, I eat like this for one reason only, to avoid diabetes. That's also why I exercise so much, quiet as it's kept. If it wasn't for that, I could happily live on hot dogs, potato chips, ginger beer, and massive slabs of pound cake," she admitted.

Paris followed her into the brick-walled kitchen that opened onto a flower-filled garden displayed through French doors. "Does diabetes run in your family?" she asked solicitously.

"Girl, 'run' is hardly the right term," Vera sighed. "It *charges* through my family like Michael Johnson running the four-hundred-yard dash. Goes through it like a freight train on both sides of my family. We all watch our diets and exercise regularly. It's not vanity, it's fear of high blood sugar that keeps me moving," she said as she located the skim milk in the refrigerator.

Paris watched closely as Vera assembled a revoltingly healthy breakfast of high-fiber Kashi cereal, a section of melon, and a handful of blueberries. The yogurt also made its appearance, something called Fit and Fancy or Lite and Lovely. *Ick.* The coffee Vera put on started making its presence known with a rich aroma. She made a slight face as she noticed Vera putting out two bowls of cereal. *Please, God, don't let her offer me that stuff. It looks like gravel and shredded rope,* she thought anxiously. She gladly left the room to answer the doorbell and returned to the kitchen with a huge bouquet.

"Here you go, Vera. I guess we don't have to wonder who these are from," she said teasingly.

Vera gave a huge smile and then cooed with happiness as she looked over the beautiful display. Lilacs, tulips, irises, and heather with lots of greenery in a huge crystal vase; only one person knew her well enough to send all her favorite flowers. Sure enough, the card read, *This is not a reward or an apology. Feel better, Marcus.*

She was still laughing as she picked up her kitchen cordless and punched in the number to his private line.

At the moment, Marcus was in a meeting with his brothers in his office. "Meeting" was perhaps too loose a term for what was transpiring; they were basically giving Marcus a hard time.

"So I hear you put on quite a show in the emergency room last night," Clay drawled in his deep voice.

Marcus threw his head back and groaned. "Aww, man, don't even go there. I'm getting ready to go out and Paris calls me and tells me that Vera fell out of an airplane. So of course I took off like a bat out of hell and go busting up in the ER like somebody's daddy. There's Vera, lying there with her leg all jacked up, claiming all she did was trip over a rock after she jumped out of an airplane. *Jumped,* thank you very much. And then there's some big overgrown clown who's supposed to be this doctor and she's just flirtin' away with the big ape. Meanwhile my heart is still going ninety miles an hour and she somehow seems to feel like *I'm* over-reacting. Me, the calmest, most levelheaded person in this family, is overreacting," he said indignantly.

Malcolm and Martin, his next oldest brothers, didn't even bother to hide their amusement; they just started laughing.

Clay looked at the two of them and swallowed his own laughter for a moment. "So what happened with your date? Did you even remember you had one?"

Marcus leaned back in his chair and raised an eyebrow. "I'm not old and senile like you jokers; of course I remembered," he said defensively. "I didn't remember right away, but I eventually called her and we hooked up later."

This statement caused all three brothers to laugh even more and the words "booty call" were heard from more than one man.

Marcus shook his head. "No, no, my brothers, it wasn't like that. An evening with me is always an event, whether it's a late night call or the full complement of dining out and whatever. Never resort to a booty call, isn't that what you taught me?" he said grandly with an expression of supreme self-confidence.

Martin was the first one to regain his composure. "Okay, you're right about that, Marcus. We did try to set good examples of how a well-bred man treats a lady. But you and what's her name are getting close to the ninety-day mark. Is she aware that she's a temporary diversion only and her contract is not up for renewal at the end of three months?"

Marcus was known for not pursuing a relationship past ninety days. Since he had no intention of getting married, he didn't believe in lengthy attachments, nor did he ever bring a woman to a family or a business function. He saw no reason to give anyone the hope that she would eventually be Mrs. Marcus Deveraux. Up until this point, Larissa had been subject to the same treatment; he was attentive, gentlemanly, and suave with any woman with whom he was involved. After last night, though, it looked like Larissa might have an edge that even he hadn't realized. The fact that she'd been calm, accepting, and affectionate had given her very high marks with Marcus, who hated scenes of any kind.

"I don't know, Martin," he answered slowly. "This might be a contract worth renewing."

Smiling at the utter shock on his brothers' faces, Marcus was about to elaborate when his private line rang, distracting him. His smile got even bigger and much more genuine as he heard Vera's effusive thanks on the other end of the line.

"Flowers? What flowers? I sent you nothing, woman! There must be another Marcus out there who's deranged enough to send you imported flowers. You got nothin' comin' from me, you crazy woman. People who jump out of planes on purpose don't need flowers, they need commitment papers! So what are you doing, anyway? Are you in bed? Is your leg propped up? Why not? Can't you do anything you're told to do?" he demanded.

The three brothers exchanged knowing looks and all three mouthed the same name, *Vera*. They rose and left the office, leaving Marcus to his phone call.

Vera didn't have time to dwell on her confusing dreams or even her aching ankle; she had a steady stream of company all day. Lillian Deveraux Williams came over to visit at lunchtime and brought more flowers as well as her world-class shrimp salad. Vera was addicted to it as was everyone who ever tasted a mouthful. Vera was happily devouring a portion while Lillian arranged the fragrant apricot roses she'd cut from her own garden. Lillian and Vera were special friends and had been since Vera first came to The Deveraux

Group. Even though Lillian was the age of Vera's mother, they were extremely close and had been from the day Vera had mistaken Lillian for a model and used her in a shoot for *Image* magazine.

Lillian had come to the office to have lunch with her sons and was crossing the main reception area when Vera spotted her. Vera, having no idea who the older woman was, had assumed she was a model who'd gotten lost looking for the studio. She introduced herself, informed her that the shoot was about to start, and led her to the models' dressing room. The next thing Lillian knew she was being photographed as a sexy woman getting married for the second time. By the time Vera realized her mistake she'd been mortified, but Lillian, who hadn't had so much fun in years, was thrilled and a true friendship was born. And the photographs were indeed used in the magazine to great acclaim.

She and Vera shopped together, lunched together, and traveled together when their schedules permitted. It was Vera who convinced Lillian that she wasn't too old to pursue the college degree she'd always wanted. Vera explained to Lillian about college credit for life experience and helped her prepare a portfolio to earn those credits. And Vera was the one person in whom Lillian confided when her childhood sweetheart, Bill "Bump" Williams, had come courting. Vera had, in fact, been Lillian's only attendant when she and Bill got married. As Lillian often phrased it in a departure from her normal ladylike speech, Vera was her "road dog."

While Lillian arranged the flowers, Vera fielded calls from various members of her staff, her parents, two of her sisters, and Selena, who was married to Malcolm. It seemed as though everyone in the world knew about her accident, thanks to Marcus. She was about to comment on this fact when the doorbell rang, causing Kika and Toby to start barking again and Lillian to go into action.

"I'll get the door, you just get on that chaise and put your foot up before it gets any more swollen," the older woman admonished her.

Vera did as she was told; the leg was really bothering her. Just as she settled in somewhat comfortably, her visitor arrived in the living room followed by Lillian. It was Benita Cochran Deveraux, wife to Clay and mother to three active boys, none of whom were with her at the moment. Bennie, as everyone called her, looked Vera over carefully, a sardonic smile on her face.

"Girl, I was expecting you to be one step away from intensive care, the way Marcus was carrying on! He made it sound as though you were at death's door," Bennie said cheerfully. "Although that does look pretty painful. Do you need anything?" she asked as she bestowed a brief kiss on Vera's cheek and presented her with a couple of hardback books and a big box of imported hard candy, one of Vera's favorite things.

"I'm supposed to give you three kisses, one from each child," Bennie said as she sat down across from Vera. "They wanted to come with me, but I think you need a little peace and quiet. Are you in much pain?"

Vera assured Bennie that it was bearable. "Marcus has a tendency to overreact as we all know. I'm going to rest over the weekend and it'll be fine by the time we tape the show next week."

Bennie and Lillian exchanged a look before Lillian spoke. "Vera, I agree that Marcus hovers over you like he's your big brother or something, but you have to admit, you've been quite the daredevil lately. I thought the bungee jumping was bad enough but this! What are you trying to do, girl? Skydiving? I know it was for charity, but really . . ." Lillian's voice trailed off.

Vera made an embarrassed face and bit her lip. How could she explain this so the two women would understand, without explaining the dreams, the list, and some other highly personal things? Luckily, Bennie came to her rescue. Bennie was herself a former tomboy and understood Vera's daredevil side.

"Okay, Vera, you have to tell me something. I never told anybody, but I've always wanted to try skydiving. If I didn't know for a fact that my husband would lock me up for the rest of my life, I still would," she said with a grin. "So what was it like? What did it feel like to take that jump?"

Vera's eyes got a faraway look and she gave the two women a dreamy smile. "It was amazing. You jump out into nothing and it's really surreal, extremely quiet and still. You feel almost helpless but powerful at the same time because you're in total command of your body and you know you're going to conquer this. And then the jump master gives you the signal and all of a sudden there's a huge jerk and your whole body goes on alert and you begin floating down and it's the most wonderful sensation you can imagine."

Lillian looked intrigued in spite of herself, but she still got in the last word. "I hate to put it this indelicately, but it doesn't sound that different from some really good sex. Couldn't you do that instead of flinging yourself out of a plane?"

Vera and Bennie burst out laughing and Vera threw a small pillow at Lillian. Vera pointed a finger at the older woman and accused her of trying to corrupt the innocent. "Here I am, a poor little widow woman, and you're trying to turn me into a hoochie! For shame!"

Lillian was completely unrepentant, though. "The only shame is you doing all these crazy stunts that could break valuable limbs instead of trying to have a nice, normal social life. You need some balance in your life, Vera. And before you ask, yes, 'balance' is another word for *men*. You need to start going out more," Lillian said shrewdly.

Vera sat up and prepared to defend herself against the familiar onslaught of loving advice from Lillian. "Hey, I go out plenty! I go to parties, to the theater, to the movies, I go dancing, I play golf—" Her indignant tirade was stopped by Bennie's voice.

"Yes, but, Vera, you do those things with us, or with your coworkers or with Marcus. It's not like you're really making an attempt to date. And having been a widow myself, I know how difficult it is to get back into the swing of a normal social life afterward. Honey, if I hadn't met Clay, who knows, I might be jumping out of airplanes, too," Bennie admitted.

Lillian watched Vera's face carefully as she posed her next remarks. "All three of us were widowed, how sad. And I agree with Bennie, it's truly difficult to try to start having a normal life again. You're not interested at first, because you're still in love with your husband. Then, when you think you might be able to tolerate the company of another man, you realize you don't really know any. Everyone I knew was married to someone else. And some of those husbands would have been more than willing to get a little action on the side," Lillian recalled with a wry smile.

Bennie nodded. "All the guys I knew were either friends of my brothers or men I met during the course of business. They certainly weren't averse to a 'hookup,' but they also wanted to network. It's not very flattering, but a lot of them saw me as a way to advance their careers." Bennie brushed her thick, glorious black hair out of her eyes before continuing. "You know what? I owe my marriage to Marcus. If he and Darnell hadn't come to Detroit and made that goofy presentation, I never would have met Clayton! Marcus is my hero," she said with a big smile.

Lillian chimed in at that. "And if Bennie and Clay hadn't gotten engaged, I might not have run into Bill again." Lillian and Bill Williams had encountered each other at the retirement party of Bennie's father in Detroit; it so happened that her long-lost childhood sweetheart was Bennie's godfather.

"So it looks like I owe Marcus a huge debt of gratitude, too," Lillian said.

Both women looked at Vera with great anticipation before Bennie spoke. "Vera, maybe you should get Marcus to introduce you to a few new guys. He knows everybody in the world and his track record is impeccable when it comes to getting people together. Look what he did for us," she added winningly.

Vera looked at her two dear friends as if they had little blue bunnies hopping out of their ears. "I don't *think* so! In the first place, I know plenty of men. Plenty. And I have a date next week, so there! And in the second place, Marcus was only the catalyst; he wasn't the agent of change with you and Clay. It was just a coincidence, that's all," Vera grumbled.

"A date? You've been holding out on us, girl!" Bennie immediately demanded details.

"Oh, it's not that much. Dante Bohannon was a teammate of John's. He always said he wanted to be a doctor and after he played pro ball for a few years he did go back to med school. He's a resident in orthopedics now and he treated me in the emergency room. I'm cooking dinner for him next week." Vera waited for reactions and got some less than enthusiastic ones.

"Oh," said Lillian. "I was hoping for something more . . . datelike, I think." She looked over at Bennie for support. Bennie, too, looked underwhelmed at Vera's announcement.

"Well, it's a start," Bennie said bracingly. "In the meantime, don't rule Marcus out. He certainly worked wonders with Lillian and me," Bennie teased.

Vera moaned and covered her face. How was she going to convince her two best friends that she was perfectly happy just the way she was? And how would they react if she told them that she never intended to be involved with another man again as long as she lived?

Chapter 3

Marcus entered the parking structure of The Deveraux Group and eased the BMW into his parking space with ease. He was returning from a week of meetings in Los Angeles and was slowly releasing the aggravation of a long, boring flight. He wasn't tired; on the contrary, he was ready to go out and do something to release some energy. Marcus thrived on his work and the continual challenges he and his brothers faced in the course of business. Unlike a person who felt trapped by a work situation, Marcus got a real kick of adrenaline from wheeling and dealing. It was Friday, the end of the workweek; his meetings had been an unqualified success and the weekend was looming large. Life was good.

He entered the glassed-in elevator through the parking structure and exited on the executive level of the building. The many-storied building was the center of a growing complex built by The Deveraux Group. In addition to the main building that housed his family's businesses, there were smaller office buildings housing law offices, doctors' offices, restaurants, shops, and the like. It always gave Marcus a slight thrill to observe the scenery from the elevator as he rose to his office; it was a terrific view. The glass and brick buildings arranged artfully in the forestlike surroundings always gave Marcus a sense of peace, pride, and accomplishment.

The elevator purred to a stop and he stepped out onto the top level of the building. The main building was a hexagonal shape build around an atrium. On this top level there were six offices and a central reception area, which was ruled with an iron fist by Tami Foster. Tami was tough, funny, organized to the point of being automated, and she made it possible for everything to run smoothly from the top floor down to the mailroom. Tami greeted Marcus in her usual humorous fashion.

"So you finally decided to come home, did you? It's about time you remembered where you belong," she added as he entered his suite. "And don't look for RaeAnn, she's having her brain sucked out with the rest of them."

"Her what?" Marcus asked with raised eyebrows.

Tami leaned against the massive mahogany door and crossed her arms. Her blue eyes lit up with laughter, and she cocked her head toward the corner office opposite the executive suite. "Her brain is being sucked out by an alien. Go look if you don't believe me."

Marcus put down his briefcase and removed his jacket. Loosening his expensive tie, he headed for the sunny corner office that belonged to Vera. It was his usual first stop when he returned from a trip, anyway. He hadn't seen Vera in about two weeks as they'd both been on the road. He could hear laughter and conversation floating out of the office, and as he entered the room he could see exactly what Tami meant. There on the long sofa was Vera, impeccably clad as always in a fabulous violet wool crepe suit with the addition of a most unlikely accessory. She had a cloth diaper thrown over her shoulder and was cuddling a small baby to it, a girl from the looks of the pink and white outfit. Also in attendance were his personal secretary, RaeAnn Powell, Paris, and Trina Johnson, Vera's permanent personal assistant, and the mother of the baby. All of them indeed looked as if they'd been taken over by another life force, all but Trina, who wore her usual down-to-earth expression with justifiable maternal pride.

"What have I told you about having babies up here?" Marcus demanded in a mock fierce voice that fooled no one. He crossed the office to sit beside Vera and take a good look at Trina's adorable two-month-old. She was a beauty, with her mother's dark cocoa skin and big knowing eyes, topped with a head of thick black baby curls.

Marcus immediately took her from Vera and held her in the crook of his arm. She rewarded him instantly with a huge, toothless smile. Marcus was exceptionally good with babies after being around his many nieces and nephews. "Babies do not belong in the office. You're a pest and a nuisance," he said sternly. "Look at you, got all these women neglecting their work just to play with you. What's your name, anyway?"

"Her name is Zandriana, isn't that pretty?" Vera cooed. "She's so beautiful, Trina!"

Marcus finally admitted that Trina had produced an exceptional child. "She's gorgeous, all right. Charles better keep a loaded shotgun at the front *and* back doors, because the boys are gonna drive him crazy chasing after her," he remarked.

Trina suggested that Marcus might want to give her back as she needed changing. His expression immediately changed to one of great horror. "See? That's what I mean about babies. You let your guard down and they poop and pee all over you. Take her!"

Vera laughed at his foolishness. "Oh, you don't mean that. You love babies, you know you do. Just wait until you have a houseful of your own, you're going to spoil them rotten."

Marcus made another face and rose from the sofa. Shaking his head vigorously, he took his leave of the assembly. "Nope, no way, not gonna happen. Being a godfather is plenty for me. No babies. Ugh."

Tami looked up from her desk as Marcus left Vera's office and smiled knowingly. "I told you, it's like having your brain dissolved by extraterrestrials. Babies make you go crazy. I should know, my nephew does the same thing to me, the little monster."

As he made his way through RaeAnn's outer office to his private domain, Marcus sat down at his massive desk and thought about what has just transpired. Seeing Vera with a baby always gave him a slight pang, although it didn't seem to bother her. Vera had suffered a miscarriage nine years earlier and had never conceived again. Marcus had been home from college for the summer when it happened and he would never forget her absolute despair. She'd been halfway through what seemed to be a normal pregnancy when for reasons unknown she lost the baby.

He remembered sitting with her for long hours after she came home from the hospital. He kept her company because her husband was away at football camp, preparing for the fall season. Everyone seemed to think it was his way of handling his grief, but Marcus thought otherwise, although he never said this to anyone. Marcus was there for Vera when she wanted to talk, when she wanted to be silent, and when she wanted to cry. It still made his heart ache a little because he knew how much she'd wanted that baby and he also knew what a terrific mother she'd make.

A knock on the huge door to his inner office made him look up as Vera popped her head in the door. "Are you busy? I brought you something," she said gaily.

He immediately rose from his desk and invited her to enter, checking out her legs as she did so. She was wearing a sensational pair of open-toed black pumps that set off her slender ankles and shapely calves. "Your ankle looks pretty good," he said.

Vera stopped in midstride and looked at him with her hand on her hip. "Marcus, that was weeks ago! Of course

it's healed, it's been all healed for a long time now. Let it
go," she said amiably. She then handed him a shopping bag
bearing the name of his favorite shirt maker. "I was in New
York so I had him make up six for you," she said. "There're
a couple of ties in there, too."

Marcus was touched by Vera's thoughtfulness. She always remembered to do little things like this for him; this
was one of the myriad of reasons they were so close. But
he always returned that thoughtfulness. "Thanks, Vera. I
was just about to put in an order for some shirts. And I
brought you something, too," he said, loving the look of
anticipation on her face.

Opening his briefcase, Marcus presented Vera with a
small velvet box that could only contain jewelry She
opened it immediately and sighed with pleasure at the
small fourteen-karat gold charm that spelled out HOLLY-
WOOD in tiny letters. "Marcus, thank you! My charm
bracelet is getting so full I'm going to have to get another
one soon," she said happily as she shook her slender left
wrist to demonstrate.

Marcus took her wrist in his big hand and examined the
bracelet carefully. Many of the charms had been given to
Vera by Marcus to commemorate some special event they'd
shared. He stared at it intently and said slowly, "I think you
could be right. This one is definitely getting full. So . . ."
With a flourish he pulled out another box, this one contain-
ing a thick gold-link bracelet suitable for attaching charms.

Vera had barely begun to thank him when his private
line began to ring. She immediately began to exit the office, making a "call me" gesture as she did so.

He nodded and picked up the phone. "Yes?" It was
Larissa, confirming their date for the evening. "Larissa,
can you hold on a minute?" Without waiting for a response
he called after Vera, "Are we still on for tomorrow morning?" Hearing her "yes" he returned to his phone call.

"So how was your trip, Marcus?" Larissa asked in her soft voice.

"Fine, fine. Everything went smoothly, so I came home happy," he responded. "What time would you like me to pick you up?"

"Well, Marcus, since you've had a long hard week of negotiations, how about I cook dinner for you and we just relax around here?" she suggested.

"Uh, I don't want to put you to any trouble, Larissa. Let's go out to a nice dinner and maybe some music, how does that sound?" he answered smoothly. "I'll pick you up about eight and we'll take it from there."

Marcus waited for her agreement and almost didn't hear her little sigh of frustration, but it was there nonetheless. He looked at the phone for a moment after he put it back in the cradle. Home-cooked dinners, cozy evenings spent at her house, he knew where this was leading and he wasn't ready to go there with Larissa or anyone else. This always happened around day sixty-five or so. So far, Larissa was right on schedule.

Meanwhile, Paris was down in the art department soliciting advice from Aidan. Since she'd begun working at The Deveraux Group the two had become good friends. They shared a warped sense of humor and a quick wit, and had a number of interests in common. Paris knew she'd found an ally when she first saw a neatly lettered sign mounted on the door to his office that read, I AM NOT NICE. I DO NOT *WANT* TO BE NICE. AND NO, IT WILL NOT MAKE ME "FEEL BETTER TO TRY." Actually he was one of the nicest people in the world but he didn't have much in the way of patience.

He looked up from his always-tidy desk and gave Paris a fierce look. "Do you ever intend to wear your hair down?"

Paris sat on an architect's stool in front of a wall-mounted drawing desk and spun around. "Probably not," she answered.

"Then why don't you cut it instead of wearing that damned ponytail all the time? You're a beautiful woman but that thing does nothing for you," he said pointedly.

Paris cheerfully shook the offending ponytail at him. They'd had this conversation many times before. Aidan was determined to give her a makeover from head to toe and she was equally determined to resist his efforts.

"Quit picking on me, I have to ask you something," she said.

"Well, thank you for not saying, 'Can I ask you a question?'" Aidan said in approval. "When people say that to me I always tell them they just did and walk away from them."

Paris ignored that and got to the point. "Suppose you knew that two people were interested in each other and that neither one of them was going to take the first step. Would you do something about it?"

"Speaking of first steps, *where* did you get those shoes?" He stared with distaste at her chunky black shoes. "Are you planning to scale Mount Everest in them? When did Birkenstock start making pumps, anyway? I've told you and told you, there are two things you do not do without me; one is decorate your home and the other is buy shoes. Why don't you let me take you shopping?" he demanded as he scanned her other items of clothing.

Paris made her usual face at his suggestion. Aidan was always impeccably attired, usually in black from head to toe. His thick black hair always gleamed with health and expensive styling gel and he had the devastatingly chiseled good looks that made people mistake him for a model, which he could have been had he not been so muscular. He was too brawny to pull off high-fashion looks and he looked too intelligent to be the scruffy lumberjack type. He had the dark hair and eyes of his Mexican mother and the porcelain skin of his Irish father complete with a deep cleft in his chin and high, stunning cheekbones.

None of this impressed Paris at the moment, though, as she was busy trying to get him to listen to her. "Aidan, pay attention! This is important. If you knew that two people were perfect for each other, wouldn't you feel that you needed to do something to get them together?"

His attention caught at last, Aidan disagreed immediately. "No. Absolutely not. If it's meant to be, they'll find each other. What are you up to, anyway?"

Paris evaded his question with one of her own. "Why is it a bad idea? Suppose there were two people who were best friends and you knew they'd probably never tell each other how they felt even though they'd be terrific together."

Aidan rolled his eyes back in his head and stood up, crossing the office to where Paris sat idly spinning around on the stool. Putting one hand on either side of her head, he stopped her from spinning and forced her to look into his eyes.

"I begged you to quit watching those chick flicks. I told you that massive degeneration of brain tissue would be the result of watching all those happily ever after drivel movies. I don't know whom you're trying to play Martha May matchmaker for, but you must *not* do it. Never try to interfere in matters of the heart, especially other people's hearts. You're plunging headfirst into disaster, I'm warning you," he said sternly.

Paris shook her head loose from his firm grip and tried to make another point. "Look, let's say you're cooking a big pot of penne pasta," she began.

"I'd never do that, I can't stand penne," he retorted.

"Okay, linguine, fusilli, whatever. The pasta is at a full boil and it's about to cook over the sides of the pot. What would you do?"

Aidan looked at her suspiciously before replying, "I'd stir the pot so it wouldn't overflow, what else can you do?"

Paris held up both hands in triumph. "See? That's precisely what I'm going to do. I'm just going to give the pot a good stir so it won't boil over, that's all."

For once Aidan was silent, but not for long. "I don't quite trust you, Martha May. This has *Titanic* written all over it. That was a disaster, too."

The next morning Vera opened her front door to find Marcus standing there with a bouquet of wildflowers. They were going shopping for a birthday present for his nephews. Bennie and Clay's rambunctious twins, Martin Andrew and Malcolm Adonis, were celebrating their birthday that afternoon with a family party. Vera had already selected her gifts and had them neatly stashed in her hall closet, but Marcus was making a last-minute dash to the toy store.

"Good morning!" Vera said happily. "I take it these are for me? What's the occasion?"

Marcus kissed her on the cheek and walked past her into the house. "No reason, I just saw them and thought of you. And to thank you for the shirts, they fit perfectly," he replied.

Vera led the way into the kitchen, where she put the flowers into a pretty pale green vase. "Well, thank you for the flowers, sweetie-pie. A most unexpected and wonderful start to my day," she said warmly.

Marcus looked around in vain for Kika and Toby. "Where are they?" he asked. They usually made their presence known immediately.

Vera smiled. "Your little darlings are on the patio. You'd better sit down, they're going to jump all over your legs as soon as they come in," she cautioned.

Marcus shrugged. He was wearing well-worn jeans, deck shoes, and a green polo shirt, so he wasn't worried about his attire being ruined. Vera was also in casual clothes consisting of black capri pants and a crisp white blouse with rolled sleeves and a pair of black canvas espadrilles. She went to the French door that led to her sunny garden and opened the door. "Marcus is here," she called.

Sure enough, the two little dogs came skittering into the kitchen at top speed, rounding the butcher-block work island so fast that they slid across the tiled floor and careened into each other. Their target was Marcus, who sat in one of the dining room chairs and waited for their attack. All Vera could hear was their excited yipping and barking as they made their delight in seeing Marcus known. She was constantly amused by the adoration the dogs bestowed on Marcus. He'd bought Toby for Vera after John died, something to bring a smile to her face. His tactic had worked admirably because caring for the puppy had truly eased some of her grief. But she couldn't bear the idea of leaving Toby at home alone during the day, so they had purchased Kika, who was about the same age as Toby although she came from a different litter. It was hard to say who took the most pleasure out of the two, although Marcus was by far the most indulgent.

"Vera, where are their leads?" he called from the dining room.

"Marcus, we are not taking those dogs shopping," she said quickly. She went to the doorway of the dining room and crossed her arms to emphasize her statement. Toby was sitting at Marcus's left foot looking up at him expectantly and Kika was sitting at his right foot with her paw in the air, her standard means of getting attention.

"Aww, look. They want to go for a ride," Marcus said coaxingly. "C'mon, Pie, let them go." Vera's habit of referring to her nearest and dearest as "sweetie-pie" had led to a game that she and Marcus played with each other. They called each other every variety of pie imaginable, from honey-pie to lambie-pie to cutie-pie. Marcus also called her just plain Pie, but no one else ever dared to venture there.

Resistance was futile with three pairs of eyes fastened

winningly on her; she finally threw up her hands in defeat. "Okay, but either put them in their carrier or you hold them. I'm not driving with them running around in the car," she instructed.

Which is how they all came to be tooling down the road in Vera's sporty little Turbo PT Cruiser with the sunroof open and the stereo blaring. Their first stop was PetSmart, a wonderful establishment where pets were welcome to come shopping with their owners. Kika and Toby were well known in PetSmart and were greeted by several employees as Marcus carried them around the store. Vera had to get some doggie shampoo and conditioner, dog food, and some of the little treats shaped like tiny lamb chops, which were the dogs' favorites. And she made the pet supplier their first stop because she wanted to get the dogs back home as soon as possible; Marcus could keep her shopping right up until time for the party. Unlike most men, Marcus actually liked shopping. Kika and Toby made their resentment known at being taken home, but Vera mollified them with the lamb chop treats. "That man has you spoiled rotten," she mumbled as she got them situated.

Marcus and Vera spent a happy, relaxed morning selecting presents for the boys, a task made more difficult by Marcus's overly generous nature. Vera vetoed him on several items including a computer, a television with built-in DVD, and a library of video games.

"They don't need a computer of their own, they're too little, for heaven's sake. Besides, there're about five computers at the house already. And you know Bennie doesn't believe in the children having televisions in their rooms, she says that's what the family room is for. And I agree with Clay that video games rot the mind. Can't you pick something that's fun and age-appropriate that doesn't cost thousands of dollars?"

Marcus was barely paying any attention to her words of

censure; his eye was caught by something that Vera actually approved, a big, colorful tent that was the size of a playhouse. It was just the kind of thing that the boys would love playing in and it was on sale besides. "And best of all, Clay's gonna have to put it together," he gloated. The giant tent did not come assembled.

"I wouldn't get too happy," Vera warned him. "Clay is not about to put that thing together by himself, and you know this, honey-pie."

Marcus nodded absently, his mind on the fun the boys would have with the tent. "Oh, I know we'll all end up putting it up, but it won't take long."

After wrestling the big box into the PT Cruiser, they went home to shower and change for the party. Marcus grumbled about having to ride in Vera's car again; he loved pretending that he hated the eccentric little vehicle. Vera smacked him on his arm. "Apologize! CP doesn't like it when you say ugly things about her," she said sternly.

"Apologize to who? Who is CP?"

"CP is my car. That's her name," Vera cocked her head slightly and dared him to say something, which he immediately did.

"CP? What kind of name is that? You named your car Colored People?" he said, genuinely mystified.

Vera burst out laughing. "No, CP is for Cutie Pie. But now that you mention the other, maybe I'd better change it."

"I have a suggestion. How about not naming an inanimate object? That's something you should look into," he replied.

"How about I put you out on the corner? There should be a MARTA bus along here soon," she said pertly.

Some hours later, the tent proved to be a huge hit with the twins. The party took place at the home of Clay and Bennie and was mainly for the family. The couple didn't believe in monstrous birthday parties held in public venues, or in inviting huge crowds of people to celebrate what was, after all, a family event. Bennie was her usual smiling, serene self, and Clay was as always a gracious host when Marcus and Vera arrived bearing gifts.

Vera barely got a chance to speak to anyone once the boys discovered her presence. Happy cries of "Aunt Vewa! Aunt Vewa!" greeted her and the birthday boys and their older brother, Clayton III, known as Trey, immediately accosted her. They dragged her off to show her their favorite birthday present, a golden Labrador puppy that had come all the way from Detroit courtesy of their uncle Donnie.

Marcus hugged and kissed his sister-in-law. "Bennie, you look gorgeous, as always. I don't have to ask if my brother is taking care of you," he said with a smile.

Bennie kissed him back and looked over at the massive stainless steel grill where Clay was showing off his grilling skills to his stepfather, Bill Williams. "Oh, sweetie, we take care of each other, you know that. But he's going to be taking extra good care of me for a while," she said quietly.

Marcus pondered that statement for a moment. "Are you . . . ?" His voice trailed off as Bennie put her finger to his lips.

"There should be an interesting announcement later." She smiled.

Marcus grinned at her and was about to speak when his mother called to him from the deck. "Marcus, could I borrow you for a second?"

He joined Lillian on the deck and sat down beside her on the big teakwood glider.

"Sorry I didn't get here sooner, Mom, but Vera was dragging me from store to store. You know how she is," he said guilelessly.

Lillian pulled her chic sunglasses down on her nose so she could look her youngest son in the eyes. "Yes, and I know *you* even better. Vera bought the boys' gifts weeks ago and you were dragging her from pillar to post trying to buy the most extravagant thing you could find at the last minute. Isn't that more accurate?" she said shrewdly.

"Maybe. Possibly. Could be," Marcus replied with no hint of shame at all. "So how's my favorite mother doing and what can I do for her today?" Marcus put his arm around Lillian and gave her a one-armed hug.

Lillian had returned her glasses to their proper position and was looking across the lawn where Vera was playing with the boys and their new puppy. Vera looked like she was having more fun than the boys. The puppy was chasing her in circles with every intention of grabbing a big bite of her long, full skirt and she was laughing merrily as she eluded him.

Lillian was watching them intently, so intently that she forgot what she was about to say for a moment. Finally she said, "Marcus, look at Vera."

Marcus looked. Vera looked perfectly fine to him; actually better than fine in a cute black sundress with tiny white polka dots and strappy flat black sandals that showed off her perfectly groomed feet with the sexy red toenails. "What about Vera, Mom? She looks okay to me."

Lillian pounded his leg softly with her fist and made a sound of exasperation. "Marcus, Vera is a young, beautiful woman. What happened to John was a tragedy, but she can't stop living her life because of it! Vera has too much love and too much spirit to live the rest of her life alone. I think she should start dating again. And I think you should introduce her to some nice men," she said firmly.

It was a good thing that she had again turned toward the happy group on the far lawn, because the look on Marcus's face defied all description.

The deck where Marcus and Lillian were chatting was situated under the kitchen windows where, if someone were so inclined, they could overhear every word being spoken. And as Paris was in the kitchen ostensibly tending to the making of lemonade, she did indeed hear every word spoken by Lillian to Marcus. And since she was watching her cousin's face, she could also see his reaction.

"Why, cousin Paris! If I didn't know any better, I'd say you were listening to grown folks' conversations. Isn't that supposed to be impolite or something?" drawled a familiar voice.

Paris quickly turned around to face her cousin Angelique, the youngest Deveraux and her partner in crime since their toddler days. "Girl! It's about time you got back in town! How was Martha's Vineyard?"

She accompanied her words with a warm hug, which Angelique returned fiercely. Angelique had been out of town for a week assisting the head fashion photographer for *Image* magazine, the renowned Alan Jay. People who didn't know Angelique well were stunned that she actually had a job, one at which she was doing quite well. People like Paris, who knew her intimately, were thrilled she'd found a creative outlet for her talent.

When they stopped embracing, Angelique gave a shrug. "It was okay. The weather was great, the food was great, Alan is always wonderful, but those models gave me fever, girl. They're nice enough but, honey, that diva attitude and drama, deliver me!" She shuddered theatrically as she uttered the last words. Then she froze as a deep voice began speaking.

"Excuse me for interrupting but isn't that the pot calling the kettle black?" The man's voice, rich with amusement, could only belong to one person. Angelique turned to face the speaker, Adonis Cochran.

"You again. I always hope for an Adonis-free summer, yet here you are," Angelique said calmly. "Why don't you ever stay in Detroit? Is there a bench warrant out for you or something?"

Paris drew in her breath quickly. Angelique generally tried to act tough, but she wasn't nearly as tough as she liked to appear. She needn't have worried, though; the tall, extremely handsome Adonis seemed to have a handle on the situation.

"Aw, sugar, there's no need to pretend like you aren't glad to see me. I came down to celebrate my nephews' birthday, bring them their present, and see my sister. And to bring you this," he said, producing a perfect rose from behind his back. "But I think this beautiful lady deserves this flower much more since you can't remember to call me Donnie, not Adonis," he drawled. Donnie turned to Paris and presented her with the flower, to her amusement.

"Hello. I'm Bennie's brother Donnie and you are . . . ?"

"I'm Paris, Lillian's niece," she replied.

"Well, I'm here for a few days and I hope we get to know one another better while I'm here," he said sincerely. Turning to Angelique, he tapped her on the end of her nose and said, "Too bad about your flower, Evie. You need to be nicer to me; then you'll get one."

Angelique turned bright red but before she could retaliate, he had left the kitchen as quickly as he had entered. She knew that "Evie" was short for Evilene, his hated nickname for her.

"Ooh, that man works my last nerve," Angelique sputtered. "That settles it, I'm going to have to punish him," she vowed in a steely voice.

Paris stared at her cousin, trying to hide the smile on her face. Between what she already suspected and what she'd just witnessed, this was liable to be a most entertaining summer.

Chapter 4

For the rest of the afternoon, Marcus was distinctly un-settled by his mother's innocent remark. All she'd done was suggest that it was time for Vera to start dating again and that it might be a good idea for Marcus to introduce her around. Harmless comments, the things one would ex-pect an old friend to say about another friend, and yet Marcus was filled with pure rage from head to toe every time he thought about the topic. For one thing, it was patently absurd to think that Vera needed to be introduced to anybody. After all of her years in the magazine business, Vera had connections all over the country.

Vera knew everyone in creation, and most of the people she knew, it seemed to Marcus, were men. Vera generally had the opposite sex eating out of her hand. They followed her around like lovesick puppies although she seemed to be unaware of her effect on her admirers. Even his nephews, mere children that they were, thought that Vera had hung the moon. They adored her and loved spending time with her. He glanced over at the deck where she now sat on the glider with one twin glued on either side of her and the puppy in her lap. Trey, he noted with grim amuse-ment, was seated on a folding chair facing her so that she was literally surrounded. Even the puppy she was holding was lolling in bliss. *Yeah, right.* Vera needed introductions like he needed more gray hair.

And as for her dating, well, that was another issue altogether. Why the idea bothered him so much, he wasn't quite sure, but for some reason it was like having a big knife in his chest. Why shouldn't Vera be dating? She was, after all, vital and charming, funny and sexy as hell. It was ridiculous to think that someone as beautiful and sweet as Vera would be doomed to spend the rest of her life in mourning; of course she needed to be out there dating so she could find the right man to appreciate her, her sparkling personality, her wit, her creativity, her . . . His reverie was interrupted by a poke on his shoulder. He'd been so lost in thought that he was unaware that Vera had left the deck and joined him at the long table that had been set up for dining.

"Hey, you. Why are you sitting here looking like you lost your best friend?" Vera gave him one of her brilliant smiles and he managed a poor imitation of one in return.

"Aren't you having a good time? I am, I've been having a wonderful time with the boys. They named the puppy Patrick, you'll never guess why," she went on. When Marcus shrugged his shoulders indifferently, she supplied the answer. "Patrick is the name of Spongebob Squarepants's best friend! You know how much they love that cartoon. So, Patrick it is. Poor doggie, I guess it could have been worse.

"Anyway, the food was wonderful, the boys loved their presents, and everyone is having a great time except you! What's the matter, Marcus?" Vera asked with real concern in her voice.

Marcus leaned forward and propped both his elbows on the table. He turned to look at Vera and was struck again by her warmth and beauty. Even though she'd been romping with the boys and the newly named Patrick all afternoon she was still as fresh and fragrant as when they'd left her house. The burden on his heart grew heavier when she put one hand over his and squeezed it gently.

"Do you feel okay, sugar-pie? If you're tired, maybe we should go home," she suggested.

Before he could muster an answer, Clay and Malcolm took up the center of the deck and Malcolm clapped his hands to get everyone's attention.

"Okay, we have an announcement to make," said Malcolm. "It seems as though we both find ourselves in the family way. That is, our *wives* are in the family way," he corrected himself.

At that point Bennie went to join Clay, and Selena, Malcolm's wife, went to his side. Clay kissed Bennie lightly on the lips before making a comment. "Our deeply loved wives," he added. Bennie smiled rapturously up at Clay, and Selena bestowed the same kind of look on Malcolm. "Our beautiful wives are doing us the honor of making us fathers again," Clay ended.

The announcement was met with cheers and handclaps from everyone. Lillian shed a few tears of joy and Bump hugged each mother-to-be and offered sincere words of happiness. Martin, Malcolm's twin brother, also embraced his sisters-in-law and shook his brothers' hands. Ceylon, his wife, was inside changing the diapers of their infant sons and was not in the happy picture at the moment. Vera was about to go up to the deck to add her good wishes when she turned to Marcus.

"Oh, Marcus, isn't this wonderful? I'm so happy for them!" And off she ran to hug her friends and offer up her sincere congratulations.

Before leaving the table, Marcus surveyed the happy group. Clay and Bennie with their three boys, Malcolm and Selena and their three daughters. Ceylon emerged from the house with a twin in each arm and was immediately relieved of her burden by Martin, although Elizabeth, their little girl, insisted on being picked up as soon as her mommy's arms were empty. For some reason the sight of the happy couples did nothing to reduce his angst; it only increased as he watched all the love and affection flowing among his family. Even Angelique had forsaken her usual hard sophistication and was wearing a huge, genuine smile. Suddenly everyone seemed to fade from his view until the only person he could see was Vera.

He could see a similar gathering at some point in the future with a similar announcement made by an unseen man and it all seemed perfectly right, a happy ending to a wonderful afternoon. So why did he feel like the bottom had dropped out of his world? He suppressed a brief shudder and rose to his feet to go and join his family in this happy moment. It was obviously time for him to take a vacation; he'd been working too hard. A few days' R&R and he'd be straight.

Convinced that he had it under control, whatever "it" was, Marcus waded into the happy group and hugged everyone in sight. He was truly happy for his family and he especially loved to dote on his sisters-in-law when they were pregnant. Marcus adored pregnant women; he thought they were the cutest and most feminine when they were in that wonderful state. His bravado left him with a quickness when he embraced Vera. Instantly he knew that his troubles were far from over. In fact, from the sensation that took over his body when he took her in his arms, his problems were just beginning.

After such a long and happy day, Vera was sure she'd enjoy a wonderful sleep that night. When she returned home after dropping Marcus off, she fed Kika and Toby and took them for their usual evening walk. Turning off the downstairs lights, Vera decided to treat herself to a long, leisurely bubble bath. She went upstairs and sat down at her 1930-era vanity with the big circular mirror. Picking up her cordless phone, she checked her voice mail and made a mental note to return the calls from her family and a couple of golfing buddies, and then was pleasantly surprised to hear Dante Bohannon's voice. He was thanking her again for the home-cooked dinner, and asking her out for dinner and a movie.

Vera sighed briefly as she laid the phone down. Staring at her reflection in the mirror, she tried to figure out what was bothering her. She should be in much higher spirits. She'd had a wonderful time that day; she in fact had a wonderful life and her dearest friends had just made an announcement that brought nothing but joy to their whole family. So why was she feeling so glum?

She abruptly rose from the lacquered vanity bench, getting up so fast that she startled Kika, who'd been lying under the stool. "Sorry, sweetie, but I've told you and told you not to do that, haven't I?" Picking the little dog up, she carried her into the bathroom to start the water for her bath. "You can sit here and watch me take a bath, how's that? And tomorrow after church, I think I'll give you and Toby one, too. Doesn't that sound nice?"

Kika barked agreeably; she and Toby both loved being shampooed. She watched carefully as Vera poured a generous amount of Perlier Peony bath foam into the tub. In very short order Vera was submerged in bubbles, trying to soak away her odd mood. She thought back over the events of the day and finally faced up to what was bothering her. Bennie was having another baby, as well as Selena. As happy as she was for her friends, she couldn't lie and say it didn't affect her. They each had three children already and Vera had none. Making a wry face, Vera muttered, "Mommy, Mommy, she had three turns and I haven't had any! It's not fair!"

Well, who said life was fair, anyway? Vera had never been happier in her life than when she was pregnant with John's child. Being pregnant was wonderful; it was the most life-affirming, exciting thing that Vera had ever done. She loved everything about being pregnant from the morning sickness to her thickening waistline. Any discomfort was worth having as long as she got a baby to love and cherish. John was equally elated, or he seemed to be; it was hard to tell with him being on the road so much with the team. When Vera miscarried, though, he was in training camp not far from Atlanta. He came home in time to take her home from the hospital, and stayed with her two days before taking off again. After that, nothing seemed to be the same for the couple.

Vera sat up straight in the bathtub and flipped the little handle that let the bathwater out. She couldn't think about that now. She stood up and turned the shower on to shampoo her hair and to rinse the fragrant bubbles from her skin. That was about all the self-pity she could handle for one evening. So she couldn't have the baby she wanted so badly, so what? So what if her sisters and her best friends had all the children they wanted? Life was just like that. Sometimes things worked out in an orderly and impartial manner, and sometimes it was totally unfair. Like the fact that her husband hadn't wanted to adopt children, the way she had wanted to when she couldn't get pregnant again. She had to learn to deal with her disappointment and go on about her business. She had loved John enough to stay married to him despite his refusal to adopt. If she'd divorced him . . . maybe she could have . . . "No!"

Vera didn't realize she'd spoken out loud until Kika, her little sentinel, barked. Vera stifled a choking laugh and stuck her head from behind the pink damask shower curtain. "Sorry, sweetie. I'm just freaking out in here." Ducking back into the warm spray of water, she rinsed the shampoo out of her hair, applying a leave-in conditioner. She turned off the water and stepped out of the shower, wrapping herself in a big, fluffy rose-colored bath sheet. Without conscious thought she went into the bedroom and picked up her phone. She consulted the caller ID and punched in the numbers she retrieved.

"Dante, how are you? This is Vera. I'm surprised to catch you at home on a Saturday night," she said in her most charming voice. "I wanted to thank you for the kind invitation and tell you, yes, I'd love to go out next week."

After chatting for a few minutes, they ended the conversation and Vera once again found herself staring into her vanity mirror. All she'd done was return a call to an old friend and accept a casual invitation to dinner. So why did she feel as if she'd stepped off into an abyss? Kika's accusing bark made her turn around. Toby, small as he was, had somehow learned how to jump up on her bed, something that drove both Vera and Kika mad. It annoyed Vera because she didn't want him on the bedspread, and Kika was jealous because she couldn't do it, too.

Without waiting for Toby to try to jump down, Vera picked him up and set him on the floor next to Kika, who promptly nipped him as punishment. They ended up chasing each other around the room until Vera shooed them out to their doggie bed in the second bedroom.

"And stay there! Honestly, maybe God knew what He was doing by not giving me kids, because the two of you are driving me insane," she said ruefully.

Vera applied scented lotion to every bit of her body and stretched luxuriously before folding back the damask duvet, the lightweight blanket and top sheet, and climbing into bed. After saying her prayers, she lay staring into the darkened room and smelling the mingled scents of gardenia and the earthy smell that rose from her garden through her opened bedroom windows. She smiled a little as she thought of something her great-grandmother had always said, "It's a great life, if you just don't weaken." And hers was a great life, it really was. There was no point in getting weak now.

A week had passed since the twins' birthday party, but Marcus was still feeling slightly unsettled. He still couldn't get his mother's innocent words out of his mind, nor could he forget the volcanic eruption of emotion the words had precipitated. His well-ordered life was slowly but surely falling into disarray and Marcus didn't like it one bit. The business side was running fine; there was nothing wrong with the part of his brain that kept The Deveraux Group prospering. The personal side, however, was getting a bit complicated. Part of the complication was the fact that wherever he turned, there was Vera.

As an officer of the company, she occupied a space on the executive level of the building, right down the hall from Marcus, as a matter of fact. The fact that she was rarely in her office was small comfort; the tastefully decorated suite bore her imprint even when she wasn't there. It wasn't any better in his office; everything in it reminded him of Vera. In fact, Marcus had asked Vera to decorate his office because he knew her taste to be exquisite and he trusted her implicitly. The end result was a uniquely modern, masculine space that expressed his personality perfectly. It was done in shades of dark blue and grays with mahogany furnishings that looked classic and imposing despite their modernity. The walls bore original works of art by major African-American artists. In a salute to his interests and his family's origins, Vera had chosen oils and watercolors that depicted scenes of New Orleans and jazz musicians. Normally his office was an energizing space in which to work, but now it only served to remind him of Vera.

At the moment he was staring out at the skyline, trying to keep his mind on business. His private line rang at that moment, and he answered it immediately, grateful for the diversion.

"It's Larissa, Marcus. I just called to say hello," she said in her sultry voice.

Suddenly it occurred to Marcus that this was just what he needed to get back on track.

"Well, hello to you, too. Listen, are you busy tonight? Would you like to do something casual and impromptu like dinner and a movie?"

Larissa immediately answered in the affirmative.

"I'll pick you up at about six-thirty," Marcus said. "You want dinner first, or the movie?"

"Oh, I'll let you decide," Larissa said breathily. "Although an early movie might be nice; then we can relax over dinner without having to worry about the time."

Marcus was feeling much better when he hung up the phone. Whatever had caused his unnatural preoccupation with his best friend was now over. He was back in control. He picked up Larissa at her Buckhead town house where she was awaiting his arrival. Her promptness was one of the things Marcus liked about Larissa. He also liked her appearance. She was pretty, petite, and as fair of skin as he was, with thick, long brown hair and a light sprinkling of freckles on her pert nose. She had slightly almond shaped eyes that gave her a rather exotic appearance, and a slender, girlish body that wore clothes extremely well.

Marcus smiled in appreciation at her appearance. She was dressed casually in a khaki skirt that ended several inches above her knees and a pastel twin set that brought out the richness of her hair. He told her how nice she looked and gave her a brief dry kiss on the cheek. They de-

cided on a movie and headed to the multiplex theater near
Lenox Square, chatting amiably until they reached their
destination. Marcus had succumbed totally to the feminine
aura that Larissa exuded and had relaxed completely. This
was going to be a nice evening, he could feel it. He had actually reached for Larissa's hand, a true milestone since
Marcus never displayed any kind of public affection, when
something caught his peripheral vision. It was Vera, standing by herself at the concession counter.

She was wearing crisply pressed jeans and one of her
many white T-shirts, this one with short sleeves and a
scoop neck that seemed a little bit too low as Marcus
imagined that he could see the swell of her ripe breasts
over the neckline. She was also wearing some of the fan-
ciful footwear for which she was known, this time a pair
of royal-blue mules with gold panthers prowling in a circle around the heels. The jeans had a small slit at the ankle
that drew attention to her feet, a small touch that made the
jeans even sexier. The sight of her standing there by herself caught his entire attention, although she was hardly
unnoticed by others.

Most of the men in the crowded lobby seemed to be
looking at her with varying degrees of lust; Vera in a pair
of jeans was something to see. The way they fit around her
firm, curvy bottom was enough to drive a strong man to
his knees. It wasn't that the jeans were tight; they just fitted her shapely form perfectly, like a coat of denim paint.
Her legs were slightly bowed, just enough to give her a deliciously sexy stance. In dresses she was devastating;
however, in pants of any kind she was a knockout. Anyone
else would have looked sporty and playful in jeans and a
T-shirt, but Vera looked sexy and desirable, too sexy to be
going to the movies by herself. Automatically Marcus
grabbed Larissa's elbow and steered her over to Vera.

Vera's face lit up when she saw Marcus. "Hi, Marcus! And hello, Larissa, how are you?"

Larissa returned Vera's cordial greeting. The two women had been introduced by Marcus one afternoon on the golf course. "What movie are you seeing?" Larissa asked politely.

Before Vera could answer, Marcus interjected. "It had better not be that horror flick, you know what they do to you. And why don't you have on a sweater? You know it's too cold in here for short sleeves," he chided. Paternal as he sounded, he had a point. Vera loved scary movies but they usually scared her to the point where she couldn't sleep. And the air-conditioning in theaters was usually too chilly for her; she always needed a sweater or jacket.

With perfect timing, Dante Bohannon arrived with an elegantly vintage navy jacket that he slipped onto Vera's shoulders with a flourish. "Thank you, Dante, I shouldn't have left this in the car," Vera said sweetly as she slipped into the garment. Its short length did nothing to diminish the impact of her butt in those jeans, something Marcus noticed right away. If anything, it drew more attention to it. The smile Vera flashed Dante in gratitude also seemed a bit too provocative to Marcus's critical eye; Vera had a one-hundred-watt smile that made her dimples flash and her lashes flutter; those smiles were more than enough to turn any man's head.

She blithely introduced Larissa to Dante and smiled up at him while the greetings were exchanged, oblivious of Marcus's disapproving expression. Dante turned to Vera and suggested they get their popcorn and get seated as the action movie they'd selected was starting momentarily. Marcus's jaw tightened imperceptibly; that was another of Vera's favorite genres. She wasn't happy unless things were blowing up or punches were being thrown every five minutes. She may have looked like a sophisticated woman of the world, but Marcus often told her there was a twelve-year-old boy in her trying desperately to get out. For some reason it was intensely annoying that this Dante person had tapped in on that fact. And that he had anticipated Vera's every need by purchasing an icy bottle of water and the biggest vat of popcorn available for consumption; Vera would forgo dinner just so she could eat as much popcorn as possible at the movies and she loved to drink water, the colder the better.

She flashed another bright smile at Dante and took the water from him, carrying it and Dante's large soda, almost forgetting to say good-bye to Marcus and Larissa before following her date to their theater. Larissa had to call Marcus's name twice before he responded. He turned to the concession counter and took a surreptitious glance at the big clock on the wall. It was going to be a long night.

Chapter 5

Vera enjoyed the evening with Dante thoroughly. After their first date, which was a casual meal in her home, they'd spoken on the phone a few times and were feeling pretty comfortable with one another. So comfortable that they'd split an entrée at Applebee's before heading to the movies. They both admitted to an insatiable appetite for popcorn and were more than willing to make room for lots of it by skimping on a meal. They both enjoyed the movie, which had lots of special effects and over-the-top fight scenes, enough to please even the bloodthirsty Vera. Afterward, Dante drove her home while they relived the highlights of the movie. Vera invited him in for an iced latte and he agreed immediately.

Kika and Toby made their usual show of hysteria when confronted with a strange man, but Dante charmed them out of their rage. He stooped down to their level and offered them his fingers to sniff. The two little dogs took their time smelling his long fingers and he took advantage of their interest to stroke both of them with his free hand. "See? I'm not such a bad guy when you get to know me," he said in a deep, soothing voice. When he stopped stroking them, and rose to his full height, Toby immediately lay down next to his feet and Kika sat up brightly with her right paw in the air to signal that she wanted more of the same treatment.

"Aww, you're just a little love-dog, aren't you? You just want somebody to play with you, don't you?" Dante obligingly picked Kika up and sat down on one of the stools next to the work island in the kitchen. Vera was still standing with one hand in the cupboard to retrieve her espresso maker. She was too stunned by what she saw to move.

"Wow, Dante. I'm absolutely floored," she said finally. "I've never seen them take to anyone like that before. They like women and children, but they are not fond of men at all. They hate all men except Marcus for some reason. You must have the magic touch."

Kika was at the moment lying in Dante's arm with her head rolled over and wearing an extremely pleased expression on her little face. Her sharp features were softened in ecstasy while Dante's long fingers stroked the fluffy ruff around her neck and massaged under her chin. Dante flashed a grin at Vera and gave her a conspiratorial wink. "It's that bedside manner thing, they teach it in medical school. You just have to know how to approach your patient, that's all."

Vera laughed and began to set out the ingredients for the lattes. "Do you want decaf or regular? Skim milk or whole?"

Dante agreed to half decaf and half regular with skim milk, which was also Vera's preferred blend. He watched in admiration as she quickly measured out the coffee and filled the little cup with its long handle and expertly attached it to the coffeemaker. While the strong coffee was dripping into the little metal pitcher, she poured milk into another metal pitcher and thrust it under the long appendage that frothed and heated the milk with steam. Dante was able to put Kika down at last and went to the sink where he washed his hands thoroughly and asked Vera what he could do to help.

"Just get two tall glasses out of that cupboard." She

pointed to one of her glass-fronted cabinets. "And fill them with ice. And could you hand me the caramel syrup from the refrigerator door, please? And the chocolate, too, I have a sudden urge for mocha."

Dante complied quickly and enjoyed watching Vera assemble two half-decaf skim-milk iced mocha lattes with caramel. "You do that like you've been doing it all your life," he commented.

"Yeah, if the magazine business dries up, I can always be a *barista,*" she said with a smile. "We just did a segment on making fancy coffee on *Personal Space* where this skill came in quite handy. I was a soda jerk one summer and I learned how to make milkshakes, malts, banana splits, you name it. Using an espresso maker isn't that different. Okay!" she said happily as she put the two tall glasses onto a small tray and filled a plate with Pirouline cookies. "Let's go into the living room, shall we?"

Dante immediately took the tray from her hands and followed her into the living room, where she indicated an ornate table between two comfortable-looking chairs. After carefully placing the tray on the table, Dante waited until Vera was seated to take a seat himself. While she tasted her latte, he looked around the living room. He had been a guest in her home when she was married to John and the style of the two homes couldn't have been more different. He said as much to Vera.

"You know, Vera, this isn't quite what I expected. Your house, I mean," he hurried to explain as she raised an eyebrow in inquiry. "Well, everything was so high-tech and modern when you were with John. This looks completely different. Completely," he reiterated as he looked around the warm, cozy interior.

Vera's home looked like a French country house somehow imported to Atlanta. The furnishings were casually elegant and inviting, with a plump love seat across from the fireplace, two slipcovered armchairs, and a chintz-covered chaise longue with an assortment of throw pillows. There were family pictures everywhere, and antique lamps with rosy silk shades gave everything a warm glow. Topiary trees in colorful ceramic pots flanked the fireplace and more plants, both flowering and green, gave the room warmth and energy. The entire front wall was a huge multipaned window, which echoed the French doors that led to the dining room and the patio. The centerpiece of the dining room was a huge cherry-wood glass-fronted cabinet filled with Thomas Blackshear figurines. More of the figurines decorated the mantel and other high surfaces in the living room; it was obvious that Vera had to keep them out of the way of the dogs.

Vera smiled as she accepted Dante's comment for what it was, a compliment. "Yes, there's definitely a difference in the two houses. For one thing, you could fit this little place into a corner of the old house! And for another, this place is much more me than the other. That's one of the reasons I sold it," she admitted quietly. "There was so much of John there, in every single room, in every piece of furniture, I kept expecting to run into him around every corner. I knew I couldn't keep living there; I'd have lost my mind. I had to start over."

Dante nodded briefly in acknowledgment of Vera's statement. He looked at her with a sheepish smile and asked if she minded him looking around. "Everything in here is so intriguing, I hope you don't think I'm being nosy," he said disarmingly.

Vera immediately assured him that he was perfectly welcome to look around. "Please, make yourself at home, Dante. I do the same thing when I'm visiting, and I'm afraid it *is* because I'm nosy!" she said with a smile. She settled back to watch Dante look at all her artwork and examine the exquisitely colorful and realistic figures of

Thomas Blackshear. The thought crossed her mind that Dante was rather a work of art himself.

He was a big man, like her late husband. Big, broad of shoulder, and imposing, he stood about six feet three and his features bore the unmistakable stamp of his African forebears. He had dark, smooth skin, skin that was almost black, with deep-set eyes and thick, shiny eyebrows. His perfectly groomed hair that was thick and tightly kinked like a Berber carpet further accentuated his broad nose and full lips. Dante Bohannon was quite a dish, especially when he smiled, as he was now doing. He had finally turned away from his inspection of the china cabinet and expressed how impressed he was with Vera's home.

"This place really feels like a home, Vera. And it looks like something out of a magazine," he said with admiration.

"Dante, how sweet of you to say that! But you'd better come and drink your latte before it's all watered down," she cautioned.

He did as she suggested and rejoined her in the comfortable chair waiting for him in the living room. Vera confessed that she had done virtually everything herself in the house.

"After John died, I gave away or sold everything," she said quietly. "And then I did what I do best, go to secondhand shops and resale shops, and I threw down! I worked out a lot of issues while I was refinishing furniture and making slipcovers. And the process helped a lot when we were formulating the first issues of *Personal Space,*" she added.

In answer to his unasked question, Vera explained. "*Personal Space* is supposed to be a vehicle for the reader to evoke change in his or her home, whether it's a dorm room, an apartment, or a mansion. And the idea is not to spend as much money as possible, but to reuse, recycle, and make over things you already have. There are a lot of hands-on projects featured in the magazine and doing this place gave us plenty of direction for the first couple of issues."

Dante's face was warm with appreciation for Vera's creativity and for her hospitality. "You know, Vera, I've really enjoyed spending time with you. It's nice to have home cooking once in a while, and to be around someone who knows why I'm doing what I'm doing," he said honestly.

Vera's face showed her concern. "Do you get a hard time about being an older resident? Was it difficult for you in medical school?" she asked.

Dante shook his head. "It was challenging, I'm not going to kid you. Yeah, I was older than most of them but it helped me out in a way. I was more focused, and to an extent, more mature. I could hit those books with no problem and I wasn't intimidated like some of my classmates. There are a lot of head games that go on in medical school and if you let yourself get caught up, you'll screw up. That wasn't going to happen to me," he said reflectively.

He stopped speaking for a moment and picked up a figurine fashioned as a young woman in a flirtatious pose. "These things are absolutely amazing, Vera. I've never seen anything so lifelike!" Gently setting the statue down, he continued his explanation.

"My fiancée and my family, they're the ones that didn't particularly appreciate my leaving a very lucrative career. Everybody was angry off when the money train rolled to a halt," he said with a hint of bitterness. "It seems like as long as I could supply my family with houses and cars and college tuition, I was their favorite son. But walking away from all that money? I immediately became the biggest fool in the history of the world. My fiancée dropped me like a hot rock. It seems she was madly in love with the idea of being an NFL wife, not so much with me. She didn't like the idea of being married to a middle-income doctor."

Vera vaguely remembered the overly made up little fiancée of whom Dante spoke. She'd wondered whatever happened with her, but hadn't asked out of politeness. Privately she'd always thought Dante could do better, but she wasn't about to say that. What she said, however, was heartfelt and sympathetic.

"Dante, I'm so sorry they haven't been supportive of you. I think your dream to become a doctor is a highly admirable one. And it's not like doctors are exactly in the poorhouse," she reminded him. "A lot of doctors make obscenely high salaries."

Dante smiled slowly and said that he wasn't going to be one of those billionaire doctors. "I started out wanting to go into sports medicine, but I'm thinking more and more about opening an inner city clinic. A place where people who need care can get it without a lot of rigmarole from HMOs and other kinds of red tape. Trust me, I'll never get rich from that. But I don't need the money. Even after paying for medical school and buying a house here and a car there, I'm hardly insolvent. If I don't act the fool I'll have plenty of money to take care of my needs and my wants. But I won't be one of those docs livin' large and flying my own plane and whatnot."

Vera's eyes were starry with admiration when Dante finished speaking. "Dante, I think that's wonderful," she said warmly. "You're wonderful! Your fiancée will never know what a prize she had in you," she added.

Dante looked slightly embarrassed but smiled again. He rose from his chair and extended both his hands to Vera. Pulling her out of her chair, he told her he had early rounds in the morning. "And since I'm getting kind of old for these late nights, I need to turn in," he said in his deep voice.

"I've really enjoyed this evening, Vera, and hope we can do it again." The words were accompanied by a kiss on Vera's velvety smooth cheek.

"Dante, I'm looking forward to it," she answered honestly. "I can't tell you when I've had a more delightful evening."

Vera locked up carefully after Dante left, and put the little dogs down for the night as she made her nightly toilette. She really did have a nice time with Dante. He was a good conversationalist, a good listener, he had a good head on his shoulders, and was darned good looking to boot. It was going to be a pleasure to get to know him better; she was anticipating it greatly.

Paris was hard at work on her computer when Aidan stopped by her office to see if she wanted to go to lunch. She barely acknowledged him when he swept in the door, so intent was she on her task.

"Hang on, I'll be done in a minute," she muttered.

"Don't hurry on my account," Aidan said mildly. "How about lunch?"

"Lunch is good," she mumbled. "Are we going to that dreadful place where they rake up the yard and serve it to you on a plate?"

"No, my little carnivore. We're going to that wonderful place where they make those delectable smoothies. Even you should find something to your taste. And there just happens to be an outlet store nearby that's worth a look," he added slyly.

Paris did look at him then. Tearing her eyes away from the computer monitor, she stared at Aidan. "You're trying to dress me again, aren't you? You just can't leave well enough alone," she said accusingly.

Aidan didn't even try to look innocent. "If everything

you owned wasn't three sizes too big for you, I'd mind my own business. Look at that thing you have on; was Omar the Tentmaker having a sale or something? You simply can't continue to dress like that. You're the only woman in the world still wearing a *burqa,* for God's sake."

Paris looked down at her serviceable cotton-polyester-blend suit that was a bit baggy here and there. It was washable, it had been on sale, and it covered her ample curves nicely, which was all she required in clothing. But she was so pleased with her project she decided to give in to Aidan.

"Okay. It just so happens that I need something to wear to Marcus's birthday party this weekend. Just let me finish making his birthday card and we can go," she said mildly.

Aidan's eyes widened in glee. "Oh, good! When you show up looking smashing, and you will, make sure you mention the name of your fairy godfather. And hurry up, I'm famished."

Paris nodded, a slow grin spreading across her face as she did one more spell check of her finished product. She hit the print key, retrieved the pages from the printer, and sighed in satisfaction. She glanced over at Aidan and showed him most of her thirty-two perfect teeth in a smile so smug and self-satisfied that it immediately set off Aidan's radar.

"I know that look, that's the Martha May matchmaker grin. You're up to something, what is it? I demand details!" he said sternly.

Paris jumped up from her desk chair, grabbed her ubiquitous and overladen tote bag, and headed to the door. "Okay, I'll fill you in on the way. But I want a smoothie before we hit the outlets; I'm starving. Matchmaking is such hard work!"

Aidan sighed deeply and shook his head as he followed

her out the door. "I knew you were up to no good. I just knew it."

Marcus surprised everyone with his choice of a birthday celebration. Instead of opting for a lavish affair he wanted a simple cookout at his parents' home. To him, turning thirty wasn't the huge milestone everyone seemed to think it should be; it was just another birthday as far as he was concerned. And one of the reasons he'd opted to have the party at his mother's house was that he'd decided to bring Larissa. Now that *was* a huge milestone; it would be the first time Marcus had ever brought one of his ninety-day wonders anywhere near his family. It seemed as though Larissa was making more progress than any of her predecessors in terms of bringing Marcus to heel. The turning point for Marcus had been the night that the two of them had run into Vera at the movies with Dante.

Marcus had been so disgruntled about that situation that he'd been moody and monosyllabic the rest of the night. Larissa actually made the best of his foul mood instead of telling him off and demanding that he take her home, something she was certainly entitled to given his behavior. Instead, after the movie Larissa had calmly suggested that they do dinner another time, as Marcus seemed to have something on his mind. Marcus gratefully took her home and spent the rest of the evening in a funk.

After a weekend of brooding, however, he managed to shake off the unsettled feeling that had come about when his mother mentioned Vera dating and that Marcus should "introduce her to some nice men." Whatever caused the spate of weird feelings was gone, over, kaput, and he didn't let it cross his mind anymore. In fact, he and Larissa actually began to see more of each other in the subsequent two weeks that led up to his birthday. He was getting more and more comfortable with Larissa, comfortable to the point of bringing her to a family party, something that had never, ever occurred before. He had even mentioned it to Vera, in an offhand way, but her reaction was less than he expected.

All she said was, "Oh, good! That will be nice, your family will really like her." This casual response from Vera prompted him to ask if she was bringing a date and her answer was again casual. She said she doubted it. "Dante has to work that night, so I'll probably come by myself," she acknowledged. The whole time they were talking, Vera was going over a layout and was barely listening to Marcus, which was slightly irritating but oddly reassuring; it meant that his unnatural state of mind regarding Vera was over. He was back in control, everything was status quo, and he was ready to move forward, to take it to another level. Life was good.

The party was to start in the late afternoon so that it could wind up at an early hour and free everyone for their own pursuits, "everyone" meaning Marcus, who had some amorous plans for the evening pertaining to Larissa. He picked her up at her town house and was once again glad to be rid of whatever had been bugging him; she looked adorable in a light pink outfit that consisted of walking shorts and a sleeveless blouse with a soft green cardigan thrown across her shoulders.

"Larissa, you look wonderful. I like that color on you," he said warmly. Leaning over to give her the usual brief, dry kiss on the check, he caught a whiff of her usual fragrance, Beautiful by Estee Lauder.

Larissa acknowledged his compliment and admitted she wanted to look her best. "Since this is the first time I'll be meeting your family, I want to leave a good impression," she said frankly.

Normally that was the kind of comment that would

make the cold chill run down Marcus's spine that signaled the end of the relationship, but not today. He actually found the remark rather endearing, although he didn't say so. Assuring Larissa that she looked beautiful, he gallantly seated her in the BMW and off they drove.

The afternoon was perfect for an outdoor gathering, clear, sunny, and pleasantly warm. Everyone was on their best behavior, which meant that no one goggled at Larissa or made some uncouth comment about Marcus bringing a date to his own party. Lillian and Bump shook Larissa's hand and invited her to make herself at home in the beautifully flowering garden area where the party was taking place. Marcus's brother and their wives were gracious and welcoming. Ceylon, Martin's wife, couldn't shake hands as her hands were full with the six-month-old twins, William Simmons and his brother Malcolm Arlington, but she smiled warmly.

"Larissa, it's so nice to meet you! Excuse my not shaking hands, but these two are a handful, as you can see." Marcus immediately took one of the boys from Ceylon and held him up in the air.

"Jiggaman! You and Biggaman are getting huge!" he exclaimed, making the baby laugh out loud.

Ceylon clucked her tongue in despair. "Larissa, excuse him. My husband started calling these babies 'Jigga' and 'Bigga' and now all of the men do. They should be ashamed of themselves, but there's no stopping them," she said ruefully.

Marcus helped Ceylon get settled on the big redwood settee under the awning on the patio of the big house and reluctantly handed over his nephew. The appetizing smell of grilled chicken and shrimp filled the air as well as the sound of lilting jazz, courtesy of the excellent sound system of Marcus's stepfather, Bill "Bump" Williams. In

addition to being Lillian's devoted husband, Bump was a
world-famous jazz musician with his own band.

The gathering couldn't have been more congenial, but
something seemed to be missing. In a few minutes, Marcus realized what it was when Vera breezed in. She was
wreathed in smiles, and she looked wonderful as always,
her hair charmingly tousled and wearing a cherry-red outfit that immediately drew all eyes to its vibrant color. It
was a tailored camp shirt with short sleeves and a pair of
high-waisted pleated slacks, but the color and perfect fit
of the raw silk outfit made it something special. She transferred the colorful gift bag in her right hand to her left
hand and waved to the group at large. "Sorry we're late,
but Dante just managed to trade shifts with someone and
here we are," she said brightly. The smiling face of Dante
Bohannon appeared behind Vera, his hands full with a
huge plastic container of crab salad.

Only someone who knew Marcus very, very well would
have noticed that his entire demeanor changed when Vera
arrived, and his cousin Paris knew him very well indeed.
Paris, who could always be relied upon to help out at a
party, was busy making sure that everyone was served and
the refreshments replenished in a timely fashion but she
kept an eye on Marcus the whole time. Besides, she had a
present for him, one that she knew he would enjoy. Vera interrupted her reverie with a compliment. "Paris, you look
fabulous! I love that color on you and I love the way it
shows you off instead of covering you up," she said
warmly.

Paris was indeed transformed, wearing a V-necked cotton jersey top with three-quarter-length sleeves in a vibrant
shade of turquoise and a sari-printed wrap skirt. Both
items served to bring out her natural vibrancy and show off

her large shapely frame instead of making it look bigger the way her normal clothes did.

"Hmm? Oh, thank you. I can't really take credit for the outfit since Aidan picked it out, but it's pretty nice, isn't it?" Paris said.

Paris made a discreet exit from Vera's side and waited until Marcus was by himself. She immediately made a bee-line for him and tapped him on the shoulder to get his attention. "Happy birthday, cuz. Here's something for you," she said, handing him a big, fancifully decorated envelope.

Marcus looked down at Paris with a smile and thanks. Paris placed her hand on his and looked around conspiratorially. "Don't open it here! Open it when you're at home, alone. You'll enjoy it much more that way," she assured him.

He raised an eyebrow but agreed. "You didn't have to get me anything, you know. Thanks, Paris," he said graciously, kissing her on the forehead.

Paris smiled to herself and rocked back and forth on her toes in anticipation. *You're really going to thank me later,* she thought.

Marcus was totally preoccupied when he drove Larissa home. So much so that he didn't notice that she was deep in her own thoughts. If he'd been paying her the least bit of attention, what happened next wouldn't have been such a shock to his system. He pulled into the parking lot and parked next to her little champagne-colored Mercedes. He was about to get out of the BMW so he could open her door and escort her in, when Larissa spoke. Her words made him go completely still.

"Hold it, Marcus. You don't have to walk me to the door. I think now is as good a time as any to tell you that I don't think we should see each other anymore," she said calmly.

Marcus stared at Larissa to make sure he'd heard her correctly. She went on, unimpressed by his intense scrutiny.

"You know, I was aware that you had a reputation for not taking relationships seriously. But it wasn't until recently that I realized why that is. You're involved with another woman, Marcus."

Marcus looked at her, incredulous. Surely she didn't believe that! Marcus may have had many relationships, but he had them one at a time. He wasn't the kind to juggle two or three women at once. He was about to defend himself when Larissa held up a hand to forestall his protests.

"I always wondered, because you talked about her so much. I actually counted the number of times her name came up one evening. You mentioned her name twenty-seven times one night, Marcus. For a six-hour date, that's quite a few times, don't you think? And it wasn't just that, I saw the two of you together just a few weeks ago. You were at Lenox Square," she said, referring to the popular mall, "and it was obvious that you were completely in tune with each other. You always make it a point not to touch me in public, but you couldn't keep your hands off her. Every other minute you were putting your arm around her, or grabbing her hand, even holding her purse when she was looking for things. You looked like an old married couple," Larissa said musingly.

"When she walked in this afternoon, it was obvious. It was all over your face, just like it was tattooed there. I didn't want to admit it before, but it's completely obvious, just as plain as day. You're in love with Vera Jackson."

Chapter 6

Marcus could feel the heat surging up to his face in a mad hot rush. Larissa was sitting there, cool and serene, making this ridiculous accusation and he was somehow rendered powerless to stop her. He couldn't seem to make his voice work; worse yet, it was like he'd forgotten how to talk.

"I saw it that night we went to the movies," Larissa elaborated. "When you look at Vera, it's like a light comes on in your very soul. Even if you're not smiling, it's like some kind of peace settles over you. That's some dangerous stuff, I must say. I thought at first that I was imagining things. After all she's a little older than you and you've worked together for years," she said, almost as if she were talking to herself. "But today? Oh, I couldn't ignore it anymore." Larissa turned in her seat so she could face Marcus fully.

"I only fight battles I know I can win, Marcus. I deserve someone who looks at me the way you look at Vera. So I think it's best that we just part now with no regrets. I'm going to get on with my life and you need to get on with your life . . . with Vera, if that's possible."

Marcus finally got his jaw working enough to speak. "What do you mean?" he mumbled.

Larissa tilted her head slightly and gave him a look of pity. "What do I mean? I mean that you're in love with

Vera, I didn't say that Vera was in love with you," she said pointedly.

Marcus drew back and stared at Larissa. There was a lot more bite to the sugar and spice of her personality, more than he would have given her credit for until tonight. Feeling like an apology was in order, he began to speak. "Larissa, I don't know what to say. I'm not saying that you're right, but it was never my intention to hurt you in any way," he began.

Larissa gave a short laugh. "Oh, stop. You had a good time, I had a good time, but it wasn't meant to last a lifetime. You aren't my destiny any more than I'm yours. Besides, the ninety days were almost up, weren't they?" Incredibly, Larissa gave Marcus a genuine smile of amusement as she stepped gracefully out of the car.

Marcus managed to move then; he got out of his side of the car with a scowl on his face and told Larissa that he'd walk her to the door. His irritation was plain, however; she was taking the fact that they wouldn't be seeing each other a little bit too well. And how did she know about the ninety-day thing, anyway? That wasn't something he broadcast to all and sundry, it was just the way things were.

Larissa stayed on her side of the car and put a hand on her slender hip. "Marcus, please. The thought of not seeing you anymore isn't rendering me an invalid, I can just about make it to the door! And don't look so surprised, the women of Atlanta can add, you know. Anyone who goes out with you knows it's a three-month arrangement," she said evenly. "Now you get in your pretty car and think about what I told you. Or go on ignoring it, whatever. I'm going in now. Happy birthday and thanks for the party."

Without another word she did exactly as she said, strolled to the door of her town house, let herself in, and closed it behind her without a backward glance at Marcus. Marcus slid behind the wheel and sat there for a few minutes, his mind a total blank. He finally started the car up and pulled out of the parking lot with no destination in mind. He had a lot of thinking to do and he needed a quiet place in which to do it.

Hours later, Marcus was having trouble falling asleep. So much so that he wasn't even trying anymore, he was sitting on the patio that faced the lake, alone in the dark with the sound of Norah Jones floating out to him from the stereo. He was still trying to get his head around the words that Larissa had flung at him: "You're in love with Vera Jackson." There was no easy way to deal with that statement. True, Vera was the closest person in the world to him, outside of his family. Other than his brothers, she was his most trusted friend and confidante. There was nothing he couldn't tell Vera, nothing that they couldn't share.

It was also true that Vera was a sexy, desirable woman. He'd known that the first minute he laid eyes on her. In fact, it was in that minute that he had indeed fallen a little bit in love with Vera. Marcus lay back on the woven canvas and leather lounge chair with his feet on the matching ottoman and abandoned himself to the sounds of Norah's raspy, soulful voice while he remembered the first time he met Vera.

Twelve years earlier

Marcus yawned widely and looked around in vain for coffee. The usually impeccable offices of The Deveraux Group were packed and ready to be moved to their new headquarters, so it was ridiculous to think that there would be coffee or anything like it available. Clay, the oldest Deveraux brother, looked up from his clipboard and saw

Marcus stretching. Like Marcus, he was clad in scruffy work clothes consisting of jeans and a sweatshirt.

"You look tired, bro; stayed out too late last night, didn't you? Too bad, we have a long day ahead of us. Why don't you go help Vera? She's got a couple of projects that need to be done before the movers get here."

"Sure, no problem. Who's Vera and where is she?"

"Vera? She's new. Go up on the third floor, that's where I saw her last."

Following his brother's instructions, Marcus made his way to the third floor of the building they were vacating and down the mostly empty corridor until he found an office occupied by a woman in jeans. She was bent over with her back to the door so that all he could see was her backside pointed up in the air, but it was a view he wouldn't have traded for anything. That had to be the best butt he'd ever laid eyes on and Marcus did a lot of looking. He was eighteen years old and about to leave for college at Howard University, so his current mission was trying to pack every moment of the summer with fun. Checking out good-looking women was one of his main motivations right now.

"Excuse me, are you Vera?" he asked hopefully.

The woman stood up and turned to face him. She was wearing a Detroit Tigers baseball cap and a FAMU sweatshirt and looked utterly adorable. She smiled and offered Marcus her hand. "Yes, I'm Vera Jackson and you must be Marcus! You're obviously a Deveraux man, so tall and handsome," she said sweetly. "Have you come to help me?"

Marcus nodded dumbly; he couldn't get a word out. This woman was gorgeous! And friendly and smart and re-sourceful, he was to find; she even had a huge thermos of hot coffee, which she insisted that he drink. "I'm having breakfast delivered here for everyone in about an hour. I can get some coffee then. You look like you can use some, though."

By the end of the morning, Marcus's heart was won forevermore. He'd never enjoyed being with someone the way he enjoyed being with Vera. She was calm, funny, and for someone so young she had real organizational ability. He was sure that she would do well at FAMU. He was about to ask her for her campus address when she made a sudden move.

"Oh, my goodness . . . oh, here they are! I took them off for safekeeping and forgot where I put them," she exclaimed. With a smile of relief, Vera reached inside her sweatshirt and pulled out a thin platinum chain. On it were an engagement ring of at least three carats and a matching wedding band.

Marcus felt his blood freeze in his veins. "Are you . . . married?" he croaked.

"Yes, for six years now," she answered as she replaced the rings on the proper finger.

"You're too young to be married," Marcus blurted out.

Vera smiled, the brilliant, beautiful smile that entrapped his heart for all time. She actually squeezed Marcus's hand as she looked up into his glum face. "Aw, sweetie-pie, that was so gallant! But I'm twenty-eight years old, or I will be on my birthday. I'm an *old* hag!"

Stepping back from Marcus, she took off her baseball cap and fluffed her short, glossy hair as if seeing her full face would convince him of her extreme age. All it did was make Marcus's heart fall even further. She was even more beautiful than he first thought and despite what she'd just told him, she didn't look a day over eighteen. Just then, Vera got a page on the still-functioning intercom to let her know that the caterers had arrived with breakfast for the workers. She dashed off to meet them, leaving Marcus alone in the box-filled office. Marcus sank down on the top of a big, broad case and covered his face with his hands, stifling a moan.

Clay found him like that a few minutes later. "What's the matter with you? You sick?"

Marcus looked at Clay with reproach. "Why didn't you tell me she was married?" he asked glumly.

Clay looked at him quizzically, and then light dawned. "Oh, you mean Vera? Yeah, she's married to a big ol' linebacker. I guess I should've warned you about Vera, she's pretty potent to the unsuspecting male. Don't worry about it, she has that effect on all men. It wears off after a few days," Clay said wisely.

Marcus shook his head. "I don't think so, dude. I think I'm permanently scarred. I met my perfect woman and she's married. I think I need to go lie down next to the pool to recover," he muttered.

"I think putting your butt in gear right here would help you a lot more, chump. Get moving," Clay growled.

Marcus stood up, looking at Clay with the youthful despair of a man whose fondest dream has been crushed forever. "You don't understand, Clay; I was gonna marry her, I really was."

Clay, like the sensitive older sibling that he was, burst out laughing. "Yeah, right. If she's ever available, I'm sure she'll take you right up on that. Now get back to work."

Marcus laughed out loud as he recalled with unerring clarity the force of his first meeting with Vera. Clay was wrong. The effect she had on Marcus hadn't worn off in a few days, not in a few months or a few years. He freely admitted to himself that he'd nursed a huge crush on Vera for years; how could he not? She was fresh, lovely, and so friendly and kind it would've been impossible for an impressionable young man not to have fantasies about her.

After college and graduate school, when he'd begun working at TDG full-time, he and Vera had collaborated on many projects and they worked together wonderfully. They could read each other's minds they knew each other so well. No matter how daunting the task, the two of them found a way to handle it. Their motto was "We can do anything!" And working as a team, they could.

In addition, there was just no one he liked more than Vera. They could talk for hours; they never seemed to run out of interesting things to discuss. They could laugh at each other and be silly with each other and they shared all kinds of inside jokes. Besides his brothers, who were his role models, and their wives, women Marcus loved and admired, there was no one he held in higher esteem than Vera. But did he love her? Suddenly restless, Marcus rose from the lounge chair and went into the house.

He prowled around the big living room for a moment, changed the music in rotation on the stereo system, and decided he was thirsty. He went into the kitchen and laughed at himself as he realized that even here, Vera had left her mark. She had supervised most of the details of furnishing his home, especially the kitchen. And the influence she'd had on him over the years was felt even in this room, he realized, as he went to the watercooler that held a jug of spring water. Vera constantly extolled the virtues of drinking large quantities of water and Marcus now drank a healthy amount every day. As he swallowed the cold water, he noticed the message light blinking furiously on his kitchen phone.

Picking up the handset, he punched in the code to retrieve his voice mail and sighed in resignation as he heard Vera's voice reminding him about the music for tomorrow and the fact that she'd put his gift in the car. He immediately headed to the garage to get his package, thinking about the next day's duet as he did so. Singing was another thing he and Vera had in common. They both had great voices and loved to sing. They'd sung together at weddings of families and friends and looked for any excuse to perform. Lillian's women's group held a charity fund-raiser every summer and it usually involved some sort of vocal performance for which she would shamelessly tap her family, which to all intents and purposes included Vera. Marcus would never admit how much he looked forward to performing with Vera, but he loved it. But that didn't mean he was in love with her, did it? Of course not.

Love was what Bump had for Lillian, what Clay had for Bennie, what Malcolm had for Selena, and Martin for Ceylon. Love was that all-consuming passion that welded people together and made them different, better, stronger than before. He knew for a fact that any of his brothers would walk through hell barefoot for their wives and would cheerfully dismember anyone who sought to cause them harm. They lived to make their wives and children happy; everything else came in a distant second. That wasn't anything like what he felt for Vera, was it? Or was it?

He wanted Vera's happiness more than anything; that was true. No one was more deserving of happiness than Vera. She was the most generous, genuinely sweet person that he knew, other than his mother. She had suffered enormous loss and managed to maintain that essential sweetness when many others would have become hard and bitter. And no one had better dare try to cause her a moment of unhappiness; he'd take great pleasure in ruining that person's life. Marcus stopped in midstride to consider what had just gone through his head. It was sounding dangerously like the kind of all-encompassing devotion his brothers and stepfather had for their women. No! It was just the concern of a true friend, that's what Marcus was feeling.

Marcus had by now gotten the large shopping bag out of

the trunk of the BMW and returned to the house. He was currently sitting on his bed opening the contents with a smile of anticipation on his face. Vera gave the best presents in the world. The two of them indulged each other to a shameful extent; they always went overboard with gifts. Vera had already given Marcus a couple of CDs at the party, but this was her real gift to him. Marcus pulled out a deep box that was beautifully wrapped and tore into it to find something that only Vera could have gotten him. She'd ordered him a dozen extra-fine cotton undershirts from an English haberdasher she'd discovered years ago. Marcus only wore the type disgustingly nicknamed "wife beaters" and these were by far the finest he'd ever encountered. Vera always seemed to know when he needed new ones.

Next came a bottle of eau de toilette, in a fragrance he'd never worn, with a note attached in Vera's distinctive script. *This smells like you,* the note read and Marcus had to agree when he sniffed the fragrance. It was cool and refreshing with a green top note, a woodsy midnote, and a metallic dry-down. Marcus had to laugh. It was amazing how well he knew terms like these, all thanks to years of hanging out with Vera when she was at the helm of *Image* magazine.

Incredibly, there was something that Marcus had been coveting for some time, the complete DVD collection of the Ken Burns series on jazz. Marcus was addicted to biographies of all kinds and every kind of jazz from swing to big band to Latin. Every time the series came on he vowed to watch it in its entirety but his schedule didn't permit it. He'd only seen parts of the series, but it was enough to captivate him totally. Just when he was feeling completely overwhelmed by Vera's gifts, he realized there was yet another package in the bag.

Opening it slowly, he felt an emotion he couldn't put a

name to as he looked at its contents. There was a picture of him and Vera, taken at the christening of Martin and Ceylon's twins. They were each holding a baby and for some reason, even though they were looking at the babies and not at each other, they looked like they belonged together. Angelique had no doubt taken the picture, as she'd been wielding a camera all that day. Vera had the shot enlarged and developed in sepia on matte paper, making it look old and cherished. There was another sepia-toned picture, this one of Vera, holding Kika and Toby, who were smiling for all they were worth. All anyone had to do was get out a camera and the two little dogs immediately started posing. The two pictures were in a joined frame made of fine kidskin and sterling silver. This time Marcus was truly wiped out.

No one knew him like Vera and certainly no one understood him like she did. Other than his family, no one had ever shown him the kind of consideration and affection and respect that Vera gave him daily. She was completely in tune with his career; she'd helped his family build the company into what it was today. She was as committed to its success as he was; more than that, she was a part of that success. He and Vera were more than friends, they were soul mates, and he'd always known that on some unconscious level. But that was friendship, wasn't it? It wasn't love, surely not. Love also involved passion and desire.

Marcus lay back on the bed and studied the pictures intently. Vera was everything a man could want, and yeah, she was damned sexy. If Marcus was going to be totally honest, he'd kept his feelings for her bottled up tightly from the moment he realized she was a married woman. Older women, sure, fine, bring it on; Marcus's idea of glamour had always been women like Diahann Carroll, Lena Horne, and the fascinating women in his mother's bridge club. Marcus had always found older women extremely sexy. But a happily married woman? Nope, no way, hell no. That was a sure way to madness. Marcus finally stopped staring at the pictures long enough to acknowledge a deep truth, that for about five years Vera had been his only fantasy. He might have been the picture of propriety during the day, but at night Vera came into his dreams with a regularity that was as intense as it was disturbing.

Marcus jumped from the bed and headed for the shower. This was crazy; he was letting Larissa's words affect him too deeply. It was just her opinion, after all. He laughed at the irony of it. If *Vera* had told him he was in love with some woman, he'd have believed her instantly because she knew him just that well. Just imagine the havoc Vera could wreak in his life if Larissa's words were true. He braced himself for the onslaught of cool water and tried to scrub away the maelstrom of thoughts that had taken him over.

It wasn't until much later that he realized how unsuccessful he'd been. He was awakened over and over again through a night filled with the most erotic dreams he'd ever had, all starring him and Vera. By the time dawn broke, Marcus was glumly ensconced in his favorite woven leather chair in the den, watching the Ken Burn series on his flat-screen plasma TV and periodically staring at the pictures from Vera. His emotions veered between extreme joy and extreme fear as he finally accepted the truth. He really was in love with Vera Jackson.

The next morning Vera couldn't have felt better. She'd gotten up an hour early, taken Kika and Toby for their walk, and then run for forty-five minutes before showering and getting ready for church. She felt energized and in control. She dressed quickly and stylishly in a simple cotton dress that would be comfortable under her choir robe. Remembering that Marcus hadn't returned her phone call, she hoped that he would remember the music for the duet. After getting into the PT Cruiser she hesitated for a second, then let the windows down to enjoy the breeze and took off for the A.M.E. church she'd attended for years. Another woman would have considered her hairstyle before all else, but Vera loved the feel of the wind in her hair too much to care if her style got a little windblown.

She enjoyed church service as she always did, even more so because the duet she and Marcus sang sounded marvelous. He'd been running late, as usual, so she didn't get a chance to chat with him before church, but she was sure they'd catch up after the service. In the meantime, she was caught up in the customary after-church throng of the Deveraux family, hugging the children, exchanging affectionate greetings with the grown-ups, and in the case of Lillian, exchanging compliments. They were standing on the sidewalk near the parking lot, chatting as if they hadn't seen each other in ages.

"Vera, that dress is wonderful! Where did you get it?" the older woman asked.

Vera looked down at her basic little black dress, a sleeveless number embroidered with small flowers in various shades of pink. "Honey, this is a TJ Maxx special. I thought it looked kind of *Breakfast at Tiffany's*, you know?"

And it did, at least on Vera. She had a positive genius for finding inexpensive things and making them look as if they cost a fortune. She was wearing Jimmy Choo sandals, also purchased from a discount store, and she was carrying a small pink leather Coach bag. The bag was the most expensive and it had been a gift, information Vera was happy to share. "You know me, the original cheap sister. Listen, TJ's clearance sale should be starting this week. When I get back in town, let's go on tour, okay?"

"On tour" meant starting extra early, going to the Waf-

fle House for an obscenely fattening breakfast, something
Vera allowed herself a few times each year, then hitting
every TJ Maxx store in the metropolitan Atlanta area, with
a few stops at select Target stores. It was a tradition with
her and Lillian, and Bennie and Selena often joined in,
although Ceylon would most likely beg off due to the babies.

"Back in town? Where are you going?"

The gruff voice at Vera's elbow made her turn around.
"Oh, there you are! You know I'm flying out today for that
conference in Las Vegas. Then I'm going to tape on location in Kansas City. I told you about that restaurant we
want to feature. Then I'm speaking at my alma mater's
commencement, so I won't be home until Thursday night.
I e-mailed you my schedule and Paris gives a hard copy
to RaeAnn every week," she reminded him with a smile in
her eyes.

Looking up at his grumpy face, she asked an innocent
question. "Didn't you sleep well?"

In reply Marcus shoved his dark glasses on and looked
distinctly out of sorts before muttering an answer. "No, I
didn't. I had . . . bad dreams all night."

Vera immediately reached for his hand and clasped it
briefly. "Aww, you poor thing. I hate it when that happens!
Next time give me a call, I'll make you feel better," she
promised.

Instead of his usual hearty laugh, Marcus nodded
gruffly and said he'd call her later. He left immediately
after that, leaving both women staring after him in amazement.

"My goodness, he must have really had a bad night,"
Lillian said apologetically.

Vera nodded in agreement. "Probably something he ate
at the party," she said with sympathy.

"Speaking of food, are you coming over for brunch? Bill

went to early service so he could make one of those elaborate feasts he loves to put together," Lillian said with a fond smile.

"I'd love to, but I have so much to do before taking off! I have to take the dogs to their sitter, finish packing, make sure my speech is in order, you know how it goes. I'll call you later," she said, kissing the older woman on the cheek before heading off to her car.

It wasn't until she was halfway home that she realized that Marcus hadn't commented on her gifts. Thinking that he probably hadn't opened them yet, she smiled as she pictured the look on his face when he did. He was going to be thrilled, of that she had no doubt.

Lillian and Vera weren't the only ones who noticed that Marcus was out of sorts. Paris had also been observing him carefully. She could tell that something was bothering him mightily, and she could also discern that her gift had gone unopened. It wouldn't be possible for him to be moping like that if he'd opened it and read the contents. She whispered, "Be right back" to Angelique and hurried to join Marcus as he went to fetch his car.

"Marcus, wait up," she called.

It took two or three repeats of his name for him to respond, and when he did, it wasn't with the gracious smile she was used to seeing on his face.

Paris, though, was the middle child of several brothers and she was used to gruff, idiosyncratic male behavior. She cut right to the chase. "You didn't open your birthday card, did you? You put it in your pocket and forgot it was there, didn't you?"

Without waiting for an answer, she went on, ignoring the look of bafflement on Marcus's face. "Look, it's a special card. Just do yourself a favor and open it when you get home, okay?"

Marcus nodded in agreement. "Okay, I will. You're right, I totally forgot about the card, and I apologize. I'll open it as soon as I get home. By the way, you look gorgeous, sweetie. I meant to tell you that yesterday, too. You look great," he said sincerely.

Paris actually blushed a little as she looked down at her outfit. It was another Aidan production, this time a fitted silk and linen blend sleeveless dress with a nice scoop neckline and a matching duster in sheer linen. Both were in a yummy watermelon-pink that made her look and feel feminine and adorable, and as a dazzling change from her usual skirt length, the outfit ended at her knees to show off her big shapely calves.

"Thanks, cousin, I do clean up pretty well, I guess. Now don't forget that card!" she said fiercely before leaving him to rejoin Angelique. She was smiling so hard by the time she got into the car with her cousin that Angelique asked her what she was up to.

"Little me? Why, it's Sunday, honey chile! I was just trying to do some good works, that's all," she said piously.

And when it works it really will be good, she thought happily.

Chapter 7

If Marcus had done as Paris suggested, he could have saved himself a lot of misery. But instead of driving home and opening the card, Marcus drove around in a funk for a few hours. He was en route to St. Simon's Island where the family vacation home was located when he abruptly changed his mind and headed back to Peachtree City. Marcus was at least rational enough to recognize that he couldn't outrun his fate, and at that point in time he was fated to be in love with his best friend. That morning after church his suspicions were confirmed when she touched his hand. With his guard down and his heart open and vulnerable, the mere touch of Vera's hand had set off a galvanic explosion of desire. Her friendly little squeeze had plunged him into a frenzy of longing that was so deep it was actually frightening.

The fear quickly gave way to exhilaration; Marcus was actually excited that he could feel the kinds of emotions that he was experiencing. Then reality reared its ugly head. What were Larissa's words? "I said you were in love with Vera, I didn't say she was in love with you." That was what was making Marcus drive around in circles, restless and frustrated. How would Vera react when he told her of his feelings? It would no doubt be a surprise to her, but would it be a pleasant one? More importantly, would she ever be able to return his feelings? She cared about him, he knew that; but could she see him the same way he saw her?

Okay, that's about enough of that! This is why I never wanted to be bothered with love in the first place, he thought bitterly. Love, especially the hopeless, unrequited kind, made an utter fool out of a man. Still entertaining these and other savage thoughts, Marcus finally pulled into his own garage and got out of the car. Upon entering the house he immediately picked up the cordless phone and dialed Vera's number.

"Hello?"

At that moment, all the tension Marcus was feeling melted away and he was relaxed and at ease again. Just hearing her voice made everything okay for some reason. "Hello yourself. I'm sorry I was short with you this morning, I had some things on my mind," he said.

Vera immediately accepted his apology, then got down to business. "Well? Did you open them? Did you like them?" she demanded breathlessly.

Marcus closed his eyes and smiled. He could see Vera in his mind's eye, as excited as a little girl. Giving presents was much more thrilling to her than receiving them, just one more thing to love about her.

"Aw, Pie, forgive me. I should have called you last night. They were absolutely amazing, Vera, I loved everything. You really outdid yourself. In fact, I think you went above and beyond the call this time," he said warmly. A delighted laugh was his reward.

"Ooh, I'm so glad you liked everything! And don't you dare say I went overboard, not the way you spoil me," she protested.

They chatted amiably for a few minutes, until it was time for Vera to head out the door to take Kika and Toby to the dog-sitter. Marcus again expressed his doubts about the arrangement.

"Marcus, please! I'm not going to stick anyone with those two, they're too energetic and demanding to just drop off at someone's house. Can you imagine Bump trying to step over them all day if I left them with your mother? They love being at Ella's, she spoils them rotten and they also get those little daggers of toenails trimmed. It's not like I'm leaving them at a regular kennel," she argued.

At this point, Marcus was merely trying to prolong the conversation so he could continue to hear Vera's voice. He hated the thought of her going out of town, but at the same time it was a relief because he'd be able to get his equilibrium back before they were together again.

"Just remember you're going to that award dinner with me on Friday," Marcus pointed out.

"I've got it right here in my planner," Vera replied. "I'll be back in plenty of time, don't worry. Listen, I've got to go, call me on my cell phone later. Or e-mail me. Take care and have a good week, okay?"

Marcus hung up the phone with great reluctance. He realized he was still in the suit he'd worn to church, but it was now rather wrinkled from his day of driving around aimlessly. He was also hungry, having skipped brunch with the family. Marcus left the kitchen and went to the bedroom where he took off the suit and placed it on the bed to go to the cleaner's the next day. Changing into a pair of drawstring pants and a faded rayon African-print shirt, he looked in the closet for some more things that needed to go to the cleaner's and took out a couple of sports coats and a couple of pairs of slacks. Checking the pockets as always, he came across the birthday card that he seemed determined to ignore. Placing the clothes in the club chair for Mrs. Daniels, his housekeeper, to deal with the next day, Marcus went back to the kitchen in his bare feet. And this time he had the card with him.

After rummaging around in the refrigerator, Marcus determined there was nothing in there to hold his interest. There didn't seem to be anything in there that wouldn't require cooking from scratch, something he was perfectly capable of doing, but something he didn't feel like tackling at the moment. He contented himself for the moment with a large glass of water, followed by another. It looked like he was going to have to go out to eat, but before he did he opened the card at last. Sitting down at the kitchen table, he pulled out the typewritten pages and looked with mild interest. Not a traditional card, after all, except for the top sheet, which read *Marcus, this is a story someone told me that I thought you might find interesting. Sometimes it's the things we don't know that hold the most promise in our lives. Happy Birthday, Paris.*

Intrigued, Marcus read the pages rapidly at first, then slowed down to make sure he understood every word. When he finished he went right back to the beginning and started over again, this time very, very slowly. He sat there at his glass-topped kitchen table for a long moment before he began to laugh, deep belly laughs that released all the pent-up emotion of the past two days. *Yes, yes, yes! Oh, hell yes!* Marcus wanted to mark this day as a national holiday, he wanted to dance in the streets, he wanted to sing. He did start singing as he hopped into his car and took off in search of sustenance. Suddenly life was good again and he was ravenous. One appetite was going to be vanquished immediately; the other would have to wait a few days. But the latter would be a banquet well worth the wait.

Vera was ready to drop. The conference had been wonderful, the location shoot went by without incident, and being the keynote speaker at her alma mater, Florida A&M, was exciting beyond measure, but she was glad to be home again. Unfortunately, she was coming in on Friday morning instead of Thursday night as she'd planned. Luckily, Paris was right on the ball, keeping everything in order the way a good assistant should. She called Vera on her cell phone to let her know that Kika and Toby were home and all Vera had to do was come home to get ready for the dinner that night.

"Paris, thanks so much for getting the dogs, that saved me a lot of time. But I'm not running home just yet. There're a couple of things I want to see to at the office before I do that. The dinner's not until eight, so if I get home by six I'll have plenty of time. Talk to you later!"

In a short time Vera was strolling into her office only to be greeted by one of her editors, Star Hopkins. Star was her real name, not a nickname, and it suited her perfectly. Tall, shapely, absolutely unflappable, and totally capable, Star had editor in chief written all over her. It was just a matter of time until the right position came along. She didn't look surprised to see Vera, but she let her know immediately that her presence wasn't needed today.

"Look at you; you got stranded by a monsoon in Florida and you turn up here looking like you just left the spa. You're kind of frightening, Vera, you really are. But you don't need to be here, you can take a day off. Go home, relax, go get a pedicure or a massage or something. Let me earn those big bucks you're paying me. Scat!"

Vera sank into the thickly cushioned Ultrasuede sofa that was the focal point of the seating area of her office. Star's words suddenly made perfect sense to Vera. What was the point of having two assistants if she didn't let them assist? And what was so important that it couldn't wait until Monday, anyway? Patting back a huge yawn, she nodded. "You know what, Star? You're right. I need to go home and get some sleep so I don't look like a swamp witch tonight. I'm going to some dinner with Marcus tonight, and for the life of me I can't remember what it's for. Some kind of award thing, I know he's giving a speech or something." She yawned again and immediately got up from the sinfully comfortable couch. "You're wonderful. Leave me copious notes on anything you think is important. I'm outtie." Waving tiredly, Vera left the building less than fifteen minutes after she'd entered it.

She actually took Star's advice, too; she stopped at her day spa and got a thirty-minute massage, a manicure, and a pedicure. She almost fell asleep while Crystal, the talented nail technician, was putting the finishing touches on Vera's usual American manicure. She turned the air-conditioning all the way up in the PT Cruiser, put on some Mary J. Blige, and blasted it as loud as possible to keep herself awake for the brief ride to her house. When she finally reached the front door she was all done in. Paris took one look at her and insisted that she get right into bed for a nap.

"You lie down and I'll unload the car. It's one o'clock now. I'll wake you at four and you'll feel like a new woman. Do you know what you're wearing tonight?" She had to almost shout the words as Kika and Toby were dancing around expressing their joy at seeing Vera again.

Vera looked startled at the question. She hadn't given it any thought at all. Cuddling the wiggly little dogs under her chin, she shrugged. "I don't know. Find me something. Anything at all, I don't care. I'm going to crash right now before I pass out on the floor. That massage just did me in! Note to self—never get a really good massage when you're really tired. Thanks a million, Paris."

Vera walked slowly up the stairs with the dogs scampering ahead of her. She didn't see the look of utter glee on Paris's face or she definitely would have rethought the idea of letting Paris pick her outfit.

* * *

After a few hours of sleep, Vera felt wonderful. She took a long hot shower that was followed by a cool rinse and by the time she emerged from the bathroom wrapped in a bath sheet she was ready for action. She quickly blew her hair dry and while she was waiting for her curling iron to heat, she got a look at the outfits Paris had laid out for her perusal. One was a halter-necked black dress with a long skirt, which Vera immediately vetoed as being too formal. One outfit was a red pantsuit with a double-breasted jacket and wide-legged pants that was rejected for being too casual. The winner was a favorite dress of Vera's, one she'd only worn once.

Vera got most of her dressy outfits at consignment stores or resale shops. She just couldn't see spending major bucks on an outfit that would be worn once or twice. She also loved to shop at flea markets and vintage stores and as a result, had an unusual collection of stunning dresses. This one was white silk crepe, the brightness of the white mellowed by age to a soft creamy vanilla. It was an elegant but simple confection with slightly extended, softly padded shoulders, fluttery elbow-length sleeves, and a deep square neckline softened by a subtle drape. The below-knee-length skirt was slit to midthigh on the left side and cleverly draped so it allowed for easy movement, but still showed off the figure of the wearer. The fit of the dress was wonderful, with darts molding the bodice and waist. It had once had a silk flower at the waist, but Vera had deemed it gaudy and removed it. The dress had none of the telltale yellowing that can occur with vintage fabrics, no broken seams or moth holes. It was perfectly preserved and perfect for the occasion.

"Okay, it looks like we have a winner," Vera said cheerfully. Paris had also put out a pair of open-toed taupe sling-back heels and a small ivory evening bag. Vera had once explained to Paris that taupe heels had the effect of making one's legs look longer and more slender, which was why they were often worn in fashion shows and beauty contests. After curling her hair, Vera sat down at the vanity table to apply the little makeup that she wore: a dab of foundation, a stroke of sheer, glimmering eyeshadow, and loads of black mascara. Shaping her mouth with a soft brown lip liner to keep her gloss from running was a necessity with the mocha lip gloss that had a hint of gold shimmer. Paris watched with fascination as Vera rapidly applied her makeup.

"Wow, you do that so fast," she murmured. "It would take me hours and I'd look like a refugee from Ringling Brothers Clown College when I got done."

Vera looked at Paris and smiled. "One day you have to come over and I'll show you how to do this. My sister worked in the cosmetic department of Hudson's while she was in school, she's the pro. If I can learn how to do this, anyone can."

Satisfied with her makeup, Vera brushed her shiny black hair and arranged it in a sophisticated style that would show off her face as well as complement the dress. She looked in her jewelry box and pulled out a pair of delicate earrings. They consisted of a small diamond stud that supported a thin chain about three inches long ending in an opal teardrop. She decided against the matching necklace, but added a tennis bracelet of opals intersected by tiny diamonds. Both the bracelet and the earrings had been gifts from Marcus the previous Christmas. Finally, after a soft mist of her favorite scent, Vera was ready to don the dress, and not a moment too soon as Paris announced that Marcus was downstairs.

To keep from getting makeup on the dress, Vera employed a trick she'd learned from her mother; she dropped a silk scarf over her head, and then slipped the dress on. Take the scarf off and voila, a makeup-free dress and a preserved coiffure. The dress, like many made in the fifties, zipped on the side and didn't lend itself to easy access. But the resulting fit was worth it, it slipped on like a kid glove. The neckline gave her a moment's concern, though, as it seemed a bit lower than she remembered.

"Paris, what do you think? Isn't this a little low cut?"

Paris assured her that it was perfect, although Vera had her doubts. "I don't know, Paris, my bosom looks like two brown puppies trying to claw their way out of a basket. Maybe I should wear something else," Vera mused.

Just then Marcus shouted up the stairs. "Woman, get moving! We ain't got all night!"

Vera shrugged her shoulders. "All right then, it's this or nothing. Let me get down those stairs before your cousin loses what's left of his mind," she said with a laugh.

After a brief compliment on her appearance Marcus hustled Vera out of the house and into the car with what she felt was unseemly haste. "Hey, slow down, are we in a race or something?" she asked pointedly.

"No, but I don't want to be late," Marcus answered.

"Hmmph. You barely told me how nice I look," she said, giving him a sidelong glance.

Marcus kept his eyes on the road, but a small smile played around his lips. "You look beautiful, Vera, like Dorothy Dandridge in her heyday. You're gorgeous," he said quietly.

Vera reached over and touched his hand. "Thank you, Marcus. And you're looking wonderful, as well. Do you have your speech?" she asked.

Marcus glanced at Vera and smiled. "Oh, yeah, I have it pretty much memorized. This will be the easiest presentation I've ever made in my life," he assured her.

They arrived at the posh hotel where the dinner was being held, and the rest of the evening went by in a blur for Vera. She generally liked to wander around and meet and greet people during the cocktail hour, but Marcus managed to guide her in the direction he wanted to follow. Which was fine, as she was still able to chat with a few acquaintances, albeit at top speed. She was excited to see that their table was full of friends: Bennie and Clay, Lillian and Bump, Malcolm and Selena, and Angelique. Dinner was superb starting with a flavorful vichyssoise, then the main course of grilled salmon stuffed with crabmeat, followed by a salad of field greens with goat cheese and an elegant vinaigrette, and ending with a lovely peach sorbet and tuiles.

Shortly after dessert was served, the speeches began. The dinner was given by the biggest civic organization in the city of Atlanta. It was their annual event that served both as a fund-raiser and a means of bestowing recognition on those the organization felt exemplified the mission of the group. The mayor of Atlanta was the first speaker, making a mercifully brief but impassioned speech on the essential role that volunteerism played in keeping the city strong. Marcus discreetly left the table during her speech to get ready to make his presentation. While the speeches were being delivered, Vera was listening to the plaudits with genuine admiration and watching Marcus's dessert plate with genuine greed. Marcus wasn't fond of sorbet, and he wouldn't miss it if she ate it. Besides, it was just going to melt, or worse yet, be scooped up by the server and tossed out. *But dare I be a pig and try to snag that plate? Can't I be a lady for once?*

She glanced up guiltily and saw that everyone at the table was watching her carefully. She could feel the heat flame up in her cheeks. Surely they all didn't know what she'd been thinking! Just then, Marcus was introduced by the emcee. Expelling a breath of gratitude, Vera focused her attention on him. He looked extremely handsome in his custom-tailored midnight-navy suit. Marcus looked like what he was, a brilliant, capable man who knew exactly what he wanted and wasn't afraid to pursue his dreams and desires. Unlike many, Marcus truly enjoyed public speaking. It was often said he'd make a great politician. Vera turned toward Marcus and readied herself to hear a stirring message.

Marcus looked out at the audience, pausing briefly when his eyes met Vera's. *My God, she's beautiful,* he thought. Forcing himself to concentrate on the matter at hand, he began to speak.

"When I was asked to present this award, I thought it was extremely fitting that I give out this particular honor. I have the pleasure of knowing the recipient very, very well and I can attest that there is no one more deserving of this recognition. This is a person who is living proof that if you want something done, let a busy person do it. Busy people have the ability to accept challenges; they seem, in fact, to thrive on them. They can accomplish things that others deem impossible, because they are usually creative. Their creativity makes them figure out a way to do something that's never been done before and they do it with style." Marcus paused for a second and looked around the huge ballroom.

"Busy people also tend to be generous. They're usually eager to help someone else, happy to share their knowledge and technique. They have a genuine concern about others that makes them want to give of themselves unstintingly," he said, looking directly at Vera this time.

"The person I'm talking about is the busiest woman I know. She's also the most generous, the most creative, the most concerned, and the most productive. If I were to tell you about all the things she's accomplished, you'd get to dislike her because I'd keep you here for another forty or fifty minutes." He paused for the expected laughter. "I'll

just name a few of the most recent things she's been involved with: raising ten thousand dollars for Habitat for
Humanity; arranging for her employer to sponsor ten
houses; Serving on the boards of Big Brothers and Sisters;
acting as a mentor with Bright Futures, the organization
she founded to encourage at-risk teens; organizing corpo-
rate donations of more than one hundred thousand dollars
for the HBCU and the United Negro College Fund; and
last but far from least, she established the John Jackson
Memorial Scholarship Foundation; which has in the eighteen months since its inception funded over one hundred
first-time college students," he added proudly.

"She does it all with style, with grace, and with enthu-
siasm. The hardest thing I've ever done was keep this
award a secret, because she generally knows everything
that goes on at TDG. But this was one time I felt like she
should have the pleasure of being surprised, the way she
surprises everyone around her with the beauty of her spirit.
If you don't know this lady, you should get to know her as
soon as possible. You'll never meet anyone like her again.
I give you the Humanitarian of the Year, Vera Clark Jackson."

Some hours later, Vera was still floating on a rosy cloud
of bliss and champagne. After her initial shock at Marcus's
heartfelt speech, she'd composed herself long enough to
walk to the dais and make what she hoped was a nice acceptance speech. There were hugs and kisses from friends
and colleagues, blinding flashes from various cameras,
dancing, and lots of laughter, and through it all Marcus
was right there at her side. Now she understood why he'd
given her a bum's rush through the cocktail hour proceed-
ing the dinner: he wanted to make sure that no one gave

away the surprise. Now they were on their way to her house, and she was relaxed, tired, and completely happy.

Marcus brought the car to a stop in her driveway, and came around to her side to open the door for her. She gladly let him lead her up the bricked walkway to the front door, and handed him her keys to open the door.

"Marcus, this was the most wonderful night," she said breathily. "It was absolutely wonderful!"

Marcus looked down at her and smiled. He closed the front door and leaned back against it. "Did you have a good time? Were you surprised?" he asked in his deep, sexy voice. "I was going to fly your parents down but they had booked a cruise a year ago. I didn't think you'd want them to lose all that money, although I would have reimbursed them," he added.

Vera had put her little ivory bag down on a small table near the door. She took one more look at the big crystal bowl that was her award, engraved with her name, the date, and her honor and then carefully placed it on the dining room table well out of harm's way. She turned to Marcus with a huge smile on her face and assured him that she had indeed had a most delightful evening and she'd been completely surprised.

Walking toward him, she counted off points on her fingers. "I looked fabulous, I had the best-looking man in the world as my escort, I had a wonderful meal, even though I didn't get to eat your dessert, you said all kinds of nice things about me, and I got a big beautiful award. And I had three glasses of champagne and everybody in Atlanta saw my boobies," she added, giving the neckline of her dress a small hitch up. "It was a swell night, Marcus."

By now she'd reached Marcus, who was still leaning lazily against the door. He suddenly stood up straight and without another word he reached out and put both his great big hands around Vera's small waist. Pulling her into his

hard, muscled chest, Marcus bent his head and kissed her.
Vera was too shocked to resist and he pulled her even
closer, until their bodies were like one.

His full, chiseled lips made hers tremble at first, and
then she found herself responding to his touch. There was
nothing tentative or coy about this kiss; Marcus opened his
mouth and teased Vera's luscious lips apart with his hot,
moist tongue. She parted her lips just enough to allow him
entry and he took full advantage of it, stroking her lips
with his tongue before mating with hers, caressing it over
and over while his hands slipped down to her curved hips
and held her against his hardened length.

Vera was so overcome she couldn't move, except to
cling to Marcus. Somehow her arms found their way
around his waist and she was holding on for dear life,
pushing closer and closer to the magnificent heat that was
radiating through him into her body. Suddenly she caught
herself and pulled away from him in total shock.

"Marcus? Marcus, what are you *doing?*" she asked
breathlessly.

Marcus looked at her with eyes made heavy with desire.
"I'm declaring my intentions, beauty. I'm claiming you,"
he said calmly. "Vera, I love you."

Vera stared at him with huge, wondering eyes. "I love
you too, sweetie, but . . ."

Marcus stepped back from Vera, but kept his hands on
her hips, squeezing them gently and moving his thumbs in
small, firm circles. He never took his eyes from Vera's as
he spoke. "No 'buts,' baby. I mean it, Vera. I'm not talking
about platonic love like you're my best friend, or you're
like a sister to me, or you're like a member of the family.
I mean, I love *you,* Vera Jackson; I've been in love with
you since I was eighteen years old and I mean to have you.
You're mine, that's all there is to it."

Vera took a sudden step backward and freed herself

from Marcus's big, warm hands. "Okay, Marcus, I think you might have had a bit too much to drink," she began.

Marcus smiled and took a step toward Vera. "No, I haven't. I wasn't drinking tonight, you were," he pointed out.

Vera took two more steps away, nearly tripping over a plump stuffed ottoman. Marcus immediately put out a hand to steady her and then led her to the love seat to sit down. Unfortunately, he also sat down and due to his size and the size of the seating, Vera was practically in his lap. He put his arm around her and leaned in for another kiss, which Vera was too weak to resist. He smelled too good, his lips were too sexy, he tasted too good; she was absolutely powerless under his sensual onslaught. Marcus's strong arms suddenly lifted Vera into his lap and she wrapped her arms around his neck. They kissed again and again, tasting each other, learning how to give each other pleasure and how to take that pleasure for themselves.

Luckily, Kika and Toby came trotting downstairs at that moment. They gleefully discovered their lord and master and broke up the heated clinch with their antics. Vera leapt from Marcus's lap and started pacing around the room like a dainty cat on a wet tile floor, alternating between clasping her hands together and mussing up her hair in a frenzy of agitation.

"Marcus, this is nuts! This is the craziest thing . . . you can't be in love with me, you just can't. How could you . . . why did you . . . oh, this is just crazy," she muttered. "And besides, you have a girlfriend, or have you forgotten about Larissa?"

Marcus gave a short laugh. "Miss Larissa dumped me. Kicked me to the curb on my birthday because she said I was in love with you. And speaking of girlfriends and boyfriends, you need to tell that Dante to push off."

There didn't seem to be anything to add to a statement like that, at least nothing that Vera could come up with.

She did correct him, though."Dante and I are not 'dating,' we are *friends*. He's too busy with his residency to date and I think he's still nursing a heartache over that ol' ex-fiancée of his," she said absently. She went back to wringing her hands and muttering.

After watching her torture herself for a minute or so, Marcus reached into the inside pocket of his suit coat and pulled out Paris's by now infamous birthday greeting. "Vera, calm down. Sit down and read this and you'll understand," he said with a smile.

Vera stopped prowling long enough to look at him closely. Marcus was sprawled on the love seat, Kika and Toby happily cuddled on his lap, and he looked as innocent as a too-handsome man intent on seduction could look. She was consumed with curiosity; but she wasn't so curious that she was going to take another step toward him. Marcus raised his eyebrows. "I'm not going to do anything you don't want me to do. Here," he said, holding out the envelope.

Vera hesitated again and Marcus laughed at the look of total indecision on her flushed, beautiful face. He carefully dislodged the dogs, setting them to the side, and stood up, bowing to Vera and putting the envelope into her trembling fingers. "Here, baby. You sit down and I'm going to get you some water," he said soothingly.

Vera watched him go into the kitchen and she did sit then, curling up on the end of the chaise with the rolled arm. Marcus came back with a stemmed goblet and an icy bottle of Fiji water, Vera's current favorite. He made a sound of disapproval as he saw her trying to relax with her shoes on. Placing the water and the goblet on the side table, he sat at the other end of the chaise and helped himself to Vera's feet, removing her delicate shoes, positioning her legs so they'd be comfortable, and putting her feet in his lap. Vera jumped when she felt the warmth of his hands on her feet.

"Hold it! You go sit somewhere else, Marcus. I mean it, go over there until I'm through with this, whatever it is," she said crossly. "I don't know that I can trust you to behave," she added primly.

"Okay, you win," Marcus sighed. "But I want it on record that I'm moving because you got the good end of the chaise, not because you're the boss of me," he said mockingly as he moved back to the love seat.

Satisfied that he would stay put for the duration of her reading, Vera at last reached into the envelope and pulled out the folded pages. She began reading and before she'd finished the first page, she gasped and looked at Marcus. He smiled lazily and assured her that it got even better. Feeling the heat blooming in her cheeks, Vera fervently hoped that it didn't.

Chapter 8

Marcus allowed Kika to inch her way up to his chest while Toby was content to rest in his lap. Both his hands were busy stroking the little dogs to their joy, while his eyes never left Vera. She was sitting on the chaise longue reading the contents of the envelope he'd handed her. It was an absolute pleasure to watch her expressive face as she took in the full import of what was typed on the pages. Marcus sank as deep into the love seat as possible given his length and let his heart fill with the sight of his beloved.

He was surprised at how relaxed and at ease he felt; he should have been terrified. Once he'd come to the inevitable conclusion that the feelings he had for Vera were real love, *true* love, he'd acted in typical Marcus fashion. Whatever Marcus wanted, he went after with a vengeance. Nothing could stop him once he decided on a course of action. If he wanted it bad enough, he could get it, whatever it was; he just had to figure out how. He didn't believe in astrology, but he indeed manifested all the traits of a Taurus man. He was tough, tender, sensual, and determined. If he saw it, if he desired it, it was his, whatever it was. And right now Vera was the only thing that filled his eyes and his heart.

A convulsive shiver came over him as he relived that first kiss, the feel of Vera in his arms, her soft lips on his, the feel of her breasts against his chest, the curve of her hips in his hands . . . it was better than anything he'd ever imagined and he'd had plenty of fantasies about her. From the time he was eighteen until he was twenty-three or so, Vera was his nocturnal pinup girl, the centerfold of his dreams. Marcus smiled as he watched his dream girl stroking her temple with her right hand while she stared at the papers in her left hand; it was a habit Vera displayed when she concentrated. And Marcus had no doubt that she was as mesmerized by what she was reading as he had been.

A few hours earlier she'd been the picture of sophistication and confidence in her fantastic outfit. When she came down the stairs to greet him she'd looked so incredible that Marcus could barely breathe. Now she looked more beautiful, more vulnerable than he'd ever seen her before. Her hair was in charming disarray, her lovely dress was rumpled, and her stunned expression was adorable. While Marcus watched Vera with his heart in his eyes, Kika took advantage of her position on his chest to run up to the back of the love seat where she could make forays onto Marcus's broad shoulder and give him little wet kisses. Absentmindedly, he scooped her up with one hand and looked her right in her alert little face. "See that pretty lady over there?" he asked rhetorically as he pointed Kika in Vera's direction. "She's going to be my wife," he said quietly.

Just then, Vera looked over at Marcus, her eyes still wide from shock. "Marcus . . . " was all she could say. Marcus understood completely. "Now do you understand, Pie? You can't play this off, baby. You know and I know this was meant to be," he said reassuringly.

"I'm going to fire Paris, I really am," Vera murmured.

Marcus laughed. "I'm giving her a private office, a Mercedes, and an assistant of her own. I'm promoting her to Executive Cousin. She's officially my favorite relative now," he said with satisfaction.

Vera wasn't paying his words any attention as her eyes locked with his and she raised both hands to her burning face. "You remembered . . . you *knew*," she whispered.

The paper was lavender parchment and it bore the unmistakable look of having been handled often, as it had. Marcus had read it enough to commit it to memory; now it was Vera's turn to read the words that had changed his life forever.

> *Dear Marcus, you remember when I was interning at* Image; *well, one of my assignments was "the Chat Room." Every month there was a new topic of discussion, always risqué, of course, where anonymous contributors would share My Most Embarrassing Moment, My Secret Fantasy, or something like that. One day I was playing around with different topics and came up with My Most Erotic Moment. I mentioned it to someone and she got a real sad look on her face. Then she told me a really fascinating story. I think you might like it. You'll understand why I decided not to use it in the magazine, but you'll also understand why I thought you should have the information. The story she told me went like this:*
>
> *"A few years ago I went to Detroit for a wedding. I was in the wedding as a matter of fact. I wasn't going to fly right back to Atlanta afterward because I wanted to visit with my family while I was in Michigan. So I rented a car when I got to town to drive up to Saginaw after the wedding. I ended up taking a friend to the airport in Detroit. He had some kind of appointment he couldn't miss. Anyway, this was way*

before that terrible September 11, back in the days when you could go right up to the gate with passengers, you know how it used to be. And my friend insisted that I walk him up to the gate because he hated waiting for planes and stuff. He has no patience, this man. He's such a good friend, of course I said yes.

"It was a beautiful sunny day in the fall, the wedding had been beautiful, we'd had a wonderful time, and we were both feeling really mellow, I guess. We were laughing and talking and going over the little details of the wedding, you know how that goes. We sang a duet at the reception and we were bragging about how good we sounded. We're both big hams. Anyway, his plane was really late and we were just talking away. He's a great conversationalist, by the way. Well, somehow our hands touched, just a little . . . just our fingers, actually. His fingers kind of entwined with mine, my left hand in his right, and we didn't pull away from each other, we just stood there with our fingers touching. Then it happened.

"I looked up at him and he was looking down at me with the most beautiful expression on his face and all of a sudden the most amazing heat started going through me, from my fingertips, all the way up my arm, through my whole body, everywhere! There was this warm, delicious, indescribable feeling like I had suddenly been submerged in warm scented oil. I say 'oil' because it was such a rich sensation, it was like being stroked all over by invisible hands. I couldn't take my eyes away from his, although I knew I should; I knew I shouldn't be looking at him like that! He looked so handsome, though, and so damned sexy that I wanted to consume him. I wanted

*to swallow him, to take every bit of him into my body
and keep him there forever, I really did.*

*"His eyes had me so mesmerized I don't know how
long we stood there looking at each other, but I
couldn't move. I couldn't breathe, I was throbbing all
over, and the moment was so perfect, so beautiful
that I still get chills when I think about it. For that
one perfect moment we were bound together by this
band of white-hot light that was radiating through us
. . . it was amazing. And I know he was feeling it too,
I know it! Well, I should say that I thought he could
feel it . . . I wanted him to feel it. Maybe it was just
my desire for him that was reflected in his eyes, I
don't know. But it was just as if I could see into his
heart and there was nothing there but me, his desire
for me. To this day that remains the most profoundly
sexual thing that's ever happened to me, it truly was.*

*"What happened then? Nothing. His plane came
in, they started boarding, he took his hand away
from mine, and he got on the plane. I sat in the rental
car for an hour and pulled myself together. It was totally wrong; wrong time, wrong place, wrong person
. . . I belonged to someone else and even if I hadn't it
wouldn't have been right in any circumstance but
I'm never going to forget that afternoon; it was like
an eternity of passion in the flicker of an eye."*

Vera was shaking in earnest as she and Marcus faced
each other across her living room. Marcus saw the depth
of the emotion she displayed and was moved to his very
soul. "As soon as I started reading that I knew it was about
you and me, Pie. How could I not remember it? You took
me to the airport after Bennie and Clay's wedding, and I
made you hang out with me because the plane was late."

Vera nodded her head slowly, her eyes fastened on Marcus's face.

"I thought . . . I thought it was my imagination," she whispered. "Wishful thinking, too much champagne . . . I don't know. I didn't know that you . . . "

Marcus again dislodged the dogs and rose to his full, magnificent height. Walking toward Vera, he made a motion with his hands that indicated she should scoot over. She sprang up from her position on the chaise, looking as if she were about to take flight. Marcus steadied her, then sat down on the end she'd vacated, the "good end" with the high back and deeply curving armrest. He pulled her down next to him and was touched anew by her open vulnerability. Holding her close to his chest, he stroked her arms and kissed her hair until he could feel her relax.

"Vera, how could I *not* feel what you were feeling? I wanted you so bad that day I was ready to explode. When I looked into your eyes, when I felt your hand, oh, God, Vera, I wanted to die right on the spot. I wanted to get on a plane with you and take off for some island and never come back. My heart was pounding, the blood was rushing through my head, and I was so hard I thought it would set off the metal detectors!" he said with a dry laugh.

"Pie, what I saw in your eyes at that moment . . . I can't describe it. I would have done anything to have you, anything. Committed a crime, donated a vital organ, anything. If I could have made love to you right then knowing I could never make love again as long as I lived, it would have been okay. You would have been enough to last me a lifetime, Vera."

He put his finger under her chin and forced her to look at him. Her long lashes were starred with tears and her lip was trembling like one of his nieces when they were very young. "Oh, baby, don't do that," he entreated her. "I can handle almost anything except your tears. C'mon, baby, don't cry!"

She couldn't answer, she just laid her head on his shoulder and let him hold her.

"Vera, you've got to get a regular sofa, baby, we can't court on this thing," he mumbled as he tried to get more comfortable on the charming but too-small chaise.

His words had an odd effect on Vera. Her head popped up from his shoulder and she looked at him full face. "Hold it, Marcus. Now just stop it! 'Court'? Who said anything about courting? This is impossible, Marcus, and you know it; you can't possibly expect that we're going to have some kind of relationship, you and—" Her words stopped abruptly as Marcus silenced her with his lips. Over and over and over he kissed Vera, the sweetest, most binding kisses she'd ever experienced.

He finally pulled away, staring deep into her eyes for a long moment. He then stood up, carefully drawing her to her feet. He didn't speak, he just held her for a long moment, gently, so she could push him away if she wanted. Instead, she hesitated for a few seconds, then wrapped her arms around his waist and burrowed closer to his big, warm body. They stood there for a long time without exchanging a word, just loving the feel of their closeness.

Finally Marcus loosened his hold on Vera. "You're tired, baby, you need some sleep. I need some sleep. I just want you to know two things. One, I meant every word I said here tonight. And two, this is going to work just fine. This is you and me, Pie. We can do anything," he reminded her.

Her long lashes immediately flooded with tears again. Marcus quickly kissed them away, and ended with a kiss on each cheek and on her forehead. "Okay, beauty, that's enough for tonight. Come walk me to the door."

Moving like a sleepwalker, Vera did just that. Automatically her arms went around his neck and she kissed him lightly on the lips, and then she drew back in confusion.

Marcus couldn't resist teasing her. "See? It feels natural, doesn't it? See you tomorrow, Pie." And without another word he was gone.

It had been a couple of hours since Marcus left, and Vera was still awake. She didn't even want to try to go to sleep because there was too much going on in her head. Ever since Marcus's amazing announcement, her mind had been racing like a videotape played in fast-forward. It was like trying to watch home movies at top speed, catching little glimpses of the past here and there, all of them images of her and Marcus over the years. *How could he do this to me? To us?*

Vera sat in the middle of her bed and stared at nothing in particular. She had gotten out of her dress and changed into one of her white T-shirts, this one about five sizes too big for her, soft and comforting to her skin. She wanted a cigarette with all her being, the desire for the taste of tobacco overwhelming her for the first time in years. But she didn't smoke anymore, thanks to Marcus. Vera had been an occasional smoker, a social smoker. She loved the taste of a nice long menthol cigarette, she loved the ritual of smoking, the rakishness she felt when taking a drag. She'd been smoking off and on since college and thought nothing of it until the day Marcus had seen her do it. He'd never seen her smoke before and the look of sadness that had come over his face was hard to think about even today; he'd looked more than disappointed, he looked absolutely forlorn watching her puff away on a Benson & Hedges menthol. "Aww, Vera . . . that beautiful body and this is how you treat it," he'd said sadly.

Vera shook her head and managed a jerky laugh as she

recalled that day. She'd butted out the cigarette immediately and never lit another one. Marcus had accomplished with one sentence what the surgeon general, her mother, and the American Cancer Society hadn't been able to do with years of nagging. She stopped smoking on the spot, not because it was bad for her, or because it was the only rational action of an intelligent woman, but because he wanted her to. And she'd done it without hesitation because she not only wanted to please him, she didn't ever want to disappoint him. Their friendship meant that much to her. Right now, though, she could have used a cigarette, or two or twenty, to calm her nerves.

How could this be happening? What in the world had possessed Paris to give Marcus that letter? How had Paris known it was Marcus she was talking about? *The little sneak.* Vera remembered the day that Paris had been casting about for a topic for "the Chat Room." Vera had been reviewing the editorial pages for an upcoming issue of *Personal Space* and hadn't really been giving Paris her full attention until she started talking about erotic memories. Something about the phrase triggered the picture of that day in Vera's mind and she suddenly started talking about it, sharing that incredible afternoon for the first time. *And she managed to remember it practically word for word, too. I didn't mention Marcus's name but she knew it was him. Smart heifer. Too smart for her own good. Just wait till I get my hands on her.* . . . Vera sighed and tried lying down on the bed, hoping a change of position would help her state of mind.

She was pretending to be upset with Paris, but that wasn't true, not really. Paris . . . was just Paris. She was curious, intuitive, and obviously extremely intelligent and she hadn't done anything terribly wrong. If this had involved other people, Paris's interference would have been considered by Vera to be a romantic intervention, a wonderful and generous act of friendship. But Paris's impetuous act had involved Marcus and Vera, not two young people who belonged together. Marcus was her dearest friend, her rock, her ally, her champion . . . he couldn't magically become the man who loved her just by saying the words.

There were so many reasons why they shouldn't be involved, so many Vera didn't know where to begin to construct a logical argument to present to Marcus. Particularly since the memory of Marcus's arms around her was making her perspire. And shiver, if she was going to be honest. Vera moaned softly and closed her eyes. When Marcus had taken her into his arms, all intelligent thought had ceased. She could still feel the heat of him, still smell his smooth skin, feel his thick moustache on her neck, his lips on hers, and she could remember exactly what tasting him had been like. It had been beyond anything she could've imagined, if she'd ever let her mind wander that way. She didn't have the will to erase his powerful words from her memory: "I love *you*, Vera Jackson; I've been in love with you since I was eighteen years old and I mean to have you. You're mine, that's all there is to it."

Vera rolled over onto her stomach and covered her head with the pillow so she could stifle a scream. Those were the kinds of words any woman wanted to hear from a man, especially a man like Marcus. Tall, handsome, brilliant, driven, so sexy it should have been a sin, generous, loving; who wouldn't want Marcus to be in love with her? *Me, that's who. This is wrong, this will never work, this is going to destroy us both,* she thought miserably. She tossed the pillow aside and scrambled into a sitting position. She took a deep, shuddering breath and was trying to decide if now was the time for a good cry when the phone rang. Startled, she glanced at her bedside clock. Impossible as it seemed, it was seven in the morning. Vera had been up all night wrestling with this. Without looking at her caller ID, she knew who it was. Making a little sound of despair, she answered the call.

"Good morning," she said quietly.

"Good morning to you," Marcus said cheerfully. "I'm bringing you breakfast. Get some clothes on, I'll be there in fifteen minutes."

"Breakfast? I don't want any fast food, Marcus," she began.

"Vera, please. Do you think I'm going to declare my love for you one night and bring you some old stank greasy fast food the next morning? C'mon, Pie. Get up, take a shower, get some clothes on, and meet me at the door with a smile on your face. Fifteen minutes."

"Thirty," Vera responded. "I have to take your little friends out."

"Okay, see you soon," Marcus answered and ended the call.

Why did I do that? Why didn't I tell him to stay away? Because she needed to see him in the cold light of day to convince him that he was completely wrong about everything. Of course, that was it! Hopping out of bed, she threw on a pair of jeans to walk Kika and Toby. Everything would be back to normal in a few hours. She would make her case, Marcus would see that she was right, and everything would just fall back into place. She felt foolish for having worried all night; in a couple of hours all would be well.

By the time Marcus came knocking on her front door, Vera was ready for him. More than ready, actually. She'd given the dogs a nice little walk as well as their breakfast. It was raining, but that didn't diminish their enjoyment of the walk. The little dogs liked rain as much as Vera did. There wasn't time for her to run before Marcus arrived, but she could always go to the gym later and take a nice run that evening. She showered quickly and dressed casually but deliberately, deciding on a pair of black linen shorts and a black-and-white blouse with a tiny gingham check. She smiled serenely as she tied the fronts of the blouse together at her waist and rolled the sleeves to her elbow. A lesser woman would have worn something concealing, but Vera was determined to act as normally as possible. This outfit was typical of what she'd have worn before Marcus's big revelation, so this was what she was wearing. She was going to inject as much normalcy into the morning as possible. That way Marcus would come to his senses that much faster.

She even put on a little makeup. First she brushed her thick eyebrows and added a teeny bit of pomade to make them gleam, then gave her thick lashes a couple of coats of black mascara. A swipe of juicy lip gloss and she was ready. She automatically picked up a bottle of the classic Elizabeth Arden fragrance Blue Grass and sprayed some on each of her pulse points and between her breasts. She had just slipped on a pair of black thong sandals when she heard Marcus's knock at the front door. Feeling more calm than she'd expected, Vera walked gracefully down the stairs to greet her friend. Already positioned by the door were Kika and Toby, jumping up and down and barking excitedly. Smiling serenely, Vera opened the door.

There was Marcus, with a big International Market shopping bag in each hand, looking way better than he needed to in old faded jeans, a FUBU rugby-styled shirt, and leather sandals. "Good morning, Vera. I hope you're hungry," Marcus said as he entered the house and headed straight for the kitchen. Vera followed him into the kitchen and immediately tried to look into the bags.

"I'm starving, you know I'm always hungry in the morning. What did you bring me?" she asked.

Marcus grabbed her shoulders and steered her away from the kitchen. "You just go into the living room and find us some nice music to dine by. I'll do everything else. You look cute, by the way," he said carelessly as he went about his business.

Vera acknowledged his compliment with one of her own. "You look pretty cute yourself. This was really sweet of you, Marcus."

She did as she was bid for a change, and went to select some CDs for their listening pleasure. She was pleasantly surprised at the serenity she was portraying, but somehow everything felt normal. That would just make it easier for her to say what she had to say, which was good. In a very short time, Marcus called her name and she went into the kitchen. She stared in fascination as she looked at the end results of Marcus's work.

There on the work island, Marcus had set two places with Vera's flea market place mats with the fruit pattern, and the green glass dishes she was so fond of. No one would have guessed that she'd paid a dollar apiece for the dishes at Target, they looked so pretty on her table. He had a salad plate at each place, topped by a dessert bowl filled with cut-up honeydew, mango, pineapple, blueberries, and peaches. Next to each setting was a bread plate that held one of Vera's most favorite and forbidden things, a glazed croissant. Her favorite French coffee mugs were there, waiting to be filled with coffee from the carafe that was also in attendance. A small jar of white nectarine jam sat next to a little pink Fiestaware jug of cream and a plate of perfectly browned turkey apple sausages. In the middle of the table was a green goblet filled with white irises, their stems trimmed to accommodate the makeshift vase. They had come from her garden and the raindrops were still clinging to the petals. The tall, multipaned windows and the screened back door were opened to admit the sound and smell of the soft spring rain, and everything looked amazingly delicious, just perfect.

"Breakfast is served, beauty," Marcus said with a smile.

Vera was so touched she didn't know what to say, which was just as well as Marcus chose that moment to kiss her. Taking her face in both his hands, he planted a sweet, firm kiss on her lips that ended much too quickly. Vera almost dropped the CDs she was carrying. "Marcus, stop that!" Vera protested.

Marcus raised one eyebrow slightly, took the CDs from her hands, and chose one to insert in the player that was mounted under her kitchen cupboard, the one that he had installed after she'd moved into the house, as a matter of fact.

"Vera, sit down and eat before it gets cold. We have plenty of time to discuss your irrational concerns, let's just have a nice meal," he said reasonably.

"I hate it when you take that patronizing tone with me," Vera said hotly.

"I know, that's why I do it," Marcus admitted cheerfully, as he seated Vera on one of the tall stools by the work island.

Vera looked at him in utter frustration, then looked at the beautiful, intimate little meal he'd prepared for her. She turned around and kissed Marcus on the cheek, long and lingering, before turning back to the table. It was going to be a long morning and she was starving.

After the delicious breakfast, Marcus and Vera amicably argued about who was going to clean up the kitchen. "You made the mess, you clean it up," Vera said pertly. There really wasn't much to be cleaned except the dishes from which they ate. Marcus was remarkably fastidious and cleaned the work area as he prepared food. He was, in fact, one of the tidiest people Vera had ever met.

"I worked like a slave and you're going to make me

clean up, too? That's just wrong, Vera. No," he said firmly, shaking his head.

While they were arguing, Vera was clearing the table of the few dishes and putting them in the sink. Marcus added what he obviously thought was the clincher as he watched her work.

"I'll tell you what, when you cook dinner for me tonight at my place, I'll clean up the kitchen. How's that for compromise?"

His sublimely confident tone made Vera stop in the middle of her task and turn around to face him. He was leaning forward with his elbows resting on the work island, wearing a mischievous smile and looking totally convinced of his words.

"Okay, Marcus, now enough is enough. You can't just assume that because you've decided on a course of action, the results are a done deal. You don't really think that we're going to start some kind of relationship because your cousin sent you that letter, do you?" Vera spoke more sharply than she intended, but she had to make him see that this was madness. Marcus's smile lost a bit of its lightheartedness and took on a more lethal character.

"No, Vera, I don't. In the first place," he said softly, "we already have a relationship. We're as close as two people can be who aren't bound by blood or marriage. And in the second place, seeing those words on paper only made me realize that you weren't indifferent to me as a man. I know you love me as a person, as a friend, but now I know that you care for me the way a woman cares for a man."

Vera stood with her back to the sink, gripping the edge of the counter with all her strength. How he could sit there and calmly utter those words? And why couldn't she talk or even move?

"It's true, isn't it, Vera? You want me as much as I want you, don't you? You want to be with me as much as I want to be with you, you want to kiss me again, to touch me, to hold me, and find out what we can be to each other, don't you?" Marcus was still smiling, but the smile had the effect of a soft caress. The music of Marion Meadows's exquisite tenor saxophone filled the kitchen to accompany the rain dripping from the eaves, and the only other sound Vera could hear was the thudding of her own heart.

She stood looking at Marcus for an embarrassingly long time and finally collected herself enough to respond. Walking slowly across the kitchen until she was even with Marcus, she finally answered him. "No. No, it's not true, Marcus, I'm sorry."

She started to leave the kitchen when she was stopped by the sound of Marcus's laughter. "You're such a bad liar, Pie."

Indignantly she put her hands on her hips and stared at him. "I beg your pardon?"

"Aww, Pie, you can't lie worth crap. Every time you try to lie you can't look a person in the eye and you were looking at the floor the whole time you were having that little Bette Davis moment. You're lying, baby."

Marcus swiveled around on the stool so that his left elbow was still resting on its smooth surface and he was facing Vera. Her arms dropped to her sides and she stood looking at him helplessly for a moment; then she walked into his arms. She rubbed her face against his unshaven cheek, loving the feel of the soft, stubbly growth. She inhaled the clean, soapy fragrance of his neck and kissed his throat softly. His big hands held her closely and slid down her waist until they rested on her hips. They remained that way for a long time, until Vera finally drew a long, shuddering breath and pulled back far enough to look into Marcus's eyes.

"Okay. You're right. But I'm right too, Marcus. This is all wrong, it just can't work," she said sadly.

By way of an answer Marcus cupped her buttocks

firmly and pulled her to him in a passionate kiss. First her top lip, then her lower one, then both her lips were treated to such a hot explosion of sensation that Vera thought she might faint. Ending the kiss with great reluctance, Marcus licked the corners of her mouth and took her lower lip into his mouth once more before letting up. "Baby, we can do anything we want. Anything. And I'm going to show you how."

Chapter 9

Marcus took Vera by the hand and led her into the dining room. "Sit down, I'll be right back," he said. He left the house and went out to the car to get his laptop computer. Whistling a jaunty tune, he reentered the house to find Vera looking at him as though she suspected he'd lost his reason. Marcus merely held up the computer and said in a theatrical voice, "Modern technology. Never leave home without it!" He then sat down across from Vera and readied the computer for use. Vera finally spoke, asking him what he was doing.

"I'm making this easy, baby. You have all kinds of reasons why you think this won't work, and I'm going to make a nice little checklist so we can mark them off one by one. Once you see how little stands between us and eternal bliss, you'll chill and we can get this show on the road," he said blithely.

Glancing at Vera's face, he saw right away that she didn't see the humor in what he'd just said so he decided to be a little less cavalier about it. Only a little, though. "All right, Vera, let's start at the top. What's your main reason for thinking this isn't going to work out?"

Vera's face continued to wear a look of disapproval and her words bore this out as she began speaking. "The difference in our ages, the fact that I'm your employee, your family, my family—"

Marcus held up his hands like a referee calling for a time-out. "Hold it! I said one at a time. Let's start with the first one and proceed in an orderly fashion," he said. "Okay, our ages. You seem to have been ten years old when I was born; that's not a problem for me. You think this is an issue, though. May I ask why?"

"Because it just is! I'm a lot older than you are, Marcus. That is an inescapable fact and one that could cause us problems down the road," she said firmly.

"Please. You're older than me, yet which one of us collects Hello Kitty toys and tapes cartoons on Saturday morning? Let's face it, Vera, of the two of us I am definitely the oldest. I had a tantrum because I couldn't wear a suit to kindergarten. Ask my mother if you don't believe me. Besides, women today make their own choices about who they date and marry. Lots of women are dating younger men. It's not like I'm your paperboy or some child you're baby-sitting! I'm a grown man and you're trying to turn this into 'How Vera Got Her Groove Back.' And on top of everything you look younger than me. I'm the one who has all the gray hair, you don't have a strand."

After that long speech there wasn't much that Vera could say, but she muttered in response, "And as long as there's a bottle of Clairol in the world, I *won't* have any gray hair!"

"I say we check off the age thing and move on. What's next?" Marcus asked.

Vera looked entirely too serious as she made her next point. "Marcus, I am your employee. It would be wrong, completely wrong for us to have a relationship while I'm in your employ."

Marcus had been ready for this point before she even uttered it. "Look, Vera, it's not like you're an hourly worker being preyed on by some horny old executive. You've been a part of TDG for over twelve years. You not only turned

Image magazine into one of the foremost fashion magazines in the world, you developed three other magazines as well as a television show. You've made us so much money it's ridiculous! You're an executive with the company, and you're on the board of directors, for God's sake! Who the hell is going to say something about you and me dating?"

Marcus paused in his impassioned speech to pick up Kika, who was waving her paw frantically for attention. If that ploy failed, she would fall over as though she were dead, which usually resulted in getting her way. Marcus went on, "There is absolutely nothing in our charter about employees dating. That was deliberate, Vera. As soon as you start telling people what they can't do with their personal lives, they find a reason to do it, just to show you they can. Then you have to start policing people and it destroys creativity and camaraderie, you know that. Besides, anybody who values their job knows they better not say a word about you."

Vera spoke up while Marcus was fending off Kika's kisses. "Marcus, I've told you before about acting like folks at TDG are wearing 'What Would Vera Do?' bracelets! I'm not somebody's icon, I just happen to love my job. And if you think people aren't going to gossip, you're nuts. They're going to talk, all right. And you can't handle it by firing people! This is something that will require gentle handling. I'm not going to be the subject of office gossip, Marcus. I refuse to be a party to that."

Marcus's face softened and he looked at the genuine distress on Vera's face. "Sugar-pie, if you think I'm going to put you in a position of ridicule, you're absolutely wrong. I'm not going to be groping you at work and giving you special treatment and making a spectacle out of our love. We're two mature adults who work in the same environment. Ultimately it's going to make our love stronger, not tear it apart. Don't forget, we have several married couples on our staff. Are they not more productive, happier in their positions, and better team players? I rest my case," he said.

"Besides, Vera, everyone knows that you and I are best friends. It's not going to be as big a shock as you seem to think it is. Trust me. I say this one is tabled, let's move on to the next one. What were you saying about my family? That one was way out in left field," he said dubiously.

Vera smacked her hand down on the table so hard it startled Kika, who was now lying on the table in front of the laptop, watching every move Marcus made. "Marcus, what is Lillian going to think? This is going to be like one of those horrid women's movies where some old divorced hag makes a move on her best friend's son! It's going to ruin our friendship, I know it! She'll hate me, and Bennie and Selena will despise me. Oh, God, Marcus, this is awful!" She jumped up from the table and disappeared into the living room.

Marcus looked down at Kika and sighed deeply. "I think your mama has lost it," he said seriously. Kika barked to signal her agreement. Putting the little dog on the floor, he went into the living room to find Vera, who was curled up on the love seat looking flustered and adorable.

"Vera, my heart, where do you come up with that stuff? Do you really think that my mother is going to despise you because I'm madly in love with you?" He held out his hand to Vera and she took it, rising gracefully into his arms for a comforting hug. He walked her backward onto the chaise longue and sat down with her in his lap.

"You know my mother loves you, you're one of her best friends. It's not like you've been hanging out with her for twelve years so you can jump my bones, is it? You haven't been cultivating the friendship of my family so you can seduce me, have you?"

Vera blushed and said, "No, of course not!"

Marcus contented himself with looking at Vera, noticing her small earrings, which were gold ladybugs with red and black enamel. She had a matching bracelet on that Marcus used to make a point. "Where did you get this from, Pie?"

Vera looked at him with puzzled eyes. "From your nieces, Amariee, Jilleyin, and Jasmine. They gave it to me last Christmas, Marcus."

Marcus nodded in agreement. "Yes, they did, because they love you. Since you call them ladybugs, they thought this was the most perfect thing in the world for you. They picked it out, they used their money to buy it, and they wrapped it for you. Not because you're my woman, or because I love you, but because *they* love you. Do you really think that's going to stop?" he asked gently.

Vera sighed deeply and cuddled closer to Marcus. "No. Yes. I don't know, Marcus, I'm so confused I can't think straight," she admitted.

Marcus tightened his arms around her for a moment, then kissed her cheek. "Vera, baby, I promise you it's going to be okay. You can have all the doubts you want, but I'm going to knock them all down. I'm going to show you step by step, inch by inch if I have to, that this was meant to be. It's going to be fine, Vera, better than fine. This is going to be one of the great loves of all time," he predicted grandly.

Vera didn't answer him right away. Finally she looked out the window and noticed the sun coming out. "It's stopped raining," she said.

Marcus replied, "So it has. Do you want to go out and do something?"

"Well," Vera said slowly, "we could go shopping."

"Oh? What do you want to shop for?" Marcus asked.

Vera gave him a huge smile along with her answer. "A sofa."

* * *

In a few days' time an opportunity to test Marcus's theory arose. In his position as CEO of The Deveraux Group, he called a special meeting of the heads of all departments. Vera took a seat between Daphne Childress and Rod Simpson in the big, sunny conference room and made small talk until the meeting started. Daphne was in charge of *Praise* magazine, one of the publications Vera had developed. It was a magazine for Christian women that featured inspirational articles as well as fashion, diet, and exercise tips and stories about family life. It had turned out to be one of the company's most popular publications and had a rapidly growing readership. Rod Simpson headed up the weekly newsmagazine, *Focus*.

"So what's this meeting about, Vera?" Daphne asked. Vera shrugged and said she had no idea. They didn't have long to wait as Marcus began speaking as soon as the last participant took a seat at the huge conference table. He looked so good that Vera had to force herself to think about the meeting, the beautiful weather, the production meeting she had scheduled with her own staff, anything at all besides Marcus.

"Okay, folks, this is an informational meeting to get everyone up to speed on the editorial direction of the August issues of our publications. I've been asked to chair the Committee for Children's Rights Coalition. Their aim is to improve the lives of children in the state of Georgia, and the biggest focus right now is on deadbeat parents. It's part of a multipronged approach to reduce the number of children living in poverty. The statistics on the number of children who are living in shelters, who are transient or living in substandard conditions are staggering. I have to tell you folks I got some of the most pitiful stories I've ever heard when they were laying this project out to me. Some of the worst, most demeaning things I've ever borne witness to," he said sadly, shaking his head. "And the number is growing at an appalling rate." Marcus stopped and loosened his tie before continuing.

"The main target for the committee is the middle-to-upper-income noncustodial parent who manages not to pay child support. They're targeting these parents because they have the money to pay the support, although they choose not to do so. There's going to be a huge advertising campaign and as chairman I will be making an editorial statement in the August issues of our publications. I won't be preempting your normal editorial statement, this will be a publisher's statement in addition to your normal article. The Deveraux Group is also going to underwrite a fund-raiser to take place during the holidays. Any questions so far?"

Vera was silent as she thought about what Marcus had just said. Marcus was deeply committed to civic matters; it was only natural that he would want to participate in something like this. And he was a wonderful choice; high profile, well known, and articulate, he'd be a great chairperson, she thought proudly. A question from Sanford Patterson, head of advertising sales, brought her attention back to the matter at hand.

"So basically this committee is declaring open season on the high and mighty who are too trifling to pay child support, right? And as chairperson, you're not only going to be the most visible member of the organization, but you're giving them a pulpit from which to speak via your publisher's statement. Just playing devil's advocate here, boss, but won't this make a lot of high-profile deadbeats pretty mad?"

Marcus gave Sanford a lethal grin that spoke volumes. "That's the whole idea."

After the meeting it dawned on Vera that this was a test of sorts, one that she and Marcus had passed admirably, for not by one gesture, one nuance, or one glance had they betrayed their new relationship. *Maybe this will work, after all.* It had been almost a week since Marcus made his declaration of love, and Vera was a mess. It didn't show on the outside, where she was her usual calm, collected self. But on the inside she was a churning mass of emotions. It wasn't that Marcus was rushing her; on the contrary, he was being kind and considerate as well as ardent, a heady combination. Other than sending her flowers and taking her out for dinner twice and lunch once, he hadn't overwhelmed her with extravagant attention.

Of course, after each date they'd kissed like there was no tomorrow. Vera thought she was going to pass out a couple of times, his lips were so potent. He called her every morning before she left for work, and they talked every night before falling asleep. In a way it was like a high school romance, sweet and chaste, but highly disturbing because they were both consenting adults. And true to his word, he hadn't acted differently toward her in the office. Not so much as a wink or a sly smile to indicate that they had a secret worth keeping. She was a little bit confused by his approach and finally told him so. Seated in her living room on her brand-new sofa, Marcus was happy to enlighten her.

The new sofa was more than big enough to hold Marcus's big body and allow the two of them to sit next to each other and neck, something they were doing at the very moment. Covered with pretty throw pillows, it was casually styled, covered in soft, comfortable sage-green sueded cotton. And one end of it extended out into a chaise so Vera was able to eliminate two pieces of furniture and still maintain the look she wanted for the room. It was a good purchase, a great fit for the room. Just like Vera was a good fit for Marcus's arms, or so he said as he kissed her cheek and neck.

"This feels absolutely perfect, baby. And by the way, have I told you that you are the best kisser in the world? You kiss . . ." He stopped to sample her lips. "Like a million bucks." He leaned back against the pillow and closed his eyes.

"Pie, I don't understand you. One minute you're convinced that this won't work, the next minute you think we're moving too slow," he said with a smile. "I think you might like this more than you realize," he said perceptively. "I think this feels right to you and you're getting used to it, aren't you?" Marcus asked quietly.

When Vera didn't respond, Marcus put the tip of his index finger under her chin and turned her face to his. He ran the finger down the side of her face, staring into her eyes with an expression of love so profound and tender that she thought she might weep.

"Look, Vera, this is no ninety-day arrangement. This is the rest of our lives, baby. Yes, I admit that I'm taking it slowly because I'm in no rush. I'm not going anywhere, you're not going anywhere, we're here for the long haul. I want to enjoy every minute of the time we're together; I want to experience every single level of romance with you from kissing and courting to making love for three days without coming up for air."

After that amazing declaration, Marcus touched his lips to Vera's, softly and tenderly, and as usual they were kissing wildly and passionately within seconds. When they finally pulled apart, Marcus smiled at Vera. "When we make love, baby, it's going to be special. It's going to be more than special, which is why I'm not trying to rush you into bed. I'm not trying to confuse you, or play games with you, I'm trying to give you everything you deserve, baby. Now do you understand?"

Vera stirred slightly in Marcus's arms, but only to move

closer to him. "Yes, Marcus, I do understand," she said on a sigh. "I really do."

Vera understood far too well, which was why she was so relieved to be getting on a plane headed far away from Marcus. She was leaving the next day to go home to visit her family for Father's Day and she needed the break in the worst way. She had a lot of thinking to do and home was an ideal place to do it. Besides, she had the perfect sounding boards waiting for her in Saginaw, her lifelong friends and her sisters. When all was said and done, nothing could get you on the right track like a long talk with an old friend. But even something as mundane as a short trip took on a new dimension with Marcus involved. For one thing, he insisted on driving her to the airport. And for another, he wouldn't hear of Vera leaving the dogs with Ella, their usual sitter. He wanted her to leave Kika and Toby with him.

"Look, Pie, we do enough traveling as it is and there's too many occasions when I can't see you off, so I intend to make the most of the few times when I can. And there's no reason why I can't take care of the urchins for you. They miss you as much as I do when you're gone."

Vera was touched by Marcus's thoughtfulness and finally agreed to his plan. "I have to tell you that you have no idea what they can get up to," she warned. "They're always on their best behavior for you, but they're extremely mischievous. I'd suggest you not leave any leather belts or shoes where they can find them. Toby eats leather like candy when he can get his little mitts on it."

"Oh, please! Those two are no more trouble than you are," Marcus said confidently. "We'll do just fine. Now me, on the other hand, I don't know how I'm going to do with you gone. Don't be gone too long, baby, I'm going to miss you too much," he said softly.

Vera looked at him for a long moment, to see if he was teasing or not. His handsome face was completely serious, and in fact, he looked a little melancholy at the prospect of her leaving. "Marcus, I do believe you mean it," she said lightly.

His expression changed to one of total exasperation and he thumped her on the back of the head. "Of course I mean it, girl, what's the matter with you?"

Vera laughed even as she was rubbing the back of her head with exaggerated motions. "Ouch! I was about to tell you how much I was going to miss you, and I was going to show you, too. Well, you can forget that, mister, I'm too through with you!"

She started to jump up from the sofa but Marcus roped her in with his long legs and arms and she found herself piled on top of him, laughing helplessly. Instantly the laughter turned to passion as she looked into his eyes. She melted against him, staring into his eyes with longing and desire all over her face. "Marcus . . . sweetheart, I miss you already," she whispered as she took his face in her hands and kissed him with all the emotion she was feeling.

When the kiss finally ended, she lay against his chest, feeling his heart pounding in rhythm with hers. *How can I ever let him go?* She wondered as she felt the beginnings of tears burn her eyelids.

Vera looked up in surprise as she entered the terminal at MBS Airport. The initials stood for Midland, Bay City, and Saginaw, and the surprise was due to her father being there to meet her plane. She immediately ran to him for a big bear hug, questioning him at the same time.

"Hi, Daddy! I told you I was going to rent a car, why did you come all the way out here?" She knew why, of course, it was because he couldn't stand the idea of her renting a car. Gordon Clark's thrift was legendary; he never spent a penny he didn't have to, and he'd taught his daughters the same habits. Sure enough, he immediately pointed out the expense of renting a car as frivolous.

"It just didn't make sense to rent a car, punkin. Not when your mother and I each have a car and there's Pinky besides," he said as they walked to the baggage claim area.

Vera cringed at the thought of driving around town in Pinky, the stately Cadillac Coupe de Ville in a bizarre metallic bronze color that was her father's pride and joy. Gordon treated it with all the reverence of a rare automotive antique, a reverence that was not shared by the rest of the family. Vera and her sisters privately referred to it as the Pimpmobile. Smiling, she looked up at her father and said mischievously, "But, Daddy, I have to go to Detroit for business. You gonna let me take Pinky to the big city?"

Clutching his chest theatrically, Gordon stopped in mid-stride. "Good Lord, no! I guess you'll have to rent one when you go to the city, punkin, 'cause my heart couldn't take it. No telling what might happen to Pinky in Detroit. I was just trying to save you some money," he sighed.

Vera looked at her tall, handsome father and laughed. "Daddy, I keep trying to tell you, I put this on my expense account. The Deveraux Group pays for this, I don't." By now they had retrieved Vera's bags and were on their way to the parking lot. Vera took advantage of the short stroll to inspect her father. Gordon Clark was over six feet tall and looked like a much younger man with his taut bronze skin and trim physique. His close-cropped hair still had the hairline of his youth although it and his moustache were more silver than black. He'd retired after years of teaching high school economics and coaching the basketball team. Due to the family propensity for diabetes, Gordon exercised daily and watched his diet vigorously as he had no intention of succumbing to what he called the "genetic booby trap" that lay in wait for the unvigilant members of his family. Looking at the two of them, it was easy to see where Vera got her good looks, and her sense of humor as well, as Gordon was known for his love of laughter.

"I see you checking me out, do I pass muster?" Gordon raised his eyebrows comically as they stowed the luggage in the trunk of his Chevy Blazer.

"Yes, Daddy, you do. You look fantastic. I can tell you've been taking care of yourself," Vera said approvingly. "How's Mommy?"

"Wonderful. You'll see for yourself in a few minutes. Although I have to ask, isn't it time that you started calling her something other than 'Mommy'? Aren't you getting a little long in the tooth to be calling her Mommy?" Gordon said with a sidelong glance at Vera.

Vera refused to take offense; this was old territory with them. "What do you suggest I call her, Mrs. Clark? I've called her Mommy all my life, why should I call her something else? I call you Daddy, why is *that* okay?" she asked reasonably. "And I'm not getting 'long in the tooth.' I hate that phrase, I really do."

"That's because you're getting older. Women get touchy as they age," he pointed out, groaning as his beloved daughter poked him in the arm as retaliation. "Daddy is perfectly appropriate for me because I'm so youthful," her father said loftily. "Your mother, however, is aging in a dignified manner and needs a more seemly title."

"Daddy, I'm telling you said Mommy is getting old," Vera said gleefully.

They continued to banter all the way to the east side of Saginaw, to the tree-lined street where Vera had grown up. Reaching the driveway of her parents' big brick home, Vera barely waited until the car stopped to jump out of the front seat. She paused a hot second to look at her mother's thriving flower beds, which encircled the house and bordered the surrounding fence, then bellowed for her mother at the top of her lungs. Her mother, the beautiful Vivian

Smith Clark, came around the corner of the house with a smile on her face. It was obvious she'd been gardening, and equally obvious that she was happy to see her middle daughter.

"Vera, child, you don't have to wake the whole neighborhood! Come give Mommy a hug," she said.

As the two women embraced it was plain that Vera had also taken after her mother. Vivian was also tall, still slender, and had the same enticing curves as her daughter, as well as the short, lustrous hair, although Vivian's had a tiny bit of white at the temples. She also had the same lissome legs, attractively shown off in denim shorts.

Vera gave her mother an extra squeeze, enjoying the faint fragrance of Red Door that always seemed to hover around her. It had been her favorite scent for years. As her father disappeared into the house with suitcases, Vera gave her mother a wicked grin and tattled on him.

"Mommy, Daddy says you're getting old! Old and dour!" she reported.

"Ha! Your father is just jealous because I still got it goin' on," her mother said pertly, with a quick snap of the hips. And she did indeed. Vivian Clark was also retired, having taught Spanish and vocal music for years in the same high school as her husband. Like Gordon, Vivian was committed to healthy living and it showed in her smooth, unlined skin and her trim figure. She and Gordon were still busy and active and enjoyed being married to each other tremendously.

Vivian also loved every moment of being a mother and was extremely good at it. So good that she knew her children intimately, much to their chagrin. So intimately that even after an absence of months she was able to zero in on the very thing Vera had been hoping to conceal.

Staring at her daughter's pretty face, flushed with happiness, Vivian made an exclamation in Spanish as she often did when she was excited. "Vera! You're in love! When did that happen and when were you going to tell us?"

Vera stared down into her glass of lemonade, wishing desperately to be somewhere else, at least for the moment. Her mother, bless her heart, had managed in the space of about thirty seconds to zero in on the very thing that Vera wanted to keep private. She shouldn't have been caught off guard by her mother's sagacity; Vivian had always been able to pull the truth about her children right out of thin air, it seemed. She should have known that Vivian would sense something was up, just by looking at her. *In love with Marcus*. Vera hadn't even said the words to him yet, but her mother knew.

Vera raised her eyes warily to give her parents a good look. The three of them were sitting around the kitchen table, having a glass of Vivian's special homemade lemonade. The appetizing smell of the dinner Vivian was preparing was all around them and everything was as it should be, but for the fact that Vera's cover was blown. And nothing seemed the least bit amiss to Vivian.

"Well, Vera, are you going to tell us about your young man?" she asked brightly.

Vera sighed deeply and rested both her elbows on the table as she covered her face with her hands. Abruptly she abandoned that pose. There was no point in postponing the inevitable. "Mommy," she began slowly, "about a week ago, Marcus told me that he's in love with me. He's been in love with me since he was eighteen, he says." The announcement didn't bring the shocked reaction that Vera was expecting. On the contrary, both her parents seemed oddly pleased with the information. They both took a sudden interest in the tall glasses in front of them, inspecting the lemon slices and ice cubes as though they were rare artifacts. And both of them wore pleased expressions that were difficult to conceal from their alert daughter.

"Okay, you two, what's up? What's with the little smug smiles?" Vera demanded.

Gordon dropped his pose and leaned toward his daughter. "I don't know about your mother, punkin, but I'm smiling because I just won a bet. I've been expecting something like this for a while," he admitted. Vera narrowed her eyes at her father and tilted her head slightly. "Oh, Daddy, you were not either. You're just making that up," she said.

Gordon suddenly looked serious, which surprised Vera. "I'm not kidding, sweetheart. I've known for a long time that Marcus has feelings for you. I knew from the way he treated you, from the way he treated *us* whenever we were in Atlanta, that he had nothing but respect and admiration for you. I've watched that young man over the years and I have to tell you, Vera, I always knew he had something that my son-in-law, God rest his soul, didn't." Gordon stopped speaking long enough to finish off his lemonade while Vera stared at him in amazement. Gordon had always seemed so fond of John. What was he talking about? She didn't have long to wait for the answer. Gordon started talking again immediately.

"Marcus has the ability to put you first, Vera. There is nothing that he wouldn't do for you, no matter what it takes. You would always be the most important person in his life, Vera. That's the quality that John was lacking. As much as I liked my son-in-law, I wasn't blind to his faults. I could see that if it was convenient for him, he'd give you a little consideration, but if there was something else going on, he came first, foremost and always. John loved you, I'm not saying that he didn't. But it was a selfish love; there is such a thing, you know. Marcus is capable of loving you unselfishly, which is what you deserve."

By now, Vera's mouth was hanging open as she stared at her father. She didn't know where to begin in her response. Should she defend her late husband or deny what Gordon said about Marcus? This was such a long and heartfelt speech from her father that she was completely at a loss. She watched as Gordon casually got up from the table and went to tend to Vivian's delicious meal. Vera was still trying to think of something to say when Vivian had her say.

She had been silent during her husband's revelations, but it was apparent that she, too, had been harboring thoughts of Marcus. "Vera, I never told you this before, probably because it's part of those things that you don't really *want* to remember. The night that John's plane went down, Marcus called us. He had known about the plane crash from the news reports, of course, but he'd just found out that John was on the plane. No one knew that yet, and he knew he had to be the one to tell you. It was a horrible thing he had to do to you, but it had to be done.

"Well, he called us as he was on the way to you. He broke the news to us as gently as possible, and then he told us a car would be picking us up within a half hour to take us to the airport where a plane would be waiting to fly us to Atlanta. He also got John's mother's telephone number from us, so he could arrange for her to be brought to Atlanta, too. Vera, he took control of that situation like nothing I've ever seen. He'd already sent someone out to California to find out firsthand what was going on, because he knew you would insist on knowing the truth, whatever the truth was." Vivian's eyes grew misty at the memory of that terrible time. She reached over and took Vera's hand.

"Honey, by the time he got to *your* door we were ready to leave Saginaw to go to you. Your doctor met him at your house in case you needed his care, and you did. Marcus never left your side during that whole ordeal. Just like he was there for you after your miscarriage. That's love, Vera. That's what made me know that this man was in love with you. It's nice to have someone you can laugh with, and play with and flirt with; that's always fun. But when you have someone who's going to be by your side during the hard times, the times of pain and sorrow, that's when you know you've got *love*.

"I'm not going to speak ill of the dead, but I never really forgave John for not coming to Big Mama's funeral with you," she said. Big Mama was Vivian's grandmother, who had lived a rich full life until she died five years earlier. Vera had been exceptionally close to her great-grandmother and had taken her death very, very hard.

This time, Vera did try to defend John. "Now, Mommy, the team was in California and John would have missed the biggest game of the season. The team was depending on him," she said.

Vivian gave Vera a look that said she wasn't buying it. "*You* were depending on him. You were his wife. And tell me this, Vera. Who was his team playing and what was the final score of the game?"

Vera looked completely blank. To be honest, she couldn't really remember if the team had been in California or Colorado and she had no idea whom they had been playing. She looked at Vivian in confusion.

"You see, Vera? Things like that aren't important in the great scheme of things. Football games, sports, scores, all of that stuff fades from your memory with time. What's important is serving God, loving your family and friends, and taking care of them. Your husband never knew that, but Marcus does. He was right beside you from the time Big Mama had that last stroke until they put her into the ground. And you think he did this out of mere friendship?"

Clearly, she didn't expect an answer to her rhetorical

question. She joined Gordon in putting the final touches on dinner, leaving Vera at the kitchen table. Vera's confusion was plain to see on her face, and Vivian was not unsympathetic to her daughter's plight. She leaned over and kissed her on the forehead, stroking her hair as she did so. "It's going to be fine, baby, it really is. Trust Mommy. And set the table, dear."

Chapter 10

It was Wednesday evening, only the first night of Vera's absence from Atlanta, but Marcus was ready to concede that she was a very wise woman. He was sitting on his bed staring at the frayed piece of braided black leather he held in his hand. Once it had been a very expensive belt; now it looked like what it was, a very expensive chew toy for Toby. How he'd gotten into the closet, Marcus didn't know, but he couldn't say he hadn't been warned. Kika and Toby were like a two-dog demolition squad. He looked at the two of them, sitting expectantly in front of him with happy expressions on their cute little faces. "You two are a mess," Marcus admitted. "Vera was absolutely right about you two, and I'm going to tell her so," he said sternly.

He took his tiny cell phone out of his pocket and said, "Vera," then stretched across the bed waiting for the voice activation to do its work. In seconds, his beloved was answering her cell phone, sounding rather subdued.

"What's the matter, Pie? You don't sound like yourself," Marcus said softly.

Vera sighed so softly that Marcus had to strain to hear her. "I just have a few things on my mind, that's all. I miss you," she added abruptly.

Marcus grinned at hearing the heartfelt words. "I miss you, too, baby. More than I can say. And the urchins miss you too. Listen to this." He leaned over the side of the big bed and held the phone out, saying, "Talk to your mama." Kika and Toby obligingly let out a series of yips and barks in the direction of the phone.

Vera was laughing when Marcus returned the phone to his ear. "You are so silly," she said fondly. "How are you guys getting along?"

Marcus didn't bother to lie, not even to save face. "I just hope the house is still standing when you get home. You didn't tell me this was like tag team wrestling! What one doesn't do, the other does without hesitation. And now I know what you mean about leather," he added ruefully.

They talked about the dogs for a couple more minutes, and then Vera got quiet. Too quiet for Marcus, he could sense that something was on her mind. "Okay, baby, what's on your mind? You're in deep thought about something. Either that or you've lost that lovin' feeling." Suddenly his voice went several octaves higher, and he started clowning as though he were a long-suffering wife. "That's it, isn't it? I work and I slave, it's not easy to make myself beautiful for you, you know, I work very, very hard at it! And you leave town for one day and you find you no longer care for me. It's just too much, I tell you!"

Between Vera's peals of laughter and the dogs anxious barking, Marcus almost didn't hear what she said next. "Hold it, baby, I didn't hear you. The urchins think I've lost my mind." Using his most persuasive voice, Marcus assured them he was just playing. "I haven't gone weird on you, guys, now be quiet, okay?"

He leaned back against the pillows at the head of the bed and gave his full attention to Vera. "Okay, beauty, what were you saying before we were so rudely interrupted?"

"I said you can check off my parents. From the checklist, remember? My parents appear to be very accepting of our new relationship," Vera said with dry humor. "Actually, they're quite happy. It seems as though they've been sizing you up for some time and they like what they see. They like it a *lot,* as a matter of fact."

Marcus smiled and tried not to gloat. He didn't really succeed. "I told you, Pie, you've been worrying about nothing. This is right, Vera. We're perfect for each other and everyone knows it. And by the way, we can check my mother off the list, too," he added.

"Marcus! You told *Lillian?* You didn't tell me you were going to say something to her." Vera's consternation was plain.

"I guess I didn't, did I?" Marcus was unrepentant, though. "It was fine, baby. She reacted about like your parents did. It seems that she's been aware that I was in love with you for years, she just never said anything. In fact, she insists that she was the catalyst behind this, that she made me 'bust a move.' I'll tell you the details of that later. Just remember, Vera, I'm not about to try to keep this some deep dark secret. At work I'll be discreet, but I'm not going to start skulking around like we're doing something we've got no business doing. Uh-uh."

He could tell from Vera's voice that she was smiling. "So you're just going to tell the whole world that we're involved, and I have nothing to say about it, hmmm?"

"Yeah, that's about right," he agreed. Suddenly he was quiet, too quiet for Vera.

"Okay, sweetie, what's on your mind?" she probed. "You're deep in thought, I can tell."

"I'm thinking about you, Pie, and how happy I am that we're together. I'm thinking about how much I miss you, and how much I want you with me right now. I should have come with you, it's too soon for us to be apart. Tell me again when you're coming back," he demanded.

Vera laughed softly. "I miss you, too, Marcus, I miss you a lot. Does that make you feel better? And I'll be back in the office Tuesday morning. I'm going to Detroit on Sunday night. I have some business there on Monday and I'll fly home that night. Does that suit you?"

"Not really," Marcus said sadly. "You just make sure you don't stay away any longer. Don't make me have to come and get you. What are you doing the rest of the week, anyway? That's a long time to be gone," he said mournfully.

"Marcus, you know I don't get home that often so I try to maximize my time here. Tomorrow I'm going to work out with my parents. They go to the Y every morning. Then I'm getting my hair shaped. And my friend Danny just bought his first house, and it's a beauty from what I hear. It's over on Gratiot over by the Country Club, which is a *very* big whoop, believe me! Years ago the only black people in that neighborhood were the domestics. But to live there in one of those big fine houses? Unheard of. Anyway, he says it needs a lot of work on the inside and he wants me to take a look. Although Danny has great taste. I can't see him needing me for much."

Marcus had his eyes closed, just savoring the sound of Vera's voice. She could have been reading a stock report and her voice would have had the same effect on him. Her throaty voice soothed him and excited him at the same time; it was as palpable as though she were touching him with her slender, capable hands. His longing for her was deep and passionate; he was right about it being too soon for them to be separated. He reached over and picked up her picture from his beside table.

"Marcus, are you listening to me?" Vera asked.

"No, baby, I'm not. I'm lying here on this big empty bed, I'm looking at your picture, and I'm wishing you were next to me," he said with complete honesty.

Vera's response was a soft "Oh."

Marcus continued to look at Vera's picture with growing desire. He'd meant what he told her about taking it slow and easy before becoming intimate; now he wondered who the hell he thought he was kidding. He'd been waiting twelve years for Vera and he couldn't wait much longer. He was about to tell her that when a sharp bark made him look down at Kika, who was staring at the bed with reproachful eyes. A sudden movement on the bed drew his eyes away from the angry Kika.

"How did you get up here?" Marcus asked rhetorically. Toby didn't answer, he just celebrated his achievement with a victory lap.

"Vera, he just jumped on the bed! How does he do that? He's only as big as a minute." Marcus was amazed. Vera was amused.

"I told you he'd been doing that. You didn't believe me, did you? I don't know if he backs up into the hallway and gets a running start, or if he jumps on various pieces of furniture to get there. But Kika hates it because she can't do it and she'll keep barking until you put him on the floor," she warned.

Marcus had already scooped up Kika and deposited her on the bed to her endless delight. "Too late, she's up here now. She seems to like it," he added offhandedly.

"Marcus, don't let those dogs on the bed," Vera fussed.

"Aww, Pie, the bed is as big as a football field, there's plenty of room for two itty-bitty urchins," he teased.

"Marcus, I'm not sleeping with dogs. There's not enough room for you, me, and those two. Don't start that habit with them, they'll expect to sleep with us all the time," she said firmly.

Marcus's face split in a smile of utter pleasure; Vera had just made an amazing revelation. She already thought of them in the same bed, which meant that she was thinking of a future with Marcus.

"Vera," he said softly, "when we're in each other's arms in this bed, you don't have to worry about anyone or anything else getting in here. It's going to be just you and me and it's going to be soon," he promised.

The next day found Vera in much better spirits. She'd had a few moments of self-recrimination when she remembered what she'd said to Marcus and his passionate response, but she slept very well, a pure, dreamless sleep that left her refreshed and relaxed. She took a brief shower and dressed in workout clothes to accompany Gordon and Vivian to the YMCA where they went five days a week. Her parents were quite serious about maintaining their good health. They shared a breakfast of high-fiber low-fat muffins, fat-free yogurt, fruit, and green tea, and then drove to the Y, which was about a ten-minute drive from their home on Cedar Street. Vivian pointed out new developments that had taken place since Vera's last visit.

"Look, that's the new medical building. I think it's going to be a real boost to the east side," she said as they went down Washington Street.

Vera admired the building as well as the new location of the farmer's market with its gaily striped tents. "Mommy, we'll have to come down here tomorrow," Vera said. She adored farmers' markets and open-air markets of any kind. She was actually more impressed with the new convenience store that was also on Washington than she'd been with the multimillion-dollar medical building. "Hot dog, our very own 7-Eleven! Now I don't have to go all the way out to Bridgeport to get a Slurpee," she gloated.

Equally impressive was the Children's Zoo, which had grown by leaps and bounds and now contained an exhibit of Vera's favorite birds, penguins, as well as a magnificent carousel with hand-carved horses, each painted by hand and decorated in a unique style. Vera said she wanted to take her niece and nephew to the zoo while she was at home, an innocent statement that caused both her parents to turn around and look at her in the backseat of the car.

"What? What's wrong with that?" she asked, puzzled. Her younger sister, Tanya, had a girl, eight, and a three-year-old boy; surely they still liked going to the zoo.

Her mother chuckled and said, "You'll see. Oh, you will definitely see." And she refused to say another word on the matter.

That afternoon, after her appointment at her friend Danny's chic, immaculate salon, the Hair Gallery, Vera finally caught up with Toni, her second oldest sister. Toni had been in Ann Arbor the previous day, helping her daughter move her things from the dormitory. She'd come home for the summer and Toni was elated because her daughter wanted to help her over the summer. Toni had her own business, she was a contractor and land developer and seemed determined to renovate the entire east side of Saginaw, one house at a time.

Toni would buy a shabby, run-down house, clean it from top to bottom, repair it, bring it up to code, redecorate it, and sell it. She kept some as rental units, and she also had a thriving real estate business. With buying and selling houses, renovating houses, and repairing houses, Toni didn't have time to reflect on the fact that her husband had lost his middle-aged mind, as she put it, and left her for his secretary. She was too busy being a great mother and a good businessperson to worry about that, or the fact that her social life was less than stellar. She had too many other things to concern herself with, like her son and daughter, her friends and family, and her church. Toni was one of the happiest, most well adjusted people Vera had ever known. And she was quite gorgeous, too. The Clark family were known for their good looks.

Toni greeted her happily as Vera walked up the driveway to her bungalow. Toni lived near her parents in the same tree-lined neighborhood in which they'd grown up. "There's my little sister! Look at you, girl, you're looking good! Turn around. Oh, yeah, you still have the Clark booty. I was afraid you were getting skinny on me!" Toni laughed.

Vera hugged her sister and stood back to check her out. "Child, I haven't lost a pound, believe me! You look wonderful, though. I thought I'd find you at the point of emaciation or something. Mommy says you're working too hard. She made it sound like you were about to keel over. And I wouldn't talk about the Clark booty if I were you. I see yours is still in full effect," she said fondly.

Toni was the same height as Vera, with the same curves, although Toni wasn't as well endowed as Vera, something she bemoaned frequently. "Why did my little sister get the extra boobs and I got stuck with a second helping of butt?" was her frequent cry. She was a rich brown, like Vera, and also wore her hair short, but hers was cut much closer to the scalp for a sleek, easy-care look. Due to her work, she was almost always in jeans and construction boots but she was so pretty that she looked cute in her work gear instead of manly.

Vera and Toni went into the house and immediately headed for the kitchen. Some of their best talks took place in the kitchen, Toni's kitchen, their mother's, Vera's; it didn't seem to matter whom the kitchen belonged to, it was just the perfect place for confiding. "So what's new in your life, little sister? What's been going on in the big bad city? How's your love life?" Toni inquired while pouring iced tea for the two of them.

To Toni's surprise Vera made a little sound and bared her teeth in a grimace that could have passed for a smile with someone who didn't know her. Toni, however, knew her very well indeed and immediately sat down across from her. "This looks serious. Dish, girl!"

And dish she did; she filled Toni in on recent events in

her life until she looked at the time. "Listen, Toni, there's more to tell, but I'm supposed to go to Danny's tonight and eat tacos. Wanna come? We can finish this afterward . . . if you're interested," she said coyly.

Toni looked at her as though she'd lost her mind. "When do I not want to eat tacos? And what makes you think I don't want to hear more of this scintillating tale? Let me hop in the shower and leave a note for my wandering child and we are outta here!"

In a couple of hours, Vera and Toni drove up to the turn-around in front of Danny's new home. It was new in the sense that he'd just purchased it; the house was almost one hundred years old. Vera got out of the car and took a good long look at the gray stucco house. It was a wonderful house; a two-storied Spanish colonial made of gray stucco, it looked imposing but comfortable. Vera took in details like mullioned windows and a small circular tower before ringing the doorbell. Danny immediately opened the door and gave Vera the once-over before letting her in.

"Okay, you've got the tomatoes. You weren't getting in without them," he said. "And look what you dragged with you," he added, referring to Toni. "I don't know if I should even let that heifer cross my threshold, she disappears for months without a word to anyone," he said, referring to Toni's workaholic lifestyle.

Vera brandished the plastic grocery bag from Farmer Jack's. "I have the tomatoes and the lettuce and they're already chopped, and I brought an extra bottle of hot sauce. Open this door before I hurt you," she threatened.

Danny Watley was one of her oldest friends. They had grown up together, gone to school together, and remained thick as thieves. Danny made it a practice to give her a hard time every time he saw her because he gave everyone he liked a hard time. If Danny was always polite and on his best behavior, it was a sure sign that he was completely indifferent to a person. Danny was extremely handsome, over six feet tall with impossibly smooth brown skin, large long-lashed eyes, and short impeccably trimmed black hair. Vera took some glee in the fact that Danny was beginning to show some premature gray in his neat moustache and the temples of his hair; he would have been too perfect without it. He was almost the same size he'd been in high school; he never gained weight and he worked out daily.

They hugged each other tightly while Vera glanced around the foyer in wonder. It was circular, and through it one could access the living room, the dining room, or go down a long hallway. It had thick, true stucco walls, and the original light fixture hung from the high ceiling. It was made of brass and stained glass in an opaline color and had fleurs-de-lis all around it. So someone had come up with the idea of stenciling fleurs-de-lis all over the walls in a metallic gold color. Vera stared at the creation, unsure of what to say. Danny saw her look as he was hugging Toni and sighed. "Oh, it gets worse," he assured her. Taking her bags, he led her into the dining room, which was magnificently proportioned but painted a deep dark blue that looked uncomfortable on the stucco walls. To make matters worse, there was a breakfast room that opened into the dining room and it was painted a bilious shade of maize yellow for a horrible contrast. Incredibly, there were also little hand-painted vines painted around each light fixture that did nothing to make the rooms look any better.

Vera stood stock-still and took it all in. "Wow. I take it the former owners were University of Michigan boosters?" she asked, referring to the familiar maize-and-blue color scheme.

A voice from the kitchen answered her query. "The pre-

vious owners had some serious issues. I think the wife
caught the husband doing something he had no business
and she jacked the house up to punish him, I really do."
The voice was that of Neesha, Danny's cousin and the
manager of his salon. Like everyone in that family, she was
good looking. Petite, with a nicely curved figure and
sleepy, sexy eyes, Neesha had a beautiful smile and a
warm personality. "You're looking good, Vera. Tell me,
don't you ever gain a pound? Couldn't you put on some
weight just to have something to complain about like the
rest of us?" she asked. "And that goes for your skinny sister, too. I hate you Clark girls, I really do," she said sadly.

Vera hugged Neesha, then laughed. "Neesha, you know
I work out every day, I have to. My grandmother always
said I was 'a baby and a biscuit' away from the plus-sized
department. Believe me, this is a result of constant vigi-
lance." She laughed, patting her behind. "And if it makes
you feel any better, I'll probably gain ten pounds tonight
from eating tacos."

Toni agreed with Vera wholeheartedly. "Girl, you have
no idea what a Clark booty can do if it's not kept in check.
If you don't work out like a dog and watch your diet, those
things will blow up like an air bag, trust me."

While they were waiting for their friend Regina to show
up so they could begin one of their favorite rituals, the
cooking and eating of tacos, Danny showed them the rest
of the house. Regina was bringing the fresh tortillas from
Vargas, the purveyor of the finest tortillas in Michigan, so
the party couldn't start without her. Vera was looking
around the kitchen with great interest while they waited.
"Danny, I love this kitchen! But wallpaper on the ceiling?"
The ceiling in question had timbers that intersected it and
would have given it a rustic look had it not been for the six
Tiffany lamps that were mounted on them, three on each
one.

Danny sighed again. "You see how much work I have to do in here? It's going to take me a year or more to get this house looking right."

Vera turned to him with a brilliant smile and said, "I have an idea. Since you're going to be redoing the house one room at a time, why don't we make it a monthly feature in the magazine? A month-by-month serial on the progress you're making on turning your house into your dream home. A lot of people are buying older homes and refurbishing them. This would be such a wonderful feature . . ." Vera's voice trailed off as she started walking around the house again, talking mostly to herself about the possibilities of the series. Danny, Neesha, and Toni were left in the kitchen staring at each other while Vera was gathering ideas. All at once, Danny's name sounded from the living room.

"So what do you think?" she asked eagerly. "Is it a go, or what?" Vera was leaning over the small balcony that looked out onto the living room. It was actually a small room that could also be accessed by a circular staircase that originated in the living room. Danny looked around the room that was filled with boxes, as was almost every room in the house; he'd just moved in, after all. "Are you sure this is a good idea?" he asked dubiously. "What makes you think that people will be interested in my fumbling around in this mess?"

Vera waved away his question. "Oh, please, honey, this is what I do! When have you ever known me to be wrong about anything?"

Danny looked at Vera and laughed. "You don't have enough time for me to answer *that* question."

Regina finally joined the group with apologies for her tardiness. She was medium height with beautiful cocoa skin, a short bob, and a ready smile. "Here you go, fresh from the oven. They're actually still warm," she said. Nee-

sha took the bag from her hands and they watched as she
began to get down to the business of making tacos. Vera
was investigating again, this time looking at the refrigerator, when Danny came up behind her.

"I think I'm getting rid of this monstrosity," Danny said,
gesturing at the wood-fronted doors that matched the cup-
boards. Vera looked aghast at his words.

"Don't even think about getting rid of this refrigerator!
This is a Sub-Zero, they're the best refrigerators ever
made! If it doesn't work get someone out to fix it, but
don't get rid of it," she cautioned.

The delicious aroma of the highly seasoned meat was
tantalizing everyone's appetites by now. Neesha was stirring the meat she'd seasoned with *cominos,* or ground
cumin as it was also known, cayenne, garlic, and onion
while she fried the tortillas. Laying one in a skillet with
about an inch of hot oil, she'd let it sizzle for a few seconds, then gently turned it over. When the oil around the
edges bubbled slightly, it was time to fold it in half. After
a few minutes, the shell would come out of the oil and be
transferred to a thick layer of paper towels to drain. Then
each person would fill the shells with the seasoned meat
and top them with chopped lettuce and tomato. None of
that yuppie stuff like cheese, sour cream, avocado, or anything else fancy. The condiment of choice was Frank's Red
Hot Sauce. And if you grew up on Fourteenth Street like
Danny, ketchup. Add a pitcher of red Kool-Aid or a Faygo
Redpop, and you were set. Tacos prepared like this and
eaten in mass quantity were strictly a Saginaw thing, as far
as any of them knew. Vera commented on the phenome-
non.

"When I'm in Atlanta, and I say I had tacos for dinner,
people will ask what else I had. When I say nothing, just
tacos, they think I'm weird. If I was in Atlanta, I'd have to
have enchiladas and frijoles and rice and about ten differ-

ent toppings for the tacos and margaritas for people to feel satisfied," she said wonderingly as she shook an ample amount of hot sauce on her next taco.

Danny, who went to New York every weekend, agreed. "When we start talking about tacos *we* get excited. Other people just don't get it, they think of tacos as some kind of appetizer."

Finally everyone had eaten their fill and were sitting around the long, oriental-styled dining room table. Danny was staring at Vera, his clever eyes taking in everything about her. With no warning, he pounced. "Vera Clark Jackson, what have you been up to? There's something different about you, what are you not telling us?"

Vera jumped guiltily and almost spilled Kool-Aid all over herself. "Dang. Is a person not entitled to any privacy?"

The others immediately said, "No" in unison.

Vera sighed deeply. "You're as bad as my mother," she complained. "I got in Wednesday afternoon and before dinner she had all my business out on Front Street. It took her about three seconds to figure out that . . ." Vera looked up to see three pairs of eyes fastened on her. Toni, having already gotten the scoop, was examining the horrific paint job on the dining room walls with a look of amusement.

Vera sighed, a deep, fake put-upon sigh. "I shouldn't tell you nosy people anything," she said with a smile. "Okay, here goes. Umm, Marcus says he's in love with me," she said quietly.

All three of them knew who Marcus Deveraux was, of course, so Vera was expecting some kind of outcry, at the very least. What she wasn't expecting was that Danny would hold out his hand and demand payment. "Ha! I told you heifers I knew what I was talking about. Pay up!"

Vera looked resigned and amused. "So I take it that this

isn't a surprise to any of you." Once again she got a choral "no" in response.

Neesha shook her head. "Oh, honey, when he came up here for your great-grandmother's funeral, we all knew. That man was eating you up with his eyes, girl. There was no doubt about it whatsoever, we could all see it. And from all the things you've told us over the years, how could we not know?"

Regina looked at Vera with amusement. "Are you telling us that you didn't know?"

Vera nodded her head. "Apparently, I was the *only* person who was clueless. I had to tell my parents yesterday because my mother the ferret figured out something was up. And she wasn't even shocked or surprised. Neither was Daddy, come to think of it. It was like they'd been waiting for this," she said bemusedly.

Toni gave her sister a sidelong glance before admitting that she, too, had long suspected something was up.

"Why wouldn't people suspect something? It was obvious to anyone with eyes. *We* certainly knew," Danny pointed out. "We've been taking bets on this for years."

"Well, it wasn't that obvious to me! I mean, I'm older than he is," she began.

Danny gave her a hard look. "So? You need a young man, can't no old man keep up with you. You'd wear out an old man. He'd want to be at home taking his blood pressure and you'd be out dancing until dawn. It would never work. And besides, you'd intimidate a man your age, you've accomplished too much. Surely you don't think there's something wrong with dating a younger man," Danny said with disgust. "Have you gone conservative on me?" he demanded. He reached under the table and pinched Vera hard, something he'd been doing since they were children.

"Ouch! Cut it out!"

An Important Message From The ARABESQUE Publisher

Dear Arabesque Reader,

Arabesque is celebrating 10 years of award-winning African-American romance. This year look for our specially marked 10th Anniversary titles.

Plus, we are offering *Special Collection Editions* and a *Summer Reading Series*—all part of our 10th Anniversary celebration.

Why not be a part of the celebration and let us send you four more specially selected books FREE! These exceptional romances will be sent right to your front door!

Please enjoy them with our compliments, and thank you for continuing to enjoy Arabesque.... the soul of romance bringing you ten years of love, passion and extraordinary romance.

Linda Gill
PUBLISHER, ARABESQUE ROMANCE NOVELS

P.S. Don't forget to check out our 10th Anniversary Sweepstakes—no purchase necessary—at www.BET.com

ARABESQUE

BET BOOKS

A SPECIAL "THANK YOU"
FROM ARABESQUE JUST FOR YOU!

Send this card back and you'll receive 4 FREE Arabesque Novels—a $25.96 value—absolutely FREE!

The introductory 4 Arabesque Romance books are yours FREE (plus $1.99 shipping & handling). If you wish to continue to receive 4 books every month, do nothing. Each month, we will send you 4 New Arabesque Romance Novels for your free examination. If you wish to keep them, pay just $16* (plus, $1.99 shipping & handling). If you decide not to continue, you owe nothing!

- Send no money now.
- Never an obligation.
- Books delivered to your door!

We hope that after receiving your FREE books you'll want to remain an Arabesque subscriber, but the choice is yours! So why not take advantage of this Arabesque offer, with no risk of any kind. You'll be glad you did!

In fact, we're so sure you will love your Arabesque novels, that we will send you an Arabesque Tote Bag FREE with your first paid shipment.

Call Us TOLL-FREE At
1-888-345-BOOK

* Prices subject to change

THE "THANK YOU" GIFT INCLUDES:

- 4 books absolutely FREE (plus $1.99 for shipping and handling).
- A FREE newsletter, *Arabesque Romance News*, filled with author interviews, book previews, special offers, and more!
- No risks or obligations. You're free to cancel whenever you wish with no questions asked.

INTRODUCTORY OFFER CERTIFICATE

Yes! Please send me 4 FREE Arabesque novels (plus $1.99 for shipping & handling). I understand I am under no obligation to purchase any books, as explained on the back of this card. Send my free tote bag after my first regular paid shipment.

NAME _____

ADDRESS _____ APT. _____

CITY _____ STATE _____ ZIP _____

TELEPHONE ( ) _____

E-MAIL _____

SIGNATURE _____

Offer limited to one per household and not valid to current subscribers. All orders subject to approval. Terms, offer, & price subject to change. Tote bags available while supplies last.

Thank You!

AN034A

Accepting the four introductory books for FREE (plus $1.99 to offset the cost of shipping & handling) places you under no obligation to buy anything. You may keep the books and return the shipping statement marked "cancelled". If you do not cancel, about a month later we will send 4 additional Arabesque novels, and you will be billed the preferred subscriber's price of just $4.00 per title. That's $16.00* for all 4 books for a savings of almost 40% off the cover price (Plus $1.99 for shipping and handling). You may cancel at any time, but if you choose to continue, every month we'll send you 4 more books, which you may either purchase at the preferred discount price. . . or return to us and cancel your subscription.

* PRICES SUBJECT TO CHANGE

THE ARABESQUE ROMANCE BOOK CLUB
P.O. BOX 5214
CLIFTON NJ 07015-5214

PLACE
STAMP
HERE

Regina added helpfully that lots of women were with younger men. "Susan Sarandon and Tim Robbins, Chilli and Usher, there's lots of women who have younger men and are extremely happy," she said.

Neesha had to put in her two cents. "Old men have worms, everybody knows that. Who wants an old wormy cuss when you can have a young, handsome man like Marcus?"

Toni said nothing, she just looked vastly amused at Vera's consternation.

Vera sighed deeply. "I don't know about this, y'all. Marcus is only thirty, he needs to be with a woman who can give him children," she said quietly.

Danny snorted. "Has he *asked* you for children? Well, why are you even worrying about it? And who says you can't have children?"

"Danny, you know I can't have kids! After my miscarriage I never conceived again, although nobody knows why. Nonspecific ovarian failure, that's what they called it. I seem to have a bumper crop of eggs. They just don't work, apparently."

Danny muttered something under his breath about her late husband's sperm. Danny was not a fan of John Jackson's. He never thought the man was good enough for Vera. "Well, maybe it wasn't *you* after all, Vera. If I were you, I'd get checked out again, and by a different doctor. They can do all kinds of things to get you pregnant nowadays."

Vera gave a short and cynical laugh. "Yeah, but, Danny, let's face it. My uterus is a relic by now. My ovaries are like fossils. If I had a baby it would look like a garden gnome, honey, with a long beard and everything. I'm going to be forty next month, you know."

"I don't know why I even talk to you," Danny said, shaking his head. "Lots of women have babies at forty and beyond, you provincial hag. But let's let that one go for the time being. The question is, how do *you* feel about *him?*" he demanded. "Are you in love with him?"

She didn't answer at once. She wondered vaguely if the rumbling in her stomach was due to the turmoil of her emotions or six tacos trying mightily to avoid digestion. With a truly forlorn expression on her face, she finally responded to Danny. "Yes. Yes, I am," she sighed.

"Well, what the hell is the problem? Why don't you look happy about the situation, you fool?"

The answer was far too complicated and far too simple to share. Luckily, Regina diverted Danny's attention by offering him her last taco. The ploy worked as Danny had never been known to leave a taco uneaten. Thanking God for the interruption, Vera busied herself by going into the kitchen for water, unaware that all four sets of eyes were boring holes in her back.

"Something is up here and I'm going to find out what it is," Danny muttered.

Toni shook her head. "This is women's work, Danny, we'll get it out of her."

Chapter 11

The next day Vera and Toni were on their way to their sister's house in Midland, a twenty-minute ride from Saginaw. Carmen Clark Brady was the oldest of the Clark girls and no discussion of any really serious matters could take place without her. She had married her high school sweetheart who was now a managing director of an international Fortune 100 manufacturing company based in Midland. After transfers to various places both in the States and abroad, they now called Midland home. Like her sisters, Carmen looked young, acted young, and took care of her health, but having four children had encouraged the legendary Clark booty to think it was a welcome guest; it had moved right in and settled down. Carmen was shapely, but definitely bigger than her sisters, which secretly overjoyed her husband, Kenneth. He was as crazy about Carmen now as he had been in high school and the fact that there was more of her for him to hang on to made it even better.

Toni and Vera drove up the sharply sloping drive and brought Toni's minivan to a halt in front of the three-car garage. Sarah, Toni's daughter, immediately got out of the car to go in search of her cousins. At the last second she turned around to get the grocery bags that were in the back of the van. "I almost forgot the reason we're here," Sarah said with a smile. "We're going to be fixing food all night," she said.

That was the main reason for Toni and Vera's visit; Carmen had elected to have the Father's Day celebration at her house, ostensibly so her parents wouldn't have the bother of cleaning up afterward. In reality, Carmen confided to her sisters, the move forced Kenneth to get the lawn resodded and to put in the deck Carmen had been wanting. The other reason for the visit was for Toni and Carmen to find out what was troubling Vera and why she wasn't acting totally thrilled with her new love. But that conversation would have to wait, from the looks of what was going on in Carmen's backyard.

The sound of laughter drew the women around the corner of the house where Carmen and Kenneth were wrapped up in each other's arms as they lay in a giant hammock set up beneath the trees. They looked and acted like a couple of frenzied teenagers rather than an old married couple in their forties. If Sarah hadn't let out a "You go, y'all," there's no telling how long it would have lasted or what level of passion would have been attained. Carmen managed to come up for air and extricate herself from her husband's long limbs with some degree of aplomb.

"Oops. Oh, well, we're young and in love, what can I tell you?" she said with a last stroke of Kenneth's lean brown face.

Kenneth fumbled around for his glasses, which were in the pocket of his shirt, and muttered, "Just remember where we left off. If y'all aren't done with this by midnight, I'm coming to get you." He rose from the hammock and pulled Carmen up with him, and the two of them straightened each other's clothes, still giggling and stealing quick smooches. Finally they walked across the lawn to greet their guests. After brief hugs all around, Kenneth excused himself to his study, although he gallantly took the bags of groceries into the kitchen for them.

Carmen hugged Sarah first, and informed her that her

cousins were at the mall. "Well, the girls are shopping. The boys were playing tennis earlier, who knows where they are now? Call the girls on their cell phone. The mall's only a few blocks from here and you can drive over to meet them," she suggested. As Sarah went off to do just that, the women went into the house and made their way into the kitchen to start preparing food and to relieve Vera of whatever burden she was carrying.

Soon the greens were being cleaned and the fruit for the gigantic salad that would serve as dessert was being peeled, sliced, and diced while small talk was made. Finally, Carmen got right down to it. "Okay, Vera, what's bothering you? I've met Marcus on many occasions and he's a fine man. I don't have to go over a list of his attributes; that would be redundant since you know them so well. And the man is obviously devoted to you. That's been evident for years. But you're acting like you just broke up with him, not like you just admitted your love for each other. What's going on?" Carmen's warm, loving tone and the look of compassion in her eyes got to Vera.

Taking a long swallow from the bottle of water provided by Carmen earlier, Vera looked at the concern on her sisters' faces and began. "First of all, I'm happy just like I am, you know? I have the best family in the world, I love my job, I have fantastic friends, and I do what I want to do when I want to do it. I don't feel like there's a void in my life that can only be filled by a good-looking man or any of that stuff. I'm just where I want to be. I'm content," she emphasized. "I think that's a wonderful thing to be and I thank God for it."

Carmen and Toni didn't say anything, they just nodded. Vera went on: "Then Marcus ups and tells me he's in love with me and everything gets crazy. Marcus is my best friend, for God's sake! He's ten years younger than me and he's my boss and I'm friends with his mother, all this other stuff, it was just a mess! Or it had the potential to be a huge mess, you know what I mean?"

Toni and Carmen had stopped cutting up the greens to listen to every word. Vera took the fruit knife and poked unhappily at the big mango in her hand while she talked. "But Marcus wouldn't take no for an answer. He says for every reason I come up with that we shouldn't be together, he's going to come up with a reason that we should. He was so sweet and confident that I let myself believe this could work, that we really could be a couple. I'll be honest, at first I was just going to play along with Marcus because he's never had a girlfriend for more than ninety days anyway! We'd have fun over the summer and go back to our normal lives and that would be it."

Toni immediately asked, "What changed your mind? Why did you decide not to do that?"

"Because." Vera paused a moment. "Because it was wrong and selfish, *and* it wouldn't have worked anyway. I find," she said wryly, "that I'm quite crazy about Marcus. I couldn't have done that to him or to me."

Carmen stood up then and went to get wineglasses. "This calls for wine, ladies. That bottled water isn't cutting it. Okay, Vera, you were going to play with Marcus for the summer but you realized that you don't have it in you to be that cruel. You acknowledge that your feelings for him are as deep as the ones he has for you, yet something is holding you back. What is it?" Getting to the truth was Carmen's specialty. As a patent attorney and a professor of law, she could cut through the bull like no one else.

Vera sighed and held up her glass of white wine to the light, admiring the amber color. "I'm scared of losing him, Carmen. After John died, I was crushed, you know that. John was the big love of my life and even though our marriage was far from perfect, he was my husband, my love. It took me a long time to get over John's death and when I could finally wake up in the morning and feel good about a new day instead of crying, I was truly grateful. I made up my mind that I was through with dating, I was through with love. I wasn't going to subject myself to that kind of torture again," she said.

Toni looked puzzled. "You're afraid to have a relationship with Marcus because you think he might die? Vera, John's death was a tragic accident. We can't put ourselves on emotional lockdown because we fear some tragedy that may never happen."

Vera shook her head and smiled wanly. "Okay, I didn't say that right. What I meant to say is this: I don't want to be in love with Marcus because I'll lose him emotionally like I lost John. I'm frigid."

There was dead silence in the room for about thirty seconds; then Toni and Carmen both started talking. Carmen said emphatically, "There are no frigid women, honey, only clumsy men."

"That's right, Vera. To find someone who's truly frigid is very rare. Usually it's a case of having an inept or uncaring lover that makes you think something is wrong with you. Why in the world haven't you told someone this before? A doctor or one of us? Why have you been walking around feeling like something was wrong with you?" Toni demanded.

Vera looked at the high ceiling and sighed deeply. "It's a long story. You know John was my first serious boyfriend. And I was a good girl right up to the wedding night, something that John didn't seem to mind. Of course I found out later that it was because he was screwing half the campus, but that's another story. The wedding night was less than spectacular. It was, in fact, the biggest letdown of my life. The honeymoon was miserable, at least that aspect of it was, and things just did not improve. I had no idea what I was supposed to be doing, all I knew was this was *not* what I'd been hearing about for years. I thought sex was supposed to be mind-boggling, life-shattering, amazing . . . Well, I thought your eyes were at least supposed to roll back in your head or something," she said a low voice.

Carmen looked at her younger sister with pity and love. "Oh, honey, they do! Your eyes really will roll back in your head and a whole lot of other stuff, too. Sex can be the most exciting, most fulfilling thing in the world. It's not just for making babies, you know!"

At that, Vera's eyes filled with tears. "Yeah, well, I can't do that either, remember? I couldn't perform the most basic purpose of a woman, according to John, and I also couldn't procreate. Two for two," she said bitterly.

"Vera, you can't let what John said affect the rest of your life. I hate to speak ill of the dead, but he was a lying baboon! He told you that something was wrong with you, that the reason he had other women was that he couldn't get what he needed from you, that you were a failure as a wife and a woman, right?" Toni's eyes were full of fire as she questioned her sister.

"How did you know that?" Vera was stunned. "Did you have a hidden camera in the bedroom or something?"

"You forget, I work with battered women at the shelter. I've been volunteering there for a long time and I've heard all kinds of terrible stories. I know the kinds of things men do to women to subjugate them, to keep them under their control. That's what John was doing to you. I just want you to know that he was lying, he's the one who was inept and incompetent in bed, not you. You just need to have confidence in yourself and in Marcus's love for you and you'll be fine," Toni said firmly.

At that comment Vera gave up any pretense of cutting fruit. She put the knife down and stared at her sisters. "Just like that?" she asked in disbelief. "I can just decide that

I'm not frigid and I'll suddenly start having great sex? I decide that Marcus and I are a hot couple and all of a sudden I'll be able to do something I wasn't able to do in all the time I was with John?"

Both sisters shouted a response. "*Yes!*"

Carmen was happy to elaborate. "When Marcus kisses you, do you like it?"

"Oh, my God, yes," Vera sighed.

"Do your knees get weak? Do you feel warm all over, sort of tingly?"

Vera smiled. "Oh, girl, my knees get so weak I can't stand up, I get hot all over, and I want to melt all over him. My whole body starts humming and I just want to kiss him forever, I really do," she sighed.

Toni looked at Carmen with eyes that were both relieved and amused and they both nodded their heads. Toni spoke for them both. "Okay, well, all you have to do is go with that. Just remember this is *Marcus,* who loves you and will do anything to make you happy. You'll experience love in a whole new way, believe me. Just remember one thing," she added. "Whatever you do, don't tell him that you're frigid."

Vera's mouth dropped open with surprise and Carmen put a finger under her chin to push it closed. "She's right. Telling a man that puts too much pressure on him to perform, and it also creates some kind of weird challenge in his head. Just don't say a word and you'll be fine."

Toni sipped her wine moodily, then blurted out what was foremost in her mind and Carmen's. "I just can't believe you kept this to yourself all these years! How could you not have confided in us?" she demanded.

Vera shrugged her shoulders. "Well, at what point do you bring it into the conversation? 'How's the job? The kids look great. By the way, I've never had an orgasm and I think I'm dead from the neck down'; is that good dinnertime conversation? Besides, it was *embarrassing!* Nobody else in this family had a problem getting their groove on! Look what you and Kenneth were doing when we pulled up here," she said in Carmen's direction. "Toni, even you admit that as lame as your ex could be, he knew how to take care of business!" Her sisters exchanged a glance and tried to say something encouraging, but Vera wasn't finished. "And Mommy and Daddy are still chasing each other around the house, you know they are. I truly felt like there was something wrong with me and I was too ashamed to tell anyone. I faked it with everyone, including John. I used to pretend that we had this hot sex life because I was too mortified to let anyone know how inadequate I was," she said with tears in her voice. "I didn't want anyone to know what a freak I was."

Carmen and Toni both rose from their seats and embraced Vera. "Well, honey, I'm willing to bet money that there's not a single thing in this world wrong with you," Carmen said confidently. "Just relax and let Marcus love you and you'll be just fine."

Marcus looked around the conference table with anticipation. Most of the staff had left for the day and it was just the four Deveraux men who ranged about the table. Marcus had decided to make an announcement that concerned only the family, and this seemed the opportune time to do it. Clay was, as usual, in a hurry to get home to his wife and boys. "Okay, what's this all about? Bennie and the kids are waiting for me, we're going to the movies," he said with a trace of impatience.

Not surprisingly, the twins, Martin and Malcolm, agreed. "I have to stop on the way home for some Ben and Jerry's. You know how Selena gets when she's pregnant. What's up?" Malcolm wanted to know. And Martin was equally restless. Ceylon didn't need any ice cream, but he needed to see her and their children. He hadn't kissed her since early that morning and he couldn't wait to hold her.

Marcus wanted to take his time with his news, but he was as anxious as his brothers to have it out on the table. With a satisfied look on his face, he said, "Nothing much. I'm getting married, that's all. Just thought you'd want to know."

All three men gave him the same look of cynical disbelief and made as if to leave the table. "Hold it! I'm serious, I'm really getting married," Marcus protested.

"When? To whom? Why?" The questions came so fast it was hard to say who was speaking, but it was obvious that none of his brothers believed a word he'd just said.

"When? I'm not sure, we haven't set a date, but it'll be soon. Why? Because I'm in love, you idiots! And to whom?" Marcus leaned back in his chair, crossed his arms behind his head, and threw his long legs on the burled-walnut surface of the table. "To Vera. I'm going to marry Vera," he said simply.

This time his brothers looked at each other and burst into loud laughter. Finally, Martin gained enough control to speak.

"Aww, man, you're not in love with Vera. You just think you're in love with her because she raised you from a pup. You wouldn't be half the man you are today if it wasn't for her influence."

Marcus took it like a man who's completely confident in himself and in his love. "Yes, Vera has been a big influence on me, I admit it. And yeah, she might have 'raised me' as you so crudely put it, but so what? She did a damned fine job. Ceylon did *more* than raise you, she tamed you and brought you back into civilization. You're the last person to be talking about a woman having influence over a man."

Martin ducked his head so Marcus couldn't see the pleased look on his face. The fact that his younger brother could rebut his argument so quickly meant that he was completely serious. All he could say was, "Touché, bro."

Clay observed the exchange with a proud smile he tried to hide. Then he, too, expressed doubts. "Okay, I'll buy that you're in love with Vera, or think you are. But what makes you think she wants you? Vera has it going on all levels. I mean I know she's a widow, but is she hard up enough to want to deal with you, the original three-months-and-out man?"

In a nanosecond Marcus was on his feet, a lethal anger visible on his reddening face. "If you ever say anything like that about Vera again, I'll take you apart. Brother or not, you can't disrespect my woman in any way, is that clear? You want to test me, say another word," he said in low ringing tones that left no doubt that he was serious.

Clay threw up his hands. "Hold on, Marcus. I apologize, I was just getting a dig at you. I love Vera like a sister, I'd never do or say anything to hurt her, and you should know that. I was just trying to get a rise out of you, man." Clay was actually elated at his brother's reaction; it told him that Marcus was completely serious about Vera.

Marcus continued to stare into his brother's eyes for a moment before relenting. Reclaiming his seat, he got in the last word. "And you can't talk. Before Benita you were the original *sixty*-day man. At least I'd give a woman three whole months of my time," he grumbled.

The Deveraux men relaxed again, but before anyone could say anything positive and congratulatory, Malcolm spoke up. "It's not like it was a big secret, Marc. We all knew you were crazy about Vera, that's why we sent you to Detroit when we did," he said.

Marcus clearly didn't understand what Malcolm was talking about, so he elaborated. "When you went to Detroit to intern at Cochran Communications, didn't you think it was funny that we'd stop your training here for that? You could have done internship in Detroit anytime, but we sent you right then because that idiot husband of hers had roughed her up. We knew that if you found out about it, you'd kill him, so we got you out of town," Malcolm said offhandedly.

It was as close to passing out cold that Marcus had ever been. His rage caused him to go hot and cold at the same time and he could feel perspiration building on his forehead and back. His stomach writhed with nausea and the veins in his neck felt as if they were about to explode.

"What did you just say? Tell me again slowly, because I don't think I heard you right the first time," he said in a guttural whisper.

Clay immediately got out his cell phone and pushed the speed dial for his home. "Peaches? Umm, I'm going to be a little late. This meeting is going to go longer than I expected," he said quietly.

Gordon looked at Vera with an expression of distaste. She was sitting on the back steps of the big brick house, wearing the worst-looking jeans he'd ever seen, an old paint-spattered T-shirt of his, and she was eating a piece of watermelon with all the gusto of a child. "That's just the height of your ambition, isn't it? Just plunked down on the steps like the ragpicker's child eating watermelon. Is that all you're going to do today?"

"Pretty much," Vera admitted with a grin. Gordon was puttering around the flowers and was impeccably turned out even for gardening. He wore jeans, but they were nicely creased, and he had on a blue polo shirt that did nice things for his skin color. Something about him reminded her of Marcus and all the time he'd spent helping her put in her garden at home. "You know, Daddy, Marcus likes to garden, too," she said dreamily.

Gordon made a face at his daughter. Coming over to sit beside her on the steps, he said in a conspiratorial whisper, "I hate gardening. I do, however, like your mother. A lot. Get it?"

"Got it," Vera conceded. She took another huge bite of the watermelon and was about to spit the seeds into the flowers next to the steps when she realized what she was doing and in front of whom. Guiltily, she put the seeds into her palm and carefully deposited them on the newspaper in her lap.

"So, Daddy, when is Miss Tanya going to put in an appearance? I haven't seen her or Alexis since I've been home."

Gordon pulled his earlobe before answering. "Well, Alexis will be home tonight. She's chaperoning the senior trip for the high school. They went to the Bahamas, if you can believe that."

Vera shook her head. "Senior trips. We didn't know nothin' 'bout no senior trips back in the day. You wanted a trip, you went to see your relatives, usually down South. Times sure have changed."

"Well, some other things don't change. Tanya is laying low because she got suspended from work."

"Again? What was it this time?" Vera asked.

"Probably being late, *again*. The girl has no sense of responsibility. She's going to mess around and lose that job and then the credit card bills will come home to roost," Gordon predicted.

"Yeah, well, she's not a girl, Daddy. She's a woman and she needs to start acting like one. She has two children to take care of," Vera replied before taking another mouthful of the deliciously sweet melon.

"You know, we never get to see you dressed up when

you come home," her father said benignly. "You're always sitting around like this," he said and tugged the frayed edge of Vera's jeans.

"Daddy, I was dressed up this morning! I went to Danny's church to hear his choir sing," she defended herself. Danny's church met on Saturday morning, and while her parents had enjoyed sleeping in, she was off enjoying the service. "I looked very nice, too."

"Yeah, well, we didn't get to see it," her father grumbled. "After all those years as a fashion icon, you'd think you could do better than *this* for your own parents."

"Okay, okay, *okay!* I'll try to make myself more presentable for dinner," she promised.

Vera did go to change clothes, but not just to please her father. It so happened that she'd been about to take a bath in the big claw-footed tub anyway, her father's remarks notwithstanding. She adored the big tub and loved taking a tepid bath in the summertime with the window open and the fresh garden smell lingering with her bath fragrance. She patted herself dry and used copious amounts of the special fragrance that Marcus bought for her. She rubbed her body with the lotion, adding another layer of fragrance with the body cream, and finished with a generous spray of the Eau de Parfum. Fingering the ivory tube of body cream with the gold leaves stamped on it, she wished with all her heart that she was getting ready for Marcus, and not just for dinner with the family.

After putting on mascara and a tiny bit of gold eyeshadow that made her eyes look bright and sparkling, Vera combed her hair and put on the dressiest thing she'd brought with her, a fabulous halter-necked sundress that wrapped and tied around the waist. It was a rayon confection she'd found in a vintage store in Palm Beach, and it was one of her favorite dresses. The bodice was boned to perfection with bra cups, and the skirt was a full circle. It was a soft aqua with seashells and other aquatic things printed on it. She twirled around in the big mirror above the double dresser in the bedroom and liked what she saw. She was about to put on sandals when her attention was diverted.

She flopped on the bed to answer the incessant chiming of her cell phone, brightening when she saw the number on the caller ID. It was Marcus! "Hello, sweetheart! I was just thinking about you," she cooed. "I miss you terribly," she said in her sultriest voice.

Marcus's voice sounded wonderful to her ear. "I miss you too, baby, more than I can say."

She sighed with happiness. "So what have you been up to, Marcus? How are my doggies treating you?"

"They're fine. I haven't been doing much, just waiting for you to come home. What have you been doing?"

Vera could hear traffic in the background and knew that Marcus was driving, something she didn't approve of when he was on his cell phone. "I've been hanging out with my sisters, well, the oldest two, that is. Haven't seen the younger ones yet. They're too busy to come see ol' broke-down me! Well, Tanya is, Alexis has been out of town. And I can hear those cars. You're not fooling me, you're driving, aren't you?"

"You got me. I'm almost home, so don't worry," he said easily. "What are you wearing?" he asked, more to change the subject than anything.

Vera was happy to describe her outfit and how wonderful her bubble bath had been. "The only thing that would have made it better . . . Hold on, Marcus. Daddy! Doorbell!" She waited a few seconds and heard the insistent chiming again. Looked like she would have to put a stop to it.

"Marcus? I'm going downstairs to open the front door. I appear to be the only person in a five-mile radius that can hear it, although I know for a fact that my parents are on the sunporch," she said with asperity. She ran down the stairs in her bare feet and entered the foyer that separated the front door from the living room. "Hold on, Marcus, it'll just be a second," she said as she looked out the peephole to see who was calling.

"*Marcus!*" In the afternoon sun, there he stood looking better than she'd ever seen him look in all the time she'd known him. She dropped the cell phone, pulled open the door, and in seconds she was in his arms, kissing him for all she was worth.

"Oh, sweetheart, I'm so glad to see you," she breathed. "Hold me, Marcus, I've missed you so much!"

When she finally let him up for air, all he could say was, "I told you I was coming to get you."

Any misgivings Marcus had about just showing up in Saginaw were dispelled by the look of joy on Vera's face when she realized that he was standing at the front door of her parents' home. There was no mistaking the excitement or the love on her face, she was unquestionably thrilled to see him. It was gratifying to know that Vera was as happy about them being together as he was, but even if she'd been upset, he still would have made the trip. After the discussion with his brothers, Marcus made the decision to come to Michigan. There were some things he needed to say to Vera immediately. But those things could wait, he wouldn't have put a stop to this greeting for anything.

Vera had pulled him into the living room and pushed him down into a big wing chair; then she sat in his lap and continued to kiss his face while murmuring endearments. Marcus couldn't do anything but react to the warmth of her body and her open affection. He returned her kisses with equal fervor and started stroking her bare back and arms with a passion that was only going to lead to trouble. *God, she feels good!* With great reluctance, Marcus came down from the dizzying level to which Vera had taken him, and tried to behave.

"Vera, baby, stop it . . . Pie, we're in your father's house," he reminded her.

By way of an answer, Vera just kissed him again, before pulling back with a mischievous smile. "Yes, we are, aren't we? I guess we'd better stop," she murmured, rubbing her nose against his. "I guess I should let them know you're here," she said thoughtfully. "Where are my dogs, by the way? Did you take them to Ella's?"

Marcus smiled lazily. He was still reveling in the fact that Vera had, in effect, declared herself when she threw herself into his arms. *She really does love me,* he thought with pride. "Your parents already know I'm here, Pie. I called them this morning to ask if they'd mind. And Lillian and Bump have the little monsters. When I left, Toby was sitting in Bump's lap eating scrambled eggs and toast."

Vera didn't seem to mind this disclosure, she was too busy running her fingers through his hair and drinking in his male beauty. "They're going to be spoiled rotten by the time I get home," she said dreamily. "I guess we should go announce you to the parents or something."

After a final kiss, she stood up slowly, straightening her dress and licking her lips longingly. "I'm not through kissing you," she informed him.

"You are for right now," he said with affection. "You'd better behave yourself or your parents will think I corrupted you."

Holding his hand tightly, Vera led him through her parents' comfortably furnished house, going through the dining room and kitchen to the sunporch that opened off the breakfast area. Mr. and Mrs. Clark were sitting on a rattan settee with pretty floral cushions, looking relaxed and casual as they watched one of their favorite shows, *Trading Spaces*, on a small television set. Marcus immediately shook Gordon's hand and leaned down to give Vivian a kiss on the cheek. He also presented Vivian with a box of Godiva chocolates and gave Gordon a bottle of Napoleon brandy. Both of them appeared to be glad to see him, he noted with relief. His impetuous trip could have had some embarrassing repercussions if they had been less welcoming. It still wouldn't have stopped him, though, this was something he had to do.

After exchanging greetings with the Clarks, Marcus said that he was going to check into his hotel and get situated. He'd made reservations at the Crowne Plaza, located in downtown Saginaw. To his surprise, the Clarks insisted that he take Carmen's old bedroom. Mrs. Clark in particular said it would be nice to have someone staying there. "We have so much room and the children are all gone so it's like the house is lonely, or something. It likes having guests and so do we," she said warmly. In short order he was carrying his garment bag upstairs to the room that had been Carmen's before she went off to college. Vera hung his garment bag up in the closet and unzipped it for him, while he looked around the feminine room with its four-poster cherry-wood bed and the handmade quilt that was folded neatly across the foot of the bed. He sat down on the side of the bed and tried to pay attention to Vera's voice as it floated out of the big closet, but nothing was registering. She finally backed out of the closet, still talking. When she turned around to face him, Marcus held out his hand to her, which she instantly took.

Pulling her gently until she was directly in front of him, Marcus put both hands around her waist and she rested her hands on his shoulders. His long legs were stretched wide so that she was standing between them; with him sitting on the bed they were almost eye level with one another. He looked at her and for a moment, he forgot why he'd made his hasty flight to Michigan. He took in her fresh, fragrant beauty and he wanted nothing more than to draw her into his arms and keep her there for a long time. But he had a job to do, one that wasn't going to wait. He leaned forward and kissed her gently, then flexed his fingers and brought her even closer. Looking intently into her eyes, he said quietly, "You should have told me, Vera. Why did you keep it from me?"

Chapter 12

Vera leaned against the passenger door and looked over at Marcus, whose visage was hidden behind a discreet pair of elegant shades with a thin tortoiseshell frame. She couldn't really see his eyes, and it was just as well. They were in the last place she'd ever pictured the two of them, sitting in the front seat of the Pimpmobile, which was parked on Ojibway Island with its top down. The afternoon breeze caressed Vera's shoulders and she would have been perfectly content were it not for the fact that she had a lot of explaining to do to Marcus. He'd made that plain in her sister's bedroom about an hour before. His words still resonated: "You should have told me, Vera. Why did you keep it from me?"

Luckily, Vera was also wearing sunglasses, an absurdly charming cat's-eye pair from the fifties embellished with rhinestones, tiny pearls, and seashells. This way Marcus couldn't read her expression as she remembered how his words had startled her. She'd immediately thought that he was talking about her frigidity and she was shocked. Then she realized it was another secret to which he was referring, the fact that John had gotten physical with her. Once she realized what Marcus wanted to discuss, she wisely suggested that they go somewhere to talk, because if she knew Marcus, his voice was going to be raised, and she didn't want her parents overhearing the argument that was surely on its way.

They had gone downstairs and Vera let her parents know that they were going for a drive. Marcus had been to Saginaw before, but hadn't really had the grand tour, as she called it. Vivian was still watching *Trading Spaces* reruns on the sunporch, while Gordon was dabbing at an imaginary spot on his beloved Pinky. Pinky spent the winters in storage and the summers under a custom-made tarp. Gordon had unveiled his prize to make sure it was in top condition as he was driving it the next day. As angry and preoccupied as Marcus was, he'd done a double take on seeing Pinky in the driveway. He'd immediately gone to take a good look at the Coupe de Ville, walking around it reverently. The next thing Vera knew, they were tooling down Genesee in the Pimpmobile, top down and Johnny "Guitar" Watson blaring out of the eight-track. It took Marcus to fully appreciate the collection of R&B that Gordon had carefully cultivated.

Vera took Marcus on a tour of the city that encompassed the downtown area, the main business thoroughfares in the township, Bay and Tittabawasee Roads, the pretty residential areas of Buena Vista and Bridgeport townships, and through Old Town Saginaw, with its quaint shops and restaurants. They crossed the Saginaw River at Court Street, heading back to the east side, when Vera told Marcus to make a left, onto Ojibway Island. The island was an oasis of green in the middle of the city. The river intersected the town and had, at one time, been its racial dividing line as well. Black folks were not found on the west side of Saginaw unless they were working there or had a doctor's appointment. Other than that, most of them lived on the east side. Now those barriers were down and the city was fully integrated, but the river still ran through Saginaw, sometimes overflowing its banks in the spring and fall and always providing recreation in the form of boating and fishing. The island was a place for summer concerts and picnics, and for some like Vera, just a quiet place to be.

Vera was counting to herself, trying to gauge just when Marcus was going to start in on her. She actually made it to seven before he let loose. "Vera, my brothers just happened to let it slip that the reason I was packed off to Detroit to intern at Cochran Communications was that they wanted me out of town after John beat you up. Beat you up, Vera. *Beat* you," he said savagely. "Why in the hell am I just finding out about it? And why am I finding out from them and not you? I thought we trusted each other, Vera, what is this all about?"

Vera took a deep breath and prayed for guidance. This wasn't going to be easy to say, and it wasn't going to be easy for Marcus to hear. "Marcus, first of all, your brothers overstated the case. John and I got into a huge argument," she said softly. "We had argued many times before, but it was nothing like this. He'd had a few drinks and things got out of hand. I told him I wasn't listening to him in his state of drunkenness and it enraged him. I remember throwing up my hand like this"—Vera demonstrated— "and he grabbed my arm, and it was *on*. If I'd just stood there and let him shake me, or slap me, it wouldn't have been as violent, but my daddy didn't raise any sissies.

"I pushed back and it was basically a shoving match, which was ridiculous. As big as John was, and as mad as he was, he had no business putting his hands on me. And it hurt, and scared me half to death as well as making me furious. I wasn't raised to brawl with men, you know? But I was raised to take care of myself and I wasn't about to let him manhandle me. When I picked something up and told him I was going to break his skull, he stopped dead. It was like he just snapped back to his right mind or something, because he calmed down and apologized, said it would never happen again."

Vera's face, what could be seen of it, was somber as she relived the terrible night. Marcus mistook her low-key recitation for acceptance and it angered him. "So that was it? That was okay with you, Vera? Why did you let him treat you like that? Why didn't you tell me?"

Vera whipped off her sunglasses and looked at Marcus with fierce eyes. "Hold it, Marcus, don't go there. First of all, it wasn't like I just rolled over and said, 'It's okay, honey, go ahead and use me for your punching bag.' I told him the marriage was over and I told him to get out. He had sense enough to leave, too; I guess he went to stay in a hotel. I really have no idea what he did. I had those locks changed so fast it would make your head spin and I went to see a good divorce lawyer. I had gone through a lot to make that marriage work but that was just the limit," she said hotly.

"I looked like I had gone ten rounds with a welterweight when it was over. I had bruises on my arms and one on my face and it was obvious that something had happened. Your mother wormed it out of me, which is how your brothers found out. And how you got shipped off to Detroit, I guess. I never put two and two together, I frankly was so caught up in my own drama that I wasn't paying attention to anything else."

Marcus wasn't satisfied with her explanation yet. "But why didn't you tell me, Vera? How could you have kept something like this to yourself?" He had removed his own sunglasses and his anger and confusion were plain.

"Marcus, I didn't tell you because it was not your concern, for one thing. What happens in a marriage is personal, it's private and it's often very complicated. Things get said, things get done that no one has any business knowing about. It's too hard to explain these things to other people and it almost always causes problems. If you get mad at your mate and you tell everybody about the horrible things he did or said, they get mad at him, too. Then the two of you make up and all is forgiven, but your friends are still mad at him and the tension is unbearable. I've seen that happen more than once," she sighed.

She looked at Marcus with great tenderness. "And there were other reasons that I couldn't tell you. I was *ashamed,* Marcus. I was raised to be a lady, a well-rounded woman with manners and style, and I was brawling with a grown man in my own house like a hoochie mama. I was also afraid to tell you; maybe I knew, like your brothers knew, that you would have beaten the crap out of him. I never told my father, either, he would have killed him for sure," she told him, looking intently into his eyes.

"Besides, Marcus, I was a grown woman, I was supposed to be able to handle my business. When you marry someone you take them on for good and bad, you commit yourself to the relationship and to your partner, and you have to be in it for the long haul. That's the way I was about John."

After a long, uncomfortable silence, Marcus spoke. "Why did you take him back, Vera? You put him out, you were filing for divorce; why did you let him back into your life? You could have been free, Vera! And what made you think he *wouldn't* do it again? The shelters and the cemeteries are full of women who were promised that 'it wouldn't happen again.' If a man hits you once, chances are he'll hit you again, you know that. What the hell made you trust him again?"

Vera was silent for a long moment, and then she took Marcus's left hand in both of hers. She stroked it, admiring the long, clever fingers and the broad, smooth palm; Marcus had beautiful hands. "I know that this hand will

never hit me, never be raised to me in anger. I know that
for sure," she said softly.

"And John knew that I would break his kneecaps if he
ever looked at me wrong again. He knew because I always
told him if a man hit me he'd better not ever go to sleep
again and I meant that. That's why he left when I told him
to, because he truly believed I was one of those 'hot grits
and lye in the middle of the night' women." She laughed
bitterly. "I probably wouldn't have cooked up something
caustic and dumped on him, but when he woke up he'd
have been surrounded by policemen, and that's for real.

"But that's not the only reason I knew he wouldn't do it
again. When he dropped his hands that night, all the fight
was gone out of him. John wasn't a violent man, Marcus.
At the moment he was a drunken man, but he wasn't violent by nature. He was a lot of things, but he wasn't
deliberately cruel.

"John's father and mother were both alcoholics. His father was an extremely vicious man and he abused John and
his mother daily. One day she couldn't take it anymore and
she retaliated by hitting him with a blunt instrument, right
in front of John, of course. She didn't kill him but she may
as well have. He had severe brain damage. He was completely incapacitated after that and died in a state
institution. John's mother went to jail for aggravated as-
sault, even though it was self-defense. His grandmother
raised John, if you can call it that. She wasn't one of those
sweet cuddly grannies, not by a long shot. She was into the
street life big time and she did a little bit of everything
from numbers to boosting, whatever. John was still being
neglected and mistreated; only now it was by the woman
who was supposed to have rescued him. His life was pretty
horrible until John realized he could play football. Oh,
man, that was *it* for him.

"He'd been told all his life that he was worthless, that he

had no value whatsoever, but he could play football like nobody's business. He was determined to do whatever it took to succeed at something and football was his ticket out. He succeeded, too. He got a scholarship to Florida A&M, he got drafted by the pros; he finally had everything he wanted. Including me, the only person to love him for what he was," Vera said tightly with the sheen of tears in her eyes.

"We had some wonderful times, John and I. We had some terrible times. But I was in it for the long haul. I wasn't going to cut and run at the first sign of trouble, I was committed to him and to our marriage. Yes, I was ready to kick him to the curb permanently, but he came to me and asked me to forgive him, to try to give our marriage another chance. He *begged* my forgiveness, Marcus, begged me on his knees for another chance. He convinced me that he would never drink or lose his temper with me again. He'd been going to AA meetings and I believed him." She sighed raggedly. "I couldn't abandon him like everyone else in his life had. I had to take a chance on him and he kept his word, Marcus. Until the day he died I never knew him to take another drink. And he never even raised his voice to me again, much less his hand."

Marcus didn't say a word. Vera took his hand, which she was still holding, and lifted it over her shoulder to indicate that she wanted to be in Marcus's arms. He draped his arm around her and pulled her close to his side. They stayed like that for a few minutes, watching the river flow past and feeling the warm breeze play around them. Finally Marcus broke the silence.

"Are you still in love with John?" he asked solemnly.

Before she answered, Vera reached over, took Marcus's other hand, and held it against her. She kissed it softly, and then pulled it around her waist so his arms were wrapped around her. They embraced tightly, and she kissed his neck, his chin, and his lips, softly, and with great tenderness. Then she spoke with an air of finality. "I will always love John. If I don't love him, who will? I can't let him be alone for all eternity with nobody caring about him. But I'm not *in love* with John. I'm in love with you. John was my past; you're my future. He was my first love, but you're the great love of my life, the man I'll love for the rest of my life." Looking into his eyes, Vera stroked his handsome face gently and kissed his lips, so softly that it felt like a kiss in a dream. "I love *you*, Marcus."

Hours later, Marcus and Vera were again alone, but this time they were on the sunporch of her parents' house. Marcus was beginning to get his bearings again; after Vera's astonishing revelations about her marriage, he'd been stunned. For the rest of the afternoon, and now the evening, he'd looked at Vera with new eyes. How could she be so accepting and compassionate about a man who hadn't appreciated her, hadn't treated her the way she deserved, the way *he* treated her? He'd been quiet and preoccupied after their tryst on Ojibway.

Vera, on the other hand, was completely serene. After they held each other for a long time, she'd kissed him with incredible tenderness and told him they needed to go out on Bay Road, the main shopping drag, to pick up a few things for the party at Carmen's house the next day. He had followed her directions and driven across town with B.B. King serenading them from the speakers. They pulled into the parking lot of Value City Department Store, and Vera had commented on the mostly empty parking lot. "We'll get in and out in a heartbeat," she gloated. Once inside the store Vera got a cart and headed straight for the seasonal section of the housewares department where she picked up a couple of casual red-checked cotton tablecloths and some sale-priced citronella candles in bamboo holders.

Marcus chuckled to himself as he recalled meeting an old friend of Vera's from high school. She was a tall slender woman named LaQuita Sims who seemed to wring every bit of enjoyment possible out of life. She was very attractive, with the soft, perfect skin of a child, an elegantly delicate nose, and full lips that never seemed to stop smiling. Her large eyes were full of amused tolerance, even when her daughter almost spilled the beans. After Vera had introduced Marcus to LaQuita, her teenaged daughter, Ranada, had stared at him closely. Ranada had an arm around "Miss Vera's" waist and suddenly her eyes had grown huge and she blurted out, "Oooh! He's the big pr—" Her words were cut off as Vera deftly covered her mouth with her hand. LaQuita just smiled and shook her head, bidding them good-bye and taking Ranada away. "We're going to talk about restraint when we get home, honey. Restraint is when we don't blurt things out in public," she said cheerfully.

Marcus had been mystified until Vera explained that Ranada had always referred to Marcus as "that big pretty man," ever since she'd seen him at the funeral of Vera's great-grandmother. "She thought you were the most beautiful man she'd ever seen. Still does, apparently, she always asks about you when I see her," Vera told him. Marcus had laughed, but it didn't stop the heat from rising in his face. *Big pretty man, my foot,* he thought.

He felt calm and oddly content now. Something about being with Vera always calmed him. He enjoyed the feel of her body next to his, her warmth, and the soft essence of her fragrance as they held each other. Vera noticed his preoccupation, though, and asked him about it. "Marcus, something is on your mind, I can tell. You haven't been yourself since we left Ojibway Island. What's the matter, sweetheart?"

He answered her as honestly as he could. "I don't know what to make of your marriage to John, Vera. When I came up here, I was thinking of him as scum, a real punk, you know what I mean. Now I don't know what to think," he confessed.

Vera smiled at him. He could feel the caress of it even in the semidarkness of the porch. "You *can't* fully understand it, Marcus. That's the nature of the institution. You're not supposed to understand someone else's marriage, it's not your business," she said gently. "John wasn't a villain, he wasn't a saint. He was a man who'd overcome a lot and had a lot left to overcome. I think if he'd lived longer, he'd have conquered some of those demons," she said reflectively.

"Tell me something that's none of my business, Vera. Tell me the nicest thing he ever did for you, and the worst thing he ever did. That's the last thing I'll ever ask about John. The subject is closed after that."

Vera tried to move closer to Marcus. She finally gave up and got into his lap. "Well, the nicest thing was that John was very proud of me. He thought I was the smartest woman he'd ever met and it fascinated him that I had this wonderful job at TDG. I'd worked for a newspaper in Philadelphia, and he was proud of everything I'd accomplished there, too. He was very encouraging and supportive of anything I did, believe it or not," she said reflectively. "The worst thing he ever did was not consent to adopting children. He wouldn't tell me why, but he refused to do it and I didn't get to be a mother. And he didn't get to be a father, either. I think he would have made a good one, too, despite his faults," she said sadly.

Marcus rocked her back and forth for a few minutes, giving her comfort. Vera raised her head from his shoulder and looked at him with damp eyes. "You know what? The day he brought me home from the hospital after the miscarriage, he cried. He had bought all kinds of stuffed animals for the nursery, it looked like FAO Schwartz in there! He went into the room and held on to the crib, and to me, and he just cried. Everyone thought he wasn't affected by the miscarriage but it hurt him as much as it did me. That's why he had to go right back to training camp. I think he would have lost his mind if he'd stayed at home with me."

"Damn, Pie, now I really don't know what to think," Marcus said. "There's nothing black and white about this, is there?"

It was Vera's turn to hold on to Marcus. "That's what I've been trying to tell you, my sweet."

Marcus brooded for a moment or two. Vera was either extremely sophisticated or she was the most emotionally mature person he'd ever met. He told her as much, saying, "I think I should be in awe of you. Maybe I should just be scared of you," he said with a smile.

Vera gave him a smile of her own. "Don't be afraid, I'm just older and wiser, remember? It's part of my charm," she said with a sexy laugh.

Marcus turned Vera around so that she was straddling his lap. "Yeah, you're right. And you've got some other charms I can't wait to sample," he growled.

Startled, Vera leaned back and the look of surprise on her face was priceless. Marcus tightened his hands around her waist and pulled her closer to his heated body. "I mean it, Pie. I can't wait to get home with you."

Chapter 13

The rest of the weekend went by in a happy rush for Vera and Marcus. They attended church with Vera's parents and drove to Midland in the majestic Pinky. The Father's Day cookout was a wonderful party, enjoyed by all. They decided to leave Saginaw at five the next morning to avoid traffic; Vera had some meetings scheduled for the next day in Detroit and Marcus decided to drop by Cochran Communications while they were in town. They spent a productive day and then flew home to Atlanta together on Monday night. Everything was perfect until the moment Vera realized they would have to go to Lillian's house to fetch Kika and Toby. She had claimed their bags at the luggage carousel while Marcus went to get the car from long-term parking. While she was waiting for him it hit her; their next stop would be Lillian's house where regardless of Marcus's version of events, she would be seeing her old friend for the first time since Marcus had declared himself.

She didn't say much on the way over to Bump and Lillian's house, she was deep in thought. Marcus glanced at her and laughed gently. "C'mon, Pie, you act like I'm driving you to the guillotine or something! We'll be there in a few minutes and everything will be fine, you'll see."

And to Vera's eternal gratitude, everything was indeed just fine. Lillian met them at the door with a smile on her face and Toby under her arm. "You two have got to see this," she said, leading them into the family room. They followed her to the doorway of the big comfortable space, where her husband, Bump, was reclining in his big leather chair with a newspaper over his face. Lillian put Toby down on the floor and whispered, "Go get him, Toby!" Toby dashed over and grabbed a corner of the paper and walked backward with it in his mouth, pulling it off to reveal a sleeping Bump with Kika curled up on his chest.

Vera and Marcus laughed at the new trick while Toby started barking as he ran around in circles to celebrate Vera's homecoming. Kika naturally woke up and started barking, too. She leapt off Bump and dashed over to Vera and all was chaos for the next few minutes. Finally things were restored to some sort of order and Vera found herself alone with Lillian as Marcus and Bump stowed the dogs in their carrier for the trip to Vera's house.

Lillian didn't waste any time, she got right to the heart of the matter. She was seated at the opposite end of the long family room sofa from Vera and she had a look of great affection on her face. "So. You and Marcus are together at last," she said in her throaty voice. "It's about time. I was beginning to think I was going to have to resort to drastic measures to make you two start acting like you had some sense. What took you so long to wake up to the fact that you have feelings for each other?" she wanted to know.

"Lillian, I have to ask, how did *you* know? How did everyone in the free world know but me? The only one surprised by love seems to have been me; everyone else was expecting this. Am I just dense?" Vera asked, the bafflement clear in her tone of voice.

Lillian laughed out loud at the expression on Vera's face. "No, sweetie, you're just Vera. But you two were as transparent as glass to the rest of us, especially Marcus."

"And this is truly okay with you? You're not going to send a hit man after me or anything, are you?" Vera had to ask.

"Vera, why on earth would I be upset that my son is happy? You're just what he needs and he's exactly what you need. Don't be silly, girl. Now come give me a hug and go home and get some sleep. You look like you're about to pass out."

The two women embraced and Vera thanked her for keeping the lively little dogs at such short notice. Lillian laughed again. "I'm surprised Bump is letting them go so easily, he went crazy over them! Wherever he was, there they were, in the studio, in the bathroom. I had to force him to let them sleep in their basket! I think there may be a puppy or two in my very near future," she said with resignation.

Finally Vera was home, and everything was the same, yet very, very different. Kika and Toby were sniffing everything in sight in case an odor had changed while they were away, which was normal. But Marcus was sitting on the side of her bed, which was not. Marcus had carried the bags upstairs for her, put them at the foot of the bed, and sat down. He looked around the room curiously, taking in the peony-pink walls, the red floral Ralph Lauren duvet cover, the crisp white-eyelet bed skirt and pillow shams, the framed botanical prints on the walls, and the row of hats hung neatly on one wall for both storage and decoration. He inhaled the sweet fragrance that lingered in the room, and smiled when he noticed that Vera had two pictures of him on her nightstand. "Pie, your bedroom is beautiful. Very sexy and feminine, but this bed isn't going to work," he said casually.

"What do you mean, it isn't going to work? It works just fine," she replied.

"For you it does. It won't hold the two of us, watch."

Marcus stretched out on the bed and sure enough, he took up the whole thing; in fact, his feet hung over the foot of the antique frame and he looked as if were in a child's bed.

Vera blinked twice, then smiled. "I guess you're right." She could feel herself growing hot all over as she took in the full implication of what Marcus was saying. Before she could get embarrassed, though, Marcus rose from the bed and walked over to Vera, who was still standing in the doorway. He gave her a brief but tight hug, and kissed her quickly. "You need some sleep, beauty. I'll see you tomorrow. Don't make any plans for dinner, okay?"

Vera nodded and pulled his head down for one more kiss, this one longer and more lingering. They went downstairs and kissed again, and she locked the door after he left. Going back up to her bedroom, she stared at the double-sized bed. It really was too small for the two of them. That meant that things were about to get serious, and fast. She only hoped she was ready for what came next.

Paris stared morosely at the contents of the bowl on the cafeteria table. It contained a steaming helping of oatmeal, one of her least favorite things. Aidan caught the look and prodded her to eat it. "If you wait it'll get all lumpy and disgusting. That just makes it worse," he advised sagely.

Paris stopped staring at the bowl and looked at her dining companion with little affection. "Tell me again why you're torturing me with this?"

Aidan sighed and reminded her of the ugly incident at the bar. "I'm sitting there waiting for Sebastian and I run into a guy I knew from college. He's gotten to be, like, *rotund*, okay? And he's asking me how I'm doing and what's new and so forth. And then he has the nerve to comment on my appearance, saying that I looked 'fabulously fluffy.

We big girls have to stick together,' he said. I almost decked him," Aidan said furiously.

"So he calls *you* fat and *I* have to diet? What have I got to do with any of this? Besides, *you're* not fat. Do you want to see fat? I've got plenty," Paris warned.

"You're doing this because I can't do it alone. I've gained about fifteen pounds and they are coming *off,* sister. Sebastian is no help; he has the most efficient metabolism I've ever seen in action. Being a professional dancer doesn't hurt, either. So you are going on this regime with me as a reward for keeping my mouth shut about your matchmaking effort," he said slyly.

Before Paris could protest, Vera and Marcus entered the cafeteria together. She and Aidan watched with great interest as Vera went to the breakfast bar to select her usual fruit and cereal, only she got two servings of each along with a bagel, apparently intended for Marcus. And Marcus got two bottles of water and two of skim milk to bring to their table. As the couple sat down together, Paris didn't bother to disguise the smug look on her face. She fingered her new necklace, a gift from Marcus and Vera. It was a long eighteen-karat gold chain with a sparkling one-karat diamond in a Danish setting.

"Don't look now, but I don't think it's going to be a secret much longer, Aidan. And they were very happy with my efforts to bring them together. Marcus said I'm his favorite cousin," she gloated. "You're going to lose your hold over me and you'll be left eating this glop by yourself," she said, staring once again at the grayish sludge in the bowl.

"Yeah, well, until then we starve together. And we have Tae-Bo tonight," he informed her.

Paris almost choked on the mouthful of oatmeal, but it wasn't Aidan's words that made her lose her composure. She was looking over his shoulder at a tall, handsome man who'd just entered the cafeteria with Martin Deveraux.

"Who is *that?*" she breathed. "I'd like to have *him* for breakfast."

Aidan didn't even bother to look up. "Don't even try it. Eat that oatmeal, woman, we still have to walk twenty minutes."

"Aidan, don't make yourself unpopular," she muttered as she again picked up her spoon.

While Vera and Marcus shared breakfast, they compared their schedules. "I'm going to be in production most of the day," Vera said, consulting her purse-sized planner. "I have a meeting with Star this morning and another one with Elise," she said, referring to her talented and capable features editor. "I'll be in the studio the rest of the day and all of tomorrow. And I'm having Dante over for dinner this week." Vera studied Marcus carefully before adding, "You're coming too, so don't get all crazy on me. What's up with you?"

"I won't be getting crazy," Marcus defended himself. "I just hope Dr. Bohannon has other plans for the rest of his life because you're taken," he said emphatically. He took a long drink of water, and then looked at his Palm Pilot. "I have two meetings this morning with my brothers, and then I have lunch with Darnell Washington. You remember Darnell, we went to school together and we both started out here at the same time. He left and became some kind of entrepreneur. He owns a nightclub. Or a restaurant, I can't remember, it keeps changing. It'll be good to see ol' Darnell," he mused. "Then I'm in meetings the rest of the day and tomorrow I have a day-long symposium at Atlanta University. What does your weekend look like?"

Vera stabbed a piece of cantaloupe and savored it thoughtfully. "I don't have anything this weekend. Next weekend, I have something planned with your mother and your sisters-in-law, but this weekend I'm as free as the breeze, why?"

"You'll see," Marcus said cheerfully. He slid his Platinum American Express card across the table and said, "How about picking up some takeout tonight and having dinner and a movie at my place? And bring the urchins."

Vera looked at the card for a second, and then picked it up. It was fruitless to argue with Marcus about money. No woman ever went into her purse when he was around, even for something as mundane as a take-out meal. She did demur on the matter of the dogs. "I'll bring dinner, I'll pick up a movie, but the dogs stay home. They run my life as it is, Marcus. Tonight it's just you and me," she said firmly, ignoring the pleased smile on his face.

"You want me all to yourself, Pie? Well, then, I'm all yours, baby," he whispered.

Marcus met his old friend Darnell Washington at a popular franchise restaurant not too far from TDG. He had suggested that they meet at the office so that his brothers could see Darnell, but that plan was vetoed due to Darnell's schedule. He was living in Miami these days, running his own nightclub with other projects on the horizon. He and Marcus had been friends since high school. Darnell had been Marcus's best and only friend, other than his brothers. They had inevitably drifted apart after Darnell had left TDG to become an entrepreneur, and only saw each other on the rare occasions when Darnell was in Atlanta visiting his family. Darnell was tall, although not as tall as Marcus. He was dark brown, handsome, and debonair, and had always had more than his share of women.

Darnell looked over at Marcus and smiled. "I can't believe you got caught up, man. You're tryin' to get married?

I can't believe you're about to turn in your player's card, Marcus. Not you," he said with a laugh.

"Believe it, man," Marcus said easily. "And I wouldn't talk about anybody having a player's card, you're the one with all the women, Darnell. I can't even compare to you, my brother, you're the one with the multiple ladies. I could only handle one at a time." Marcus held up his hands, signifying that Darnell had won this round.

"Yeah, but I'm not the one who had four prom dates. That was you, my brother, or have you forgotten?"

Marcus laughed loudly at the memory. "You say that like it's a bad thing, Darnell. You know that they were all friends. We all went together because we wanted to have fun and we did. You make it sound like I was some kind of Casanova. It wasn't that serious," he added.

Marcus had always had more female friends than male. And he had indeed taken four of his best friends to the prom, all riding in the same limousine together. Darnell was still laughing and shaking his head over the event.

"And they named you Prom King on top of it! Tell me this, Marcus, does your lady know about that part of your past? That you were the true player even way back in the day?"

Marcus scratched his neck while he thought. "Vera? I don't know if I ever told her that or not," he mused. "But she'll find out in a few weeks. Cassandra's getting married and I promised her I'd sing at the wedding. So Vera will meet the Fearsome Foursome and all my dark secrets will be out because you know can't a one of them keep their mouths shut," he said fondly, referring to his four running buddies from high school.

He took another swallow of his mineral water while Darnell looked him over and smiled. "Look at you. CEO of the family business and all but engaged to Vera Jackson. I'll be damned. Who would have thought that you'd end up with Vera, man? Vera Jackson, the finest woman to ever walk the earth, and you got her. How did you pull that one off, man? How did you get to be so lucky?" The look of envy and admiration on Darnell's face was amusing, but not so amusing that Marcus was going to reveal a single personal detail about him and Vera. He almost regretted telling Darnell they were involved, period.

Marcus smiled and replied, "Clean living and a pure heart. So tell me what's been going on, Darnell. How's the nightclub business treating you? I sure hated your leaving TDG, but you've done very well for yourself. What is this, your third nightclub?"

Darnell looked like a proud father. "This is actually the fifth one. But I have something in the works that's going to top the clubs, something with some serious money potential. In fact, that's partly why I wanted to meet with you today. This one is too good to miss out on, Marcus."

Intrigued, Marcus raised an eyebrow, leaning back slightly as the waitress put his Cobb salad sans bacon in front of him. "Oh, yeah? Tell me about it," he invited.

After his meal was served, Darnell did just that.

Hours later, Vera sat enjoying the evening breeze on Marcus's patio. "Patio" was almost a misnomer as it was actually an outdoor room. The wall between the house and patio was all glass, with the addition of a double fireplace. One side worked in the family room, the other worked on the patio, so that the space could be used even in the winter months, as Georgia winters were usually mild. There were also glass walls on either side with a canvas canopy that could be rolled out or left rolled up in fine weather. Huge clay pots of tropical plants were arranged along the walls and the comfortable, chic furniture made it a perfect place to relax. This addition to the Frank Lloyd Wright–

influenced home had been Vera's idea, one for which Marcus was completely grateful. It was yet another way that Vera had left her indelible mark on him.

They had eaten by candlelight on the patio, enjoying a nice meal and glass of wine, talking about this and that. Marcus had just finished clearing the table and he stood in the doorway for a moment, watching Vera. Her hair blew in the gentle breeze and the subtle scent of her perfume caressed Marcus's senses. She looked casual but very pretty in a loose-fitting pink top that was fashioned from a thin gauzy fabric accentuated with three big shell buttons down the front. The top was short, short enough that every time she moved he could see her small, firm waist exposed above the matching hip-hugging long skirt she wore. As if she felt his eyes on her, she turned to face him. "Hello, sugar-pie. Are you ready to watch the movie?" she asked.

Marcus gave her a slow smile in return. "Yep. Let's go," he said, holding out his hand. She walked over to him and took the hand he offered, surprised when he didn't stop in the family room. "Where are we going, Marcus?"

"My room," he said casually. "The set down here doesn't work."

Marcus's home was built on four levels that intersected with each other at angles so that the house wasn't excessively tall, but cleverly arranged to look like a three-story house. The highest one consisting of a master suite with a huge bedroom, a sitting room, and a bath suite with separate lavatory and bathing facilities. It was comfortable to the point of being sybaritic, and Vera had also helped design it. They stopped in the doorway of the room to admire Marcus's bed. "Now, Pie, *that's* a bed," Marcus said with a smile. And it was, a huge, custom-made edifice that was bigger than a California-king-sized bed. It had a panel-style headboard that was made of big squares of hand-stained teakwood set at cross angles to show off the

grain of the wood. The footboard was made of the same
material and the bed was at least half a foot higher than
Vera's bed. In the winter the bed was covered with a heavy
damask covering in rich navy blue, but it was currently in
its summer dress of sand-washed silk in a soft blue gray
like the ocean. Marcus liked his creature comforts and was
not in the least embarrassed about it.

He went to the cabinet that held his video equipment
and stereo to put in the DVD that would play on the flat-
screen plasma TV that was mounted on the wall directly
across from the bed. He turned around to find that Vera
had taken off her sandals, climbed onto the bed, and made
herself comfortable with the pile of pillows at the head of
the bed. Marcus wanted to stand there and relish the picture she made in his bed, but instead he joined her, kicking
off his sandals and stretching out beside her. He reached
over on the bedside table and pitched something into her
lap before turning on the movie.

"What's this?" Vera asked curiously.

"Tickets. We're going to Jamaica on Friday morning,
beauty."

Marcus didn't know which he liked the best, the look of
surprise on Vera's face, or the abandon with which she
threw herself into his arms. "Ooh, Marcus, that sounds
wonderful, sweetheart," she cooed.

Marcus tossed the remote control aside and took Vera
into his arms, kissing her passionately. He would never get
tired of kissing Vera. Her soft lips and moist, juicy mouth
drove him crazy. He would have continued kissing her, too,
but she wanted to talk.

"Marcus, wait a minute, sweetheart, umm, that's nice,
but stop for a minute," she said breathlessly. "Why Jamaica? Why this weekend?" she asked.

Marcus sighed and lay back on the high-piled pillows.
He held his arm out to Vera and she immediately went to

him, curving her body next to his as if they'd been doing it forever. Slowly he answered her question. "Because I want to be with you, Vera, in every way. I want to make love to you and I want you to remember it for the rest of your life as the most perfect night of your life. That's why I'm taking you away to a beautiful place where we can explore everything there is to know about each other," he told her, his voice filled with passion.

"That's why I wanted to be up here tonight," he confessed. He rolled over so that they were facing each other. Vera's face was serious, her eyes huge and fixed on his. "I wanted you to get used to the feel of me next to you, Vera. That's why we're in this bed right now."

Vera raised an eyebrow. "I thought you said the TV downstairs didn't work. What's wrong with it?"

"I unplugged it," he said guilelessly. "I wanted you up here in my bed. Is that so wrong?"

Vera stared at him for a long moment, and then started laughing. "You sneak! Why didn't you just say what you wanted instead of going through changes like that?"

Marcus grabbed her and rolled onto his back so that she was on top of him. "Because this was more fun," he admitted. "I like trying to put something over on you, Pie."

Vera didn't seem to be listening to him; instead, she was stroking his big shoulders and looking into his eyes. She lowered her head and kissed him on the chin, then the neck, and she began unbuttoning his shirt. Suddenly she realized what she was doing and stopped. Before he could stop her, she scooted off his body and ended up kneeling next to him, her eyes huge and bright.

Marcus sat up and gave her a slow, sexy smile. "You want this off, baby? Here you are," he said, removing the garment and exposing his broad, muscular chest to her view. She reached out tentatively and gently touched the solid wall of his bronzed flesh covered with silky hair.

"Don't be gentle, baby, it's yours, do what you want with it," Marcus said softly.

Vera came closer to Marcus and straddled his body, stroking his chest with both hands. She leaned forward and kissed him again, his lips, his chin, and down his neck to his chest, her hands still rubbing and caressing his hot skin. Marcus put both his hands around her waist and slid them up her rib cage, drawing her closer to him. He made quick work of the three big buttons on her blouse, and sighed with happiness when he realized she was wearing a front-hooked bra. He quickly unsnapped it and freed the firm brown globes from their lace prison. He looked his fill at her perfect breasts before caressing them with his big hands. Pulling her even closer, so that their bodies were crushed against one another, he kissed Vera with all the love and passion he was feeling, using his tongue to pleasure her mouth and her lips; then his mouth traveled down her neck to the sensitive area he'd just uncovered. Suddenly Vera jerked away from him, covering her breasts with her hands.

"Stop, Marcus! I-I-I can't," she said with a choked sob.

Marcus instantly sat up, his face full of concern. "Did I hurt you, Vera? What's the matter, baby? Tell me," he urged.

To his amazement, Vera was blushing; a bright red hue suffused her face while she struggled to get the words out. "Marcus, I, I'm . . . umm, I'm frigid," she whispered.

Marcus didn't say a word; he just looked at her while she tried to explain to him that she was unable to make love. "I'm like dead from the neck down, Marcus. The whole time I was married I never . . . it never . . . " She drew a deep shuddering breath and went on. "I don't have the normal reactions that a woman has when she's making love, Marcus. I don't feel anything, my body doesn't react the way it's supposed to." She never took her eyes from his as she was telling him in halting words how inadequate she was, which let him know that she believed the ludicrous words she was saying. When she finished, a lone tear worked its way down her stricken face while she waited for Marcus's reaction.

"Vera. Baby. This is what you went through the whole time you were married? Your husband"—he couldn't bring himself to say John's name—"let you suffer like this?"

He immediately pulled her into his arms and placed her on his lap. He held her and kissed her tears away. Finally he spoke. "That was then, my heart. This is now. I don't know exactly why you think something's wrong with you, but it's going to be fine. There ain't anything wrong with you, from what I can see. Trust me, baby."

Vera allowed him to comfort her for a few minutes, and then took her head off his shoulder. "How can you be so sure, Marcus? I want to make you happy, really, *really* happy in all ways, and I don't have a very good track record in these matters," she said softly.

Marcus didn't respond, he merely kissed her again, softly letting his tongue play around the most sensitive part of her lips. She parted her lips to allow him access and the resulting soft, pulsating rhythm seemed to echo the pounding of their hearts. When they finally broke apart, she wanted to close her eyes and nestle into his neck, but he wouldn't let her. "Look, Pie, I want you to see something," he said. She looked down to see her nipples distended to a size she would never have believed, looking ripe, sexy, and totally foreign to her eyes.

"Holy smoke! How'd you do that, Marcus?" she breathed.

Marcus gathered her to his chest and held her while he laughed gently. "*We* did that, baby. We did it, and that is just the beginning of what we're going to do. In Jamaica.

We can do anything, remember? Button up, I'm taking you home right now," he added.

Vera looked totally dismayed. "Aren't we going to watch the movie?" Her eyes betrayed her words, though; she was looking at Marcus's muscular chest as if it were a delicious dessert and she was being deprived of a treat. Marcus set her aside gently and reached for his shirt, which he had tossed on the floor.

"You don't want to watch that movie, you just want to take advantage of me. I'm taking you home before things get out of hand," he said with a wink.

Vera grumpily refastened her bra and buttoned up her blouse. "I do too want to watch that movie," she mumbled. "And you can't take me home, I drove here."

"Oh, yeah? What's the name of the movie?" he challenged.

Vera, who had selected and rented the DVD, looked completely blank. "Ahh, umm, it's . . . umm . . . I don't remember," she confessed. She stared at the TV, trying vainly to make sense of the scenes flashing before her. It had been running the whole time and neither one of them had paid it one bit of attention.

"You lose. I'm following you home in my car to make sure you get there safely. I need some air, anyway. We will resume this discussion," he said as he helped her off the bed, "in Negril, Jamaica."

And despite her efforts to the contrary, Marcus prevailed. He followed the little PT Cruiser right up to Vera's driveway, and waited while she unlocked her front door and went into the house. Marcus sat in the driveway for a few minutes, still trying to get his bearings. He should have gone into the house with Vera, but in his present state he couldn't trust himself to be alone with her. He was still trying to assimilate the information Vera had given him. Vera, the sexiest, most sensual woman he'd ever met, was under the impression that she was frigid. The merest touch of her hand was enough to get his juices flowing and when she had caressed his bare chest for the first time that evening, he almost lost control right then and there.

He finally pulled out of her driveway and headed for home. He had a lot of planning to do because he was going to make sure that Vera's initiation into real lovemaking was perfect. After this weekend, she wouldn't have any doubts, any questions, or any fears. Marcus was going to make sure of that.

Even though it was a short week, to Vera it seemed to go on forever. Having Dante over for dinner definitely helped, though. It was a nice midweek break that served as another milestone of sorts with her and Marcus. She made flounder stuffed with crabmeat and served it with fresh green beans and little red potatoes, along with a garden-fresh salad. Fresh was the operative word too, the lettuce had come right out of her garden. The evening could have been the worst disaster since the Hindenburg, but it was a pleasant, relaxing night of good food and good conversation. Marcus was a wonderful host, and put Dante at his ease immediately. Kika and Toby were on their best behavior, which meant they seemed to remember Dante was a friend and didn't attack him. After the dessert of blueberry crumble and ice cream, Dante had to leave to go on duty at the hospital. Marcus admitted that he was every bit as nice as Vera had claimed. "Just so long as he knows that you might be *his* friend but you're *my* woman, we'll get along fine," Marcus emphasized.

Vera gave Marcus a look of amusement. "Okay, Tarzan. I still don't think he's interested in having a relationship right now. I told you, I think that fiancée of his really broke his heart," she said sadly. "It's really too bad, too, because he's such a nice guy."

Further conversation was cut off as Marcus started kissing her, something that never failed to get all of her attention.

The rest of the week was devoted to preparations for the trip. And she got help with those preparations, albeit in a most unusual way. She came home to find a big package from UPS sitting on the dining room table. Luckily it had arrived on a day that her twice-a-week housekeeper, Mrs. Evans, had been there to receive it. Vera looked at the package curiously, and then noticed the Michigan return address. She immediately tore into the box, realizing it was from Carmen. In minutes she had dissolved into helpless laughter. It looked as though Carmen and Toni were still taking their big sister duties seriously.

The box contained three of the sheerest, most feminine nighties Vera had ever seen, all made of silk and all fabulous. One was soft ivory, a short, simple confection that was barely more than a camisole with matching bikini panties that tied on the side with a silk ribbon. The black one was floor length with side slits all the way up to the lace bodice; it too, had a matching panty, which was nothing more than a string thong. The last one was her favorite; it consisted of a short top with fluttery sleeves and only a thin ribbon tie at the neckline, no other fasteners at all. The bottom was a pair of tap dancer panties with full legs that also had sexy slits on the sides.

That wasn't all, there was an assortment of paperback books in the box too. Several titles were historical romances by Beverly Jenkins and there was the Hideaway series by Rochelle Alers and three books by Janice Sims including *A Second Chance at Love* and *Desert Heat*. Puzzled by what seemed to be an array of Post-it notes sticking out of each book, she thumbed through the nearest one and realized that her sisters had highlighted all the juicy parts for her perusal. And there were highly aromatic scented candles and a well-wrapped bottle of massage oil, to boot. She didn't know what to make of the small razor that was also in the box. She was about to call them to express her thanks when her phone rang.

"Hello?" she said breathlessly.

"Did you get it?" Carmen said at once.

"Oh, my Lord, yes! I don't know what to say to you two. Is Toni there?"

Toni's voice responded, "Of course I am, you know I had to deliver some words of sisterly wisdom. They are as follows: don't feel compelled to wear those gowns, as pretty as they are. If the spirit hits you, go naked, he won't mind a bit. And make sure you read all of those books, at least the parts we highlighted. They make a wonderful study guide," she said with a chuckle.

Carmen added, "Just remember to relax and take it easy. Marcus will do all the rest, trust me. I was watching you two pretty closely and that man is deep-deep-deeply in love with you! You two look so pretty together it's actually kind of sickening."

Vera laughed. "Well, according to Tanya and Alexis, the whole idea is pretty sickening, remember?"

Her younger sisters had indeed been less than supportive when they realized that Vera and Marcus were a couple. Tanya, ever outspoken, told Vera that she was out of her mind to get involved with a younger man because the first young thing to come along was going to snatch him away from her. Even Alexis, the youngest Clark sister and the least like the others, had an issue. "It just seems unnatural, Vera. Women are supposed to be with older men, not younger ones. Marcus is barely older than me, for heaven's sake! How am I supposed to meet an eligible man if women like you are trying to take them all?"

Carmen clicked her tongue in disgust. "Alexis is just jealous, she'll get over it. Tanya, well, ever since she took up with that creature she's dating she's become Saginaw's Queen of the Ghetto Fabulous. I still haven't gotten over that outfit my niece was wearing! And as for my nephew, I was just too through!"

Tanya's eight-year-old daughter, Raquel, had shown up for the party wearing a leopard-printed halter top and a fake leather miniskirt with platform sandals. She had preened around and at one point remarked that "J. Lo wished she had some of this here," referring to, of all things, her narrow, arrow-straight body. As if that wasn't embarrassing enough, Tanya's three-year-old son, Rafiq, was clad in FUBU from head to toe, a head that included long braids like a popular rap star and pierced ears. And he had the patented scowl on his face, too. Vera had been shocked at this transition, to say the least.

"Yeah, well, it's not their fault that their mother dresses them like a junior hoochie and short Doggy-dogg. Although I see now why Mommy said they wouldn't be interested in going to the zoo, they're too grown for that! But, honey, Miss Tanya and Miss Alexis didn't bother me any," Vera said airily. "Like I told them, 'Don't hate me 'cause you ain't me.' They'll get over it. Or not, I don't care."

Abruptly changing the subject, she announced her upcoming trip to Jamaica and held the phone away from her ear while her sisters squealed in unison.

"Vera, this is perfect! Girl, that box came right on time, didn't it? Take everything in the box, well, maybe not the books, just memorize them. But make sure you pack everything else, you hear me?" said Toni.

"The dead can hear you, Toni. You don't have to holler. By the way, what's the razor for? I already shave my legs, are you trying to drop a hint?" Vera said with a smile.

Carmen cleared her throat. "It's not for your legs, dear. It's for another part of your anatomy entirely," she said delicately.

Vera automatically threw her hip out and rested a fist on it while she made a face at the phone. "Excuse me, but I've been getting bikini waxes for years, honey. You're a little tardy with the razor, sister!"

Carmen and Toni's silence spoke volumes. Finally Carmen said, "Well, all righty then! You seem to be good to go! Take care of each other and have a wonderful time. And call us the minute you get home, we want details!"

"Read those books," Toni insisted. "And pick up some Francis Ray and Brenda Jackson, too. If you're not ready *then,* you never will be!"

Vera laughed and laughed as they disconnected the call. She was ready, all right; she'd never been more ready in her life.

The flight to Jamaica wasn't markedly different from any of the flights she had taken with Marcus over the years. They had traveled together many, many times on company business and this was much the same, although there were subtle differences. When she fell asleep on the flight, as she always did, Marcus just lifted the armrest between their first-class seats and she curled into his shoulder as though she'd been doing it for years. When he kissed her awake as the plane began its descent, it felt natural, as though his kisses woke her every day. There was definitely something to be said about being involved with your best friend. The comfort level was unmistakable.

Marcus had naturally reserved the most posh accommodations for them. They were staying at a five-star hotel and spa, but they were in the private villas, not the main hotel. The villa was stunningly beautiful, it had floor-to-ceiling windows in every room, with filmy white curtains blowing in the ocean breeze. There was a large living room with a comfortable sofa and love seat, as well as a wet bar, a big-screen television with a DVD player, and stereo equipment hidden in the cabinet beneath the TV. There was a small kitchen, for those inclined to prepare a meal or light snack, and a dining area with a pretty glass-topped table and chair upholstered to match the sofa and love seat.

The bedroom, though, was what made Vera stop and catch her breath. Almost everything in the bedroom was white, the four-poster bed, the dressing table and dresser, the tile in the big bathroom that opened off the bedroom; everything seemed to be white. Even the big ceiling fan that turned sedately above the bed had white blades. The walls, however, were a warm peach and the carpet was a darker shade of the same color. There were accents of peach here and there, and the exquisite oil paintings that depicted island life added warmth and charm to the decor. It was charming, with big French doors in the living room and bedroom that opened on to the brick patio that surrounded the villa. The patios were graced with colorful flowers growing in big pots and there was a short path that led directly into the ocean. Vera was enchanted with the villa and told Marcus so, her eyes sparkling.

"Marcus, this place is wonderful, sweetheart. I love it!" she exclaimed as she hugged him.

Marcus couldn't answer for a moment as Vera was kissing him with great gusto to show her appreciation. The day hadn't dawned when he would prefer doing something other than kissing Vera, so he gladly went along with the embrace. Finally, they came up for air. "This place is a world-famous spa, as you already know, Pie. What you don't know is that we're going to have an afternoon of treatments. Mud baths, salt scrubs, and facials and stuff, anything you want to have done, we're doing it," he said enthusiastically.

"Oh," said Vera. She immediately tried to generate more excitement, but it was very difficult when her mind was in another place altogether. *The treatment I need isn't going to be found in a mud bath, Marcus.* Stifling this and other ungrateful thoughts, she went along with Marcus's plan to be pampered all afternoon. And it wasn't nearly as torturous as she thought; it was actually fun to be patted and soothed and given expensive beauty treatments. They went in two different directions for some of the treatments as there were separate facilities for men and women. There were some coed areas, though.

It was particularly fun when she and Marcus ended up in the same place at the same time, like when their facials were completed and the cosmetician tried to talk her into thinning her brows. Vera's eyebrows were perfectly arched, but thick and glossy. Vera knew for a fact that Marcus adored them; he'd always commented on them. Vera merely smiled and pointed at Marcus. "You see that big man over there?" she asked sweetly. "He likes them just the way they are." The cosmetician actually shivered as she looked at Marcus, who was scowling for all he was worth. The scowl wasn't just for the benefit of the woman who dared tried to trifle with Vera's brows. His own attendant was suggesting that he color his hair. "No," he said flatly.

"But you would look so handsome, so much younger with dark hair," she exclaimed. Marcus turned to face the woman, speaking as though to the feebleminded. "You see that beautiful, sexy woman over there? She likes me just fine the way I am, gray hair and all, and she's the only person I want to impress in any way, okay?"

Catching the way Marcus and Vera smiled at each other, the woman did indeed understand. "Of course, sir, please forgive the suggestion," she murmured while thinking that Vera was a very lucky woman indeed.

Finally it was time for Vera's massage, something she was truly looking forward to since it signaled the end of the afternoon of treatments and because she was also in need of a relaxing rubdown. She was led into a pale blue room with a high massage table in the center. The lights were dimmed and there was soft music playing, while a soft fragrance spewed from a mister at regular intervals. Vera used the little steps next to the table to get on top, lying down on her stomach and removing the spa-provided robe she was wearing. The attendant adjusted a sheet over her naked body, and told her that the masseuse would be in any moment. Vera's face was in the opening at the top of the table that enabled her to breath normally while she maintained the proper position for the massage.

She vaguely heard the door open and close, but she did register a person coming to stand beside the table. Her masseuse was here at last. She took a deep breath as warm scented oil was squirted on her back, and braced herself for what was to come. What she felt next brought her nothing but joy. "Marcus," she breathed.

"Yes, baby, it's me," he admitted. "I paid the guy off so I could take his place. I couldn't have another man touching you like this," he said gruffly.

"Like what?" Vera asked coyly. Marcus was happy to demonstrate by stroking her back with long, strong movements of his arms, using his thumbs to manipulate her spine and kneading her muscles until they were completely relaxed and pliant. He went down each leg and included her feet in the sensual manipulation, caressing the soles and gently rotating each toe in turn so that even her feet were tingling. As he made his way back up her long, strong legs, Vera wondered briefly if he was going to include her more sensitive areas, like her derriere. She didn't have to wonder long as he gave each brown globe its own personal treatment, which made her want to claw her way through the table.

Every touch of Marcus's hands was like magic. Where they touched her she was left tingling and vibrant, inching closer and closer to a state of total abandon. By the time he had massaged her entire body, she was trembling and weak from needing more. When she could stand no more she turned over on her back and begged him to stop.

"Marcus . . . this is driving me crazy," she gasped. Marcus was magnificent, wrapped in a towel and nothing else; she could see he was as ready for her as she was for him. "Marcus, you've got to do something," she whispered. He answered her plea by kissing her passionately as he stroked her breasts and flat, taut stomach with the same long sweeping stroke he'd employed on her back. The thin cotton sheet was slipping farther and farther down her hips and she moaned aloud from the sweet torture she suffering at his skilled hands. The soft sound of her moan made Marcus realize how far they'd gone.

"Hold it, baby, our first time is not going to be in a public massage room on a hard old table. Especially that one, if I jumped my big butt on that thing I'd turn it into kindling. Let's get out of here, baby, right now," he urged.

Somehow they dressed and got back to the villa in what must have been a land speed record for such activity. In minutes they were back in the villa, blessedly alone and ready for something wonderful to begin. Marcus held out his hand to Vera and she walked into his arms.

Chapter 14

After holding each other closely, Marcus gently released Vera and said, "Why don't we get more relaxed, baby? Let's get out of these clothes."

Vera agreed and they went to get ready, Vera using the big bathroom off the bedroom and Marcus using the smaller one off the living room. With hands that were surprisingly steady, considering how nervous she was, Vera brushed her teeth, added her special fragrance, the one that Marcus loved, and debated about what to put on. She certainly had enough seductive outfits from which to choose, thanks to her sisters. In the end, though, she made the one choice that seemed right. She finger-combed her hair and after one last look in the mirror, she was ready.

She entered the main bedroom, expecting to see Marcus waiting for her. And he was, but he was standing on the lanai watching the sunset. He was wearing a linen and cotton blend robe that she'd bought for him the previous birthday, a white robe that made his skin warm and rich by contrast. He turned when he heard Vera behind him and held out his arm. She went to him immediately and they held each other in the gathering twilight, watching the waves lap against the shore. He looked down at Vera with such love and tenderness in his eyes that she suddenly felt like crying; instead she pulled him down to her for a kiss.

Their lips touched softly, then more intensely as the passion they'd sought to hold at bay began to surface. The warm ocean breeze caressed them, the music of the surf matched the pounding of their hearts, and time seemed to stand still for a moment. When their lips finally stopped touching, they looked at each other solemnly, wordlessly. Vera gently drew her arms away from Marcus and slowly put her hands to the belt of the pale green robe she was wearing. She undid the belt and opened the robe, letting it slide off her body. She stood before him completely naked, wanting only him to make her complete.

Marcus looked at her as though she were an exquisite work of art, as though he'd never seen anything as beautiful in his life. She held out her hand to him and he took it; then picked her up as though she weighed nothing at all. Carrying her over to the big bed that awaited them, Marcus gently placed her on it and removed his own robe. It was Vera's turn to look at him with awe. Marcus's hard, muscular body looked even bigger and more masculine with no clothes on. Especially the most masculine part of his anatomy; Vera couldn't look away from it as Marcus lay down next to her on the bed. Marcus seemed to sense her hesitation and gathered her into his arms.

He stroked and caressed her arms and shoulders, and she instantly relaxed, reveling in the feel of their naked bodies touching each other. Marcus wasn't finished with her, though. He kissed and caressed his way down her body, stopping at her ultrasensitive breasts. When Vera felt his hot tongue encircling her nipple, she thought she might faint from the sensation. He gently kneaded one while he licked and kissed the other, gradually reversing his position. Vera's head went from side to side on the pillow as she tried to assimilate all the new sensations she was feeling. She gasped and moaned aloud as Marcus continued his relentless exploration of her body with his big, gentle hands.

When he grasped her hips, she felt the world tilt and then right itself as he used his clever fingers to explore the most feminine part of her. Her eyes flew open and the shock of what she was feeling was replaced with ecstasy as Marcus's lips followed his fingers into the most intimate exploration possible between a man and a woman. Her whole body tensed and she couldn't breathe. The pressure that was building inside her, the exquisite sensations that Marcus was creating were growing, spiraling through her body until she couldn't stand the pleasure anymore. Just then something pulsed through her that felt like a shower of stars raining down on her. She screamed his name over and over as the tremors continued, over and over again, until she was trembling and sobbing his name aloud.

He finally released his hold on her and kissed his way back up her body. She put her trembling arms around his neck and kissed him, long and passionate, while she wrapped her legs around his. When the kiss finally ended, she opened her eyes to find Marcus gazing at her with the sexiest expression she'd ever seen, and she returned the look with a loving, tender smile. "More," she whispered.

"Your wish, beauty, is my pleasure," he replied.

He rolled over onto his back and reached for the box of condoms that awaited him. Taking a flat, gold-foil-wrapped disc out of the box, he began to open the packet when Vera took it from his hands. Kneeling next to him on the bed, Vera set the packet aside for the moment; it was her turn to explore Marcus. He lay there like a golden titan, beautiful and sexy and all hers. Boldly, her hands caressed every inch of his broad chest while her lips returned the favor he had granted her, kissing and licking her way down his body until her soft, caressing hands found what they sought and she acquainted herself with his manhood, hard and heavy with desire for her. She stroked it, fascinated with the smooth, warm feel of the sensitive skin, and daringly, she rubbed it against her cheek before tasting Marcus the way he had tasted her. In what seemed like seconds, Marcus was calling her name.

"Vera, baby, please put that thing on me, put it on *now*," he said hoarsely. Vera reluctantly did as she was asked and was richly rewarded when Marcus took a deep sigh and held his hands out to her. "C'mon, Pie." She took his hands and he guided her on top of his big body, steadying her hips with his hands as he entered her, slowly, tenderly, but with a sensual pressure that drove Vera mad. All concern about whether or not he would fit her went away as her body began to know his, their bodies moved together like the surf pounding outside their door, the rhythm of love took them over and guided them to a completion that was as strong and pulsing as it was right. This time it was Marcus who screamed Vera's name over and over as they crossed into the stars together.

Much later, after much more loving, Vera uttered her last coherent thought before falling into a deep sleep. "Marcus, I love you. I love you so much more than I knew. I'm so glad you were right about us," she murmured before falling asleep in his arms.

Vera lay on her stomach, her arms and legs spread gracefully even in slumber. Marcus lay next to her, running his index finger down her spine. When that didn't produce the desired effect, he replaced the finger with his tongue, licking her sensuously between her shoulder blades. She finally stirred, giving a sexy giggle that immediately aroused him.

"What time is it?" she said sleepily.

"Twelve," he answered.

"Mmm, it's midnight already? That was such a nice nap," she said with a delicate yawn.

"Pie, it's twelve noon. You've been asleep for almost fourteen hours," Marcus said with amusement.

"Noon? But it's still dark," Vera said groggily.

"That's because your eyes are closed, baby. Open them up and see the sun," he invited.

Vera buried her head in the pillows instead. "No, I look like a swamp witch, I just know it. Why did you let me sleep so long?" she wailed. With no warning she leapt from the bed and dashed into the bathroom, slamming the door behind her.

Marcus rolled over on his back and laughed aloud. Vera was something else, something rare and special, his own personal treasure. He shivered as the aftershocks of their loving coursed through him again, the way they'd been doing since last night. He'd never experienced anything like the night he'd spent with Vera.

Vera finally emerged from the bathroom, with a freshly scrubbed look about her. Her eyes were bright and happy, and she bore the unmistakable signs of having showered. She smelled fresh and soapy and her skin was slightly damp. She was wrapped in a large bath sheet and, he was relieved to note, she looked anything but nervous. Marcus hadn't moved from his position on the bed and she joined him, draping her arms around his neck as she kissed him in greeting.

"I can't believe I slept so long," she said between kisses. "I'm so embarrassed! How could you let me sleep this late?"

Marcus kissed her back and laughed at her chagrin. "That just means I did my job right, baby. You were supposed to get a good night's sleep," he said with more than a touch of pride. "I used my time wisely, though. I got a lot of work done for the Children's Coalition. So now I'm ready to play," he said with a sexy grin.

The grin faded slightly when Vera jumped off the bed. "Well, *I'm* ready to eat. I'm starving, Marcus, feed me!"

They spent a playful, relaxing afternoon together and took the opportunity to explore the hotel and its many amenities, although they didn't feel compelled to do any sight-seeing. They were perfectly content just to be with each other, talking and laughing and making love for hours on end. Neither one of them wanted the weekend to end, they wanted to prolong this time away from everything and everyone except each other. The day before they were scheduled to leave, Marcus expressed this to Vera. They were in the big bed holding each other, a sheet covering their nude bodies.

"I'm not ready to go back, baby," Marcus confessed. Vera, who was propped up on one elbow stroking his broad chest, said that she didn't want to leave either.

"Marcus, this time has been so special, so perfect, I could stay here forever," she agreed. She moved slightly so that her head was pillowed on his shoulder and her long legs came into more intimate contact with him. Marcus groaned with pleasure as she rubbed against him.

"Okay, beauty, stop that unless you mean business," he warned her. To his delight, she didn't stop but gave him more proof that business was indeed what was on her mind. He rolled over and pinned her underneath his big body, giving her a long, wet kiss. "No turning back, baby, are you sure you can handle more of this?" he asked. "I don't want you to be sore and miserable."

Vera smiled wickedly and kissed him back. By way of an answer she reached under the pillows and pulled out a foil-wrapped packet. "You do it so well, I haven't felt anything but pleasure," she said.

She started to open the packet when Marcus stopped her. "Not just yet, Vera, you won't need that for a while," he told her and swallowed her sound of surprise into his kiss.

Later, much later, they were drowsy with completion and once again resting in each other's arms. Marcus was sated and happy and awash with love for Vera; he'd never experienced anything in his life like the feelings he had for her, which explained what happened next. Marcus dropped a kiss on top of Vera's head and pulled her closer to his side. "Vera?"

"Yes, sweetheart?" she answered sleepily.

"Marry me."

Some time later, Vera and Marcus were in the big Jacuzzi tub in the bathroom. The windows were open to admit the fragrant island air, the ceiling fan was turning lazily, and there were big glasses of fruit juice over crushed ice on the edge of the tub. Vera reached for hers and took a long sip from the long thin straw. She looked long and hard at Marcus while she was drinking; then she abruptly set the glass down. Marcus was aware of her scrutiny, and asked why she was staring at him.

"Because you're the best-looking man I've ever seen," she said honestly. "You're so handsome that you ought to be on a coin, or a stamp or something," she said appraisingly. She moved closer to him as she spoke, getting into his lap and rubbing her wet body against his. She locked her soapy arms around his neck and kissed him, one cheek, then the other, then a soft, wet kiss on his hungry lips. "And that's why it wouldn't be fair for me to marry you," she said with finality.

Marcus groaned and put his forehead against Vera's while he tightened his arms around her. Over the past few hours he'd heard every reason in the world why they shouldn't get married and he wasn't buying any of them. This one, however, was a new twist.

"Vera, what does that mean?" he asked wearily. "You're getting obtuse on me, baby."

"It means that you have an obligation to pass on those genes of yours. I can't give you children, Marcus. You're too young to get stuck with a woman who can't have your babies. You need to be with someone who can make you some pretty babies to carry on your family name and those exceptional genes of yours," Vera said quietly.

Marcus felt a pain deep in his heart at Vera's words. She'd mentioned something about not having kids earlier, but this time he had to convince her. "Look, Pie, I think it's a true tragedy that you can't have babies of your own. I can't think of anyone who'd be a better mother than you. And if you want to, we can adopt. But I have to tell you, Vera, having children isn't on my short list of things to do. Or my long list, for that matter. I've never told anybody that I want to have children, now, have I?"

Vera sat back from him a little so that she could look deeply into his eyes. He looked back, steady and convincing. "Look, Vera, the family name is just fine. I've got a whole passel of nieces and nephews and they're all crazy as dancing mice. Most of them look just like me, too, so the gene pool is doing just fine. Having babies is the last thing on my mind, Vera. People get married for reasons other than having children," he reminded her.

Vera was occupied with smoothing the silky hair on Marcus's broad, muscular chest. "They do? What other reasons do they have?" she murmured as she rubbed her palms in circular motions over his sensitive nipples.

Marcus moaned his pleasure and shifted Vera so that she was straddling his lap. "Lots of good reasons. Like love." He shuddered as Vera slid up and down against his groin. "And passion." He groaned as Vera deliberately leaned for-

ward so that her breasts were rubbing against his chest.
"The desire to take care of the other person, to share with
them," he whispered as she licked his earlobe and pulled it
into her hot little mouth. "The . . . the . . . oh, to hell with
it." He stood up and Vera locked her legs around his waist,
laying her head on his shoulder. He wrapped his arms
around her tightly and carried her into the bedroom.
"Marry me, don't marry me, I don't care, Vera. You belong
to me, Vera, and I belong to you, and that's all there is to
it. You're mine," he said in a voice choked with passion.
"Mine."

Vera clung to him just as tightly and smiled, although
there were tears in her eyes. "And you're mine. I love you,
Marcus, I do," she confessed.

His last thought, before abandoning himself to their passion, was that one day she'd say "I do" in an entirely
different context. There was nothing he couldn't get if he
put his mind to it, and having Vera as his wife was his only
desire. She was going to be Mrs. Marcus Deveraux, and
soon.

As they were packing to go home to Atlanta, Vera suddenly turned to Marcus with a deeply serious look.
"Marcus, I absolutely can't marry you," she said. He
whirled around with a look of panic on his face. Vera took
him by the hand and led him over to the bed, where they
sat down.

"What's my name, Marcus? My *whole* name?"

Marcus looked puzzled. Not many people knew that
Vera was a nickname, but of course he did. "Your name is
Devere Alicia Clark Jackson, why?"

"Say my first name and your last name," she said.

"Devere Deveraux," he said promptly. He stared at Vera
and burst out laughing. "Devere Deveraux! That's hilari-

ous!" He got so tickled that he fell on his back and laughed until his stomach hurt.

Vera was laughing, too. Her given name Devere, pronounced *Dev-ah-ray,* was an impossible match to Deveraux. "See? I'd sound like a dancer in a booty bar or a soap opera heroine or something. It won't work, Marcus!"

Marcus continued to laugh, although he was gaining control. "So I'll change my name, what difference does it make?"

"Change it to what?" Vera laughed.

"Who cares? I'll call myself John Jacob Jingleheimer Schmidt if you want me to. As long as you're my wife, that's all that matters," he said seriously. Before she could answer he pulled her into his arms for a kiss.

"Marcus, we can't, we have to pack," she said as his intentions became plain. They were both nearly undressed, Vera in a little robe and Marcus in a towel. Marcus didn't answer; he just took off the towel and let Vera gaze on his magnificent body.

"Oh. Well, in that case, maybe we can take a later flight," Vera murmured as she removed her robe. All thoughts of leaving the island vanished as they reached for each other.

Chapter 15

Marcus gave a courtesy knock on Malcolm's office door and entered without waiting for an invitation. Malcolm didn't even look up from his computer screen, he just mildly asked why Marcus felt like he could just barge in any time he felt like it.

"I knocked," Marcus defended himself.

Malcolm looked at his younger brother with disgust. "Yeah, you knocked, but then you came busting in here. How do you know I wasn't with someone?"

"You weren't," Marcus pointed out.

"Yeah, but . . . never mind," Malcolm sighed. This particular debate was never going to end.

Marcus leaned back in the leather chair across from Malcolm and put his feet up on Malcolm's desk. "We got any money?" he asked.

"Some. Why?" Malcolm asked curiously.

"Enough to buy a plane? We need a plane, man. This flying commercial is ridiculous. How much money do we spend and how much time do we waste flying the airlines? It's time we got our own jet," Marcus said flatly. The trip to Jamaica had been the deciding point for Marcus; it was time his family came into the twenty-first century in terms of travel. To Marcus's surprise, Malcolm agreed with him wholeheartedly. He'd been preparing some data to support that very idea. They discussed it and agreed to bring it up at the brothers' weekly meeting.

Marcus was quite cheerful as he left Malcolm's office and headed down to the production area to talk with Clay. Clay, as head of the television and film division, spent a great deal of time down there, as did Vera when her television show was taping. She was, in fact, taping that day as Marcus found when he made a detour to stop by her set. He watched from the sidelines as Vera and her guest, a decorator from a local home supply store, put the finishing touches on an exquisite hope chest. It had started life as a plain wooden storage box with a hinged top. Now it looked like an heirloom; they had added ball feet, decorated each flat surface with molding to give it a more defined profile, and custom-painted it after upholstering the top with foam rubber, batting, and a beautiful fabric that was actually a remnant from the fabric store. The end result looked like a million bucks when the project had actually cost about twenty-five dollars.

Marcus watched in fascination as Vera worked her magic. She specialized in showing the viewer how to live graciously without breaking the bank. Her guests were booked months in advance and there were a surprising number of celebrities among them. Appearing on *Personal Space* to show off home projects and hobbies was quite *de rigueur* these days. It was no wonder that the syndicates wanted to lock up *Personal Space*; the show was hot, just like its creator. There had been several offers made to syndicate the program for cable television. It remained only to pick the best offer. How long he stood there watching he didn't know, but he would have been content to do so for a lot longer. Clay found him, though, and indicated that he should follow him off the soundstage.

When it was safe to speak without danger of interfering with taping, Clay told Marcus to come with him. "Where are we going?" Marcus asked. By now the two men had left the building and were in the parking lot that serviced the studio area. Clay gestured to a huge vehicle and grinned. "We're going for a test drive," he said with glee.

The two men got into the ungainly SUV and pulled out of the parking lot. "So where have you been, man? Haven't seen you in a few days," Clay commented.

"I took Vera to Jamaica over the weekend," Marcus said with a satisfied smile. "We just got back a couple of days ago."

Clay looked over at his younger brother and returned the smile. In his deep, gravelly voice he asked, "So when you gonna make an honest woman out of her? When are you two taking the vows?"

"I asked, man. I asked while we were in Jamaica and she hasn't given me an answer yet. Hey, are you actually thinking about buying this monstrosity? This is the ugliest thing I've ever seen," he said as he looked around the interior.

"Nope, Bennie's not gonna let me get it," Clay said ruefully. "She says it looks like a tank and it's an environmental disaster. But we need something like this for those rowdies we're raising. You have no idea what those boys can do to a car. Wait till you and Vera pop out a few, you'll see. You'll need something big and indestructible like this."

Marcus looked at Clay with a mixture of love and pain on his handsome face. "Vera and I won't be having any kids, Clay. Vera can't have children, and that's why she hasn't given me an answer. She says it wouldn't be fair to deprive me of fatherhood."

Clay raised his thick eyebrows. "Vera can't have babies? I knew she had that miscarriage, but I didn't know she couldn't have any more children. Damn, that must have been hard for her to take. Vera loves kids," he said thoughtfully. "I wonder why she and John didn't adopt."

Marcus took a deep breath and leaned his head back, or tried to; the SUV didn't offer up much in the way of comfort. "She wanted to adopt but John wouldn't hear of it for some reason. After the miscarriage she never conceived again and he just refused to cooperate with the idea of adopting so they could have a family. She got cheated big time, Clay."

"So what was your answer when she told you she couldn't give you babies and that was why she couldn't marry you?" Clay asked.

Marcus sighed. "I told her the only lie I'll ever tell her in our lives. I told her I didn't want kids. She still hasn't given me an answer, though."

Clay didn't respond immediately as he maneuvered the huge, homely SUV through traffic. Hearing the lengths to which Marcus would go to reassure the woman he loved made Clay understand the depths of his love for Vera. Finally he spoke, reassuring his brother. "Just give her time to get used to the idea, Marcus. You love her, she loves you, and neither one of you is going anywhere. Be patient, everything will work out," he counseled.

"And if it doesn't?" Marcus asked. "What do I do then?"

Clay looked over at his youngest brother and smiled. "Trust me, Marcus, before the year is out you'll have a ring on Vera's finger to match the one in your nose. Bet on it."

It was a sign of how far gone Marcus was that he didn't lash out at the ring-in-the-nose comment. He did take the bet, though, and he would have been gratified to know that the odds were in his favor.

Despite their efforts to appear casual and uninvolved at the office, it was obvious that something was up with Marcus and something was definitely up with Vera. She became the object of speculation all over the building by virtue of the fact that she was glowing like a shooting star when she and Marcus returned from their trip. Besides being sun-kissed and relaxed, she looked sexier than ever. Finding true sexual fulfillment with Marcus had definitely left its mark on her. Tami Foster was the first one to comment on it.

"Okay, Miss Vera, what's up with you? Where have you been, what have you been doing, and who have you been doing it with? And don't lie, I always know when people lie," she said. Tami had taken one look at Vera when she returned to the office and promptly followed her into Vera's spacious and colorful office.

Vera tried to play it off, which didn't work with Tami. Tami would have made an excellent interrogator during the Inquisition. She left no stone unturned in her quest for information. To her credit, though, once she had the dirt it traveled no further. People had been known to offer her large sums of money for inside information and she laughed in their faces. Tami liked knowledge, but she hated sharing information. Knowing Tami quite well, Vera wasn't worried that she would gossip about her, but she wasn't ready to share, either.

"I don't know what you're talking about, Tami," she said airily. "I had a long weekend, that's all. Just a little R and R."

Tami came closer to Vera and looked deeply into her eyes. "Okay, keep it to yourself. But don't think you can fool me, I know you too well for that. Someone in this room got real busy over the weekend and it wasn't me. I had to take my senior to Callaway Gardens with her peeps," Tami said ruefully. "I spent the last three days fighting off doddering old men waving their Viagra prescriptions. I'll bet *you* weren't fighting anyone off," she added pointedly.

Vera blushed pink and refused to answer. "Look, I'm going down to production, where I'll be most of the day.

And you should get your mind on something *productive,* like your own love life." She laughed.

Tami tossed her taffy-blond hair back and said, "Ha! That's the most nonproductive thing about me. I got more action from the geezers on Callaway than I've had in months!"

She and Vera left the office together, Tami stopping at her desk in the reception area and Vera continuing to the elevators. Vera, for once, got in the last word. "Well, you better get busy, Miss Tami, before you're stuck with the geriatric set for real. Time's a-wastin'!" she said merrily, just before stepping into the elevator.

Her own words echoed strangely in her ears throughout the day. She went through all the usual motions as she taped the segments that would later be edited into a whole program, but her mind was busy. She was still on the set, making postproduction notes while seated at a small desk that was part of the set. Her main set resembled a great room, casually outfitted with an extra-long sofa and the normal furnishings one would expect. There was also an open-plan kitchen with a big work area that had a cooktop and grill, for demonstrating recipes. There were a couple of secondary sets that were used for woodworking and other home projects. Vera was often on the set more than she was in her office upstairs. Right now, though, she could have been anywhere at all, for her mind wasn't on her surroundings. All she could think about was *time,* the principle of time, the concept of life measured out in tiny parcels.

Time was the one thing that couldn't be treated like a commodity; no one knew for sure how much time they had. It certainly wasn't promised to anyone, as she knew only too well. She had a sudden flash of insight as to why Marcus was pressing her for marriage. He simply didn't want to have their life together parceled out into a series of dates and evenings of hot sex. *Very, very hot sex,* she admitted.

Memories of their Jamaican weekend made her flush with passion when certain scenes came to mind. She still couldn't believe how easily Marcus had awakened the dormant sensuality that now was an essential part of her life. But it wasn't just the sex, she knew, it was everything about the relationship, everything about being with Marcus, loving him. He wanted more from her than access to her physically. He wanted access to her heart, to her soul. He wanted to be her partner in life, in everything . . .

Her mind was so occupied with these thoughts that she didn't realize that someone else had come onto the set. She jumped as she realized that Martin was sitting on the sofa with his long legs stretched out in front of him. "Martin, you scared the life out of me! Hang on, let me put this stuff in my tote and I'll come chat with you," she said. She stacked her papers neatly and put them away in labeled folders, then stowed them in her black leather tote bag. "Okay, I'm all . . . oh!" Vera looked up to see that Malcolm had joined Martin on the other end of the sofa. They looked like two extremely handsome bookends.

Vera knew something was up but she was so comfortable with the brothers that it didn't give her a moment's pause. "I see. You're down here to get all in my business, aren't you?" she said with a smile. She placed the tote bag on the desk and walked over to the sofa with her hands on her hips. Stepping over Malcolm's long legs, she sat between the two men. "I'm guessing that Marcus spilled it, hmm? There's no such thing as a secret with you boys, is there?" she said fondly.

Malcolm and Martin gave her identical grins. "No comment," said Martin like the attorney that he was. "We did, however, want to extend our loving welcome to you. We get the impression that you're going to be a very important part of our lives for quite a while," he said with sincere charm.

Malcolm nodded and extended his own good wishes. "You always felt like a sister anyway, so it's not much of a stretch," he said, ending with a kiss on her cheek. "Besides, we all knew that Marcus was in love with you. We're just glad that you could find it in your heart to love him back," he said with a laugh.

Vera immediately got indignant. "Hey, that's my man you're disparaging. Why wouldn't I love him? He's brilliant, handsome, sexy, charming, he treats me like a queen, and he loves my family like they were his own! He has integrity and morals, and a social conscience, and . . . and . . . you're just messing with my head, aren't you?" Vera said with a sheepish smile.

Martin was too busy laughing to answer her, but Malcolm did with great affection. "Yes, Vera, I'm messing with your head. I've always known that Marcus was crazy about you, but I knew it was true love when he put that garden in for you," he told her, his deep voice full of amusement.

Vera looked puzzled as Malcolm told the tale. "When he was a kid, it was his job to keep the yard up. We all had to suffer through it. He was the youngest and it was his turn. Marcus hated yard work so much that he subcontracted the job! He would get paid fifteen dollars to do it and he would pay his buddy seven to actually cut the grass and stuff," Malcolm recalled. "This was when he was, like, nine or ten years old, believe it or not."

Martin told the rest. "Well, they got a little business started. Marcus had the lawn mower, the edger, and all the tools. He made the contacts, going around in the neighborhood and getting clients. His buddy David was the one who did the work. They eventually got a couple more helpers and they ended up doing lawn care all over the neighborhood. In fact, his buddy David liked doing it so much he became a landscape architect and he has a huge landscaping business. You've met him too, his firm keeps the lawns at TDG."

Vera's eyes were wide with this information. "I thought Marcus just liked to garden," she said softly.

Both men laughed again. "No, Vera," said Martin. "If we'd had more land, Marcus would've had sharecroppers out there. He hates anything to do with dirt. But he's willing to do anything to please you, to be with you. That's why I knew he was really sincere about you," he said with a smile.

When Malcolm and Martin got ready to leave, Vera said she had a few more things to attend to and she stayed behind. She just needed time to assimilate what she'd been told. Thinking about Marcus's motivation for helping her in the garden reminded her of another very special man and a slow smile of recognition spread across her face. Full of resolve, she gathered her things together and left the studio. She didn't return to her office, but went straight to her car. She had a lot to do and not a lot of time in which to do it.

When Marcus pulled into the driveway of his home, he was gratified to see Vera's sporty little car already there. She'd had a key to his place since he bought the house; she needed to have access to it while she was overseeing its decoration. The fact that she felt secure enough to use the key made him feel wonderful. He entered the house through the garage, smiling in anticipation. What he saw made him smile even more. Vera was in the kitchen, putting together a green salad. She glanced up from her task, a look of welcome transforming her face. She immediately stopped what she was doing and came to greet him.

"Hello, sweetheart," she said, kissing him softly. "How was your day?"

He put down his briefcase and pulled Vera against his long frame to kiss her more thoroughly. "I don't remember," he said. "I have no recollection of anything that transpired today. You've erased my short-term memory, beauty."

They continued to embrace for several long moments, until Marcus became aware of the tantalizing aroma that was permeating the air. "What's that wonderful smell? And to what do I owe this pleasure, anyway?"

"The smell is roast chicken. The reason is that I love you and I wanted you to have a nice, relaxing evening," Vera replied. "You have just enough time to take a shower and get into something comfortable," she added.

Marcus took a step back and looked at Vera, who had apparently taken her own advice. She was wearing a rayon sarong with a pattern of tropical foliage in shades of green. She had on big gold hoop earrings and little green thong sandals and she looked cool, relaxed, and adorable, despite the fact that she'd obviously been working for some time.

"How long have you been here?" he asked as he removed his tie and started unbuttoning his shirt.

Vera filled a glass with a white wine sangria made with peaches, pineapple, and star fruit. Handing it to Marcus, she told him she hadn't been there that long. "I left the office early, went home and got the dogs, and came over here. I put the chicken in the oven, took a shower and changed, and waited for you," she said. "Now, go take a shower and get comfortable so we can enjoy this evening together."

He had one more question for Vera as he left the kitchen. "Where are the urchins?"

"They're on the patio. Let them in, they'll be thrilled to see you," she answered.

And they were, dashing around his feet in circles and yipping madly. They accompanied him to the master suite and sat on the bath mat while he took a long shower made fragrant by the green Vitabath bath gel with which Vera kept him supplied. Marcus was singing as he got dressed in khaki shorts and a favorite polo shirt. He rescued a leather sandal from Toby and put it on along with its mate. He was singing an Al Jarreau tune as he entered the kitchen, carrying the glass that had contained the sangria.

He came up behind Vera and put his arms around her waist, kissing the back of her neck as he did so. "You're the best, Pie. I was feeling okay when I left the office, but now I feel like Superman. Thank you, baby."

Vera turned around in his arms and hugged him. "It's my pleasure. Now help me take these things out to the patio where we're eating, Superman."

The meal Vera made for him was simple, low fat, low carbohydrate, and entirely delicious. She didn't get to cook often, given her busy schedule, but when she did, everything she made was fabulous. Marcus was a notoriously picky eater, but anything Vera made tasted perfect to him. Like tonight's menu: green salad with his favorite dressing, red wine vinaigrette; a succulent herb-roasted chicken with roasted potatoes and fresh green beans; and for dessert, a shared bowl of Edy's lemon sorbet with chunks of juicily ripe honeydew melon. In a very short time, Marcus was relaxed on the double chaise on the patio, digesting his very fine meal.

He had insisted on cleaning up the kitchen for Vera and had done so quickly and efficiently while Vera relaxed. Now they were entwined in each other's arms and listening to Kurt Elling on the stereo. Kika and Toby were amusing themselves by attempting to catch the fireflies that were floating in the fragrant twilight. Marcus was almost overwhelmed by the sense of euphoric calm that he was experiencing.

"Vera, baby, this is what I'm talking about. Just you and me, like this every night for the rest of our lives," he said persuasively.

"Every night?" Vera was curled up next to him, her head nestled into his shoulder and her soft hand traveling under his shirt to stroke his hard, muscled stomach. "Even when one of us has had a rotten day? Or one of us is sick, or has to be out of town or—"

Marcus stopped her words by kissing her senseless. "Dang, Pie, I don't think you have a romantic bone in your body," he complained. "I'm trying to think about how wonderful our life could be and you're cluttering up my fantasy with practicality."

Vera smiled at him in the light of the candles that were arranged on the patio. "Fantasy? I've got a fantasy for you," she said in a sultry purr. She placed her soft lips right on his ear and whispered to him, "Do you know why I wore this dress? Because it comes off so easily," she sighed, licking his earlobe. "You can slide it right off my body, right here, and we can make love under the stars with . . ." She stopped speaking because Marcus was shaking his head no.

"That's why I have that big giant bed upstairs, Vera. If I learned nothing else from my brothers I learned this: you do it outside, you get caught. No way, Pie. Uh-uh."

Vera sat up and stared at him. "Who's going to catch us, Marcus? Nobody can see anything back here!"

"Believe me, it'll happen. I went over to Clay's house one morning to get his golf clubs and I came around the corner of the house and there he was with Bennie, right in the middle of the yard!"

"Marcus! What did he say when he saw you?"

"Are you crazy? I got out of there so fast I don't even

Melanie Schuster

think I left footprints! The only reason I'm still breathing is that to this day he has no idea I was there! One time some of us were at the house on St. Simons and I got up early to go run on the beach. When I came back, guess who was in that outdoor shower? Martin and Ceylon, that's who, and they were doing a lot more than bathing, trust me! I didn't even stop, I turned around in midstride and went right back to the beach until I figured they had time enough to cool their jets." Marcus chuckled at the memory.

Vera was fascinated as well as amused by the stories. "What about Malcolm and Selena?"

"Oh, please, I caught those two so often it wasn't funny. In his old bedroom at home, in the pool after everyone had gone to bed, in his office at the old headquarters, I swear every conversation I had with him started with 'Get a room.'" Marcus laughed and pulled Vera back into his arms. "That's why I go crashing into his office whenever I take a notion, it's my way of getting back at him for traumatizing my adolescence.

"So, beauty, I will be more than happy to take you upstairs and make love to you until we don't know our own names but it's not going to be out here. It might work for other people but in this family you get busted every time," he said with regret in his voice.

Vera was about to rebut his argument when a voice came around the corner of the house.

"What are y'all doing out here in the dark?" asked Angelique. "Why can't you answer the doorbell? I've been out there for five minutes," she said with exasperation.

Vera looked surprised while Marcus looked resigned. "See? I'm never wrong about these things, baby."

A short time later Vera and Marcus were standing in the foyer where they had just said good-bye to Angelique. She had dropped by to retrieve one of her cameras, which Marcus had borrowed to take to Jamaica. And for once in her young life, she didn't have anything mean or sarcastic to say about the fact that Vera and Marcus were obviously in love. As a matter of fact she gave every appearance of being happy for the two of them. She played with Kika and Toby for a few minutes and only Vera heard her whisper, "It's about time they hooked up. You guys can stay with me when they're on their honeymoon, okay?"

After watching for Angelique's little car to leave, Marcus took both Vera's hands and held them, then wrapped her arms around his waist while he pulled her as close to him as possible. With real regret he said softly, "It's getting late, baby."

Vera smiled and kissed the hollow at the base of his throat, a place her lips adored. "I know it is, sweetheart."

"We have to work tomorrow," he said sadly. "So you need to be getting to bed, Pie, you know how you need your sleep."

"Yes, I do," she agreed. "So I think I should be getting into bed, and so should you."

Without another word, she pulled away from Marcus and took his hand, leading him to the stairs.

"Does this mean you're staying here tonight?" Marcus said wonderingly.

"Yes, it does. Unless you think I should go home," she said, giving him a look that could have melted a glacier with its warmth. "I brought a change of clothes, and my toothbrush and I don't need jammies, so, unless you have some objection, I'm spending the night with you."

Instead of answering, Marcus simply picked her up in his strong arms and carried her into the bedroom where he deposited her on the bed with great care. He stooped to scoop up Kika and Toby and took them to the guest room on the lower level, closing the door behind him. When he returned to the bedroom, he looked like a hero who had vanquished a marauder; he was all but pounding his chest with bravado.

In his brief absence, Vera had lit several scented candles and put on a CD of love songs by Miles Davis. She was in the process of turning down the bed when Marcus returned.

"You're still dressed," he observed.

"Yes, I am. And I'm going to stay that way until you undress me," she said. "What's taking you so long?"

Marcus pulled the polo shirt over his head with one hand and undid his khaki shorts with the other, both garments leaving his body in one smooth motion. He stepped out of the shorts without breaking stride and reached Vera's side in seconds, clad only in black bikini briefs.

His swift response to her playful challenge took Vera's breath away, and so did the speed with which he removed the thin, pretty sarong. When he discovered that she wasn't wearing anything under it, it was his turn to catch his breath. He picked her up again and slid into the massive bed holding her with one arm while he used his free arm to remove his briefs, a task made more difficult by the presence of a huge erection. Vera took his face in both hands and kissed him to slow him down.

"I'm supposed to be doing that," she said with affection. "I had this whole seduction planned and you're not cooperating."

Marcus immediately stilled his frantic movements and rolled onto his back. "I'm yours, baby. Whatever you desire, I'm yours."

After removing the uncooperative briefs, Vera knelt next to Marcus and looked her fill at his long, magnificently made body, turned warm gold in the candlelight. She stroked his long torso, admiring the contrast of her brown hands against his skin. Then she surprised him by kissing his navel, lavishing it with the same thoroughness she would his mouth. Marcus groaned aloud at the sensation that resulted, the liquid fire that licked along his veins at her touch. Vera kept on kissing him while her hand sought and found his engorged sex, caressing and fondling it until Marcus reached a point of desperation.

"Vera, please, baby, please," he moaned.

Vera stopped kissing his navel long enough to move to a more sensitive part of his anatomy, which wrought an even stronger reaction from Marcus. The feel of her lips and tongue on him was driving him to the point of madness, to the point where there could be only one return. Crying her name, he found the strength to move away from her and pull her up until she was on top of him. "Baby, if you want to keep seducing tonight you need to stop for a minute or that's exactly how long this will last," he panted.

Vera didn't believe him for a second. She knew by now what Marcus was capable of and his appetite was insatiable. She rose up so that she was straddling him, driving him to the brink again and again with the slow gyrations of her hips. His eyes were half closed in pleasure as he watched her taut body raise and lower itself on his. With great difficulty he reached for a condom and put it on with Vera's assistance. Then he was ready for her, ready to take everything she was giving him, and ready to demand even more. His upward thrusts started a new rhythm, one that Vera easily matched. His hands held her hips as the spiraling sensations that signaled the inevitable explosion started rocketing through their bodies. His name became a chant on Vera's lips, a chant that culminated in a cry of pure release as she found fulfillment. In seconds it was his turn to call her name, over and over, as he joined her in ecstasy.

Vera collapsed on his chest, both sighing with satisfaction and trying to catch her breath. "Marcus . . . it just keeps getting better, doesn't it?" She kissed his chest and snuggled closer to him as he wrapped his arms around her.

"Yes, it does, baby. And it's going to keep getting better and better and better. Just think, Vera, if we were married this is how it could be every single night of our lives," he said softly.

The only answer he got was the soft, even breathing that told him Vera was asleep. He closed his eyes and inhaled the sweet fragrance of Vera's hair, the earthy muskiness of their lovemaking coupled with the scented candles, and he soon followed her into slumber.

Chapter 16

The days that followed found Marcus and Vera getting closer and closer. They spent almost every night together and every weekend, except for the weekend after they'd gone to Jamaica. That was a girls' only weekend that had been in the works for some time. That was the weekend that all the sisters-in-law, Lillian, Angelique, and Paris, were getting together to decorate and furnish the twins' bedroom at Martin and Ceylon's house.

All of the women were devoted to *Trading Spaces* and *While You Were Out*, and they decided to combine forces and create a beautiful room in two days using some of the precepts of the two shows. While they were doing this, the men, and this included Marcus, were going to the house on St. Simon's with all the children, except for the babies. Ceylon had expressed her doubts about little Elizabeth going since she was so young, but Martin scoffed at the idea of leaving her at home. Up until the morning they departed, Ceylon was ambivalent about the trip. It took Martin a while to convince her that Elizabeth might be the youngest of the girls but she was also the toughest. When Vera arrived at the house she found Martin in the act of persuading his wife that all would be well.

"Butter, baby, it'll be fine. First of all, if she stays here you all won't get a thing done for watching her. Second of all, I can take care of her, you know this. And third, she wants to go with us," he ended. "And the girls will be there to watch over her, too, although God knows they might need some protection. She's pretty rough."

They were standing in the sunny kitchen of their midtown Atlanta home and Martin had his arms wrapped around Ceylon as he ticked off each point. Ceylon admitted that he was right, but she still had misgivings. "Martin, I've never been away from her even for one night," she fretted. "And she's so little! Vera, you know what I mean!" she said, looking to her friend for support.

At that moment, Bump, Ceylon's father, entered the kitchen with Elizabeth on his back. She was wearing Oshkosh overalls and her grandfather's fishing hat and looked adorable. "Let's go, Daddy! Hurry up, we go now!" she bellowed.

Martin and Vera both looked at Ceylon, who threw up her hands. "Oh, fine then." Reaching for the little girl, she placed her on her hip and kissed her soundly. "Are you going to be a good girl for Daddy and Grampa?"

Elizabeth smiled winningly and kissed her mother back with gusto. "Yes!" she promised. "I *very* good girl. Let's go!"

Vera soon found herself upstairs surveying the bedroom that would be transformed into a place of beauty for the twins. The other women joined her to escape the chaos that reigned below. The sight of Malcolm, Martin, Clay, and Bump trying to organize a caravan with seven Deveraux children, a couple of extra pals of said children, Martin's Akita, and the excitable birthday puppy, Patrick, and all the assorted paraphernalia that was required for the weekend was downright tiring. Lillian was gamely trying to offer advice and direction while the children ran around noisily and Patrick barked incessantly. Their voices could be heard through the opened windows of the house.

Ceylon turned to Vera and smiled. "Welcome to the

family, honey. This is what you can expect for the rest of your life," she said warmly.

Vera felt the heat surge up her neck, even though she was with her dear friends. She tried to respond casually, but she was flustered. "Um, what do you mean, Ceylon?"

Ceylon grabbed Vera's hand and laughed. "I'm sorry, I wasn't trying to embarrass you! But you have to know that this is your destiny, Vera. You're going to be one of us, one of the *Deveraux wives,*" she said with a comical face.

Selena joined in the laughter. "She's right, Vera," Selena said gently. "You're in this for life, girl. Deveraux men do *not* let go once they've got you. Marcus has been crazy about you for so long, it's a done deal as far as he's concerned."

Bennie seemed to sense Vera's confusion. She looked at Vera warmly and asked her a question. "Vera, did you truly not know how Marcus felt about you all these years?"

"I really didn't, Bennie! We were such pals, you know? And there's the age thing, and the work thing . . . and I'm not his type, anyway. He never looked at a woman like me before, so I . . ." Her voice trailed off as all the women started laughing.

Bennie explained the cause for the laughter. "Honey, you are his *only* type! Marcus used to date those little skinny girls only because he couldn't have the woman of his dreams. The Deveraux men are the original 'big brown booty boys'; they like a woman who's got a real shape to her. And they like a woman with a healthy appetite, too. These men are obsessed with food, that's why they all give you some food-based nickname," she added carelessly.

Vera looked at the three women strangely. They all nodded their heads. "Clay calls me Peaches," Bennie said. Selena volunteered that Malcolm called her Cookie. Ceylon blushed and admitted that Martin's pet name for her was Butter. "So when you get named after some food, you'll know it's the real thing." Bennie laughed.

Just then, Marcus's voice boomed up the stairs. "Pie! Where are you?"

The sisters-in-law burst out laughing while Vera felt as if her head were on fire, she was blushing so hard. "That's not why he calls me Pie," she protested. "It doesn't have anything to do with food!"

Marcus entered the room with eyes only for Vera. "Baby, let me take the Cruiser to the island, there's more room in the back. You can take my car, is that okay?" Accompanying his words with a quick kiss, he dropped the keys to his BMW into her hand. Only then did he notice Bennie, Selena, and Ceylon smiling at them for all they were worth. "Okay, what's up?" he asked warily.

Ceylon spoke right up. "We were wondering why you call Vera 'Pie,'" she said nicely.

Marcus immediately answered just as nicely. "None of your business," he said cheerfully. "We've got to have *some* privacy," he reminded her. "Everybody knows too much of our stuff as it is."

Bennie and Selena immediately rubbed their tummies and sighed. Marcus could never deny a pregnant woman anything. He gave a long-suffering sigh, and then answered their unspoken query.

"Okay, if you must know, it's because she's *like* a pie. She smells as good as peach pie, she's as sweet as pecan pie, she's as sharp as a Key lime pie, and as delicate as lemon meringue. You all know that pie is my favorite dessert and Vera," he said, pulling her into his arms and kissing her neck, "is my favorite person, so she's my Pie."

Vera was too bemused to say anything. Just then a chorus of plaintive male voices alerted the women to the need for their presence and Marcus and Vera were left alone. "I always thought it was because of that sweetie-pie thing," she murmured.

Marcus didn't answer, he just looked at her with great

desire and kissed her lips, her cheek, and her neck. "I don't want to leave you," he said quietly. "I want to be with you all weekend, all week, all the time, baby."

What Vera was going to say was lost as Trey came bounding up the stairs in search of his uncle.

"Come on, Uncle Marcus, I get to ride with *you*," Trey said enthusiastically. Like most small boys he was in love with Vera's car.

They all went downstairs and joined the throng in the circular drive as last-minute hugs and kisses and admonishments were being exchanged. Ceylon and Vera each had a twin on her hip, while Marcus bemoaned the fact that Kika and Toby weren't making the trip.

Vera gave him a look and shook her head with a smile. "They've appointed themselves guardians to the twins. They seem to be fascinated with the babies and I don't think you could pry them away," she said. Sure enough, they had positioned themselves by the women's feet and were staring anxiously up at the babies, who were laughing and cooing at the little dogs.

Meanwhile, Bennie had to pat down her boys one more time to make sure that Chubby, their gerbil, wasn't hidden somewhere. Chubby had been smuggled into church, he'd been to school, to the mall, and on one memorable occasion, he had greeted Clay by leaping out of his briefcase in the middle of a big meeting. The boys were known for hiding the creature in various places to accommodate what they felt was his desire to travel.

Marcus commented on this to Clay. "You have to admit, man, that thing is indestructible," he said with a laugh. "I had no idea that gerbils were so hardy."

Clay looked at his brother with an odd expression. "He's not indestructible," he said at last, "but he is *interchangeable*."

Marcus looked horrified as the full import of what Clay was saying sank in on him.

Finally the caravan pulled off with the children distributed among the three vehicles and lots of honking and waving. Paris and Angelique had arrived with more supplies and the big transformation was ready to begin. Vera had a feeling that more than the room would be transformed by the end of the weekend; she had an idea that the women had more revelations in store for her. They all went upstairs to get started on the day's projects with no comment, however.

Lillian glanced at her watch and suggested they get a move on. "We need to get as much done as possible, girls, because you know those jokers aren't going to stay away two whole days. They'll be back here before noon tomorrow."

All the women laughed except Vera, who looked puzzled, and Paris, who had gone back downstairs to answer the doorbell. Bennie explained the cause for the laughter. "Honey, these men can't really stand to be away from home. This is a valiant attempt on their part, but they'll be back sooner than scheduled, you can bank on it. Deveraux men don't like to be away from their wives any more than they have to," she said with the supreme confidence of someone who is adored by her spouse.

Vera raised her eyebrows slightly, suddenly curious about other traits of the "Deveraux men." She knelt on the floor and began to open the small cans of paint that would be used in the mural they were painting on the wall of the nursery. Malcolm and Martin had already painted the ceiling and walls since they didn't want Bennie and Selena doing anything crazy like getting on a ladder. Finally Vera looked up at her friends and asked the question that would take all afternoon to answer.

"So what other things should I know about Deveraux men?"

* * *

In the meantime, Paris had opened the front door and found herself speechless. There in front of her was the man she'd been drooling over at TDG, the mystery man she'd seen with Martin earlier. He was tall, about six feet four, and exotically handsome in an unusual way. He had tawny skin, coarse sandy blond hair, high cheekbones, and oddly Asian looking eyes of an intense gray. Or were they blue? They kept changing in the afternoon light. He was casually dressed in jeans and a polo shirt and yet he looked as powerful and controlling as a man wearing a Savile Row tailored suit.

Paris forgot her manners completely, and had pretty much forgotten her own name, she was so captivated by what she beheld. She might have kept on staring if he hadn't spoken.

"Is your uncle at home?" The amusement in his voice and the fact that he mistook her for one of Martin's nieces jarred Paris back to reality. It also reminded her that she was wearing a pair of grubby overalls with a pink T-shirt and had her long hair in a ponytail on either side of a center part. This ensemble coupled with her pink flip-flops, and she probably looked like a gawky teenager. And sounded like one too, as she stammered a response.

"No. He's not. Home, I mean. Or my uncle," she said quickly.

To her chagrin the man looked even more amused. He passed her a large manila envelope. "Can you give this to him for me? Wait, never mind, I'll just call him later," he said easily, taking the envelope back.

Paris nodded dumbly at the same time that she reached for the envelope. She looked at her empty hand, and then looked at the man, puzzled. "Oh, that's right, you're going to call him. Right. Who shall I say is calling?" she asked breathlessly.

The man smiled again, transforming his angular, pleasant face into a thing of seductive good looks. "Tell him Titus stopped by and that I'll call him later," he instructed gently.

"Titus," repeated Paris. "Titus," she said again as she watched him go down the walk to his car, which was parked on the street.

It was a time of wonderful surprises for Vera, not the least of which was feeling like a complete woman for the first time. The power of the sensuality that Marcus had unleashed with his patient, passionate lovemaking continued to amaze Vera. Sometimes their connection was so strong that it frightened her. The intensity of their lovemaking seemed to merge them into one person. Then she would remember that this was *Marcus,* the man who loved her and treasured her and would do anything to make her life beautiful and complete. She would sometimes feel her eyes fill with tears as she realized the depth of his commitment to her. And at other times the passion he incited in her would overwhelm her.

One afternoon she was working in her office at TDG when a wave of longing for Marcus swept over her. The feeling was so poignant, so intense that it startled her. Suddenly she couldn't concentrate on anything but the sound of his voice, the feel of his skin, the touch of his hand, the moist pull of his mouth. Vera was so aroused that she began fanning herself with a manila folder as she went to the corner of her office and opened the small mahogany-fronted refrigerator. She took out a bottle of mineral water and dropped the folder in her haste to open it. She drank the entire bottle at once, gulp after chilled gulp, but it did

nothing to assuage the burning sensation the thought of
Marcus had aroused. Discarding the bottle, she left her office and walked down the hall to Marcus's suite.

RaeAnn, his assistant, smiled when she saw Vera. "He's
in there and he'll be glad to see you. He's been on conference calls all day," she said cheerily.

Vera nodded absently and tapped lightly on the door. At
Marcus's invitation she entered and closed the door behind
her. She leaned against the door and just stared at Marcus,
drinking in his solid appearance just as thirstily as she had
tossed down the icy water. And looking at him was no
more satisfying than the water had been. She needed more,
much more from the man she loved.

Marcus immediately rose from his desk and smiled at
Vera as he always did. There was never a time when he
wasn't glad to see her. He noticed right away that she
seemed flustered, which was contrary to all he knew about
his beloved. She was normally the most serene person in
the building.

"Is everything okay, Vera?" he asked with concern in his
voice. He came around his desk and held his hands out to
Vera, who, he noticed, was trembling. "What's the matter,
my heart? Did something happen?"

Vera shook her head without saying a word, then realized how idiotic she must look. "No, nothing's wrong. I
just . . . I just . . . oh, Marcus," she sighed and put her arms
around his neck.

Marcus heard the tender sigh that floated from her lips
as he put his strong, comforting arms around her body. He
didn't say anything at first, he just held her tightly. Then
he put his lips against her ear and whispered, "Is this what
you wanted, Pie?"

He was gratified to hear her answer, a throaty yes.

"Marcus, I don't know what came over me," she confessed. "I was working on next year's projections for the

show and all of a sudden I couldn't breathe, I couldn't think, all I wanted was you," she said softly. "I had to see you, to touch you, to—"

Her words were cut off as Marcus kissed her hotly and passionately. It was over much too soon and she found herself looking up into his smiling face.

"You know what I think, baby? I think we need to go away this weekend," he told her. "Let's go to St. Simon's, Vera, just the two of us. We can leave tomorrow afternoon, what do you think?"

"I think yes, my love. And I think you'd better kiss me again so I can go back to work," she said with a smile.

The trip to St. Simon's was, like everything else about those enchanted weeks, wonderful. They drove to the island with much laughter and intimate conversation, although Marcus vowed to control the CD player on the return trip. Vera's choice of music included Paul Simon's *Graceland* and the entire Steely Dan boxed set.

"You like Steely Dan, too, go on, admit it!" Vera teased him.

"Yes, I do, but not as a steady diet. And the urchins hate it, too," he added, and then glanced into the backseat where the two little dogs were sound asleep. "See? They passed out from horror. If you change that, I'll give you something nice, Pie," he offered. "Something really nice," he added in desperation.

"Anything I want?" she said cheerfully. "I might want something really extravagant," she warned him.

"*Anything,*" he said fervently. "Just take that CD out and don't put it back in!"

Vera complied immediately, inserting an Al Jarreau compilation in its place. Marcus didn't notice how deep in thought she was, he was just glad not to hear any more of Steely Dan's esoteric lyrics.

When they got to the island, Marcus unpacked the car in record time, and Vera insisted on fixing him a nice dinner. They ate on the deck, cleaned up the kitchen together, and spent the evening making slow, languorous love as they expressed their happiness at being together. It was turning into the perfect weekend; they ran on the beach every morning, they cooked wonderful meals together and talked for hours when they weren't making love.

The morning before they were to leave the island, Vera mentioned that she'd left something outside and went to get it. Marcus nodded absently as she spoke; he was reading the instructions for his new cell phone, one of the ones with a digital camera built into it. Marcus loved gadgets of all kinds, the more complicated and expensive, the better he liked them. He was completely engrossed until he heard Vera call his name, and he went to see what she wanted. When he reached the back door he saw the most amazing thing he'd ever witnessed; Vera was standing in the morning sun wearing a seductive smile and not another stitch.

"Marcus, does this ensemble give you any ideas? Any at all?" she asked innocently.

Marcus was out the door in a flash, his eyes huge and filled with lust. Vera was damned incredible, that was the only way to describe her. Her taut brown body with its lush curves was right out there in the open in front of God and everybody, he couldn't believe it. He loved looking at every inch of her form, but to be in the great outdoors like that was crazy!

"Vera, baby, are you nuts? What are you doing? Anybody in the world could see you!"

Vera walked over to Marcus and stretched her body in the most provocative manner possible. "No, they can't, Marcus. I've been scouting around here every morning when we went out to run and there is no one who can possibly see back here." She walked closer to him, sliding her hands under his T-shirt and stroking his back suggestively. "And this feels amazing, Marcus. Like when we were in Jamaica, remember? It's wonderful and I want you to try it. Besides, you said I could have anything I want and what I want is a nice long shower with you in that lovely shower stall," she said, looking at the infamous shower enclosure.

By now, Marcus wasn't listening to her words; he had kicked off his sandals and was stepping out of his jeans. He stripped off the T-shirt and cast it to the side, then pulled Vera against him for a slow, wet kiss that went on for a long time while the fresh morning air blew across their bare bodies. With a groan deep in his throat he walked Vera backward into the shower and in no time the warm water was cascading over them as they lathered each other with the Vitabath that Vera had previously placed in the enclosure. His hands rubbed over Vera's slick wet body in slow, sensual circles while she returned the favor, sliding over his muscular chest and down his hips while they continued to kiss each other.

"Vera, we've got to get one of these at home, baby. As soon as possible," he said in a voice thick with passion.

Vera wanted to agree with him but she couldn't get the words out. His hands were driving her to a point of sublime arousal unlike anything she'd yet experienced. Just then his long fingers began an even more intimate exploration of her feminine recesses, which made any kind of conversation impossible. She clung to Marcus and cried out her release, crying with happiness and collapsing against him. As the last convulsive shivers coursed through her, Marcus pulled her even closer to him as he turned off the shower and picked her up in his arms for the few steps it would take them to reach the house. She heard Marcus concede, in a husky whisper, that there was definitely something to be said about making love with nothing but nature around them. She buried her face in his neck, still damp from the shower, and agreed from the bottom of her heart.

Even before Marcus had declared himself to Vera, the summer months were a never-ending parade of events for the Deveraux family. Cookouts, parties, and celebrations of all kinds abounded. Bennie's birthday was on July 1, followed by the annual company cookout for the Fourth of July. It was normally held on the Saturday before the Fourth so that people who planned to leave town for the holiday wouldn't miss out. By then it was rather apparent to TDG employees that Vera and Marcus's close friendship had progressed to a more personal level but no one was crazy enough to comment on it. They all valued their jobs. There weren't any overt gestures or words that gave them away at work, but everyone seemed to know that these two were a couple.

An event like the cookout served to remove any doubt from anyone's mind as to their status. Marcus and Vera worked together at the buffet tables making sure that everyone was served. They looked and acted as much like a married couple as any of the other Deveraux couples. And realistically, most of the longtime employees of the company had been expecting it anyway. They felt it was only a matter of time before they found each other, and seeing the two of them at the party laughing together and even exchanging a quick kiss seemed only natural, just like it was natural that Marcus do something splendid for Vera's birthday.

Vera's Fourth of July birthday was a special one, since it was her fortieth and the first time she would celebrate it with Marcus. The last three birthdays had gone by with virtually no celebration as she just hadn't wanted to bother after John's death. Now, though, she was feeling nothing but joy and Marcus wanted to do something to enhance that happiness. He asked her how she wanted to celebrate, and she wasn't sure.

"I guess we could go out to dinner or something. Maybe we could go to Savannah or New Orleans for the weekend. I don't really need anything but your company for a celebration, sweetheart. As long as we're together, I'm happy," she said honestly.

Marcus acted as though he were taking careful note of everything she was saying, but he had his own agenda as she found out on the Fourth. He took her over to Bennie and Clay's house and she walked out into their enormous backyard to find her parents, her sisters, Danny, Neesha, and Regina all waiting for her, as well as Paris, Aidan and his partner Sebastian, and a host of other friends. Her mouth flew open with shock, and happy tears immediately started flowing. "Marcus! I can't believe you did this," she cried.

"Hey, what good is having a company plane if you can't make your beloved happy?" he asked rhetorically.

The party was the most wonderful she could ever remember, and it turned into a wonderful weekend. Everyone stayed over the holiday with the exception of her parents, who drove to Birmingham, Alabama, the next afternoon to visit with Vivian's mother. Odalia had surprised everyone by deciding to move back to Birmingham after her mother, Vera's Big Mama, had passed away. She lived in a lively and active senior citizens' community and seemed to be thriving, but Vivian worried about her nonetheless. As Birmingham was so close, it would have been foolish not to visit. Everyone had a marvelous time, even the reticent Alexis and the ebullient Tanya, who seemed more like the sweet younger sister she used to be before she started dating her current boyfriend whose main ambition seemed to be thuggery. The children had an especially wonderful time racing around like puppies and playing loud, noisy games.

Marcus also took that opportunity to point out that his nieces and nephews were all nuts. "Look Vera. Look at Trey over there dancing his butt off. I told you he was crazy, they all are."

Vera looked at Trey, who was wearing headphones and was indeed dancing with mad abandon. "So he's dancing, what's so crazy abut that?" she asked, puzzled.

Marcus pointed at the oblivious child and made Vera look, too. "What's he dancing *to*, Pie?"

Sure enough, the headphones weren't connected to anything except the music in Trey's head. The connector was trailing along the ground and Trey was moving to his own beat. "I told you, they're all crazy, so don't worry about not being able to make more of them. Let's just get married and be happy, damn it." He kissed her hard and long, making it unnecessary to answer at the moment.

The presents were many and wonderful, too many in Vera's opinion. But none were as memorable as the ones Marcus gave her. The two of them were alone in Bennie's solarium as he presented her with a beautiful gift bag that was full of enchantingly wrapped things. The first gift took her breath away. It was *The Storyteller*, the first figurine of the Thomas Blackshear series, the rarest one that was impossible to find. Somehow, Marcus had located it for her. After Danny had gotten her started on collecting the pieces Marcus had the joy of presenting her with a new piece for special occasions. It was a joy he wanted for himself alone, too. He was known to get quite irritated if someone else gave her a Blackshear piece. He enjoyed the look of awed surprise on Vera's face when she realized what he'd given her.

"Marcus, my goodness, I don't believe it! Oh, baby, this is so wonderful! Wait until Danny sees this, he won't believe it!" Vera said happily.

"Oh, he'll believe it, he's the one who tracked it down for me," Marcus admitted. Danny had actually found the first *three* statues of the series; the other two would be given as Christmas gifts. He smiled to himself as he tried to picture her reaction. "C'mon, Pie, you're getting behind. There's more stuff in there," Marcus reminded her.

Vera continued to investigate her gifts. There was a year's worth of gift certificates to the spa she frequented, and gift cards to her favorite stores, Target, Bed Bath & Beyond, and Pier One Imports. Her favorite fragrance from The Thymes was presented in candles, soap, body crème, bath gel, and Eau de Parfum. Three sets of exquisitely sheer and feminine lingerie by La Perla, the maker that she favored. Vera was known to pinch pennies on everything else but she had a weakness for expensive underwear.

She was sighing with happiness as she examined each item. "Marcus, this is lovely, it's so wonderful," she said tearfully. Vera always cried on happy occasions.

Marcus lifted her into his lap and kissed her tears away. "You're not through yet. Keep going, Pie."

Vera reached into the bag and took out a small box that looked like it held jewelry. Sure enough, there were a pair of amazing earrings, three diamonds graduated in size that hung in a delicate tier to light up her face with their sparkle. And if that weren't enough, there was a matching necklace with three stones, the smallest of which had to be at least three-quarters of a karat. The largest stone was easily a karat and a half. Vera bent her head so that Marcus could fasten the shining eighteen-karat chain about her neck. She looked into Marcus's eyes and sighed with happiness. "You spoil me," she whispered.

"I *love* you," he countered.

"And I love you," she answered fervently. The kiss might have gone on forever if it hadn't been for the appearance of Tanya, who'd come in search of her. "Come cut the cake, girl, we're waiting on you. Wow, check out all this loot! Ooh, Marcus, don't you have another cousin or brother somewhere for me?" she exclaimed.

Marcus laughed. "I've got tons of cousins, but I'm the last of the Atlanta Deveraux brothers and we're all taken, I'm afraid."

Tanya inspected the thoughtful, expensive, and highly personal array of gifts and looked at Vera with new respect. "I may have to let you school me, girl. You seem to have some skills," she said with awe in her voice.

Vera immediately got off Marcus's lap and led her back out to the party, shaking her head. "Tanya, girl, what am I going to do with you?" she muttered.

Marcus and Vera were inseparable, doing everything together including attending the wedding of one of his dear friends, Cassandra Bourdon. He'd promised her for years that he would sing at her wedding and now the time had come to make good on his promise. The wedding rehearsal was on a Friday, the day before the wedding, and Vera accompanied him. There was also going to be the traditional rehearsal dinner that they were to attend. Marcus had warned her beforehand that she was going to meet his best friends from high school and that there was no telling what they might say or do. "Just remember they're all crazy as road lizards so don't pay them attention. Actually, they kind of remind me of your sisters," he said with a grin.

Vera laughed. "Well, we should get along famously then."

She almost changed her tune after entering the church.

Among the participants of the rehearsal were three stunning women who had to be the bridesmaids, and naturally, the bride herself, who was also quite lovely. Vera took a seat near the back of the church, hoping to be unnoticed, but no such luck. As they waited for the wedding director to arrive, as well as some of the groomsmen, the four women made a beeline for Vera while Marcus was going over music with the pianist. Vera found herself surrounded with one woman on each side and two on the pew in front of her, turned around so they could get a good long look. She was fervently glad to be looking her very best in a white strapless sheath with a bolero jacket that showed off every curve.

Vera smiled in spite of herself. There was certainly no shame in their game. "I'm Vera," she said to break the ice.

A slender, dark-skinned woman with shoulder-length dreads nodded and said that she was Suzie. The woman to Vera's left had a creamy complexion, thick shoulder-length curls, and announced that she was Camille. The woman on her right was tawny and freckled with stylishly cut red hair that looked natural. She smiled and said, "I'm Sophronia, but call me Sophie, please." Vera nodded and turned her eyes to the pew again. The only one of the four left was undoubtedly the bride. "I'm Cassandra, in case you haven't figured that out." Cassandra was about Vera's complexion with long, rich brown hair and a pretty, dimpled smile. "Sorry to be so bold." she said, not sounding sorry at all. "But we had to come check you out. Marcus was like our brother in high school and we had to meet the woman who won his heart," she said frankly.

Vera couldn't help it, she giggled. "Okay, so do I pass?"

They all looked her up and down and nodded as one. "Oh, yes, definitely. We saw you walk in with that Jessica Rabbit body and we could see what Marcus saw in you, all right," Suzie said artlessly. "But Marcus was not like *my* brother in high school. I spent four years lusting after him. *I* was supposed to be Mrs. Marcus Deveraux," she said, looking Vera dead in the eyes.

Vera didn't even blink. Suzie was just trying to give her a hard time and all the women knew it. Vera was more than equal to the challenge, though. With a smile she said, "Aww. Sucks to be you, doesn't it? I'd say I'm sorry, but I'd be lying. But fine as you are, I know your dance card is full. Just pick the best one and put the rest of them out of their misery, honey."

All four of the women burst out laughing and gave each other high fives. Vera had apparently passed some kind of test, because they all started chatting as if they'd known her for years. By the time Marcus made it back to their little corner they looked like old friends. "Okay, what are you harpies up to? Are you corrupting my lady and telling her things that may have no basis in fact?" he demanded.

Camille was happy to answer him. "No, we're telling her the truth, like the fact that we were all your prom dates," she said cheerfully.

Marcus reddened along his cheekbones and pulled at his collar. "Okay, that's enough ancient history for one night. You better tell me what you want me to sing or I'll get up there and do 'YMCA,' " he threatened Cassandra.

" 'Your Precious Love' is our favorite song. And 'Amazing Love,' " she said breathlessly.

Marcus looked disgusted. "Those are duets, nitwit. Who would you like me to sing them with?"

Cassandra looked sad for a moment. "I was really looking forward to hearing those songs," she sighed. "Okay, I'll pick something else. Unless you happen to sing, too?" she asked, looking at Vera with hope in her eyes.

When Marcus and Vera let go with "Your Precious Love" at the wedding the next day, there was total, awed silence, to be followed by sighs of appreciation when they

Melanie Schuster

did "Amazing Love.'" They proved so popular that Cassandra begged them to sing one more at the reception, which they were happy to do. As the dancing started they took the microphone and sang "Let It Be Me,'" which happened to be one of Vera's favorite songs. As their magnificent voices caressed the lyrics, their eyes caressed each other with such naked passion that the rest of the room seemed to disappear. It was just Marcus and Vera, pledging their love for an eternity.

That same dreamy sensation carried over as they left the reception and went to Vera's house. They'd found that if they were careful, they could actually get through a night in her much smaller bed. In the kitchen Vera was preparing something cold for them to drink when Marcus began speaking.

"Vera, you see how happy Cassandra and her husband were tonight? That could be us, baby, you and me. When are you going to say yes?"

Vera was so intent on her tasks that she missed the wistfulness in his voice. "Marcus, I think you want a wedding more than you want a marriage," she said thoughtlessly. "I think you love me, but I also think you just want what your brothers have," she added. She looked up in time to see fury all across Marcus's face.

"Damn, Vera, this isn't some kind of game I'm playing with you! Of course I want what my brothers have, they have happy homes, beautiful wives, and they have loving marriages. Those are good things, Vera, the only good things in the world. Why wouldn't a sane man want that?

"But that's not the point here, is it? You're just not taking me seriously, Vera. I've given you my heart over and over again and you're still acting like this is some kind of fling. I can't take it much longer, Vera. I can't."

Vera dropped the glass she had in her hand as she watched him abruptly leave the room. With a silent prayer for guidance, she went after him, finding him standing in the living room, anger and pain radiating off him like heat from a sunlamp.

"Marcus, my darling, I apologize," she said softly. "I think it's time I told you something," she said as she took his arm and led him over to the sofa. They sat down and Vera turned so that she was facing him, curling her legs under her as she did so.

"Do you remember when we went to the Black Ski Summit a few years ago?" she asked.

Marcus looked confused at the rapid change of subject. "Yeah, five or six years ago, sure, but what has that got to do with anything?" he said bleakly.

"Just hear me out," she pleaded. "We had all gone up there to cover the event for *Image* magazine and I was the only one who could ski. I kept telling you to stay on the bunny slope but you were bound and determined to ski the same slope as me and you ended up spraining your ankle, remember? And while everyone else was at the big party that night, I took pity on you and stayed with you in your suite until you fell asleep," she recalled, her eyes misty with the memory.

"I was getting ready to go back to my suite and I wanted to make sure you were all covered up. So I pulled the blanket up and I was standing there watching you sleep and you were the most beautiful thing I'd ever seen," she said with a slight catch in her voice. "I leaned over and kissed you, Marcus. I kissed you, knowing it was wrong, knowing that I was another man's wife, that nothing could ever come of it. But for that moment you were all mine and I kissed you because I knew I was in love with you," she said so softly he almost didn't hear her.

"That's right, Marcus. I was in love with you and I knew it. I knew it was wrong, but I wanted you so badly I couldn't think. I had feelings for you that I should only have for my husband, but I didn't have that kind of love for him anymore, it had just died away over the years from indifference and his infidelity," she said, dashing away the tears that were now coursing down her cheeks.

Marcus sat perfectly still during her words, not daring to move a muscle. "When John died I was torn up inside from sheer guilt, because of my feelings for you. Before he went to California, he had come to me and asked me for another chance to make our marriage what it should be. He begged me to set aside all the hurts and disappointments and arguments and start fresh. Incredible as it seems," she said with a bitter laugh, "John had fallen for me all over again, so he said. And I hesitated, Marcus. I told him I would give him an answer later, but there wasn't a later because he was killed. I didn't give him the answer he wanted because of my love for you. I didn't have a whole heart to give him because I had given part of my heart away to you, and you never knew it, I could never, ever tell you," she sobbed.

Marcus couldn't stand it anymore, he put her on his lap and held her, murmuring endearments and confessing his love. Vera wasn't finished, though. "That's why I haven't given you an answer, Marcus. I'm afraid. This means so much to me, darling, it means more than you could ever know. I couldn't take it if something went wrong between us, if we were to get married and not be happy with each other. This is the most important thing I've ever done and I can't mess it up, Marcus. I just can't."

By now Kika and Toby had discovered their humans were home and were expressing their concern over Vera's state with frantic whines and barks and in Toby's case, a heroic leap onto the sofa. Marcus continued to rock Vera for a few minutes, then called for silence. "Pipe down, you two, I'm about to say something profound and I want my beloved to hear every word." Amazingly, both dogs quieted at once.

"Vera, my heart, those were the most beautiful words anyone's every spoken to me and the fact that they came from your lips makes them all the sweeter. My beauty, you can't possibly be afraid that I'll stop loving you, or that some other person could ever take my attention away from you for a second. You're the only woman I've ever wanted, the only one I've ever loved, and that's not going to change. Not now, not ever. Just let me love you, Vera, and I'll prove it to you, every day, in every way," he vowed.

Vera's tears had slowed to the occasional hiccup. "God, I must look a mess," she said self-consciously.

Marcus agreed. "You've looked better. But you still look beautiful to me. Are we going to church tomorrow? Because if we are, I think we need to get some sleep. At least one of us does," he amended as Vera gave a huge yawn against his shoulder. She told him she definitely planned on going to the service the next morning, and gasped as Marcus swung her up in his arms. He carried her upstairs and helped her undress. She was asleep as soon her head hit the pillow, although it took Marcus a lot longer to drop off. He had too much to think about, too much to process to succumb to slumber at that point. But when he did fall asleep, it was with a smile on his face and Vera in his arms.

Church service the next morning proceeded as always. Vera and Marcus sat together on the pew with Lillian and Bump at the other end. Paris was in attendance, although there was no sign of Angelique. Clay and Malcolm were ushering and Selena's choir was singing. It was a peaceful calm morning of renewal, disturbed only slightly when Trey appeared at the end of the aisle with the twins in tow. Without a word, little Martin stepped on everyone's feet as he made his way down to Vera, joined in seconds by little Malcolm. Martin looked at her with no remorse and reported that his mother had put him out of Sunday school class. This was a fairly normal occurrence. At least once a month his high spirits made it necessary to send him upstairs. His milder-mannered twin would come too, in a show of solidarity. They always sought out Vera and Marcus, sensing that these two were the least likely to give them a swat.

So that Sunday, like so many others, found Vera with little Marty sprawled across her lap, sound asleep, while little Malcolm leaned against Marcus's side also deep in slumber. She blotted the beads of perspiration from Marty's brown forehead and watched his deep, even breathing. A feeling came over her that was indescribable, except to say that she felt completely protected and loved. Marcus was beside her, his arm thrown across the back of the pew as always, just close enough for her to feel its protective warmth. He loved her, his family loved her, and she loved them all, too, but especially him, her Marcus. She turned to him and during the last part of the sermon she looked at him intently and said one word. "Yes."

The love on Marcus's face was as complex as the emotions she was feeling. She would have expected him to look proud, triumphant, or smug, but all she could see in his eyes was a fierce joy and a profound happiness. His hand rose to caress the back of her neck and she felt his big thumb stroke the vulnerable bump at the top of her spine. Just once, one tiny touch, but it spoke volumes. Marcus gently removed his hand and smiled at Vera. No other words were necessary. There were none that could express his joy at the moment. At last, the deepest dream of his heart was going to come true. The words hadn't been invented that would tell of his happiness. The only thing that would suffice was a prayer.

* * *

After church service was over, Vera and Marcus went over to Bump and Lillian's house for brunch. Marcus hadn't really reacted to her acceptance of his proposal, other than letting his joy radiate all over his face. It was just as well, too, since the way he wanted to react couldn't have been demonstrated in a church parking lot without causing a major scandal. But he never let go of her hand from the time they left the church; their hands clung as if glued together. When they reached the house, Marcus pulled out his cell phone, the new one that took pictures, and consulted the time.

"You think your parents are home from church yet?" he asked Vera.

"Absolutely," she answered. "Daddy likes to go to the early service in the summer so I know they're home by now. Why do you ask?"

Instead of responding, Marcus hit the speed dial for the Clarks' number and greeted her mother affectionately when she answered the phone. He asked her to get Gordon and to get on-line with their computer.

Vivian, bless her heart, didn't ask any questions, she just got Vera's father and accessed the Internet while Gordon and Marcus talked. By the time everything was set up to Marcus's specifications, he and Vera were in the back-yard surrounded by family.

Looking directly into the camera, he said, "I didn't want you all to miss this. As you know, there's only been one love in my life. I've been in love with Vera for a long, long time, and God has given me the gift of her love in return. Today Vera has given me the extreme honor of allowing me to love her unconditionally for the rest of our lives. She finally said yes, and we're going to be married."

While tears of joy filled Vera's eyes, he reached into

his pocket and pulled out a distinctive Tiffany's blue box. He handed the phone to Bennie, who was nearest, so she could keep the camera on the couple while he opened the box and slipped the ring onto Vera's finger.

"Mr. and Mrs. Clark, I graduated with honors from two very good schools but right now I don't remember enough words to say how happy this has made me. Thank you again for entrusting me with your daughter and rest assured that from now on, nothing in this world is more important to me that her happiness." Marcus never took his eyes from Vera's as he made this lovely speech.

Vera meanwhile was beyond teary-eyed, she was crying with joy. "Marcus, you already make me so happy I can't see straight. It's my turn to show you how much your love means to me, and to promise you that I'm going to give you the same love and care that you've always given me. I love you with all my heart, Marcus, and I can't wait until we're man and wife," she said.

They went into each other's arms and held each other tightly while everyone sighed and more than a few wiped tears from their eyes. The children were less enthralled with the goings-on.

"Why is everybody so excited?" Trey asked Amariee.

"Because Uncle Marcus and Aunt Vera are getting married," she sighed.

"I thought they already were," Trey said indifferently. "They make pretty eyes at each other all the time and Uncle Marcus always wants to kiss her. *All* the time," he added in awe. He still didn't get the kissing business, although his parents did it constantly.

"Well, they're getting married for real," Jilleyin said with satisfaction. "I'll bet we get to be in it, too!"

By now the family had surged around the happy couple and congratulations and hugs and kisses were the order of the day, from everyone except Angelique, who stood slightly apart from the rest of the family. She had joined the group from the pool house behind Bump and Lillian's house, which was where she lived, and had arrived just in time to hear the big announcement. Her expression was unreadable; she merely stood and watched the joy without speaking.

Chapter 17

Marcus had no idea that life could be this sweet. Ever since the Sunday morning when Vera had turned to him and said the word that changed his life forever, he'd been walking on air. There were still details to be worked out, like when the wedding would be and how big an affair it would be, but those were mere details. For now it was enough to know that Vera was wearing his ring and that they would be man and wife in the very near future. He woke up in the morning with a smile on his face, mostly because he was waking up next to the woman he adored, but also because everything else was working just the way it was supposed to.

He'd had to deliver some disappointing news to Darnell, but he could still feel good about how he'd done it. Darnell's big proposal concerned casino gambling in Mississippi. He had a great opportunity to take over a casino there and he was looking for investors. Marcus wasn't particularly taken with the idea, as he wasn't a big enthusiast of gaming. When he was in college his older brothers would kidnap him for the weekend and they'd go to Atlantic City or Vegas for a prizefight. They would usually stroll the casinos while they were in town.

Once in a while they would play a game of baccarat or blackjack, but nothing more. Clay was the only one who was really proficient at it and he considered it a big waste of time for a rich man and frankly dangerous for a poor one. Marcus had gotten it ingrained in his head that gambling wasn't worth the risk of losing hard-earned money. He didn't have any argument with casino gambling, but he wasn't about to invest in it. But he told Darnell that he'd present the proposal to the brothers to see what their opinion was in the matter. As he guessed, they were all opposed. As much as they liked Darnell personally, the prospect wasn't one in which The Deveraux Group had any interest. With sincere regrets, Marcus explained to Darnell that the project wasn't one that the family wanted to take on.

The two men were in Marcus's plush office when Marcus gave him the news. Darnell looked disappointed, but he quickly rallied. "Not a problem, man. Maybe we can work together on something in the future, how about it?"

Marcus agreed readily. "You know it. I miss working with you, Darnell. If you ever get tired of being the big-time club owner and restaurateur, look me up. You could have made it big in the publishing world if you'd stayed," he added generously.

Darnell shrugged. "Well, you live, you learn. I like being my own boss, calling the shots, you know," he said modestly.

Just then Tami buzzed Marcus to announce that Vera was waiting to see him. "Send her in by all means," he said.

Vera entered the office looking like a cover model in a chic, trim-fitting suit, her hair becomingly tousled in a new style, and surrounded by the faint fragrance that Marcus thought of as her signature. After greeting Darnell, she turned to Marcus. "I'm sorry to interrupt, but my friend Mariel called me from the television station. Look at this," she said with a smile. She picked up the remote control from Marcus's desk and changed the station. The three of them watched in fascination as a forlorn little boy sat on the steps of what appeared to be an inner city apartment building. Marcus's voice was heard as a voice-over, intoning, "When does a man stop being a man? When he stops taking care of his own."

The sixty-second spot went on to talk about the need for parents to support their children not only financially, but also with caring. The Children's Coalition hot line number scrolled across the bottom of the screen as Marcus himself appeared in the last frame. "Being a man means acting like a man. Take care of your children, it's the right thing to do."

Vera applauded with gusto, to Marcus's embarrassment. "Oh, man, do I look like an idiot?" he asked no one in particular.

Vera assured him he did not. "You look authoritative and very handsome, doesn't he, Darnell?"

Darnell had to agree. "Yeah, man, I hate to admit it, but you look good up there. Next thing I know you'll be running for office. Senator Deveraux, Governor Deveraux, what's it gonna be?" he said laughingly.

Marcus stood up and embraced Vera. "It's going to be Mr. and Mrs. Deveraux very soon, and that's about the limit of my ambition for the time being," he said, smiling down at Vera.

Darnell reacted at once to the news. He stood up and said, "Well, congratulations, my brother. And best wishes to your future bride. Do I get a hug, too?" he asked, holding out his arms.

Marcus gave a long-suffering sigh and released Vera. "Well, if you insist," he said in a martyred voice and threw his arms around Darnell.

"Cut it out, fool, you know I meant your fiancée, not you!" Darnell sputtered.

"Oh," said Marcus innocently. "Well, in that case, ab-

solutely not, keep your big meat hooks where they are."
Only Vera knew that he really wasn't kidding, no matter
how jovial he sounded. He didn't go for people putting
their hands on his wife-to-be, old friend or not. She waved
good-bye to Darnell and left the office quickly, using a
meeting as an excuse. The two men watched her exit, both
admiring the graceful sway of her hips as she walked.

"Deveraux," said Darnell slowly, "you are about the
luckiest man on the face of the earth."

Marcus, savoring the slight fragrance that Vera left behind, had to agree.

Vera's reaction to being engaged was slightly different
from Marcus's. She was the one who had to do all the planning and strategizing, after all. She had anticipated a tiny,
tasteful wedding, but that seemed to be an impossible
dream on her part. It was going to be a huge affair from the
looks of things. Everyone who had any connection to the
couple at all wanted to be involved and she simply didn't
have the heart to say no. Especially after her conversation
with Angelique, who had come to her office the day after
the announcement.

Angelique had peeked around the door and asked if
Vera was busy. "No, honey, I'm not. Even if I was, I'll always have time for you. What can I do for you, Angel?"

Angelique entered the office and refused a seat. She
wandered around looking at the photographs on Vera's
walls. Vera had, in lieu of expensive artwork, enlarged and
framed copies of special covers of *Image, Praise,* and *Personal Space* magazines. Angelique paused in front of
Vera's very favorite, the portrait of Bump and Ceylon that
had graced the Christmas issue of *Image* a few years before. It was taken not too long after Bump and Ceylon had

found out that he was her birth father, and the love and joy in their expressions was wonderful to behold.

Angelique stared at the portrait for a long moment, then finally slumped on the end of Vera's couch, looking, of all things, diffident and humble. She cleared her throat a few times; then she spoke. "Vera, I wanted you to know that I'm very happy about you and Marcus," she said in a near whisper.

Vera was struck by Angelique's tone of voice and rose from her desk to go sit with her on the couch. "Why, thank you, sweetie-pie. I love your brother very, very much and I want to make him happy for the rest of his life," she confided.

Angelique looked at Vera as if to say, "So what else is new?" but she smiled wanly and replied in the same little voice, "Aww, Vera, he's been crazy about you for years and years. Even *I* knew it and I'm not known for being perceptive, just for being a bitch."

Before Vera could protest, Angelique hurried on. "I know I'm not a very nice person, but can I ask you a favor? Can I be in your wedding? I've never even been to any of my brothers' weddings. Malcolm and Selena eloped, so nobody got to see it. I was being a bitch to Bennie when she and Clay got married, as you well know since you took my place in that wedding. And I was feeling sorry for myself when Martin and Ceylon got married and I left town. I just realized that I never even saw any of them get married and I thought that if you didn't mind, maybe . . . maybe . . ." Her voice stopped as Vera moved over on the sofa to give her a big hug.

"Angel, I want you to be my maid of honor, sweetie! And don't you ever let me hear you call yourself the b-word again, I won't have it. You're very special to Marcus and to me. To the whole family, honey, even if you don't realize it. Of course you're going to be in my wedding! And I'm going to need your help with a lot of things, too, so I'm going to keep you busy! Are you up for it?"

The smile that Angelique gave Vera was one of pure happiness. "Yes, I am! When do we get started?"

In a couple of weeks the troops had been mobilized and the production was under way. Neesha, who in addition to managing the Hair Gallery was a professional event co-ordinator, was in charge of the decor and invitations, assisted by Aidan, who had volunteered for the job. Paris and Angelique were planning the bridal shower and the bridesmaids' luncheon, and Angelique was also chronicling everything photographically. She had taken Marcus and Vera's engagement pictures and they were without a doubt the best portraits Vera had ever had made. Alan Jay, the head fashion photographer for *Image,* would be shooting the wedding, however; Angelique would be much too busy to assume that task.

Vivian and Gordon spent a huge amount of time in Atlanta helping Vera move her things into Marcus's home. She had decided to keep the carriage house and lease it out, reasoning that a sale would bring her a finite amount of money, but the rent would provide an income. Gordon and Bump insisted on providing the rehearsal dinner and the bar, since Vera and Marcus were paying for everything else. He and Bump got along like a house afire, as did Lillian and Vivian. They enjoyed each other's company so much that the four of them made plans to spend the holidays together, with Thanksgiving in Michigan and Christmas in Atlanta.

Carmen and Toni were perfectly happy at being hostesses for the wedding. Vera admitted to being just superstitious enough not to want to have the same attendants for her second wedding as her first. That meant none of the Clark girls could participate, which was fine with the two older sisters. Her younger sisters, though, had a different reaction. They made their displeasure known when Vera came home to Saginaw to strategize with Danny and Neesha. Danny had agreed to direct the wedding, although Vera also insisted that he stand up for her. He whined and wailed and threatened, but she was implacable. He was her best friend and he was going to be at that altar with her if she had to make him the ring bearer.

"So you just gonna kick us to the curb, huh? You know that's not right, Vera. I can't even believe you're not going to let me be in your little raggedy wedding," Tanya said, sniffing.

Alexis didn't say much, but her anger was clearly visible under a thin veneer of icy politeness. Vera sighed deeply and tried once again to reason with her siblings. "Look, you two were both in my wedding to John. I do place all my faith in God to make things right in my life, but I want this to be a clean slate, girls, and that means nothing from the first marriage into the second marriage. The only thing that's going to be the same is Daddy walking me down the aisle. But this time Mommy will also walk with me, so that will make it different. Besides, as hostesses you get to mix and mingle with everybody and there's going to be all kinds of people there. People in the music business, the movies, politics. Marcus and I know all kinds of folks," she said casually.

It was enough to get Tanya to thinking and even Alexis was slightly mollified. "And I don't have to remind you that there are a whole passel of fine Deveraux cousins from Louisiana who will be there as well. And quite a few professional athletes, too. So could you two please do me the honor of being my hostesses and making sure that everything runs smoothly for me? You know you're each getting a new outfit out of it and you get to pick them yourselves. I don't care what you wear as long as they're bronze in color," she reminded them.

They were all grouped around Vivian's dining room table with fabric swatches, wedding books, and books of floral designs piled everywhere. Paris and Angelique were also in attendance. Angelique was being more vivacious and cooperative than Vera had ever seen her. She had come along not only to help with the planning, but to take more photographs of Danny's house in the "before" stages as the series about his remodeling was going to launch in the January issue of *Personal Space*.

Paris had come to assist Vera and to assist on the shoot, but she had an ulterior motive for being in Saginaw. She was trying to work up the nerve to get Danny to cut her hair. After the encounter with Titus Argonne, she decided to make sure she looked her age at all times. And she also wanted to make sure that Titus would be at the wedding. She broached the subject to Vera.

"Vera, that friend of Martin, that Titus Argonne, is he on the guest list?" she asked in what she hoped was a casual voice.

"I'm sure he is," Vera answered while she and Neesha were looking over and rejecting decorating themes. "If he isn't, it sounds like you'd like me to put him there," she said gently.

Paris looked at Vera full in the face then, and started asking questions. "Who is this guy, anyway? Is he married? Is he straight? Where did he come from? What's he like? What are his interests? What—"

Vera looked at Paris then, a smile of amusement on her face. "Slow down, girl! I've met him on more than a few occasions, and I know he's very intelligent, extremely intelligent, as a matter of fact. He has a good sense of humor, the quiet, dry kind. I don't think he's married, but I could be wrong. He has very nice manners and he's very, very good at being an investigator. And that, sugar-pie, is all I know about the man. You'll have to launch an investigation of your own, I guess." Vera laughed as she turned back to the books with Neesha.

The look of determination on Paris's face said that she was going to do that very thing and as soon as possible.

With everyone working like galley slaves, the wedding was taking shape in an indecently short amount of time. It was going to be held in November, the week before Thanksgiving. Angelique would be the maid of honor and Lillian the matron, with Paris, Neesha, Regina, Ceylon, Bennie, and Selena as bridesmaids, as well as Sara, Toni's daughter, and Carmen's two daughters. And Marcus's nieces, Amariee, Jilleyin, and Jasmine, would be junior bridesmaids along with Tanya's little girl. Danny would be at the altar but he would be one of the groomsmen. Trey was in charge of rolling out the white carpet on which Vera would walk, and the twins would be the ring bearers. Everyone felt there was safety in numbers and that Malcolm would influence Marty to behave. The wedding was going to be huge, bigger than huge, but Vera couldn't have cared less. This was a celebration, darn it, and it *needed* to be huge.

It was amazing what had been accomplished in such a short time. Vera and Selena were on their way to meet the other bridesmaids for a final fitting and Selena remarked that people were going to think that Vera was in the family way due to the speed of the nuptials. Vera gave an ironic laugh at that remark. She wasn't hurt by it, she knew Selena meant no harm. "Well, honey, they'd be dead wrong about that one, now, wouldn't they? There's no baby to be had here!" she said jauntily, although Selena detected a tiny pang in her voice.

Selena immediately apologized. But as a friend and a very qualified OB-GYN, she did have a suggestion. "Vera, that was so thoughtless of me! I'm so sorry I said that. But as long as I've got one foot in my mouth, I want to ask you if you've ever considered more testing. There are all kinds of things that can be done these days to help you conceive. Your diagnosis, the 'nonspecific ovarian failure' thing, that's considered very old school these days. I would be happy to act as your physician if you'd feel comfortable with it, but if not I can recommend some fertility specialists who are tops in their field."

Vera felt a faint stirring with which she was unfamiliar, a stirring of hope. Squashing it down quickly, she thanked Selena for her advice and said she'd think about it. "But not until after the wedding! I've got to keep focused on the task at hand or I'll never get through this. Everything's going so smoothly I'm afraid something horrible is going to go wrong. With everyone helping us, this thing has just come together too easily, something is bound to happen," she said with a smile.

Selena laughed and shook a finger at Vera. "Girl, take it back! Don't invite ugly thoughts like that in and give them energy," she chided.

Vera bowed her head and acknowledged that Selena was right. "I take it back, I take it back! Nothing is going wrong, it's going to be perfect!"

A few weeks later, Aidan was also congratulating Vera on the efficiency of her wedding planning. "You know, if I ever have a small country to run you're going to be my first choice as leader. You certainly know how to mobilize and delegate. I'm in total awe. Too bad you don't use that power for evil," he joked.

He and Vera were on their way to Boston on a location shoot with Charles Waters and his beautiful wife, the legendary Toni Shaw. The estate where they lived was known for its fabulous gardens as well as its art collection, and the fact that they were willing to let *Personal Space* photograph the home was quite a coup. Vera was quite excited about meeting Toni Shaw; she was one of Vera's favorite authors. And dedicated gourmet that she was, Vera had also consumed more than her share of Waters' Foods. Charles Edward Waters had owned a multibillion-dollar food company from which he retired, just to be able to spend more time with his bride. Vera was truly giddy about meeting the Waterses. They were dashing, exciting people and terribly romantic, in her eyes. She was less excited about being away from Marcus, however. He was in Washington, D.C., on coalition business and they planned a romantic rendezvous in New York that weekend.

Vera smiled at Aidan's remark about using her power for good and not evil. "I don't know about that, Aidan. When Marcus sees how much money I've been spending he may think it's evil!"

Aidan made a face and threw up a hand. "Oh, please, woman, you're the most frugal creature I've ever seen! Besides, your betrothed is also besotted with you; you could triple your spending and he'd just hand you more money. With a smile on his face. Hmm, maybe you *are* using those powers for something less than good," he said with a comical leer.

They were met at Logan Airport by a chauffeured limousine and driven in luxury to the Waters estate, with the crew following in a huge van also provided by the Waterses. The couple greeted them and made them right at home, expressing their excitement over meeting Vera at last.

Toni told Vera that they were both big fans of her work and that not only was *Personal Space* a prized publication, but also the show was one of the few things they watched on TV. "My daughters are addicted, too," Toni confided.

"Bree and Georgie are both very busy women, but they make time for *Personal Space*."

Vera was about to return the compliment when Toni noticed the fiery flash from Vera's engagement ring.

"Oh, my goodness, that man meant business, didn't he?" Toni took Vera's hand and stared at the seven-karat stone in its simple Tiffany setting.

Vera smiled with more than a hint of pride. "Yes, he did. He said he's been in love with me for twelve years and this is just a token of how intense that love is," she told the older woman.

Toni was impressed. "Charles and I were college sweethearts who were separated for over twenty years," she said easily. "And I fought like a tiger about getting married, even after we had worked out all our differences and acknowledged that we were in love. It took him a long time to bring me around, but I'm so glad that he did. Marriage to someone you love is wonderful, Vera. But to have that marriage culminate a lifetime dream, that's just too wonderful for words," she said quietly.

Charles, or Chuck as he was known, joined the two women in the sitting room. "Too wonderful for words?" he repeated. "That would indicate that you're at a loss for them, sweetheart, and I've never known that to happen," he said lovingly.

He turned to Vera and told her that a press conference was about to air regarding the Children's Coalition and suggested that she might like to watch since her fiancé was so involved. She and Chuck and Toni went into a den with a large-screen television while Aidan continued to walk around with the crew making notes and giving directions. In a few minutes she'd see Marcus on television and she felt the familiar happy thrill that came whenever she saw his face. She resolved to do something about all her traveling; she realized that she wouldn't be able to stand being away from him for any length of time.

Marcus was counting the minutes until he could leave Washington. The meetings were over and he had endured the luncheon and the endless speeches with good humor, albeit tinged with impatience. He was impatient to leave, to get home to Vera. She'd been on his mind all night and all day. He wanted to see her, to hold her, and make sure she was all right. It was the second time they'd been separated since their engagement; the first time was when she'd gone to Saginaw. He'd discovered both times that he hated, absolutely hated being away from her. He looked around the big hotel ballroom where the press conference was being held and suppressed a smile. If anyone knew what he was thinking about they'd think him a lovesick fool, which he definitely wasn't. He was just a man who was passionately in love with the woman he was going to marry, that's all.

Finally the chairman of the national board made his remarks and introduced Marcus as the new national spokesperson for the Children's Coalition. Marcus stepped up to the podium, made a few remarks about what he hoped to accomplish in his new role, there was polite applause, and the floor was opened for questions. After two or three polite, brief inquiries from various members of the press, Marcus nodded to indicate that he would take another question.

The woman who raised her hand stood and introduced herself. "Lauren Rabscot of the *Atlanta Star,* Mr. Deveraux. My question is this, doesn't this represent a conflict of interest for you?"

Marcus paused and raised a brow. "I'm sorry, I don't understand your question," he said in his deep voice.

The woman elaborated: "Doesn't your being a spokesman for an organization that protects children from deadbeat fathers raise a conflict for you since you fathered a child out of wedlock thirteen years ago? And since your father also fathered an illegitimate child in an extramarital affair years ago in California? How do you justify your involvement with this organization?"

Chaos erupted in the ballroom as people began shouting questions and camera flashes starting going off so rapidly it looked like a display of fireworks. Marcus had to work very hard not to explode from sheer rage. Instead he looked out on the gathering of frenzied newspeople and said, "There is absolutely no basis in fact for any of those allegations. I have nothing further to say at this time."

It was hard to say who was more appalled, Chuck or Toni. They had watched the press conference with looks of horror on their faces and immediately offered to turn off the set, which Vera refused. Ironically, she was the calmest person in the room. She turned to her gracious hosts and explained.

"I guess only someone who knows Marcus as well as I do would understand this, but there is no possible way that he fathered a child and kept it a secret. Marcus would be out trying to name a street, an airport, or a college after his child. In any case, secrecy is not his strong suit; he couldn't possibly have kept something like this a secret for what, thirteen years? I'll tell you this, though, I almost feel sorry for whoever planted this story because they're going to rue the day they picked him as their target. It was the worst move they could possibly have made," she said with assurance.

Toni was impressed with the younger woman's poise and confidence. She had a chance to observe Vera closely while she excused herself to answer her cell phone. How would she, Toni, have reacted if Chuck had been named as the absentee father of a secret child? She flashed him a look and was relieved to see that he was smiling at her tenderly; it seemed that the irony of the situation was not lost on him, either.

Vera did more listening than talking; as expected the call was from Marcus. When she was finally able to get a word in, she told him that she loved him, that she believed in him absolutely, and that she would be home the next day. "I can get finished here tomorrow and I'll be back tomorrow evening. No, don't worry about the plane, I can fly commercial. But . . . but . . . oh, okay! Okay, we'll talk tonight. Everything is going to be fine," she said firmly. "I love you. Now go get whoever did this, darling. Take care of yourself."

Chapter 18

Marcus was once again happy that he'd decided that a plane was a necessary investment for TDG. If he'd had to fly back to Atlanta on a commercial jet he would have lost his mind. As it was it was difficult to get through the Hartsfield to his car without attracting attention. He thought that he heard his name being called but he ignored the voice in his haste to get to his car. The late afternoon sun was giving way to dusk as he made his way to Clay's house. Clay lived the closest to the airport and during a midair conference call with his brothers, they had agreed to meet there to discuss the obvious, what was to be done about the situation.

Except for when he found out that her late husband had manhandled Vera, Marcus couldn't ever remember being as angry as he was now. His blood pressure was undoubtedly high, he was still flushed and hot with rage. It was clear that someone meant to sabotage him, make him look like an idiot, and they didn't care how they did it. The *Atlanta Star* was a rival newspaper that had a vested interest in running down TDG as they owned several publications that competed for the same readership as the *Atlanta Star*. But why would the *Star* act in this manner now? And where had they gotten their distorted version of the facts?

By now Marcus had reached the long private drive that led to Clay's home. He pulled into the drive and drove up the wooded length just a bit too fast, his recklessness clearly reflecting his mood. His anger had driven all conscious thoughts from his head, except for his need to know who concocted the story and where they got their information. Fury had made him forget what nothing else could do; it made him forget for the moment his longing for Vera. Right now his mind was totally focused on one thing and that was getting to the bottom of the maelstrom of vicious rumors that now surrounded his family.

Stifling a savage curse, he parked in the large turn-around at the top of the drive and remained in the car for a moment, trying to compose himself. Letting his temper run away with him wasn't going to do any good at the moment. He needed a cool head so that he and his brothers could formulate a plan for getting to the bottom of it all. He took a deep breath and got out of the BMW. He was at Clay's front door in seconds, his long legs making short work of the distance. He hesitated a moment before ringing the doorbell. In those few seconds the door came open to reveal Martin standing in the doorway. "Come in, Marcus. I was watching for your car," he said, his somber mood evident.

Marcus merely nodded. He followed Martin into the house and both of them went directly to the oversized office that had been added to the house when the solarium was put in. It was normally a large, sunny space conducive to creativity, but now it held all the warmth and appeal of a county morgue. Clay was there, sitting behind the desk custom-made to accommodate his size. There was a long leather sofa along the wall. Malcolm was sitting on one end of it. There were two leather chairs in front of Clay's desk. Martin sat in one and Marcus took the other. Marcus started to speak first, feeling that he needed to say it once and for all so that there would be no mistake about the true facts of the story. But before he could say anything the legal counsel for the family and for the corporation, his brother Malcolm, began talking.

"Marcus, if there is any truth to what was said today we need to know it now so we can address this. We haven't issued a statement of any kind, we couldn't until we heard your side of the story," he said in a carefully neutral voice.

The fury that Marcus had been holding at bay erupted. He leapt to his feet, bellowing, " 'Any truth to what was said today'? Man, what the hell is this? Do you actually think I'd father a child and not say a word about it for all these years? Do you think I'd have a child and not marry the mother? Do you think a child of mine would be out there with a name other than mine? You act like we just met, Malcolm! And what the hell do you mean you haven't issued a statement of any kind? You didn't have to wait for me to confirm or deny anything. I'm your damned brother, you should know me better than this, man!"

His anger spent, Marcus dropped heavily into the leather chair and rubbed his left hand over his forehead. "I don't know how this crap got started, but I'm damned sure going to find out," he vowed. "I've never had unprotected sex in my life. That was the one thing you drilled into my head from the time I was old enough to know what girls were," he said in a low, tight voice. "I knew the consequences of sleeping around and this was before everyone was worried about AIDS and HIV and all that. This was just back in the day when getting a girl pregnant could mess up both your lives forever. I'm not stupid, you know; I did listen to you all.

"Besides," he went on, looking directly at Martin and Clay for the first time, "who is the mother of this alleged child? Where *is* the child? And most importantly, where are they getting this crap from?"

Martin glanced at Clay before speaking. "The mother of the child is someone you know, Marcus, which is why

Malcolm said what he said. He meant no disrespect to you, he was just being a lawyer. You have to understand, Marcus, the wire services picked this up, it was all over the cable networks as well as the regular networks, and of course it was the front-page story in the *Atlanta Star*. Look for yourself," he said, handing Marcus a folded newspaper.

Marcus unfolded the paper and saw a big picture of himself holding a young woman wearing a long formal gown. There were also pictures of a young boy wearing next to nothing standing barefoot in the mud, looking like a child from one of those commercials about international relief for impoverished children. To the amazement of his brothers, Marcus laughed. And laughed so hard that they feared his mind had snapped. "Oh, man, this is rich. This is too much," Marcus mumbled.

He looked up at his brothers and pointed to the picture. "You don't recognize her, do you? That's Camille, one of the girls I took to the prom. Camille Yancy, the one who had the real fine sisters and the mean daddy, remember?"

All three men nodded as Marcus's words brought them into the picture. "Camille was the reason I decided on a group date for the prom. You know me, I couldn't have cared less about going to the prom. I was so busy hanging out with you guys that all the high school stuff wasn't of any interest to me. But poor Camille came to me and told me she was pregnant. She was so scared; man, it was pitiful. I offered to go get the guy and beat him up, but she wasn't having it. I offered to go talk to her parents or have Ma talk to her mother or something, but she said no. She just wanted to get through graduation without anyone finding out and then she would take the consequences.

"She was tough. She was scared half to death, but she was tough in her own way, because you know what it was like when a girl found herself pregnant back in the day. It was somehow all her fault. The guy would get away scot-free, maybe get off with a lecture or something, but nobody ever made him bear any real responsibility. And if he was a popular kid, an athlete or something, forget about it. His parents, his coaches, everybody would do everything possible to make sure that nothing interfered with his career. To hell with the girl, as long as he could still play ball," Marcus said bitterly.

Suddenly realizing how dry his mouth was, Marcus looked around for something to drink. He settled for water from the cooler near the desk. He stood and crossed over to the unit and drank several cups of the icy-cold water before continuing.

"I felt bad for Camille. All of us did, Suzie, Sophie, and Cassandra, we all hung together and we knew what kind of hell she was going to have to go through in the next few months. Because there were two things she wouldn't do, one was get rid of the baby, and the other was tell who the father was. To this day, I have no idea who fathered that child, although I have my suspicions," he said broodingly.

"Anyway, we all wanted to cheer Camille up and we knew how much she'd been looking forward to the prom. So we decided to all go together. I rented a limo and bought corsages for everybody and I went to each girl's house and posed for pictures, the whole shot. That's where that stupid picture came from that makes us look like a couple. And that *is* a picture of her kid, but it's not what it looks like. She went to live with her aunt in Alabama after graduation. She actually ran away to her aunt because her parents would have flipped out. Anyway, she stayed there on her aunt's farm while she was going to college. She managed to put herself through on scholarships. That picture was taken one day when Marcus was playing in the mud after a hard rain. He's not some impoverished little boy who doesn't know where his next meal is coming from, he's a very successful kid," Marcus said proudly.

The lawyer in Martin made him interject. "Did you say the child's name is *Marcus?*"

Marcus reddened along his cheekbones. "Yeah, well, she named him after me. That's his middle name, though, his first name is Nathaniel. The point is, Camille finished her degrees and she went on to become a college professor at Tuskegee, which is what she always wanted to do. Marcus is almost thirteen and he's a smart, well-adjusted kid. Very grounded, very good looking, but not *mine*. You hear that? I have no children. I'm not that careless or clumsy, man. And if I was, I'd be man enough to admit it, damn it."

"Will Camille say that this child is not yours?" Malcolm persisted.

"Of course she will, she's probably no happier about this than I am," Marcus replied.

"Okay, then we issue a statement tonight and tomorrow we start the lawsuit. We're going to sue the *Atlanta Star* for a whole *buncha* money," Malcolm said with satisfaction. "Defamation of character, slander, libel, you name it. And don't even get me started on the pain and suffering for the family after what they said about Pop."

Clay had been strangely silent during most of the interchange. Now he spoke and his words were not what anyone expected. "I'd hold off on that one if I were you. There's a distinct possibility that they could be right about Pop."

By the time the meeting had concluded, Marcus was wiped out and so were his brothers. He drove all the way out to his home in Peachtree City. He waited until he was in the house and lying across his big bed before calling Vera. Due to the lateness of the hour, he debated about calling her, but he knew she'd be furious if he didn't call her at all. She deserved to hear about what was going on from his own lips, even though it was old news by now, he thought, glancing at the CNN broadcast on his television.

He called Vera's cell phone, gratified that she answered on the first ring and that she sounded more concerned than angry.

"Marcus, darling, are you all right?" she asked immediately.

"I'll live," he said dryly. "Listen, Pie, I know you must have heard and seen all the crap that's all over the media by now. I want you to know it's not true," he began.

Vera stopped him before he got any further. "Marcus, please. Don't you even dare start that again, you know that I know this to be completely untrue. Don't you dare defend yourself to me," she said hotly. "Please, surely you know me better than that! I certainly know *you* better than you seem to realize. There's no way in the world you'd have fathered a child and not claimed it, I *know* that. I also talked to Camille at Cassandra's wedding, remember? She told me all about the prom and why you all went together. She's a very tough lady, Marcus. And she's mad as hell that they put that vicious story out about you. She called me tonight and told me so," Vera said calmly.

Marcus was at a loss for words. Once again, Vera was showing him that she was the perfect woman for him. She knew just what to say and how to say it. He actually felt better as she spoke, something he would have thought impossible a couple of hours ago.

"Marcus, honey, why don't I fly home right now?" Vera suggested. "I don't think you should be by yourself tonight," she said in a voice full of concern.

Marcus was charmed that she was so concerned for him, but refused to hear of her trying to leave Boston at that hour. "We'll be together tomorrow and that's all that matters, Pie. And by the way, I'm not resigning as head of the

Children's Coalition. I offered to, but they wouldn't hear of it. In fact, they want to use the fact that I was falsely accused of paternity as a new platform for increased responsibility on the mothers. They want to emphasize that it's this kind of thing that makes it harder for men who really want to do the right thing. So it's going to work out just fine, I think."

After saying their good nights, they hung up the phone. Marcus, overwhelmed by the events of the day, did indeed fall asleep almost immediately, after prudently turning off his cell phone and turning the ringer off on his landline. There was no way that he was going to deal with the barrage of calls that were sure to start coming in. Tomorrow he would have to see about getting his number changed.

The next few days were like nothing Marcus had ever experienced in his life. TDG was in a state of siege practically. It seemed that reporters had nothing else to do but hang around the building hoping for a scoop. Even though the legal department had issued a terse statement, the buzz continued. Camille had also issued a statement and had been on *Larry King Live* to decry the lies that had turned her life, the life of her son, and Marcus's life into a circus. Marcus had indeed remained as the national spokesperson for the coalition. They had issued an eloquent statement saying that their faith in him was unshaken and they still felt he was the most appropriate person for the job. Overall, the most galling aspect of the whole thing was that even after irrefutable evidence came forth to prove that Marcus was innocent of all allegations, the *Atlanta Star* continued to snipe at the Deveraux family, insisting that the stories about Big Clay Deveraux Sr. were true.

The thing that was galvanizing the brothers was the possibility that there was a child of Big Clay Deveraux out there. When he was twenty-one, it had fallen to Clay as the eldest to go to California and deal with his father's death in less than honorable circumstances. His father died in the bed of his longtime mistress who was herself a married woman. Clay had been forced to go through all manner of machinations to protect his mother from the truth and to keep it out of the media. And he'd done an excellent job on both counts until now. The irony was that Lillian knew all about her husband's infidelity, as Marcus had recently found out.

He and his brothers had gone to Lillian to somehow gently explain to her the reason behind the attack on her late husband's character, and to their utter shock she already knew. She and Bump had been seated on a love seat in their graciously furnished living room with her sons ranged all about the room, uncomfortable with the topic at hand. Lillian had taken control of the conversation by saying that the stuff in the *Atlanta Star* was old news to her.

"I'm not very proud of the fact that I knew that your father was unfaithful to me," she said. "In my defense, I loved him dearly and I wanted our marriage to work. I'd had children with him and marriage was, and is, sacred to me. I did everything I could to make it work, I really did. But he had a wandering eye and he could never control those impulses," she said matter-of-factly. "I don't want you to think it didn't hurt, because it did, it truly did," she acknowledged. "But over the years, I've learned to let it go," she said softly, looking into her husband's loving eyes as she squeezed his hand.

Clay spoke up then. "But, Mom, this rumor that Pop had a child somewhere, what about that?" he asked.

Lillian slowly shrugged her shoulders. "I'm not saying that it's true. But I heard rumors from time to time and it *could* be true. You could very easily have another sibling out there, I'm sad to say."

Although the news made the men pensive and uneasy, it was worse for Angelique, who became enraged when she realized that her brothers had kept the secret of her father's demise all these years. Her point was that she had a right to know, the same as the rest of them. Clay tried to reason with her, pointing out that she'd been a tiny child when he died. The men all felt there was nothing to be gained by telling her the story later, there didn't seem to be a point.

"The *point?* The point is that I'm an adult, I'm not an idiot child, and there was no reason for you to keep this from me once I grew up. I'm tired of being treated like a useless idiot by this family," she raged.

It looked like she was going to pull another one of her famous disappearing acts and just leave town until she felt better able to handle what was going on. She was so angry and hurt, in fact, that this one might last longer than all the others combined. Surprisingly, though, she turned to Vera for counsel and guidance. She just showed up at the house in Peachtree City on the Saturday morning after the news had broken, looking confused and in need of comfort, which is what Vera offered her.

After a warm hug and the offer of pineapple juice and coffee, both of which were refused, Vera sat down with Angelique in the big sunny kitchen. "Look, Angel, I can't tell you how to feel about all of this, I wouldn't be that presumptuous. But I'm asking you to look at this from the larger perspective. Let this crisis bring you closer to your family, don't let it drive you away," she said softly.

She reached across the table and took Angelique's hand. "I honestly don't know how I'd be reacting right now, if I were you. I don't know how I'd be feeling either. I'm sure I'd be hurt, like you are, and angry, like you are, and I'd be very disappointed that I was being kept in the dark about an essential part of my life," she told her. "But feelings aren't facts, Angel. Feelings are *feelings,* they're how we react to events in our lives. How we act on those feelings, the steps we take when we're learning to live with those events, that's what's most important. Take the right steps, Angel. Even if they're baby steps, little-bitty steps. Take them one at a time and you'll be the better person for it when all is said and done."

Angelique squeezed her hand tightly and the sheen of tears in her eyes startled Vera. Angelique almost never cried and the thought of a torrent of tears was daunting to say the least. Vera quickly changed tactics.

"Besides, girl, if you think you're weaseling out of this wedding you've got another think coming. I need you! You can't abandon me now," she said dramatically.

Amazingly, Angelique laughed and reached over to hug her friend, the woman who would become her sister in a very few weeks. "I wouldn't dream of it, Vera. You're sure gonna need help now because every nosy idiot in the state of Georgia is going to try to crash this wedding!"

Vera sat up straight and stared at Angelique. "You know, you're right? Oh, my goodness, this is turning into a circus right before my eyes," she moaned.

Angelique set her jaw and looked grim. "Not if I can help it. This thing is going off exactly as planned without a hitch, just wait and see."

Chapter 19

Paris and Aidan were enjoying a few minutes of leisure before leaving for the wedding. Aidan couldn't stop complimenting Paris's transformation. "I know I've said it before, but you look wonderful. I have three words for that new haircut: Fab. U. Lous! You look like a real woman, my dear, and it's about time."

Normally she would have given Aidan grief, but she was feeling so mellow she let it go. She'd gone to Saginaw again to help with wedding issues at "Bridal North" as Neesha and Aidan had taken to calling the Clark home. This time she gathered her courage and asked Neesha if she could schedule an appointment with Danny to get her hair cut. Neesha immediately got her one for that Thursday evening, and with great trepidation Paris ventured to the small, stylish salon on Genesee Street near downtown Saginaw. As soon as she entered the shop she felt at ease.

The salon was small, completely decorated in black and white and immaculately clean. The floors in some people's houses didn't gleam with cleanliness the way the black and white tiles did at the Hair Gallery. The only touches of color were the colorful magazine covers in the rack by the door and the huge live ficus tree that took a prominent place in the reception area. Danny immediately greeted her and had her sit down in his chair so he could inspect the heavy mass of hair. When he took down her ponytail and all the wavy hair tumbled down around her, he smiled.

"You came in here like Cousin Itt, but you're leaving here a star. Leave everything to me," he told her with assurance.

And in the soothing ambience of the salon, Danny cut almost a foot of hair, leaving her with a layered cut that still fell past her shoulders. He shampooed and conditioned her and gave her a roller set that took forever to dry, but the results were worth it. She looked fresh, sophisticated, and the family cheekbones were thrown into prominence at last. He also arched her eyebrows, which lent an air of mystery to her face. She was speechless when he was through, but she was able to throw her arms around him for a big hug, which he accepted graciously.

With a little catch in her voice she said, "I never thought I could look like this. I really look nice, don't I?"

Neesha, Danny, and the other patrons all scoffed at her humble statement. "Girl, you look beautiful!" Danny said indignantly.

Paris was still smiling a dreamy smile as she thought about that afternoon. Aidan, of course, knew what she was up to.

"That poor man doesn't stand a chance with you, does he?" Aidan said wryly, referring to Titus Argonne.

"A chance of getting away from me? Not likely, unless he's married. If he's single, all bets are off," she said brazenly.

"Well, my money is on you, honey. Go get him!"

Vera was by far the most serene occupant of the huge dressing room where everyone was getting dressed for the wedding. Ever since the astounding revelation of the identity of Camille's child, nothing had bothered her in any way. After seeing the story on TV and seeing the pictures in the paper, the real father of Camille's child stepped up to make an announcement. It turned out that he was none other than Derrick Brandon, the Hollywood heartthrob whose last five movies had set box office records around the world.

Derrick was the oldest son of the Brandon family who owned mortuaries in Atlanta, Macon, Birmingham, Alabama, and other cities throughout the South. His family had always felt that Camille was beneath him, and the fact that she got pregnant in their senior year was enough of convince them of this fact. It didn't seem to occur to them that Derrick was equally responsible for her condition. Derrick was young and spoiled and easily convinced to abandon his responsibilities to his unborn child; he was willingly shipped off to finish the rest of senior year by correspondence and enroll at Howard University on schedule in the fall. The Brandon family heaved a sigh of relief at the outcome, assured that their scion was safe until he could inherit the family business, and that nothing more would be heard from the girl, who, after all had been bought off with a generous sum.

What they didn't count on then was that Derrick would slip from their control and drop out of school, taking off for California and an acting career. Or that Camille Yancy would throw the money in their faces and tell them she couldn't be bought for any amount of cash. And what his family certainly hadn't counted on now was that he would have the internal fortitude to hold a press conference and announce that he was the father of the child and that he was tired of living the lie of a cowardly youth and he wanted to be a man. He publicly asked Camille and their son for forgiveness and had made arrangements for thirteen years of child support to be sent to the child.

His gesture was still the talk of the tabloids, the entertainment magazines, and the gossip columns, but it was old news as far as Vera and Marcus were concerned. All they cared about was getting married and going on a long and secluded honeymoon. And now they were just hours away from their goal. Vera sat quietly while Tanya expertly applied her makeup.

Even the normally reticent Alexia felt compelled to tell her sister that she looked beautiful. "Marcus is going to be stunned, Vera. I've never seen you look so gorgeous."

Vera looked in the mirror and had to agree. Tanya had worked her magic to a flawless degree. She was indeed going to knock his socks off.

Marcus was as relaxed as Vera, although he was much more impatient than she at the moment. Clay, the best man, had his work cut out for him to keep Marcus contained.

"Man, can you relax for a minute? You're going to work yourself into a sweat and my future sister-in-law would not appreciate having a sweaty groom in the least. Sit down!" Clay admonished him.

Marcus sighed deeply and sat down on one of the comfortable club chairs in the dressing area reserved for the men of the bridal party. He was completely still for all of two minutes; then he was up again, pacing the floor. He wanted to be married right then, right there, he could barely contain himself he was so happy.

Clay gave up. He looked over at Martin and Bump and told them it was their turn to calm him down. "See if you can't get him into his tux or something, that might slow him down, " Clay suggested.

Bump shook his head and laughed at Marcus, who was now looking at himself in the mirror and trying to decide if he needed to shave again. "Boy, you really need to chill! How's that hand, by the way?"

That had the effect of making Marcus stand still while he showed the hand in question to Bump. The swelling had gone down and the hand looked almost normal except for some slight bruising. Bump examined the hand, commenting that he still couldn't believe the identity of the person who had leaked the false information to the *Atlanta Star*. It was none other than Darnell Washington.

Donnie, who was acting as a groomsman for Marcus, hadn't heard the whole story until now, and Marcus was grimly supplying him with details.

"Hard as it seems to believe, it was my best friend, my cut buddy Darnell. The reason he knew Camille was pregnant was that he knew who the father was. They were real tight in school, almost as close as Darnell and I were, so Darnell was the only person that Derrick confided in about the situation. The reason Darnell told the big lie to the *Star* was that he was bent out of shape after we didn't want to go into the casino business with him. It seems like his nightclub is in foreclosure and all the tales he's told me over the years about making bank just aren't true. I kinda feel sorry for the guy but I still want to kick his ass," Marcus admitted.

"Well, you did pretty good at the bachelor party," Martin said dryly, and it was true. When Darnell had made a boozy, tearful confession and tried to explain, Marcus had decked him with one punch. And now Titus Argonne was taking his place in the wedding party, something for which Vera was very grateful. Suddenly it was time for Marcus to don his tuxedo and get to the altar to await the woman he would love for the rest of his life. He smiled a perfect and peaceful smile. The long wait was almost over.

Vera stood in the anteroom, waiting for her cue to walk down the aisle. The junior bridesmaids, wearing peach frocks, followed the perfectly behaved twins to the front of the church. The bridesmaids in a deeper shade of peach, which was almost a coral, followed. Then the maid and matron of honor in a shimmering shade of tangerine that would have looked odd on anyone but Lillian and Angelique; they looked radiant. They all carried exotic bouquets of tiger lilies and tropical orchids that set off the unusual colors of the dresses. Then it was Vera's turn to go to the man she loved.

The music that accompanied her was completely untraditional, "Our Love," a song that had been written by Stevie Wonder and sung as a duet by Stevie and Julio Iglesias. This time Marcus's brothers, who harmonized so beautifully that there was hardly a dry eye in the entire church, sang it. With her mother on one side of her and her father on the other, Vera floated down the aisle in her incredible dress, an ivory silk charmeuse suffused with gold. It was daringly strapless, although there was a sheer jacket that gave it some modesty. The bodice was tight as was the draped skirt that showed off her incredible figure. The train that trailed behind her concealed the back slit of the dress. She wore, in lieu of a veil, an amazingly constructed diamond, pearl, and citrine tiara that Marcus had commissioned for her. It was made so that it could be turned into a necklace after the wedding, and it matched the delicate earrings that were also custom-made just for Vera.

They finally reached the end of the aisle, at which point Marcus came forward to claim Vera. After shaking her father's hand and kissing her mother with great affection, Marcus took Vera's arm and they took the rest of the journey to the altar together. With tears of joy sparkling in her eyes, Vera recited the vows that Marcus had waited a lifetime to hear. He never took his eyes from hers as he told her through the sacred words that she was his until death took them from this earth. When the minister pronounced them man and wife, Marcus cupped her face in his big hands and said, "I love you, Vera, more than I can ever show you," then kissed her tenderly to a chorus of oohs from the guests. Vera looked at him with her heart in her eyes and laid her hand on his heart before saying, "And I love you, Marcus, more than you'll ever know."

She would have drowned him in happy tears right about then if a familiar sound hadn't caused her to look around. There was little Elizabeth in a fantastic pale peach gown with ribbons in her hair and Kika and Toby on their leads. Each was wearing a festive peach bow and a flower and they were barking eagerly to join the recessional. Vera looked reproachfully at Marcus as everyone laughed.

"Aww, Pie, we couldn't leave them at home! Look at them, they wanted to come," he said persuasively.

"Marcus, what am I going to do with you?" she asked with loving exasperation.

"Love me forever?" he suggested.

"Works for me, baby, Let's go!" she said as they started their first walk as a married couple.

Chapter 20

Like everything else about the couple, their reception was definitely untraditional. For one thing, the music was outstanding. Bump's band provided the music for the first part of the evening with a DJ taking over later. With so many beautiful voices right there in the family, there were an abundance of musical tributes to the couple. And Marcus and Vera sang to each other; he sang "At Last" while she serenaded him with Anita Baker's "You bring Me Joy." They also sang a duet of "Let It Be Me" and the simple lyrics of the song took on a new meaning due to the love in their eyes as they harmonized.

The food was fabulous and everyone had a wonderful time; it was like being at the best party in the world. When the dancing started it never seemed to stop. The music drew everyone out to the floor and no one wanted to leave. Even Angelique and Donnie ended up dancing together, having declared a truce for the evening. Paris was chatting away with Aidan and Sebastian when someone tapped on her shoulder; it was Titus Argonne, asking her to dance.

Her eyes opened wide with surprise and she turned into his arms as he danced her out onto the floor. It was a slow number and she found she was able to follow his lead easily as he was an excellent dancer. He might also have been a great conversationalist, but Paris was suddenly overcome with shyness. She couldn't think of a thing to say, she just tried not to look like a total idiot while they were dancing. She wanted to say something clever, something sophisticated, but it was as though she were struck dumb. He looked down at her with the same expression of gentle amusement and she felt her cheeks flame up. Thanking God when the dance was over, she mumbled a thank-you and abruptly left him standing on the dance floor.

Aidan and Sebastian were waiting for her at the edge of the dance floor. Sebastian didn't say anything, but Aidan pounced on her. "What in the world was that all about, Miss Girl? Have I taught you nothing?"

Paris sighed deeply and looked around for the nearest waiter. Taking a flute of champagne from the tray, she tossed it back as if it were water. "I guess not. Apparently, I haven't learned a thing," she mumbled in response.

Marcus and Vera had more fun than anyone at the reception; they danced until the very end and finally left in a shower of rose petals and confetti. In the back of the limousine that would take them to the hotel where they were spending the night before leaving on their honeymoon, Marcus took both of Vera's hands and kissed each one, then looked into her eyes.

"Vera, my heart, this has been the best day of my entire life. Thank you again for loving me enough to be my wife. You'll never, ever regret this, Pie. I'm going to try to make you happier than you've ever been in your life," he said solemnly.

"Marcus, my love, you already do," Vera assured him. "Thank you for being smart enough to know we were meant for each other and for coming after me. If you hadn't I would have missed the greatest joy of my life, being with you and becoming your wife."

As the long, expensive car sped toward their destination, they kissed each other with great and abiding passion.

* * *

After the joyful wedding and the fabulous reception, the honeymoon was like nothing Vera had ever imagined. Marcus had planned every bit of the honeymoon, refusing to let Vera know anything about where they were going and what they would be doing. He whisked her off to a very expensive, very private resort in Bali where they could enjoy the luxury of starting their married life in complete solitude. It was a lovely, tender, and extremely romantic time for them, a time that would always be remembered. But once the honeymoon was over, Vera was ashamed to admit that being married was something of a letdown.

She was constantly tired, was sleeping poorly, and her appetite was off. Foods that she used to savor made her cringe and she was always slightly nauseated. She had a horrible feeling that she knew why. Her face looked pale and unhealthy and she'd lost about fifteen pounds with no effort whatsoever. *If I was trying to lose weight, it would stick there like it was glued on,* she thought sadly, feeling herself close to tears. She fought off tears on a regular basis lately; it seemed that everything made her cry. She had to pick Danny up from the airport and she dissolved in tears right in front of him, to her shame.

Danny was alarmed to say the least. "What's wrong with you? I told you I could rent a car. Did the traffic do this to you? Has Marcus done something to you, what?" he exclaimed as he hustled her through the doors to short-term parking. "Here, sit down on this bench and I'll go get the car. There'd better be a good explanation for this, heifer. People probably think we're breaking up or something," he grumbled as he went to get the car.

In a short time they were at the house in Peachtree City, drinking iced tea and talking. At least Danny was drinking iced tea. Vera was gulping water like there was no tomorrow. Her thirst was constant and could barely be contained even with the copious amounts she now drank every day. Danny had come down to tape a portion of *Personal Space* that would introduce the feature revolving around the gradual makeover of his home. He was vacationing in Savannah, so this was the ideal time for him to stop in, enjoy a day or two with Vera, and then drive over to the coast. After her gulping stopped, Danny fixed her with a steely glare. "Now, then, do you care to tell me what that was all about? And can you tell these dogs that I don't like them?" He looked down at his feet where Kika and Toby were relaxing, each draped across one of his feet. They adored Danny although he repeatedly insisted that he hated them and all other small yappy dogs.

Vera drew a long, hiccupy breath and told Danny what she suspected. "I'm in perimenopause," she said sadly.

"What the hell is that?" Danny asked.

Vera sighed and explained. "Before your body goes into full-fledged menopause you start going through a series of changes that precede the big change. Mood swings, loss of appetite, insomnia, a lessening or cessation of the menses, it's like the warm-up for the final change, menopause. I'm entering early menopause, Danny."

"So you're having these symptoms, I take it?" Danny said in a voice of clinical concern.

"Yes. I wasn't sure until I missed my last two periods. Well, the one was really light, so it almost counts as missing one. But I definitely missed the last one," she said tearfully. "They were as regular as clockwork, too, which I could never understand, since I can't have children. It was like delivering mail to an empty house." She sniffed. "I mean, the house is vacant, been boarded up for years, and yet the postman keeps coming."

Danny lowered his head to keep from laughing at her

melodramatic delivery. "So what did the doctor say about this? Did he put you on hormones or something?"

Vera shook her head miserably. "I haven't been to the doctor yet, partially because I don't want to hear the words. I'm just postponing the inevitable, I guess. I just feel so old and haggard all of a sudden. Marcus is going to be so sorry he ever asked me to marry him," she sobbed. "I'm going to turn old and dried up right before his eyes," she wailed.

Danny stared at her with amazement. "Look, heifer, until you go to the doctor, you need to cut all this drama out. You're making yourself sick with this nonsense. Now your raggedy behind is going to the doctor tomorrow if I have to drag you there by your hair. And for the record, just because I love you does *not* mean that I want to know about your cycles! That's just a little bit too much information for me to handle, woman."

Despite her angst, Vera laughed. Danny could always make her feel better. And he'd brought with him their time-honored cure-all, Vargas tortillas. In no time he had a batch going, scenting the house with the spicy aroma of her beloved tacos. Vera was suddenly ravenous and put away three of them in minutes. In less time than it took for her to eat them, she was in the bathroom giving them up.

Puce with embarrassment, she made her way back to the kitchen, where Danny was waiting for her.

"Oh, yeah, you're definitely going to the doctor tomorrow," Danny said decisively. "Any time you can't keep down a taco, something is definitely wrong."

Too miserable to disagree, Vera just nodded. Danny distracted her by examining her engagement ring again. "Let me see that boulder again, girl." Vera obligingly stuck out her left hand. Suddenly she sniffed again, signaling that water was going to flow again from her reddened eyes.

"I've lost so much weight it's too big now," she wailed.

Danny looked distressed for a moment; this was definitely not Vera!

"Quit bawling for a minute. Do you have any Vernor's?" he asked. No one reared in Michigan ever ran out of the sweet, peppery ginger-flavored soda. It was good for indigestion, flu, and tummy troubles of all kinds and was considered medicinal; Michigan doctors practically prescribed the stuff, it was so efficacious. Vera kept it on hand at all times as did Bennie and Ceylon, who'd also grown up on it in Detroit. In minutes Danny had her lying down sipping Vernor's over crushed ice. "Doctor's office, first thing in the morning, Miss Thing. Thank God Marcus is out of town, he'd be dragging you in there right now," Danny said. "You look like death eating a soda cracker."

As it turned out, Vera was feeling much better in the morning, well enough to insist that they tape before she went in to the doctor. "My appointment isn't until three and I'd go nuts sitting around that long. We'll tape your segment and be productive until it's time to go to the doctor," she said with her usual practicality.

Practicality flew out the window, however, as the segment was ending. She managed to get through the whole interview with Danny before turning a pasty yellow and passing out cold in front of everyone. Before she could rally enough to protest she found herself on her old stomping grounds, the emergency room. This time Paris and Danny accompanied her as she waited for the doctor.

"Too bad Aidan isn't here, we could have a reunion," Vera said whimsically.

Danny was taking great glee in telling her, "I told you so," as in, "I told your stubborn butt you were sick, woman. Now look at you!"

It so happened that Dante was on duty and he was the one to give her the results of her blood work. Danny and

Paris went out to the waiting room, while she lay on the narrow cot feeling utterly foolish.

"We've got to stop meeting like this, Dante," she said with an attempt at humor.

He smiled briefly to acknowledge the joke, then started asking her questions. "Have you experienced excessive thirst lately? Excessive urination? Any dizziness or blurring of vision? Weight loss? Nausea?"

Vera's head was bobbing up and down like a marionette's by the time he got through with her. "Well, your preliminary tests bear out what I suspect, Vera. With your family history it's not surprising, gestational diabetes is almost to be expected in these situations. You need to schedule an appointment with your own doctor as soon as possible so that you can begin the proper course of treatment immediately," he said in a reassuring tone of voice.

Some time later, Vera was dressed and ready to leave. Paris, assured that Vera would be fine, went back to the office to confer with Star Hopkins on rearranging Vera's schedule as she obviously needed a couple of days off. Vera left with Danny, who kept looking at her as if she were going to start speaking in tongues or something else unexpected. He waited until they were safely at the house to begin the interrogation, however. With Vera once again stretched out on the sofa, Danny stationed himself at the other end.

"So? Do they know what's wrong with you or not?" he asked impatiently.

Vera nodded without saying a word.

"Well, are you going to tell me or what?" he said with a slightly raised voice.

"I have diabetes," Vera said quietly. "Gestational diabetes."

Danny looked genuinely distressed for a moment and suddenly the distress was replaced by confusion. "I thought gestating was what you did when you were pregnant," he said.

Vera folded her hands in her lap and looked at Danny with an unreadable expression on her face. "It is. And I am," she said quietly.

When Dante had blithely given her the diagnosis of gestational diabetes, she'd been stunned. Shocked was a better word for her reaction; she went completely still. Then she started talking.

"Dante, that's not possible! I can't have children. I have something called nonspecific ovarian failure. I've never gotten pregnant since the miscarriage. How is it possible for me to suddenly be pregnant?" she demanded. "This can't be happening, this is a mistake," she said, raking her hand through her hair with agitation. "Please do the tests again because they have to be wrong. I have to be sure of what you're telling me, Dante, I really do."

While Vera was expressing her doubts and her incredulity, Dante's calm, impassive face underwent a radical change. Shock, embarrassment, and pity flashed across his face so rapidly that Vera, in her distraught state, didn't notice. He waited until she calmed down, then took her hands. He pulled his stool right up next to her cot, so she could hear him clearly without anyone overhearing.

"Vera, what I'm going to tell you is something you should have known a long time ago. I'm not violating a doctor-patient privilege by telling you this, because when I was given the information, I wasn't a doctor. But John confided in me, Vera. He used to call me 'Doc' because he knew I intended to go to medical school, and he knew that I had taken a lot of premed courses. Vera, John had an extremely low sperm count. It was so low, in fact, that him getting you pregnant that first time was a fluke, a one-in-a-million deal. His low sperm count was why you couldn't get pregnant again, it wasn't anything to do with you," he said softly.

Seeing the look of utter shock on Vera's face, he continued. "He felt like a failure as a husband, Vera, which is why he was so determined to give you a child instead of adopting one. He thought, like a lot of people, that unless you give birth to a child, it's not really yours. In fact, Vera . . ." He hesitated before continuing. "He had found some kind of specialist in male fertility in California and he was going out there to have another try at getting you pregnant in what he called the 'natural way.'

By now Vera's head was spinning with the information Dante had just given her. It was just too much for her to absorb and she started crying. As Dante stood up and awkwardly hugged her, she suddenly started laughing, although she didn't sound hysterical, to his utter relief. "I thought I was going through the change," she explained. Wiping the tears away, she took a deep, teary breath. "Oh, my goodness, Marcus is going to be so surprised," she murmured.

After she finished explaining everything to Danny, it was his turn to be stunned. "My God, girl, you're gonna have that garden gnome after all, aren't you? I'll be damned!" He sat there, contemplating the enormous news, and then he stared at Vera. "So why aren't you reacting, woman? Aren't you happy?" he demanded.

Vera sat up straight and her face was slowly transformed into a visage of pure joy. "Danny, I'm so happy I could dance on the ceiling! I'm going to have a *baby,* Marcus's baby. Oh, Danny, I can't wait to tell him," she sighed.

"So? Pick up the phone and tell him, woman, what are you waiting for?" he demanded.

Vera shook her head no, her eyes still full of stars. "Absolutely not! I've got to tell him in person, Danny. He needs to be with me when I tell him he's going to be a father. And I need to see the look on his face when I tell him." She looked troubled for a moment, then confessed that Marcus didn't really want children. "I just hope he'll change his mind when he hears the good news," she said worriedly. "I hope it *is* good news to him."

Danny looked at his dear friend who was completely convinced of her words. How could someone so intelligent be such a dope when it came to the man she loved? "Oh, I'm sure he'll be just as happy as you are," Danny said dryly. He had a feeling Marcus would be dancing on the ceiling right along with Vera.

"So when is he coming home?" he asked.

Vera's normal demeanor came back as she told him of Marcus's travel plans. "He had to go to D.C. for a meeting with the national board of the Children's Coalition. It seems that the new program that shaped up after the so-called scandal has been a great success. There's a press conference this afternoon and he's flying back then. So I only have a few hours to put together a celebration for him," she said with a huge yawn.

"It sounds like you need a nap more," Danny said. "Why don't you go to sleep and I'll wake you up in a couple of hours? We can figure out something after you get some sleep. I can help you get it together before I leave for Savannah. You have a lot to deal with right now, you need to conserve your energy," he added wisely.

In minutes she was sound asleep with a sweet smile on her face.

Marcus wasn't suffering from the same angst as Vera; he found everything about marriage wonderful. He loved going to sleep with Vera in his arms each night and waking up with her still there the next day. He loved all the prosaic little things about being married, even the way Vera squeezed the tube of toothpaste from the middle. The richness of their conversations, the warmth and passion of their nights, even their morning commute was wonderful as far as he was concerned. The only thing that concerned him was the fact that Vera seemed a little run-down lately.

She couldn't look haggard, she was far too beautiful for that, but she was definitely tired and a little pale looking, he'd noticed. He was determined to get her to a doctor and as soon as possible. He was driving home from the airport after taking a short trip to Washington and he thought again that somehow he was going to have to curtail his traveling. He was just too miserable when he was away from Vera. He smiled with utter relief as he pulled into the driveway at home; in a few minutes he'd be in the only place that mattered, the loving arms of his wife.

He entered through the back door and was pleased to find Vera in the kitchen putting the finishing touches on what looked to be a very festive meal. She immediately came to him and embraced him, kissing him sweetly.

"Hello, my husband. I'm so glad you're home, Marcus! I missed you," she said with a warm, loving smile.

"Not as much as I missed you. Do I have time for a shower before dinner?" he asked as his eyes drank her in.

"Absolutely. Take your time, baby. Would you like a glass of wine?"

In a very short time Marcus was getting dressed in comfortable casual clothes, having taking a relaxing shower. Kika and Toby were watching his every movement with great interest and he was talking to them as he got dressed.

"I hope you little urchins realize what a lucky man I am. I have it all, you know. I have the most beautiful, loving wife in the world, I have the best family in the world, I have a career I enjoy thoroughly, a beautiful home, and the most wonderful, exquisite wife in the universe," he said with satisfaction.

Melanie Schuster

Kika barked sharply, as if to point out that Marcus had mentioned Vera twice. "Yeah, I did say that twice, didn't I? Well, I could say it ten times a day and it wouldn't be enough," he said firmly.

Picking up his now-empty wineglass, he left the room with the little dogs scampering after him and joined Vera downstairs. The table in the dining room was beautifully set with candles and their best china and crystal. Marcus raised his eyebrows and looked at Vera, who was also looking extremely festive in a long, shimmery caftan. She didn't look tired or pale; she looked radiantly happy, that much was plain.

"This looks great, Pie. And you look exceptional, as always, baby. Is this a celebration of some kind?" he asked.

Vera led him to the table and made him sit down before answering. She handed him a small, prettily wrapped gift box before speaking. "Yes, Marcus, this is a celebration. Before you open that I want to tell you something. You are without a doubt the most wonderful thing that has ever happened to me. I love you so much, and I'm so grateful for your love and affection that I can't express it. I look forward to every single day of our lives together, Marcus. You make my life richer and more exciting than I ever thought it could be, and I hope that what you find in that box does the same thing for you," she said softly.

He looked at her face in the flickering candlelight and had to swallow hard before answering. "Vera, my heart, that was beautiful. But you don't—"

Vera interrupted him at that point, by begging him to open the box. "Right now, Marcus, I can't wait!"

Puzzled, he did as he was bid and found a small white plastic wand with an indentation at one end. The indentation had a small cross in it. He turned to Vera, confusion on his face. "What is this, Pie?"

The smile that Vera had been holding at bay broke

through. "It's an early pregnancy test. A positive one," she said softly.

Marcus stared at the object in his hands, then at Vera. "Does this mean . . . Are we pregnant, Vera?"

She nodded her head, the happy tears starting to fall from her eyes. "I went to the doctor today. He confirmed it, Marcus. There was never anything wrong with me, it was John who had a low sperm count," she said, although it's doubtful that Marcus heard her.

He let out a shout of joy and leaped from the table, scooping Vera up and hugging her so tightly she gasped. He immediately released his tight grip on her and held her loosely, bending his head to kiss her over and over with all the happiness he was feeling.

"A baby! You and me, Pie, we did it! I told you we can do anything and we did. Oh, baby, please say you're happy about this. Say you don't mind having one, Vera, because I'm so happy right now I could cry," he said, unaware that tears were indeed streaming down his face.

"Marcus, how could I not be happy?" she asked him. "I'm so thrilled I can't stand it. To think that I'm going to have your child, that we created a life together, Marcus, I'm so happy I can't even express it!"

Suddenly Marcus picked her up and carried her into the living room. He sat down on one of the big couches and just held Vera in this arms, kissing her and saying thank you over and over again.

Vera lay in his arms, loving his warmth, his tenderness, and his joy. Suddenly she sat up and cupped his face in her hands. "Marcus, we made a *baby*," she said in awe.

Marcus smiled at his beloved wife and kissed her again. "Yes, baby, we did. A beautiful baby," he said quietly.

Vera smiled at him with great affection. "How do you know it's beautiful, Marcus?"

"Because it belongs to us. Because we made it together.

How could it not be beautiful, Vera? You just wait and see, we're going to have the prettiest baby anybody ever saw, Pie."

And in a few months, Marcus was proved to be absolutely correct. Their baby girl, Anastasia Angelique Clark Deveraux, was generally considered to be the most beautiful baby ever born in the state of Georgia, as her father was very happy to inform anyone who hadn't heard the news.

Epilogue

Marcus was absolutely entranced by the women in his life. When he wasn't doting over his beautiful, loving wife, he was being the world's most doting father to his little daughter. Vera often despaired of him, saying he was going to spoil Anastasia to death, but he insisted it was impossible.

"I want her to have self-confidence, Pie. I don't think you can spoil a baby by giving her too much love and attention," he said earnestly.

Vera was seated at her dressing table and turned around to look at her big, handsome husband lying in their big bed. She smiled at him tenderly. "Sweetie-pie, she's eighteen months old! She's getting to be a little girl," she teased him.

Marcus returned the look of affection his wife was giving him. "She can be eighteen *years* old and she'll still be my baby," he informed her. "Just like *you're* my baby. Always have been, always will be, Pie."

By now Vera had crossed the room, taken off her silk peignoir lavished with lace, and joined Marcus in the bed. Her figure was back to what it had been before the baby. Even the legendary Clark booty had cooperated with her post-baby exercising and returned to its normal form. Vera wasn't too thrilled, though, that her tummy had developed what she called a little pooch, something that was invisible to her loving husband. She changed the subject from Anastasia to her tummy as she cuddled next to Marcus.

"You know, Marcus, I exercise and exercise and it won't go away. I want to have a tummy tuck," she said.

"A *tummy tuck?* Vera, that's . . . well, I think it's ridiculous. I love you just the way you are, I always have and I always will. But if that makes you happy, fine," he said, the doubt in his voice still evident.

Vera, however, was more than satisfied with his response. "Okay, then. It's settled. I'm having a tummy tuck. Right after this baby is born, I'm going to make an appointment," she said quietly.

"All right, Pie. As soon as this baby is born . . ." Marcus's voice trailed off as Vera's words sank into him. He sat upright, pulling Vera up with him.

"Are you serious, Vera? We're going to have another baby?" The joy and awe were plain in his voice.

Vera threw her arms around his neck and they held each other tightly. "Yes, my darling, we are. Are you happy, Marcus?"

"Aww, Pie, I'm so much more than happy. I'm so in love with you and Anastasia I can't see straight half the time. I'm so happy I can't say the words, Vera. But," he said in a seductive whisper, "I can show you how I feel."

And he did, that night and for the rest of their lives.

To My Readers,

Thanks again and again for all your kind letters and e-mails. I continue to be humbled and very appreciative of all your support. I hope that you enjoyed Marcus and Vera's story. It's always a joy to bring two people together who truly treasure each other as they do.

I took the opportunity in this book to talk about diabetes because this is a disease that is killing far too many people. So many people; family, friends, celebrities, so many have succumbed to "complications of diabetes." The best way to combat the disease is to be informed. You have to know the enemy before you can defeat it. I say this because I am a diabetic and every day of my life is spent fighting it off. If you have the disease, keep working to get those numbers in line. If you don't have it, do everything you can to never get it. Exercise and watch your diet carefully—don't invite it in, it's a most unwelcome guest in anyone's life! And if you know someone who has it, encourage them; support from family and friends is some of the best medicine in the world.

In answer to your many questions on the subject, yes, it is finally Angelique's turn to find love. The high-spirited, slightly spoiled, and very headstrong youngest child of the Deveraux family may have already met her match. But is she going to be wise enough to know true love when it's staring her in the face? You'll find out later this year in *A Merry Little Christmas*.

Until then, be well and stay blessed, everyone!

Melanie
I Chronicles 4:10

P.O. Box 5176
Saginaw, Michigan 48603

ABOUT THE AUTHOR

Melanie Woods Schuster currently lives in Saginaw, Michigan, where she works in sales for the largest telecommunications company in the state. She attended Ohio University. Her occupations indicate her interests in life; Melanie has worked as a costume designer, a makeup artist, an admissions counselor at a private college, and has worked in marketing. She is also an artist, a calligrapher, and she makes jewelry and designs clothing. Writing has always been her true passion, however, and she looks forward to creating more compelling stories of love and passion in the years to come.